PRAISE FOR
TRIPTYCH

"A beautiful and moving exploration into the human soul... An outstanding debut novel and a welcome and refreshing addition to the genre of Canadian science fiction."
— Dr. Jennifer Brayton, associate professor in Sociology at Ryerson University, and scholar in Canadian popular culture studies

"Frey delivers gloriously unpretentious science fiction, with enough fun and romantic intrigue to make you forget that something smart is going on until the closing pages."
—Liana K., Co-Host, Writer & Producer for *Ed The Sock*

TRIPTYCH

A NOVEL BY J.M. FREY

Triptych

Copyright © 2010 J.M. Frey
Cover Art © 2011 Charles Bernard
Edited by Gabrielle Harbowy

ISBN 13 978-1-897492-13-0

Printed and bound in the United States

www.dragonmoonpress.com
www.jmfrey.net

UFO dingbats are from the font
SpaceStationHokusPokus © Manfred Klein

TRIPTYCH

J.M. Frey

www.dragonmoonpress.com

Before

A BODY COLLAPSING WITH NO muscular control onto plush carpeting makes a kind of muffled thudding, all raw meat and cut strings. Doctor Basil Grey had heard other, more terrifying sounds in his thirty-three years. He'd heard screams more gorge-raising, had felt more threatened by the piercing shriek of experimental components as their structural integrity began to fail in close proximity to, well, his very valuable self. He'd heard the grating whines of undergrads, the sobs of grad students over the latest drafts of their theses, and the heated yelling matches between colleagues with differing grasps of a theory.

They were all horrendous sounds, and he had ranked them, once, by order of how much they made his teeth ache. But now he quickly reevaluated his internal top-ten list.

This particular sound was above and beyond the worst he'd ever heard in his life.

Something in his gut burned, like a punch had landed solidly to his solar plexus, and Basil doubled over, breath forced from his lungs.

For a ridiculous, dissonant second, he thought *he* was the one who had been shot.

1

"No," he moaned, and only realized after the fact that it was he who'd made the soft, wounded animal sound. It was unnaturally loud in the aftermath of the flat, empty crack of a bullet leaving a barrel.

Already partway down, he let gravity pull him the rest of the way to the floor. He reached out before he could stop himself, scrabbling, shaking, and forced his hand into Kalp's, laid a palm across Kalp's cheek. His throat closed up and he struggled to fight against the revulsion from the limpness of the fingers wrapped around his hand; from the already waxy feel of the skin under the bristles on Kalp's jaw.

Kalp blinked, just once, and turned his head towards Basil. And then, somehow, he was gone. There was no death rattle, no dramatic final breath, just...life in his eyes, and then...none.

Kalp was dead.

Kalp was dead on the living room floor.

Basil jerked backwards, away from the *thing* that he now touched, the thing that wasn't...that was still so warm, and dead bodies weren't supposed to be *warm*. They were never warm in the movies. But Kalp radiated heat like a little rain forest. *Had* radiated, no longer in the present...goddamnit all to *hell* and goddamn the tenses too. Then Basil's other instinct, the desperate need to *deny*, jumped to the fore and he surged forward to try to shake Kalp back into breathing. The purple-red blood was still oozing out of a fist-sized wound, growing ever more sluggish as the seconds ticked by, becoming sharply chilly in the still air. Basil jammed his hand over the blooming injury, pushed in his fist in a desperate, futile effort to stop the flow. Limp blue fur tickled his knuckles. Dark skin cooled irrationally rapidly, making goose pimples burst upwards along his arms.

Basil called to Kalp, kept calling long after it was obvious that Kalp could never respond, because no, this couldn't be it, this couldn't be *all*. Not after everything else, not after all they'd lost, he couldn't accept it, he couldn't just let Kalp *die* in their own house, in the one place that the Institute had promised they would be *safe*, god*damn* it.

He looked up. Standing in the fore of the tightly packed group of three Special Ops soldiers from the Institute, a veritable phalanx of Kevlar and scowls, Agent Aitken had gone ashen and grim. Her gun was pointed at the ceiling now, but her finger was still on the trigger, her knuckles white around the grip. Basil imagined that he could see smoke curling out of the barrel.

"Why?" Basil shouted, and everyone in the room jumped at the sudden submachine spray of words that shot out of him. "What the *fuck* did you do that for!"

Aitken swallowed and her grim composure cracked for half a second. "The hostile was—"

"My *husband* was—"

"No, you don't understand. He *had* to be—"

"Shut up. *Shut up!*" Basil shrieked, forgetting about staunching the blood flow. It was so cold against the backs of his fingers, the beds of his nails—cold already, too late. He lunged up to wrap clawed fingers, purple as Kalp's blood dried, around Aitken's neck. She dodged back, and the two other soldiers from the corps surged forward and dragged him bodily away from her. Basil kicked out, furious, his face hot and his head burning.

Kalp, God, no, *Kalp...*

"Gwen! Where are you?" Basil screamed. "Call an ambulance, *fuck,* someone arrest that crazy woman! She killed Kalp!"

Aitken stepped back, into the kitchen and out of the way. She holstered her gun and lifted her hand to probe around her neck, then the other hand went to her ear-mounted transmitter and clicked it on. She whispered urgently and softly into the microphone, expression twisted into a sneer even though her lips were dead white. Basil saw the words "backup" and "meatwagon" fall like cannonballs from her mouth. Nobody made a move to stop her.

Basil looked around at the faces of his fellow agents in disbelief. Some averted their eyes. The rest just frowned. Behind them, Basil's living room suddenly looked surreal and *wrong*. A teacup was resting on its side on the coffee table, and beside it, stacked neatly, there was a small bundle of files. They looked like some review work someone had left for half a second, just to nip up to the loo, and meant to return to. On the dining room table sat a torn piece of paper and some strange lump of twisted metal that Basil only half saw but couldn't force his shocky brain to recognize. It all seemed too...*domestic* for what was lying on the floor.

Basil lunged at Aitken again.

At least, he tried, but a matched set of agonizing grips on the insides of his elbows wrenched him back. A fleeting thought ran across his mind—a complaint about whiplash, pulled muscles, maybe something particularly snippy about manhandling—but Basil couldn't spare the brainpower for his habitual bitchiness just now. He bent his knees, trying to regain forward momentum, trying to pull with his center of gravity.

"Calm down, Dr. Grey!" one of the grunts shouted in his ear, yanking him back so hard something in his shoulder twisted and popped and began to burn.

Basil yelped, feet skidding out from under him in his surprised pain, and they wrestled him towards the front door.

He thrashed from side to side, ignoring—no, *revelling* in—the biting needles that were broadcasting out of his shoulder socket, concentric circles of throbbing agony and clarity. The pain made everything clearer. It made the truth too true to bear.

He jabbed out with his elbows, but he only succeeded in getting himself all the more tangled in the soldiers' unforgiving grip. The soles of his boots slipped and skidded against the polished hardwood floors, along the white tile of the house entryway. They caught the corner of the dirt-dull shoe carpet, dragging it across the threshold along with the three struggling men, out onto the cement stoop.

But he could not make them *stop*.

"Kalp! Gwen!" he screamed, and he felt something rip in his throat, the hot burn of anger and grief and pain.

Kalp couldn't, he just...it just...*no*.

"He's dead, Dr. Grey," the same grunt said, and he didn't even try to say it nicely, didn't even try to soften the blow.

"You don't, you don't know that," Basil insisted, digging heels ineffectually into the concrete of the stairs, trying to haul himself and his captors bodily back through the gaping front door. He could see, see the slow spread of browning purple, the ghastly streak of turquoise lying still, motionless in the pool. "You don't know about them, maybe, we don't know anything about their physiology, maybe he's in a coma, or, or his breathing is irregular, he could be fine, God, just let me, let me!"

"No, doc. He's gone."

"*No!*" Basil screamed, and suddenly his knees went out from under him, like they couldn't stand the thought of functioning anymore, not when Kalp was…

One of the soldiers let go, and the other guided him to the softer scrubby turf of the postage-sized front lawn. Basil's whole body felt heavy and shaky, like it wasn't his. It was too *hot*, too shivery, too much by far right now to have ever been something that Basil lived in.

He put his face in his hands and sobbed.

And Gwen, where was Gwen?

He called out her name, looked up, around. She wasn't there. Across the street, Mrs. Baldwin stuck her nose out of the door, blanched, and darted it back in.

Basil wept. Alone.

There were no sirens when the Institute arrived. There were only big, square black SUVs coming up the side road, pulling up in front of the house, a cube van behind. All the windows were black, black. A man in a coroner's tee-shirt climbed out of the van's cab. It was Doctor Zhang, mortician.

"No!" Basil said again and surged to his feet. He turned back to the house, but his way was blocked by one of the soldiers.

Gwen appeared in the doorway then, finally, and Basil took a step towards her before he registered the look on her face, and stopped; grim, closed down, nothing. She was dressed in full swat gear like a doll of a soldier: eyes empty, every new strap unfrayed, every buckle still blindingly factory-issue shiny. Her mouth was painted in a flat line, her lips held so tightly together that they had taken on the same shade of pale as the rest of her vacant face.

She was not angry. She was not sad. She was…nothing.

The coroner and men in suits piled out of the SUVs and she let them into the house. They shut the door behind them. She stood on the stoop.

"Gwen!" Basil shouted.

He shoved at the soldier and the man still would not let him by.

"Let me go," Basil snarled. "That's my *wife*."

Gwen descended the stairs, one hand curled over the butt of her gun in its thigh holster, and stopped a good few feet away. He reached out to her.

"There's blood on your hands," she said. "Come on, we're going to the Institute."

"No!" Basil said, jerking his hands back and folding them against his chest, tucking his knuckles under his armpits. This was it, this was all he was ever going to get of Kalp ever again. He couldn't—he couldn't just *wash it off*. Like it was dirt.

Like it was *filth*.

Gwen grabbed his sleeve, nodded to the soldier, and together they herded Basil into the first SUV like a mulish child. More neighbours had their faces pressed to glass, had their hands over their children's eyes as they stood together on front steps and by driveways. Basil resisted getting into the SUV, locking his arms at the elbows, refusing to let them whisk him away, to make him leave behind...

But Basil wasn't exactly the most stunning example of male physicality, and it was three against one. Between the soldiers and Gwen they got him stuffed into the back. The driver hastily engaged the child lock. Gwen zipped around and nipped in the other door before Basil had even registered that she was getting in with him.

He pounded at the window, scrabbling at the latch, and screamed, "No, no, Gwen, they killed him, we can't, we can't just go with them, we can't just *let them...!*"

"Shut up, Basil," Gwen hissed from beside him. She raised her fists and Basil shied back. She caught herself, eyes popping wide, showing white all around. She swallowed heavily once, twice. She looked like she was about to be sick. She dropped her hands to her hips, forced the fingers into a fanned flex. "Just...shut up," she whispered, and turned her body away, firmly directed her face out the window.

The SUV began moving. The quiet rowhouse suburb rolled by the windows. Basil wasn't sure he was ever going to see it again.

He folded over on himself, felt the burn and the fury and the too-hot surge of more tears crawl up his throat, then push at the back of his eyes. He clenched his fingers into his hair and wailed, and screamed, and sobbed until every muscle in his back throbbed with the effort of remembering to breathe. Until the back of his throat felt shredded. He swallowed and tasted blood.

When Basil's cries wound down to soft, fat hitches and the continual roll of tears down already soaked cheeks, the slow slide of snot across his upper lip, he felt Gwen reach out. She reached over, slid her damp palm down his neck, across his collarbone, igniting the ache there; then down his bicep, over his elbow. She twined her fingers around his.

He grabbed back, held on, held on, held on.

Kalp's blood was itchy between their palms.

THE DEBRIEFING cell was cold and grey. Basil stared at the painted floor between his knees. Gwen was there with him, he could see her out of the corner of his eye, noted more than registered. But he couldn't seem to lift his head. Not for her words, not for the cup of now-stone-cold tea she'd brought in for him, not for anything.

He was angry enough to throw something—the chairs and table, maybe, only they were metal and bolted to the floor. At any rate, he was too exhausted to move, to put furious thought into violent action.

His throat was killing him. He wanted water, or something, he wasn't sure. Maybe orange juice. That would make the pain worse, wouldn't it? Fill the small cuts in the soft tissue of his throat with an acidic bite. Yeah, that could be good; make the pain on the outside match what was eating him to pieces on the inside.

Gwen had suggested they "talk about it" well into their first hour. How long ago that was now, Basil didn't know. He hadn't replied. It hurt to reply. He just sat there with his forehead on the edge of the table, hunched over his own brown-purple hands, staring at the painted floor.

Who the hell paints a concrete floor, anyway?

His brain said: *seals in dust lessens airflow deadens echo and the travel of sound easier to clean,* and he shook his head. All the little fragments of thoughts scattered out of his ears like pepper from a mill. He went back to being empty.

Alone.

Basil shifted his eyes to his hands. Palm up on his thighs, curled slightly. He looked like he was trying to catch words, the same strange non-verbal gesture that Kalp did to indicate that he was listening, paying attention, focussed. The same way Kalp *used* to.

Hell.

Basil quickly turned his hands over.

Some of his own blood was mingled with…with *his.* Basil had cut himself with his own fingernails while making a fist, impotent in the black void that was the back of the SUV. Yesterday he would have been worried about cross contamination, his blood mingling with another species', but now all he could think was *yes, inside me, he's safe there, yes.*

Gwen sat down beside him. He knew it was Gwen, would know even if he was deaf and blindfolded. Even if he'd had all his senses deprived, taken, he'd know Gwen. The skin on his face tried to crawl away from her, goosebumping painfully.

"Basil," she said softly, and then her fingers were curled into his palm, soft and surprisingly cool. She clucked her tongue once, the tip of her own nails tracing the punctures his had made. "Oh, Basil," she said again, and this time it sounded like a pet name, like a soft and meaningful "sweetie" or "baby." But Gwen had never really indulged in pet names, and Basil had felt stupid calling her "pumpkin" when the most she ever called him was "Baz." So, no pet names for them. Sometimes he called her "colonialist," but that was when they were teasing.

Now she made his name sound…what? Like it was the name of a moping child, or a pouting lover. Like he was foolish. Condescending.

Basil straightened and yanked his hands out of her grip. He turned his face away. He didn't want her to see how chapped his upper lip was, how swollen his eyes were. He could see how miserable he looked in the speciality glass that made up an entire wall.

Stuck on the mirror side for once, Basil thought. Self-pity turned to anger. *I didn't do anything wrong! It wasn't me!*

Something soft and wet and warm touched the side of one of Basil's knuckles, and he looked down. Gwen had one of her hands in his palm, a wet washcloth cutting a peach slash through the rusty burgundy that was flaking off of his skin.

He wanted to pull back, scream *no!* and push Gwen away.

But even Basil knew that he'd have to wash off Kalp's blood sometime. Logically.

Gwen turned his hand over and Basil let her, slow and reverent and ritualistic as she scraped at the clots that had gathered in the wrinkles of his joints, the small turquoise hairs that were caught under his nails. She had a shallow bucket of warm water. Basil wasn't certain when it had arrived, but then it wasn't exactly like he'd been paying attention, was it?

The water grew progressively more violet as Basil's hands turned white with scrubbing. He watched morosely, eyes dry and sore, the tip of his nose throbbing. Gwen slowly, gently ran the cloth across the backs of his hands, along the tender thin skin under his wrist, between his knuckles and along the fine webbing of his fingers, across the intimate mound that was the base of his thumb.

Gwen took her time with his nail beds, chasing after every speck before turning his hand over and slowly and just as carefully cleaning out the fingernail wounds. When she was finished, she left the limp rag draped over the side of the white bucket, dripping watered-down blood onto the grey table top.

Basil had to turn his head away to keep from retching.

Gwen pulled a small tube from her tactical vest. It was the liquid band-aid that all Special Ops personnel were assigned in their field med kits, the one enhanced with alien technology. Basil hissed as the antiseptic in the opaque jelly went to work first. Gwen smoothed a small amount over each cut with the small brush and Basil refused to whimper. He bit his bottom lip until the sting on the cuts gave way to the warm tingle that meant the epidermis repair nodules had gone into effect. In a few hours, no one would even be able to tell that he had harmed himself at all.

Make the cuts again, he thought rebelliously, *make the pain on the outside match!*

But no, Basil didn't like pain. Especially the self-inflicted kind. And he hurt so much right now that it seemed redundant to just add more...

Gwen reached out and took up the cloth again, turned it over, folded the dirty side in, and wiped gently at the salt water dried onto Basil's cheeks, the leftover snot at the sides of his nostrils.

She leaned forward and pressed a kiss to the tip of his abused nose.

"Kalp's dead," Basil said softly.

Gwen paused, lips still touching his skin. Basil felt them stiffen along with the rest of her posture. She pulled back, eyes down, not meeting his desperate gaze. Desperate, yes, for confirmation, for sympathy, for grief, *fuck,* for some sign that Gwen was hurting as much as Basil was, that she was hurting *at all*.

Gwen turned away and dropped the cloth into the bucket. She stood and went over to the door and left it by the corner of the jamb, on the floor. Basil couldn't help but notice that it was in such a place that made it easy for someone to fetch it and slam the door back closed without opening the door too wide or for too long.

At first Basil thought that Gwen hadn't heard him, but then, with her eyes on the door handle, shoulders slumped, she said, "Yes."

Basil took this for a good sign, that Gwen had come out of whatever weird stoic shock she had thrown up like a shield, that she was going to start crying soon. Just, any proof that she was grieving, too.

Basil stood and went over to her, ready for her to turn her face against his neck and weep. He held his arms out slightly, and tried not to think of the last time they'd clung to each other like that, in the graveyard on the night they'd buried Gareth.

God, Gareth. Kalp would have to go into the plot beside Gareth.

Wrong, Basil's mind screamed. *It was supposed to be me next!*

What Basil's tongue tripped out was: "We should...organize... oh God, I don't know what to do, for the Ceremony of Mourning, we have to..."

"No."

She didn't turn to face him. She didn't even *sound* sad.

Basil wrapped his fingers around Gwen's hands, squeezing hard. "Of course we...why not?"

"No," Gwen repeated, and pulled her hands away, slowly but firmly. Detaching. "Not for traitors."

"Gwen!" Basil gasped, so surprised as to be scandalized. "You can't really think—"

"Don't tell *me* what I really think!" Fire lit her eyes, flamed her cheeks for half a second and Basil hoped that now was the time when she'd finally start to react...but no. She shut down again, went cold and constrained.

Basil felt like an MP3 player left on loop. "Gwen!"

"No." She moved to the other side of the room, put the table between them. She folded her hands over her stomach and bent her head.

Gwen stared at him, long and hard, and Basil was startled to see the white lines wrinkling the skin around her eyes, the corner of her mouth. There was silver streaking her temples, the little inlet of hair that peaked around her scar. Basil was sure, so sure that it hadn't been there at all this morning. Gwen looked weary. Old.

"He was my husband, too," she whispered.

"Then...then c'mere," Basil whispered. He held out his hand. Gwen slowly, as if she feared what the touch of his skin might do, reached out, up. Their fingertips touched.

She didn't step into him, didn't fold her sweet soft arms around him or pillow her cheek against his chest, but for now that little bit of contact was enough. It was better than nothing.

Basil closed his eyes and wished that he could start this day all over again. What he needed was a cosmic reset. A big red button that he could press or a trigger that he could pull that would let him go back in time and...and...

Basil gasped.

"The thingy!" he shouted and clicked his fingers. "Someone get me that metal component thingy from my dining room table!"

Part I: Back

THE DAY DAWNED CRISP and (too early) sweet.

September light dropped heavily over the stretching acreage of the farm, drenching the quiet world in the warm sepia of all the best nostalgia. The sky was the sort of open blue that prompted content, indulgent thoughts of a step-ladder and a spoon, just to see if it tasted as ripe as it looked. For a breathless second, even the birds and the insects seemed to share in the gentle glory of the early autumn sunrise, too awed to break the hush with the busy matter of attracting a mate.

It was, of course, promptly shattered by Gwennie's shrill demand for breakfast. She was always better when someone else did the waking, lazy-eyed and pillowy and pliable.

"S'comin', s'comin'," Mark mumbled into the comforter. He heaved himself upright. His wife cracked a sandy eyelid in sympathy as he poked sleep-warmed feet into the chill morning air. Dawn feedings were Mark's responsibility. He had to get up to do the milking, anyway. He hinged upwards like a rusty door, legs crooked and then holding him up as if gravity was some sort of recent miracle and he hadn't quite gotten the hang of moving with it just yet.

TRIPTYCH

Safe from the comfort of her down duvet, Evvie winced as Mark ricocheted off the corner of the solid wood dresser—an heirloom from his own grandfather's farm, if you could call such a battered and scuffed piece of sturdy wood an "heirloom"—as he struggled to pull on a pair of jeans that he'd left crumpled on the foot of the bed the night before. A year ago, Evvie would have appreciated the flex of his biceps, the fact that he'd neglected to put on anything else under the denim; that meant he was feeling frisky and nothing but good things would come of it when he got back in from the chores. Now it meant that he was too bleary to remember anything as banal as underwear.

The only things Mark and Evvie were doing in this bed nowadays were cuddling the baby, failing to sleep, and cultivating a lovely matched set of shiny purple bruises under their eyes.

Awake now, Evvie tracked the sound of her husband stumbling downstairs, the clatterbang of the fridge door opening and closing, the gurgle of a small pot being filled with tap water, the metallic swish of it being placed over an element, and the slow crescendo of bubbling as it boiled on the stove. Gwennie's cries subsided into desperate, miserable sniffles and breathy gasps; it took everything Evvie had to stay in bed, denying the itch in the marrow of her bones to go and gather her daughter up, press her close, and soothe.

Dawn was for Mark and Gwennie, special daddy-daughter time. They'd agreed.

The stairs creaked as Mark padded back up them, bare feet on bare wood. The door to the next room made a soft hiss in counterpoint as the wood slipped over the new carpet in the nursery. Mark said something gentle, his voice a low, crooning buzz filtering in through the wall that separated Gwennie's room from theirs, repeated in surreal electronic stereo on the other side of her head through the baby monitor. Finally, Gwennie's hitching wails wound down into even, soft breathing.

Evvie unclenched her teeth and worked her fingers out of the knots they'd balled into the blankets, amazed that even after so many months Gwennie's discomfort could cause such acute anxiety in her stomach.

Selfishly, Evvie considered the day ahead: raspberries to rescue from the cooling nip of nights outside, to wash and sort through and start to mash up for jams; vegetables to pick and preserve; weeds to pull; a garden to tuck in safe under a blanket of home-grown fertilizer and straw for the coming winter. All with a baby strapped to her back. She snuck out of bed, chilly toes creeping along hardwood floors, to steal the first warm shower and a few moments of privacy.

She loved her husband. She loved her daughter.

But God, did Evvie Pierson love hot showers, too.

THEY HAD a brand new cordless telephone.

They'd made good on the spring's run of calves, and indulged in the expense of the unit because of the baby. It was top of the line, and Mark had been very proud when he had installed it last month. Very few people around them had cordless phones. Now Evvie could go up or down stairs while talking any time she liked. She could keep the phone with her even when she was in the nursery, in the pantry, or downstairs folding the laundry. If she activated a feature on the base, it acted as a two-way walkie-talkie. Mark took the handset out to the barn every morning in case there was a call or an emergency with Gwennie.

Knowing Mark was just a button-push away, Evvie spent the early morning cleaning and preparing bottles, using the food processor to mash up some vegetables into a glutinous mass soft enough for Gwennie to smear artfully on every surface except her own tongue, and preparing lunch. Gwennie was very tactile, loved touching things, brushing her fingers against the tails of the barn cats, the trunks of the trees, curling sweetly in the ends of her mother's hair. Evvie made grilled cheese sandwiches for the adults. Waiting for Mark to come in to eat his lunch, she passed the time—far more time than she'd probably like to admit to her circle of friends—playing a game of dishtowel peek-a-boo that Gwennie tired of before Evvie did.

Mark appeared briefly for the sandwiches and some underwear. "Zipper's rubbin'," he complained, this time with a hint of the smirk that his wife remembered so well—then struck out again to finish clearing all the bales out of the hayloft before dark. The boys from the neighbour's farm would be by tomorrow afternoon to help Mark pull up the moulding floorboards and replace it; wet hay caused everything else around it to go off, and paradoxically, started fires. It was the MacKinnons who'd bound and stacked the hay before it was properly dried in the first place in their haste to get the work done last year, and their father said they owed.

The MacKinnons were good for that—paying back.

When Mark had disappeared, Evvie washed each dish carefully and stacked them in the plastic drying rack under the window. The sun glanced off the rapidly evaporating water, filling the small kitchen with light. Gwennie tried to grab at a reflection of the sun off Evvie's watch, patting her fat palms against the wall beside her high chair with futility. They played that game for a while, too, Gwennie laughing, trying to smack the light between her hands or grasp it with fingers still smeared with green paste.

Evvie moved Gwennie into her carrier at noon and they spent the next hour shuttling baskets, garden tools, water pitchers, a soft, much-gummed plush frog, and a wheelbarrow of fertilizer out to the garden at the bottom of the backyard. It butted right up against the marching line of corn stalks gone golden with the end of summer. That would be Mark's next task, ploughing under the stripped stalks. The world smelled of clean dark soil, the faint perfume of the apple orchard belonging to their neighbours far upwind, and the crisp lingering after-scent of the morning's brief hoary dew.

With Gwennie content with her frog, Evvie bent to her task, old gathering baskets dappled with the brownish and pink stains of many years duty at hand, carefully reaching around the thorny tendrils of the raspberry bushes, plucking the dark fruit away from the leaves and lifting them gently into their new homes to keep her fingers mostly free of sticky juice. She had to reach and stretch carefully so the prickly edges of the leaves never got to close to Gwennie.

And then.

The buzzing sound was soft enough that Evvie didn't notice it right away. She flapped a glove-clad hand at her ear, hoping it wasn't a late-season mosquito trying to get in one last meal, or a fly bothering Gwennie. It grew louder, too loud to be an insect, too large. She thought maybe it was Gwennie, making sounds with her chubby baby lips, and Evvie craned her head around to smile at her.

What she saw was Gwennie looking up, mouth open in awe, wide blue eyes reflecting the sky and...

The aircraft swooped down so low that Evvie couldn't deny the urge to duck. It buzzed the top of the corn, sending the crowns of dried seed husks flying in clouds of pellets. The plane turned in midair, belly up like a swimmer at the end of a pool, then waggled and flipped upright with a barrel roll straight out of the movies, sharp nose pointing at them. *What the hell kind of plane looks like that?* Evvie thought. *What aircraft can even manoeuvre like that?*

Something hard and sharp welled against the underside of her ribs.

She flattened herself against the ground, tugging desperately at the straps of the carrier, wriggling to pull Gwennie around, shield her under her body as the craft came at them again. Thoughts of sprays of bullets and missiles pressed fervidly against Evvie's forehead, and she felt her face get hot, heard Gwennie squeal. Blood pounded against Evvie's skin, and she could taste her heart in the back of her throat.

What the hell was *happening?*

The world erupted in a bang.

Evvie squeezed her eyes shut, but she could hear the skidding slide of the aircraft digging into the turf of the backyard, some sort of scream, the shrill protest of metal being bent away. There was a vicious tug on the baby carrier and she felt the straps tear. It took Gwennie, ripped her out of the carrier, a foot on the strap, slamming Evvie's chest back into the ground.

"Gwennie!" Evvie screamed.

Suddenly Evvie was flying through the air. As soon as she had registered the cold pull of bare, dry fingers—too long, too thin, too strange—on her arms, they were gone. Tossed away like an empty corn husk.

"Gwennie!" she shrieked again, then "oof!" as all of the air was driven out of her lungs, her ribcage coming up hard against the ground.

Stars sparked against Evvie's eyelids. Blackness swooped up but she pushed it away, desperately, everything burning as she tried to suck in air, tried to flip over, to push herself up, to crawl, but she had no air, couldn't move at all...

Gwennie! Gone, gone.

Evvie's vision swirled into single focus. The craft was...it...

There was a flying saucer in her strawberries.

Gwennie screamed.

God, *screamed* and Evvie...

She reached out, up; she was still on the ground, legs too shaky to support herself. Evvie sucked in a breath and suddenly it was like the stones had been lifted away from her limbs, and she had the ability to move again. She pushed onto scraped hands and knees, scrabbling to get close, arms up, and *no, please, a knife, it has a knife* and...against her little throat, pale and...her chest heaving, jerking, and it was holding Gwennie by her arm, like it...

That's not how you hold a baby!

Evvie swallowed, trying to work up the spit to speak, to *scream*, to beg, oh God, and it tasted like ash. "Give her back! *Please!*"

The thing looked at Evvie, only *looked* at (through) her.

What the hell is it?

The short snout wrinkled, the bat-wing ears flattening against its head, like the barn cat's. The ears were ridges of articulation, fingerling joints, a yacht sail of flesh and bone, but oh so very expressive. Angry.

A flash of fangs and the knife and Evvie screamed too, because you can't—someone can't cut out your heart without making you scream.

She's a miracle, look at those little fingernails, Mark had once said, and the words rang between Evvie's ears like a frosted gong. *Can you believe we did that?*

We didn't invent it, Evvie had replied. *But it sure as hell feels like it.* Then.

Evvie sensed, suddenly, someone behind her.

"Please, please, no!" and the knife flashed again, only it wasn't a knife flash, it was an explosion, just a small one, and the air reeked suddenly of cordite and fireworks and copper. There was the flat crack of a gunshot.

The thing's head ceased to exist.

The long padded fingers spasmed once, went limp, trailed behind the body as it slumped backwards. Evvie reached out, still kneeling, and grabbed her daughter out of the air where the thing's hands used to be. Relieved, she said, "Mark!" Because who else could it have been?

Gwennie howled again and Evvie tucked her in close to her chest, running a hand over the baby's shoulder, her throat, looking for blood, for broken bones, just to feel Gwennie's skin (*hot and tingling, whole, alive*) against her own. Something red and sticky on Evvie's fingers, but she couldn't see where it was coming from. Whose was it?

Was Evvie hurt? Would the adrenaline fade and would some bone suddenly protest its previous ignored agony? Her ribs, her whole side throbbed, raw and scraped and bruised, and she spared a second to hope that bruises were all she'd gotten.

"Mark," Evvie said again, and stood up, turned to him, to bury herself in his arms, to hold Gwennie between them and shelter her. "Something's wrong. Call an ambulance!"

"M' not Mark," said the woman with the smoking gun.

Evvie goggled. *How many clichés could I live through in one afternoon?* Evvie thought. *Barely live through—God, Gwennie!*

"W-who," Evvie managed to stutter, and Gwennie was screaming still, furious and terrified and unable to understand, and frustrated at her own inability to articulate her terror. "*W-what?*"

"The less you know, luv, the better, innit?" another voice behind Evvie added, and she turned to face it. A man this time, but he was dressed the same as the woman: all dark and durable with no loose hardware. Just tough pants, thick boots, a vest with too many pockets and straps, a blank black ball cap. No badges. No emblems. No indication of rank. Only empty Velcro fuzz where they might have sat on the top of each arm. Wind- (explosion-) blown and militaristic. Guns in hand, big and boxy. Official-looking, but without any insignia that she knew; it reminded Evvie of the Navy Seals.

Something so (covert) dangerous they had no need to advertise. Their clothing freaked her out. Evvie decided to freak out as quietly as possible.

Dry and dusty horror swept down her. She felt her cheeks get cold, the heat and adrenaline of anger and fear sliding away. Her joints seized and the bottoms of her feet itched; Evvie wanted to run, wanted to yell, wanted to cry and all she could do was stand and shake, and shake, and shake.

Evvie tightened her grip on Gwennie and the baby didn't seem to notice.

The man started to lift one arm, winced, and switched to the other. He pointed at the plane-ship. "Did you see where it came from?"

"N-no," Evvie admitted, because she hadn't; because she had been looking at the tired old baskets, and the thorns and the fat raspberries, now smashed and pulpy; red and black innards sprayed all over the lawn. Grotesque.

And what the hell was *it*? As if real life was a movie, but nothing she had ever seen before. It was like in the commercials for that new Spielberg film with the bicycles.

A sudden whistling sound rent the air, high and long. Silver, tinnish, dying. It hurt Evvie's ears. They were wincing, the man and woman in black, but seemed otherwise unaffected; more concerned with catching their breath and arguing with one another than the shrill cry of the machine.

The sound made Gwennie wave her fists and *howl*.

Not happy, Mom, her squished face and watery blue eyes said. *Seriously not happy.*

The air reeked in turns of burnt plastic, churned turf, and the faint, sickening tang of blood and raw meat as the wind shifted, blowing the smoke first towards and then away from the pack of too-still people. A long, thin line of blood arched over Gwennie's smooth forehead, down her little neck. Evvie pulled her close, hiding her face, covering her ears.

Maybe Evvie should have been more concerned about the ship, the twenty foot divot on the lawn, the *noise*. She wasn't.

Big blue baby eyes and a squall—*Seriously, Mom, not happy.*

Evvie jogged her once and thought, *Hush, sweetie. Let Mommy cope. We've nearly been killed by aliens.*

Aliens.

There was a flying saucer in the *strawberries.*

The word crashed around between her ears, echoing and squealing like icy mice.

Aliens.

Gwennie went silent and white, her little chest jerking with terrified gasps; something, maybe, in the tenseness of Evvie's body as her mother clutched her close, an instinct not to fuss, not to bring attention to herself in a time of danger. But the two strangers were both staring at her anyway. The small gash on her forehead bled freely.

The man pulled a square of gauze from the miniature first aid kit in his over-packed vest pocket. He handed it to Evvie. The kindness of the action jolted her out of her paralyzed terror, out of the vacant numbness of shock and sound.

Evvie took the gauze. Pressed it down. Her daughter whined.

"Oh my God," the woman breathed, looking down at Gwennie, and why, why was Evvie suddenly struck with the thought that this woman looked *familiar?* The stiff soldierish facade cracked and the woman showed a real emotion for the first time, a sort of confused horror, her eyes still zeroed in on the baby.

"I don't get it," the man said, without acknowledging that she had spoken. He was on a rant, too absorbed in an argument with himself to listen. It didn't look like that surprised her. "Why?"

Smile, Evvie thought, resisting the urge to just stare at the woman. *Smile so I know who you are. I'll know you if you just smile.*

But that was terrifying too, because who did Evvie know that could do what (kill like) this woman just had?

"Basil—" the woman said softly.

"*Why?*" the man repeated, hands zooming around like scared birds as he tapped at something that looked like a palm-sized notebook, but had a face like a television. He gestured at Evvie, at the divot, at the sky. "Why go to all that trouble to trigger a Flash—a *temporal* one no less, and who knew they could do *that*—and, and then just…attack some random family in the middle of Nowheresville the moment you get here? I mean, if they were going back in time to, I dunno, invade the Earth or sommat before we had the technology to fight back, why balls it up by attacking some random family? Why not *hide?* Why not go back *further?* It doesn't make *sense.* They're smarter than that, the little sons of a—*Kalp* used to be smarter than—"

"It's not random," the woman snapped off, interrupting. "And don't talk to me about Kalp after…" She trailed off, sucking in a breath. Scrubbed an eye with the palm of a fingerless glove, fingertips brushing along her hairline. She stopped, felt something there. Realization and cold disgust made her eyebrows caterpillar upwards. "They weren't after the mother."

The mother.

Like Evvie was a mannequin, or a chess piece.

(Trivial.)

"No?" Basil asked, unsure.

He frowned, studied Evvie, his own face pale and round-eyed, with spots of colour still high on his cheeks from the exertion of shooting down the ship. He peered at her as if Evvie were vaguely familiar too, and all he needed was to get a good look.

I know how you feel.

Evvie tried not to roll her eyes. It took some doing.

Mark was still in the barn with the phone. He had to be. Where was he? Had he heard any of it? Evvie's scream? The shots? The engine, now? Had he already called the cops? Or did the thump of rotten hay falling to the floor mask every other sound? Did he hear the grinding wail of the…

There's a *flying saucer* in the strawberries.

And finally, finally, the wailing sound began to fade, like a fan blade just unplugged still sluggishly exerting the last of its momentum. *Thwip-thwip thwip…thwip…thwiii…*

Where was Mark?

Gwennie whimpered once, mashing her face unhappily into her mother's bicep.

"They were after the baby, just the baby," Basil said, realizing the truth behind what they had seen: what had happened too fast, what was too fantastic for Evvie to digest just yet. The woman got whiter. Evvie's brother Gareth used to collect Asimov. But how could Evvie possibly be *living* it?

Basil tapped his notebook television hard. "Why the baby? Why babies at all? Blimey, do you think they're targeting babies?"

"No," the woman breathed. She took off her ball cap and crumpled it up in a white-knuckled fist. Reddish brown hair, and a tumble of unmanageable pseudo-curls—not unlike Evvie's when the summer humidity got to it—were pulled back hastily into a clip, scrambling for freedom in all directions. The woman reached shaking fingers up, brushed the thin white scar at the edge of her hairline. On her forehead. "They're not going after random babies."

She ran her nails through her hair, scratching her scalp lightly. When she hit the clip she tugged it out, angry now; she tossed it at the flying saucer. It made a sharp pinging sound where it hit the side. The engine chugged once as if in reproach, an ugly thick sound. The high-pitched whine cut out abruptly, and Evvie felt the tension in her shoulders ratchet down a notch, fall away from her ears.

"Dammit," the woman hissed into the sudden, shocking silence. "They're going after *us*."

"Us?" Basil repeated, unsure. The woman jerked her chin at the wound on Gwennie's forehead, and touched her scar again.

"They're going after the Institute," she said softly. "That's not just a random baby, Basil. That's *me*."

But the woman looked like she was about the same age as Evvie, so how could—but, not at all because…

A snap somewhere in Evvie's chest, sudden tightness in her throat because yes, yes, of *course*.

That's who she was.

THIS SORT of thing had never been covered by the old etiquette books.

What would Miss Manners have to say about vanquished alien invaders? Meeting your own adult children decades too early? Was Evvie supposed to offer tea? Cookies?

(Sanity?)

Mark and Evvie had already decided not to call an ambulance; nothing was broken on either Gwennie or herself, and Gwennie's head had stopped bleeding. Evvie's ribs ached and her palms and knees were scraped. They stung every time she took a step or picked something up, but were otherwise ignorable. What the Piersons hadn't agreed on, yet, was the issue of the police.

"I'm calling the cops," Mark said from across the kitchen table.

"Mark," Evvie began, but then stopped because she wasn't entirely sure that calling the cops wasn't an excellent idea, now that she'd had a chance to take stock of what had happened.

"No." Basil held out a hand. "We'll take care of it."

"Take care of it *how?*" Mark demanded. "There's a *UFO* in the backyard!"

"We'll bury it," the woman who was Evvie's baby offered. Evvie's fingers itched to touch her, but she was occupied with baby Gwennie, and too scared that touch would make it real. "We're way out in the country. You own this land. You won't sell it. It flew in low; the neighbours won't have seen it. I know that for a fact, at least. We'll bury it."

"You reckon it's as simple as that?" Mark shouted, red-faced with impotent fury.

"Simple as that," she said, unaffected by his anger. She was nearly insolent; practiced with his bad moods. "I'll fetch it when I go back."

Evvie swallowed once. "Back? Back to the…" she said softly, clutching baby Gwennie close to her chest. She was sucking contentedly on Evvie's knuckle, all right with the world now that she'd been hushed and patched. "Back to the future?" Evvie said the words, didn't quite believe them, even as they came out of her own mouth. People didn't time travel. That was not the way the world worked. Period.

Grown-up Gwennie (Evvie's hair, Mark's eyes, pale like Mark's sister) and Basil exchanged a look filled with raised eyebrows and half-hidden smirks. Had Evvie said something funny?

"Could say that," Basil conceded. He tapped a little more at the surface of his strange notebook. If Evvie craned her neck, she could see that he was making something happen on the screen, like changing the channel on a TV, but by touch and not with a remote. She'd never seen anything like it outside of sci-fi afternoon creature features. "Look, when I first got my hands on their tech, I expected there'd be a locational but not a temporal divide between where we were and where we are." His free hand made chopping motions on *were* and *are*. "Then I expected that there would be a return function, but…" He held up a jumble of blackened circuitry and ridiculously small wires. A sleek black shell was half melted around them. "Looks like we'll never know now."

"Is *that* what the Flasher does? Jesus." The woman groaned and pinched the bridge of her nose. "Dammit, I didn't think of that. And there's no Array, is there? No just calling for a lift. Just us. *Here.*"

Basil, without lifting his shoulder too high, prevented again by a sharp pain that his wince broadcasted, pointed to a small piece of black plastic wedged into the hole of his ear. "Glorified decoration. Story of my bloody life," he said, as if that explained everything.

To the grown-up Gwennie, it did.

"Can you use what's here?" she asked, tapping her own piece of ear-plastic with a blunt fingernail.

They were speaking a different language.

Evvie understood their words, but not the way they were using them. Was this how Evvie's mother felt when she listed to Evvie and her friends conversing? Hell of a generation gap.

"I'm getting nothing."

"Of course you're getting *nothing,* you great *git,*" Basil snapped. Evvie blinked at his condescending tone and turned back to gauge grown-up-Gwennie's reaction, like a Wimbledon spectator. She was merely watching him blandly, not at all stung, accustomed to his sharp tongue. "That's because it's the year nineteen eighty…" he trailed off, looked over at Mark in askance.

"Three," Mark supplied with a tiny sputter, as shell-shocked by their brisk, intimate efficiency and strange vocabulary as Evvie was.

"Nineteen eighty–three, and as such, I am only four years old, and I have absolutely no desire for you to see me in short pants and my hideous school jumper—"

Gwen's smile grew momentarily, surreally natural, trying to crack through the brusque mask. "Bet you were hot," she teased, but the light tone was strained.

"You're sick." He grinned, wide and amused. Either he didn't catch the hitch in her mood or he was ignoring it. "So, though I *am* a certifiable genius at any age, as of now I have yet to actually design and *build* the highly-advanced-even-for-two-thousand-and-twelve Communications Array for the Institute. Hence." He lifted a sharp finger to the ceiling in emphasis, then swivelled his wrist and pointed at his earpiece. "Glorified decoration."

The woman sucked on her lips, amused, and poked his arm slowly and deliberately. "Let's not talk about stuff that's classified in front of the civvies, sweetie," she said softly. Immediately Basil looked contrite and ducked his head, the high spots of mottled pink on his cheekbones sliding away. "So back to my original question: think you *can* use what's here?"

Basil rocketed out of the kitchen chair, happy to have a distraction, a task, and picked up the phone hanging on the wall. Basil shook it, listened to it rattle slightly, then sneered at the handset critically like it was a cockroach found swimming in the peanut butter.

"Use it, nothing!" Basil said irritably. "Blimey, do you *see* this phone? I can't use this! It's a bloody beige *brick*, innit? It'll never interface!"

"Hey!" Mark protested. He was damn proud of that phone.

"Sorry," Basil said, and didn't sound like he meant it at all. "But it's so far beyond obsolete it might as well have been carved out of granite. The components just don't *fit*."

"Why?" Mark asked. "Are your telephones, what, bigger in the… the future?" He tasted the word "future," rolled it on his tongue, then made a face suggesting it was nasty.

The woman pointed to the small black piece of plastic fitted snugly inside the shell of her ear. A tiny little microphone that Evvie had missed the first time was poking down along her jaw, delicate and as thin as a guitar string.

"Smaller," she corrected. "Much."

"And this? Is not small," Basil said, shaking the phone to make it rattle again. "It's bigger'n my *head*, Gwen."

Evvie sucked in a breath, and beside her, Mark did the same. He sat down heavily on the kitchen chair Basil had abandoned.

Her name.

Gwen, not Gwennie, turned her attention back to the Piersons. "Oh," she said softly, as if just realizing now that they were still in the room with her. "Oh, jeeze. I'm…I'm sorry. This has got to be *bizarre*. I totally forgot that you have *no idea*…I mean, me, I'm used to bizarre, but you…"

"Who *are* you?" Mark said softly, and Evvie heard equal parts anger and confusion in his voice. Warning perhaps, a little bit, as well.

Gwen sat up, straightened her spine and smiled at her parents, but it wasn't the same easy smile she'd employed in chiding Basil, the one that looked like her Uncle Gareth's. This was regimented, precise, practical. Regulation.

She slipped a black leather square out of a pocket in her vest, flipped it open to reveal an ID card with a postage-stamp sized picture. She held a careful thumb over everything but her own face and name. "I'm Specialist Gwendolyn Pierson. That's Specialist Doctor Basil Grey. We work for…well, I can't tell you who we work for," she said with a rueful little headshake. With a practiced wrist flick the ID and leather wallet vanished back into her pocket. "We'll call it the Institute for now, because you've heard that name already."

"An' you're from the future?" Mark said, clearing his throat with a cough, as if that could clear his head, too. He didn't look like the taste of the word "future" had gotten any sweeter.

Specialist Doctor Basil Grey, already ripping the Piersons' new telephone to pieces with a set of miniature screwdrivers that he had pulled out of who-knows-where on the vest, said, "Twenty-nine years, give or take a few months."

Evvie just barely resisted the urge to scrub at the bridge of her nose with the heels of her hands. Her daughter was *two years* older than she was.

Mark watched with a tightly set mouth, but didn't protest. Evvie wondered if it was because he was secretly awed by Basil's quick efficiency and familiarity with the electronic tinkering that so befuddled her husband—the microwave clock still flashed 12:00, three years after they'd purchased it—or because he was simply steamrolled by Basil's blunt personality.

"And you're...you can't get *back* to the future?" Evvie asked, trying to clarify, to quantify, to (accept) understand. Gwen and Basil snorted and giggled again, respectively, and Mark narrowed his eyes, got that look in them like when he didn't like the punks in the fields tipping the cows and let them know it. "What's so funny?"

"The... 'Back to the Future,'" Gwen began, then stopped, gasping in a breath and floating it out in a chuckle. "Never mind. Classified. Sort of."

"Sort of," Basil agreed around the screwdriver in his mouth. He kept tapping the screen of his hand-held television, pulling pieces out of the phone and comparing them to the images on the machine. "Blimey, my BlackBerry for a Flux Capacitor."

"And a swanky DeLorean." Gwen grinned as if Basil hadn't just babbled something totally incomprehensible about fruit. She made a motion with her hand, a horizontal cutting through the air like describing the path of an airplane.

"Can you tell us what that thing was?" Mark asked, shaking his head at the strange terms the two kept tossing at each other, trying to pull them back into conversation that made sense—as much as a conversation about aliens and time travel *could*. "The flying saucer in the garden?"

"Classified," Gwen said again, with the practiced ease of someone who'd used the word a lot (too much). "Though the term 'flying saucer' is considered derogatory."

"Though *technically* the organization that classified it hasn't actually been started yet," Basil pointed out, mimicking her flippant tone.

"Shut up, dear," Gwen said amiably.

"It was coming after...you?" Evvie asked, some of the clues slotting into place. She looked at the scar on Gwen's forehead, then down to the blood-spotted bandage on Gwennie's. "Her? To...I mean, to stop whatever you do in the...then."

Basil frowned at the screen, face suddenly stormy. "It don't seem right, does it? That they'd come and get cozy just to...to do something like *this*."

"I agree that it's *completely* unexpected, given their earlier behaviour," Gwen said with a nod, and Evvie blinked at the professionalism of it. "They were warm and very...very *open*."

"*Gwen*," Basil warned.

Gwen deflated a little, shutting down on what she'd intended to say, tucking away an old can of worms that had been about to be reopened. "But that's based on us actually *knowing* them." So bitter.

"Unfair," Basil whispered.

They glared at each other over the table—the kind of silent battle that only an intimate couple can have; the kind of battles Evvie had with Mark. Basil was the first to look away, turn his back, and return to dissecting the telephone.

Gwen stared at his back for a moment, eyes narrowed, as if trying to force her opinion in through the back of his skull with just the power of her glare. When that failed, she rolled her eyes and her shoulders, sighed, then leaned over the table to stare into the baby's face. For a long moment two pairs of wide blue eyes regarded each other. Gwen reached across the table and Gwennie lay perfectly still in Evvie's arms, completely unconcerned.

"Don't touch her," Basil said without looking up. "You'll make space-time go kablooey."

"Bullshit," Gwen said. "What do you think this is, an episode of 'Doctor Who'?"

Gently she ran the very tips of her fingers up the baby's soft, still arm. Tapped the pudgy nose. Then she shivered all over once and sat back, staring at the tip of her finger like she was expecting the skin to melt off, despite her own self-assurances.

"You're taking this very well," Gwen said abruptly, dropping her hand to her lap.

"No, I ain't." Mark ran a hand through his hair, making the already over-stimulated tufts stand up in all directions. "I'm in shock." His eyes widened a bit. "An'…an' don't swear, young lady."

Gwen chuckled. "Yes, Dad."

Mark's stern expression melted into something akin to wonder. "Dad," he repeated breathily. Neither of the Piersons had expected to hear that word quite so soon. The exhalation was his way of bumping back down to Earth, the truth of what was happening starting to settle. Evvie wasn't far behind.

"*You're* taking it well, at least," Gwen said, her words aimed at Evvie.

"How could I not?" she asked, because it had landed in her the same time as it had in her husband. She knew, she *knew* that this woman was her child, felt that *mine* sensation, down in the same place where she felt Gwennie. "You have Mark's eyes. My hair. Gareth's smile."

Gwen lifted a hand and covered her mouth, and there was something of shame in the gesture. "Gareth died in—" Her eyes were drawn back to the bandage on the baby's head. "You told me I fell down the basement stairs."

"You what?" Evvie blurted, thrown by the *non sequitur* and the horrible thought that her brother Gareth was going to…no, Gwen hadn't finished that sentence. It could have been anything. Could be *years* from now (tomorrow).

"The scar. You told me I fell down the stairs."

Basil craned his head around the wall, to the small flight of steps that led to the basement family room. The basement was just a sublevel sunk a little lower than the kitchen, entirely visible through the white metal railings that separated it. Evvie could stand beside the sofa and see the table they were seated at now. Basil frowned, crooked mouth arching down, eyebrows following.

"What? A scar like that?" he asked, pointing at his forehead to the place where Gwen(nie)'s mark was with the tip of his screwdriver.

"It's four steps. Oh, my God, Gwen, look at that telly! It's so *fat*. Is that a *Betamax?*"

Gwen dropped her hand and rolled her eyes. "Trust Basil to geekgasm all over the eighties."

EVVIE DIDN'T have much in the way of things to make up a meal in her house. The nearest store was more than a fifteen-minute drive up the country road, and even that was just a glorified family-run market stand. Neither she nor Mark wanted to leave the other alone with Gwennie and these two. Just in case.

Aliens and spacecraft and time travel aside, they were just hard to understand. Trying to hold a conversation with two people who knew you better than you did, who spoke in strange half-idioms and references to things you were unfamiliar with, while cheerfully ripping apart every piece of technology you owned was...tedious, to say the least. Terrifying, at the most.

So Evvie pulled Hi-liner fish sticks and McCain French Fries out of the freezer, and Basil muttered mutinously about how they were *not* real fish and chips, but Gwen clipped his ear and he ate everything she put on his plate, and more besides.

Evvie was starting to see how he may have gained his soft middle.

Was this really the man that Evvie's daughter, her baby Gwennie, was (going to be) with? Brilliant, acerbic, nerdy, pudgy, rude, with a back-pedaling hairline? Evvie had envisioned a farmer with dirty blue jeans and a lazy smile that he flashed at her whenever he asked for more apple pie, or a cop with bright white teeth and a penchant for bringing home flowers, or the manager of a supermarket with dependable hours and a good benefits package. Instead, Gwen had found a squirrelly, potty-mouthed British mech-head.

They were easy around each other, touched casually and insulted affectionately, but Evvie couldn't be certain they were *together*. If they were, then what was wrong? They weren't even engaged yet, if her bare fingers were anything to go by, and Gwen was nearly thirty!

And Gwen herself…? Soldier? *Specialist*? (Nerd?) Evvie knew it was a horrible motherly cliché, but she wanted Gwennie to be a ballerina. A nurse. The prettiest girl in school, with all the boys after her but smart enough to know that a man wouldn't marry used goods. Instead, Gwen was single, childless, her social life lost in the secret bunkers of a covert military operation. That was not the life Evvie had in mind for her daughter. She was supposed to be the Fall Fair Queen, not a…a *killer*.

Killer, Evvie said again to herself, to be sure that it was the word she meant. Yes. Gwen had looked at the knife so precariously close to Gwennie's tiny throat, and shot that thing point blank in the face. In the *face*. No warning shot, no demands for surrender. Cold.

Just a pulled trigger and the spray of stuff (brains) all over the grass.

For a split second, empty.

This was Evvie's daughter.

Trained killer.

Her baby.

The fish sticks make a bid for freedom and she swallowed once, heavily.

The milk glass clutched in her hand groaned, and the eyes of everyone at the table—save for Gwennie, who was solemnly massaging her ketchup into her hair—turned to Evvie. Mark cleared his throat, which he only ever did when he was nervous, and asked, "Evvie? Honey? You okay?"

"Yes," Evvie lied. She set down the glass carefully. "I'm not… hungry." She stood, cleared away her dishes, scraped the half eaten fries into the garbage and dropped the plate into the sink.

My daughter is a killer, Evvie tried not to think.

Gwen's mouth went tight around the edges, her eyes blue marble.

Unable to resist the motherly impulse, Evvie grabbed Gwennie up out of her highchair, pulled her close, sucked in the scent of starchy sugar and processed tomatoes and baby. "I'll give her a bath," she said to no one, and fled upstairs before anyone could protest or see the way her hands shook.

THE SOUND of the water running to fill the bathroom sink drowned out the conversation downstairs. Evvie hated abandoning Mark to a room filled with strange words, but she couldn't, couldn't stay in that kitchen with that uncanny woman. Unnatural.

That *stranger* who was her child.

Gwennie blew contented snot bubbles until the water was ready, fingers grasping alternately at her mother's shirt or more of the ketchup, turning Evvie's clothing into a palette of red and green smears. *An artist maybe?* Evvie thought, smiling down at her.

With a jolt of startled horror, Evvie realized that no, no, of course Gwennie wasn't going to grow up to be an artist. She was going to be a soldier. A Specialist. She was going to wear black and bullet-proof vests and telephones in her ear. She was going to carry a boxy gun on her hip. She was going to *use* it.

Evvie began shaking hard all over, and if weren't for fear of hurting or startling Gwennie, she probably would have collapsed to the floor and had a good self-indulgent screaming fit. As it was, she sank down and sat on the toilet lid and cried quietly, miserably into Gwennie's little neck. It felt awfully wonderful in that wrenching cathartic way and it made the back of Evvie's eyes and throat burn.

Gwennie patted Evvie's cheek with sticky, saucy fingers; a small, soft comfort. *It's okay, Mom. It'll be okay.* And then she smiled at Evvie with her uncle's (dead) smile.

What will happen to Gareth? Evvie didn't dare try to answer herself.

"I love you," she whispered into Gwennie's reddened wisps of ketchup-matted hair. "I love you and even though I want you to do what makes you happiest, don't be like her." The words stopped up her throat, felt disingenuous and unfair and tasted horrible but only because they were true, true, *true*. She sobbed harder, hiccoughing against Gwennie's shoulder. "Please, please, please, don't be like her. Be better. Be good."

And that was a stupid thing to say because nobody ever was, not as easy as that, but it was unfair, so unfair that Evvie had to *see* it, so totally, so perfectly, so *soon*.

Beside her, the water in the sink began to overflow, pattering a syncopated staccato against the floor as it fled over the corner of the counter, and Evvie stood up quickly, yanking on the taps before the bathroom rug got soaked. Gwennie looked torn between confusion and amusement. The back of her eyes still hot with the rest of the tears that she didn't let fall, Evvie drained a bit of water from the sink, then set Gwennie down on the damp countertop and stripped her quickly of her onesie with shivering hands. She dropped it into the trash. She never wanted to look at it again. She didn't want to remember. Even if Evvie did ever get the blood stains out of it, every time she saw the little elephants on the cotton candy clouds, all she would think of would be aliens and knives and how Gwennie had almost…almost…

Evvie removed Gwennie's diaper as well—soiled but not too dirty—and then the gauze bandage on her forehead. Gwennie squealed when the tape came away with some of her hair and Evvie gathered her close, whispering soothing nothings against her head. Gwennie sniffled miserably, not entirely sure if the pain was worth full-blown tears. Evvie talked her out of them and sat back to take stock of the cut.

The flash of white bandage caught her attention instead. She stared at the gauze in her hand. A piece of the future.

She was about to throw it into the trash before it was ever created.

A strange urge to keep it, treasure it, to secret it away flooded up in her and she sighed.

Evvie shook her head at her own silliness and forced herself to discard the bandage. It wasn't special in any way, and it was soiled. It wasn't worth keeping. She refused to feel something as absurd as *regret* about it.

She turned her attention back to Gwennie and her wound. It was longer than Evvie thought it would be, judging by the scar on Gwen's forehead. On the adult Gwen, it arched back into her hair—that same hair covered it on the grown-up, but Gwennie's was still baby fine, and it was visible. The cut was a little deeper than Evvie thought at first glance, too. The tip of the knife had done more than nick her. *So close.*

It wasn't bleeding any more, and clotting just fine, but Evvie wondered if perhaps they should go into the hospital for some stitches after all. The thought of having to try to explain to the doctor that an alien from twenty-nine years in the future had been trying to cut her baby daughter's throat to prevent her from growing up and blowing its face off was too much, and Evvie scrubbed at her eyes with the heels of her hands.

No, Evvie knew how to take care of cuts. Her brothers had gotten hurt enough around the farm when they were children, and with her father out in the fields all the time and her mother sometimes in town running errands, it was up to her to patch them up. Some gauze, some tape, and a careful eye to avoid infections, and Gwennie would be none the worse for wear.

Save for the puffing white scar that would mar her perfect little forehead for the rest of her life.

Gwen wore her hair long on the right side of her face. She kept patting it down in a sort of reflexive, compulsive manoeuvre. Evvie hoped fervently that wasn't the result of some sort of bullying or a complex about her appearance that she had developed during her childhood. She wasn't sure how to even *think* about Gwennie at school, much less Gwennie at school getting bullied. Evvie didn't want to dwell on it, but with all the technobabble she and Basil spouted at each other, there was a distinct possibility that her (prom queen) daughter would turn out a geek.

Picked on. Loser. Outcast.

Was that why she was in some nameless military branch, involved with such a...horrible, rude man? Was she hiding? Did she feel she didn't deserve better?

Did she run away?

Don't think about it.

Testing the temperature of the water in the wide bathroom sink and deeming it cool enough, Evvie set Gwennie down to sit in it. Immediately Gwennie began slapping the surface of the water joyously with the palms of her hands, splashing the mirror, the wall, and Evvie. Tenderly, Evvie worked the mild shampoo into Gwennie's hair, avoiding the cut carefully, and rinsed it off with a scooped hand.

The water turned ketchup-red.

Evvie stared at it for an unmoving second, then she pulled Gwennie out. She had just enough time to pull her daughter, dripping wet, against her side and flip open the toilet lid before she puked.

It tasted like fish sticks and ketchup and disappointment and Evvie hated, *hated* that this was happening to her. Gwennie was completely still against her body, clinging with curled fingers like a sloth. Evvie flushed, unplugged the sink drain, and set Gwennie down on a thick towel on the floor of the tub before she cast about for the dusty bottle of mouthwash that was jammed against the back of the cupboard under the sink.

Just as she spat the lumpy, sticky green liquid out of her mouth, for once happy for the overpowering medicine, the sweet alcoholic burn at the back of her teeth, Evvie heard a voice float up through the half-open window. With a glance at Gwennie, who was happily mouthing her big toe, eyes getting droopy, Evvie went to the window, folded her hands over her fluttering stomach, and looked down.

Down in the yard, the lower half of Basil was poking up out of the ruined cockpit of the spaceship, and he was tossing electrical components up into the air, over his shoulders, to fall with a distant thud against the turf like in a cartoon. He was complaining—loudly—about how he was a *scientist* and not a *grunt* and the hiding of evidence was not *supposed* to be his job.

It was hardly eavesdropping if he was speaking at such a volume.

"Well, whose job is it supposed to be?" Gwen asked, rubbing her hands on the thighs of her pants as she emerged from between the rows of corn. A quick glance at where the alien's body used to be told Evvie what she had been doing out there. They had stripped off their tactical vests. In just their black pants and jackets they looked small and strangely fragile.

Human again.

"Wood's job," Basil said. "She's our clean-up man." Then, "*Bugger.*"

"What?"

"I'm stuck. My—*bollocks*—my bloody sleeve! Grab my trousers."

Gwen snorted. "What now? Here?"

"*Perv*," Basil said happily. "Pull me out."

Gwen complied, grabbing a good handful of his belt. With a mighty tug, Gwen had Basil out of the spaceship and sprawled half on the lawn and half on her. His left sleeve was in complete tatters, revealing more pale skin beneath and a sharp, angry red scratch. He rolled over, took advantage of their position, and kissed Gwen thoroughly. Evvie felt like a voyeur, even more because this was her daughter and her—what, lover? Boyfriend? Fiancé? Evvie didn't even know, anymore. But she didn't stop watching. Gwen's hands ran up the back of Basil's neck, carded through his thinning hair.

Still tactile Gwennie.

"I'm happy to see you smiling again," Basil said softly. Gwen replied by ducking her head down, tucking her chin against her own chest, curling up.

Evvie shivered, a feeling of soft foreboding settling over cool skin.

Basil sat up and waved something triangular in Gwen's face that was silverish and sprouting wires like feathers. "*Got* it," he said triumphantly, trying to win back the easy banter that his admission had quenched. "Now we can go back inside and I can murder your father's overcompensating excuse for a video player, and get us the bloody hell out of here."

Gwen's grin was wide and twinkling and oh-so-much like Gareth's and at the same time baby Gwennie's that Evvie's stomach lurched sideways and she thought maybe she was going to be sick again.

"Look," Basil added, digging into his breast pocket and coming up with a small metallic disk. Evvie was too far away to be able to tell, but it looked like it was made out of some sort of multicoloured, shining plastic or steel. "They even left us music to work by." Basil snorted and shoved it in his pocket without looking at it again. "What would I play it in, anyway?"

"Certainly not the Betamax." Gwen rolled her shoulders. "You know, when we get back, Dad will make you pay for it."

"With interest. Balls." Basil scratched the side of his nose, leaving a long smear of rainbow-slick engine fluid along his cheek. "I'll buy him an HDTV—one of the 'spensive ones that fold out and go flat against the wall, yeah?"

Gwen pulled a tissue from her pocket and scrubbed at the smear, and though he winced, Basil suffered manfully.

"I can't wait to see the look on his face when he sees us again," Gwen said, eyes on his cheek.

"On *both* their faces," Basil added happily.

And as quickly as that, the laughter was murdered.

"I can't do this," Gwen admitted brokenly, in a rush, and that was when the shaking started. She buried her face into Basil's neck, her back hitching with visible wrenching, dry gasps that struck Evvie, made her heart hurt and the back of her throat close up.

She was torn.

She wanted to go down, hold Gwen, touch her and soothe, but this woman was not Evvie's child and Evvie wanted nothing (everything) to do with her and her misery.

She was (Evvie's) not what she wanted.

Gwen's eyes were wet, but Evvie saw no tears on her cheeks, and she was blinking furiously, refusing to let them fall as firmly as Evvie had moments earlier. A family trait?

Had Evvie's mother ever cried in front of her? She couldn't remember.

"Shhh, shhh," Basil said, running his fingers through the hair at the back of Gwen's head, toying with the small curls that were really Evvie's curls, flipping them across fingernails etched with the guts of electronics and the mechanical oils (blood) of the spaceship. He nudged Gwen's forehead gently with his nose, murmuring directly into her ear, too soft and intimate for Evvie to hear. He raised his chin, kissed the scar once, kissed each dry eyelid, then Gwen's mouth, comforting and crooked and so filled with *want* that Evvie had to look away, at the floor, at the damp rug. She peered over the edge of the tub at Gwennie dozing, snuffling haplessly against the fuzzy towel.

"Right then," Evvie finally heard Basil murmur. "What can't you do?"

"I can't go back in there. I can't…" and the sucking of breath started again, a bit slower and a bit quieter. "Pretend that this is easy. That this is where I want to be. It's all too much, on top of…" When Evvie turned back to look again, Gwen's face was pale, sheeted with cold sweat, but there were still no tears on her cheeks. "I can't face her."

J.M. FREY

"Who, your mother?"

It felt like a punch in the chest.

"Did you see the way she *looked* at me? Basil…she hates me."

A tidal surge of guilt and grief passed through Evvie, and she wished that the words would wink out of existence; as much as they hurt, they were true, true, true, and that's what pained her most of all.

"I didn't choose this!" Gwen hissed, her shoulders hunched up by her ears, defensive, angry, spitting. "I only translate stuff! No one told me when I signed that confidentiality form that they were going to *split apart my world* and then hand me the puzzle and tell me to reassemble it with a *gun*."

"None of us did, Gwen. Be fair," Basil said softly.

"I'll be fair when she's fair! *Fuck*."

Evvie blinked at the cuss, wondered idly which one of her parents Gwen had learned it from, because she couldn't, *didn't* want to see the rage that it translated instead.

"The way she…I didn't want to be a…a *soldier*. I didn't want *any* of this!" She threw her arms out, gestured at the backyard, the hole in the ground, the place where the corn bordered the grass of the backyard. "I am in the past, *my* past, where I caused the scar on my own forehead by blowing off the head of an *assassin* from another *planet* and my mother *hates* me, and this is just way too freaking science fiction for my comfort level!"

Didn't want to?

Evvie saw the half smile try to slide into the corner of Basil's mouth. "Does that make me the acerbic genius? Or, no, I most definitely am the engineering geek. Ha! We are 'Stargate.' I am so Rodney McKay! And that makes you Samantha Carter. 'Cause, Amanda Tapping? Hot."

Evvie resisted grabbing the side of her head. What were they talking about now? Were these things she would read about in the news one day? A knot of panic pushed against her sternum and she took a deep breath. Their idioms and similes were making Evvie's head hurt, making an already baffling situation so viscerally confusing as to be nearly physically painful.

Evvie didn't *understand.*

Instead, Evvie focussed on Gwen, perched vulnerable and scared in the arms of the man she obviously loved, just as confused as her mother. *Wasn't a soldier.*

Gwen punched his arm. "Kinda having an existential crisis here!" *Mistake.*

"Ow," Basil muttered morosely. Instead of hitting back, he wrapped his arms around her shoulders, reeling her in, holding her against his chest and kissing the top of her head, the shell of her ear, the line of her neck. "I love you," he said. "And I'm here with you, and for now, that's good enough, innit?" he said.

Saved my life.

"I miss…" she whispered into his shoulder.

Saved her own.

Basil's breath hitched. "I miss him, too. I wish he was here."

Isn't a…

"That wasn't what I was going to say," Gwen snapped, perhaps a bit too quickly, too vehement in her denial. Basil's mouth slanted in such a way that said he had noticed it, too. "I don't. I can't believe… the least he could have done was *admit* to it. Let me hate him all the way, instead of playing fucking innocent up until the moment they blew a hole in his—"

"You don't *mean* that, Gwen," Basil said, his voice high and a little desperate. He pulled her close, buried her face in his neck, rocking her, muffling the rest of her sentence. "Yeah? You don't mean that."

Only doing what she has to.

Basil pressed his cheek against her hair, swaying them back and forth, one hand around her head, one arm tight around her neck. His own breath was short and uneven, panicked. "You don't really mean that, you can't, you *loved* him."

What she has to.

Gwen pushed him away, enough to look up into his face, head craned like a furious, puce-faced Scarlet O'Hara. "Just rig up a damn Flasher. Get me the hell out of here." She sniffled once, then hiccoughed. It would have been a laugh if it hadn't been so wet-sounding. "Before we descend into more bad sci-fi clichés."

Basil snorted out a little puff of laughter, which ruined the Rhett Butler pose, but he still tilted his head so their noses wouldn't bump, then kissed her long and slow and sad.

"They just shot him," Basil said against Gwen's lips, shaking like an addict, pulling back just a fraction to give his mouth just enough mobility to form words. "There was nothing I could do. Aitken panicked and just…just *shot him.*"

"Kalp sold us out," Gwen said back, a bitter, chiding reminder.

"He didn't, you *can't think*—"

"Can't think *what?*" Gwen hissed. "They *knew* that we started training the microsecond after the first assassination. *Somebody* told them what kind of training we were doing. *Somebody* was selling them information."

"That doesn't mean it was Kalp—"

"Well *who else?*" Gwen snarled. She pressed her hands against his shoulders like she was trying to push him away, but he wouldn't let go. He fisted his hands in the fabric of her shirt. "There was the letter. And that…that *thing* you used in the Flasher to get us here. All that time he was with us—"

"No."

"All that time he was *in our bed*—"

"No, Gwen."

"All that time he talked about *units* and *'it's the person, not the plumbing.'* He made us look like *fools.*" Basil kissed her temple, the top of her head, her cheek, silently, with desperation. "The Institute stood up on *international fucking television* and condemned the protesters for being such racists, such goddamned homophobes, *for him,* defended what we had *for him,* and he…he…"

She buried her face in his neck again, and her shuddering grief was palatable in the night air. Evvie imagined she could taste the salt of Gwen's unshed tears, feel her daughter shaking against her own hands. Basil reached up, brushed the pad of his thumb across Gwen's forehead, tracing the scar.

"He did that to me. It's his *fault*," Gwen said.

It sounded to Evvie like Gwen was trying to squash whatever affection Basil still clung to.

Enough.

Evvie left the window, gathered Gwennie up and put on a new bandage and some antiseptic cream. The baby protested with a dozy whimper, and Evvie went to put her down in the nursery. Mark was already there, standing beside Gwennie's open window, staring at the backyard, clutching the teddy bear he had bought Gwennie before he had ever met her.

For a moment they stood together, suspended between the dark of the room and the sudden dawn of understanding.

"I don't hate her," Evvie confessed, quietly, as she set Gwennie down in her crib. "It's not hate, it's…" How could Evvie hate her when she was suffering just as much (more) as Evvie was? "But I'm *scared* of her. What she's brought with her."

"Reckon she's scared, too," Mark replied.

TWILIGHT, AND Mark went out to the barn to do the last of the day's milking. Evvie went upstairs to check on Gwennie and wake her for her feeding. She didn't expect that either she or Mark were going to sleep any time soon, but the little rituals of the world didn't stop just because two strange people had dropped out of the sky. Evvie found Basil standing in the dark at the foot of Gwennie's crib, staring, watching silently as the baby slept. It should have made Evvie uncomfortable—instead, she found it strangely endearing, though still mostly creepy.

Evvie shifted from foot to foot in the doorway, then made a decision.

"Do you want to hold her?" she asked.

He raised his head slightly, not surprised by Evvie's sudden question, and she realized that he had probably known Evvie was there the whole time. He was (scary) special ops trained.

"Don't want to wake her," he said.

"She's going to wake herself in about five minutes." Evvie padded across the wooden floor to stand beside him and stare down at her child. She held out the bottle. "I've discovered that if I do the waking, she's less cranky than if she does it on her own."

Basil took the bottle with another small, crooked grin. "That's truth for the next twenty-nine years, too," he admitted.

Evvie reached down into the crib, rubbed Gwennie's tummy gently until she cracked a sleepy, hopeful eye. *Food time, Mom?*

Basil chuckled. "I know that face. That's the *where's-my-damn-coffee* face."

Gwennie suffered Evvie scooping her up, offering nothing more than a gummy yawn when she transferred Gwen to Basil's arms.

"Mind her head," Evvie said softly, and obviously needlessly; Basil already had a large, gun-calloused palm cradling her expertly.

He lifted the bottle to her mouth, hummed a bit when she took the nipple without protest, and smiled. "She looks like a tennis ball. Just like my sister's kids," he said.

"You have a sister?" Evvie asked, seizing on the tidbit of information; wanting desperately to make (it right) conversation.

"Mm," he said, nodding once, slowly. His eyes never left Gwennie's face, mesmerized, probably looking for the woman he loved in the baby fat and button nose. Evvie had done the opposite earlier. "Two. Older. Right horrors to grow up with—teased me for years. We got close after they both got married, and I realized how…empty my life is. Was." He smiled softly, and Evvie knew he was seeing things, people behind his eyes, that she could never know. "Used to be."

Another question danced around the room, and Evvie ignored it, even as she felt it crawl into her mouth.

"What's a Kalp?" She asked instead, frantic to keep the sound of voices in the semi-dark, or she might forget that he was human, might forget that they had saved her, might forget that he was hurting, might forget everything but her own irrational fear and that these people were strange. And that she (pitied) loved Gwen anyway.

Had to love her because Evvie couldn't hate her.

"Who," Basil corrected glumly. "He…he was killed by, uh…

another Specialist. He was…he was smart. He was…" Basil swallowed hard. "He used to mean a lot to Gwen and me. Before…well, before."

He looked up, eyes finding the silhouette of the corn against the darkening sky, seeing people and shadows and things that made the corner of his crooked mouth pull down. "Kalp lived with us. We were a…an Agl—a team," he said, correcting himself before he actually made the verbal slip, mindful of his audience. He gave a little huffing chuckle. "We shared a house. Kalp wanted to get chickens, 'cause the people in the movies always have chickens. British gardens and estates and all that. He devoured movies, liked the way the hum of the electronics felt against his skin. Never mind that we only had a small garden. A fox got at one, and Gwen had to strangle the poor thing with her bare hands. I couldn't bear to watch, but the sound was enough. Kalp made mushroom sauce and I refused to go into the kitchen until its eyes were gone. Gwen thought it was the funniest thing…"

He frowned again, trailed off, closed his eyes.

Basil seemed disinclined to say anything more.

The other question weighed heavily on Evvie's tongue, pressing until she would suffocate from it if she didn't ask: "How can you love her?"

Basil looked up, really looked Evvie in the face for the first time, and stared at her with cold, firm eyes. "Do you think I would still be with Gwen if I didn't? Especially after Kalp?"

"I didn't mean—"

"Yes. You did."

The loud sucking pop of Gwennie smacking her lips off the nipple startled Evvie, and she bundled her close when Basil passed her back, lifting Gwennie to her shoulder to rub the baby's back. Evvie wanted to run, out of the room, out of the house, out of this strange "Twilight Zone" episode that was suddenly her life, but Gwennie needed burping, needed tucking in, and Mark would want to wash up, then Evvie had dishes to do, bottles to prepare…Too much.

"I should be working," Basil said. "We need to get back. *Fix* this."

"What about the other people?" Evvie asked. Already Gwennie's eyes were getting heavy, but Evvie wouldn't put her down until she had belched. She patted Gwennie's back encouragingly, perhaps a bit too vigorously.

"What about them?" Basil asked coldly.

"Aren't you worried that other people are ceasing to exist all over the place?"

Basil sighed, rubbed his eyes with the thick pads of his fingers. "Not to be callous, but the only people I'm worried about right now are me and Gwen. The other people, the babies being murdered? Well, I don't know them. They never grew up, never became Specialists. The world shifted and someone else took their place, and those someone elses are my friends, aren't they? I never knew them, so if they die I don't—I *won't* care."

"That *is* callous," Evvie said angrily, pulling Gwennie tight against her chest. Gwennie responded with a little *urp!* in Evvie's ear. "You may not know them, but they're still *someone's* child."

Basil looked at the floor. "Look, the machines only have enough power to Flash every few days, which doesn't really mean a lot when it comes to time travel, but it's a better hope than anything else. So if we can get back there before they go off again, then we'll do what we can, okay? I don't want people dying anymore than you do, but I also have a duty to the Institute. "

Evvie stared at him, tasted her heartbeat on the back of her tongue. "Will they come back here?"

"They probably know that their assassin failed by now. So yeah, might do. Which," he ploughed on, interrupting her next question, "is why I must go and make shiny, complicated things now. You have tea?"

"Lots—in…in the cupboard next to the fridge. Six kinds."

"Lovely. Really. Another sleepless night for the amazing Doctor Basil Grey." The corners of his bright eyes crinkled slightly with a small grin. "I tend to do the not-sleeping thing a lot. Lots of close deadlines. Sort of come to live on the adrenaline rush. Drives Kalp and Gwen *mad* when I crawl into bed at dawn—" He made a sour, choking face. "Drove. *Bollocks.*" He shook his head once, viciously. Then he sighed, low and long, like a tire leaking. "There's just me, and they literally have time on their side."

"I don't hate her," Evvie blurted, apropos of nothing. "I just don't understand."

Basil didn't even blink. "So go *talk* to her," he said. "God knows what she needs is more trust issues right now."

GWEN WAS sitting at the kitchen table in the dark.

She was leaning back in her chair, the front two feet raised above the linoleum, wavering with each indrawn breath. Her knees were braced against the edge of the wooden table, and in her hand was a mug of milky tea. Her jacket and her heavy vest were piled artlessly on the end of the table, leaving her in a black tee-shirt that revealed well-toned arms.

Did the musculature come from lifting books or bullets?

Her feet were bare, and Evvie could see that under her military tightness she still had a bit of girl left—Gwen's toenails were a fun but elegant purple. Her hair was down, half flattened in the back where she had presumably been lying on it, unsuccessful in her attempt to catch a few minutes of sleep, and she still wore the little black piece of plastic in her ear.

Is it permanent, Evvie wondered, *can it even come out?*

Gwen heard Evvie walk in. Evvie didn't make a secret of it, didn't want to be spying on her daughter (except not her daughter) in the night. Gwen looked down at her mug, the remnants of a wistful smile ghosting across her mouth before it flattened again. "Chamomile tea, with a splash of hot milk," she said, holding the mug up slightly before letting it drop back into her lap, and wrapped both hands around it to leech on its warmth.

"That's what I drink," Evvie offered, "when I can't sleep." Evvie turned on the light. Gwen didn't wince.

"I know."

Yes, of course she did.

Slowly, out of respect for Gwen's bone-deep weariness and her high-strung paranoia, Evvie moved gently and deliberately around the kitchen to fix herself a matching mug. When Evvie had tea of her own, she sat in the chair opposite Gwen and sipped.

Evvie had questions. Obviously Evvie had questions. Hundreds. Millions. *What was your first word, who was your best friend, when was your first kiss? What were your grades like? Did I buy you the prom dress you wanted? Do you get on with your Dad? How long have you been with Basil? Have I met him already? Do you love (hate) your mother?*

Did Evvie like Kalp?

Did Evvie (approve) ever meet him?

Are you happy?

Evvie wasn't going to ask them, because then where would the little joyful surprises of her life come from? Evvie had already hurt Gwen (herself) enough with her carelessness and curiosity, and judging by what Basil had said, someone else hating her was the last thing Gwen needed right now.

"You know…" she said slowly, and almost so softly that Evvie didn't hear it. Evvie stilled, let Gwen chew on her thoughts like she was chewing on the bottom of her lip, peeling at a little flake of dry skin with her teeth.

"You know," Gwen said again, "those movies where the aliens come to Earth, and they…I dunno, they try to steal our natural resources, or create a nuclear winter so they can turn the Earth into slag, or they melt the polar ice caps and New York is under fathoms of water, or they clone us for slaves, or create terrifying bioweapons and wipe us all out and use our cities for farmland, or…all that stuff?"

Evvie's heart trembled. She could taste her pulse and her fear, thready and metallic on the back of her tongue. "Yes," she said softly. (Please, no.)

Gwen looked up. "It was nothing like that."

Evvie let out a breath she didn't realize she'd been holding, forced her shoulders down, away from her ears, exhaling the (terror) stale air.

Gwen sat forward, and the legs of her chair landed with a soft thump. She set her mug down with a muted *thock*. Then she looked up, eyes Evvie had known for only eight months meeting eyes that Gwen had known for twenty-nine years. She folded her fingers on the table top, stretched them out like a fan, curled them in again. Evvie waited.

"They were refugees," Gwen went on softly, out of deference for Basil toiling so diligently down in the sub-basement with his clinking tools and muted cusses, for Gwennie, asleep upstairs, for the ghost cast by Mark's absence. "Their world, it had gone out of whack. You know about centrifugal force?"

Evvie shook her head slightly. Gwen reached out; fingers splayed along the rim of the cup, turned it slowly clockwise.

Gwen exhaled loudly and then said, "Planets spin like this, right? That's what keeps them…together. That's part of what makes gravity, like…like when you swing a bucket of water up over your head."

Evvie nodded. Yes. That, she understood.

"Well, something—an asteroid, meteor, whatever, *space junk*—crashed into the planet, big enough to change the speed of their revolutions." She jerked her mug to the side, let it spin and bounce wildly for a second, but caught it before it crashed to the linoleum.

"Oh," Evvie said.

"Part of their world suffered from the debris cloud—no sunlight, little air. So many of them suffocated, and those who didn't were well on their way to starving to death. Like the dinosaurs. It was cracking apart, tectonic plates rupturing, magma thrown into the air, pieces of mountains just cracking off and going spinning into space at the end, just from the speed of the gyrations. The force was too great, the gravity became crushing, and the dust cloud was spreading. They escaped. Just one small, overcrowded, reeking ship. A population of billions reduced to one thousand, three hundred and thirty-seven."

Gwen traced a circle in the small spot of tea that had been jostled out of her mug, drew something that could have been a smiley face, could have been an alien refugee vessel.

Evvie waited.

"They found the Voyager probe out past…uh, you still call it a planet, don't you? Huh. Well, past Pluto. The probe, it…it had the coordinates of Earth, a message of peace, samples of music and plants and atmosphere. They learned about Earth and just…showed up. And it's not like we could say 'no,' not really. I remember that day. You remember days like that. The day Chernobyl went up, the day Princess Di died, the day the Twin Towers fell, S.A.R.S., the day the eastern seaboard went black, all the flu pandemics…"

Evvie sucked in a breath at that list, and couldn't decide if she should commit it to memory or try to forget it entirely. Gwen didn't seem to notice.

"The day they came, I was eyeball deep in the library, chasing some obscure translation out of the Welsh for my PhD thesis. I yelled at my best friend for running in and shutting the book on my fingers. She dragged me to the window and pointed up and said… 'Look.' Just '*Look*.'"

She stopped playing with the spilled tea, glanced back up at her mother, shrugged slowly and sort of sideways. "An international committee was formed, the U.N. ran it, and they started recruiting as many people as they could get—linguists, mechanics, engineers, cultural anthropologists, biologists, physiologists, social workers, botanists, sci-fi geeks. We became a *force*. The Specialists."

"The Institute."

Gwen smiled once, warm. "The something-something Institute of blahdity-blah-blah, actually. We just say 'The Institute' for short. I was so proud when they tapped me. Specialist Pierson. Has a nice ring to it, doesn't it? So happy to be *human*, to be *representing* us. It was all very top secret of course, hush-hush, didn't want mobs freaking out or anything, so I told you that I had been given a study grant to do an extra few years of my PhD at some university in Europe." She looked back at the empty mug by her hand, at the sad damp teabag in the bottom. "We fought. You didn't want me to go. We haven't spoken since. I thought you…"

I was trying to protect you, Evvie wanted to say. She knew that was why; she would say it because she knew what was going to happen. That Gwen would end up (miserable) here.

Evvie bit her bottom lip, then stopped when she realized that Gwen had been mimicking the motion mere moments earlier.

Silently, Gwen stood, took up her mug. She turned for the kettle and refilled it, placed it on the burner, and waited for it to boil. She said nothing, and neither did Evvie, both paused like a cassette, waiting, waiting.

Basil had said that other people would have stepped in at the Institute to take the place of the babies who were murdered. If there were any others. Would time and the universe and whatever else make sure that no matter what Evvie did, or what she tried to do, Gwen would still end up here, hurting and alone, in the past?

Could Evvie actually change *anything*?

Or, because it was happening now, would it have to happen again? Was there really any way to break this…this inevitable cycle?

And if there was…would Evvie know what that thing, that one decisive action or comment would be? But if Evvie did that thing, if she stopped…all this…then she would never have met Gwen and she would never know that she had to do something to keep her safe and happy, and then it would just happen again, wouldn't it?

Or…

Evvie pinched the bridge of her nose. This was complicated.

When Gwen came back to the table, her mug steaming again, she took a sip and contemplated what to say next.

She settled on: "We were doing *good work*." It looked like she wanted to say more, say something else, say something (personal) important. Instead she went on with her story: "There weren't many of them, see, so it was easy—they settled in Canada mostly, or in European countries; communities used to people who are different coming in and setting up camp. To immigration. We taught them how to use zippers, which side of the road to drive on, social etiquette, street slang. We taught them that baring your teeth is considered polite, not a threat—a smile. Kalp thought I was doing some strange tuneless singing the first time he heard me laugh. It gave him goose bumps because…oh, you know, they hear with their skin, sort of like…uh, echo locations and—and it's actually kinda thrilling when they touch you and…you know what? Never mind."

She pinked a bit, shy and feminine under the military shell.

"They taught *us* how to build vehicles that run on solar power, how to predict major earthquakes up to seven months before they're going to hit, the best way to throw a curveball and shoot a slapshot. How to form a cohesive family unit. How to get over our piddling gender issue bullshit; the countries that hadn't legalized same-gender marriages wised up fast." Another quick and guilty eye flick. "But the Institute, that's where I met Basil. He was trying to reverse engineer a sort of mechanical wind-surfer and kept futzing the directions because he couldn't read all of the alphabet. They sent him to my office and...*God*, he was an *asshole*. I actually dreaded the days he was scheduled with me. Then one day he asked me to translate this really dirty poem he'd found and...I guess I just liked his laugh."

She blushed again, the same shy pink that let Evvie know that there was still a woman under the academic patter, the regimented brusqueness. Evvie sipped her tea and said nothing, afraid that whatever came out of her mouth would be (prejudiced) ridiculous.

So much that Evvie couldn't follow.

"Then they sent us Kalp—he was an engineer, too—and we all met at the Institute. They made us into a research team, but Kalp thought it was...like, some cultural arranged marriage thing...so he kept *touching*...It was a huge disaster." The corners of her eyes crinkled a bit. "Kalp couldn't understand why I was so *angry* that he was trying to dance with Basil. On their planet it's in threes. Makes it easier, because how can two people possibly raise a child alone without sleep deprivation and going broke, or nuts? He didn't quite understand that here we...he was so...*innocent*. So sincere. He was so good for us. It was *too* perfect." Her pale eyes flashed with sudden bleak fire. "I'm such an *idiot*."

She trailed off, and Evvie tried to swallow her heart. Gwen's gaze roamed up the wall opposite, dark and shaded and once again unreadable. No, not unreadable; just used to being judged.

Both of them?

Oh, God.

Evvie wanted to say *no,* and *that's disgusting*; she wanted to, but she could see the pain in Gwen's eyes, see that she had loved him, missed him, even as she hated him.

TRIPTYCH

Can the world stay the same, after aliens show up and your best friend tells you to "look"?

"He was...*it* was...it was nice, really nice. Our time together." One hand stole down, fingers spread and then curling over her belly. Then they snatched up, back to the table top, to her hair, along the scar, then to pat her hair down over the thin white mark, and back to the side of the mug, heavy with guilt and sorrow, and then anger for feeling those. "There was opposition, of course, there's always opposition. But it's the Institute's job to spearhead change—change on Earth when it's better, change among them when it wasn't. They had to get used to new things too, but then...*it* changed."

Evvie wrapped her hands tightly around her own mug, white-knuckled, because otherwise she would get up and go around the table and wrap Gwen in her arms, and Evvie wasn't sure if Gwen would want (need) her pity or comfort. Evvie's sudden aching guilt. Regret.

"What happened?" Evvie asked instead.

Gwen shrugged again, looking more helpless this time. "I don't actually know." The downward slope of her shoulders matched the small miserable curve of her mouth. "One minute I'm translating alien blueprints and the next I'm in an underground bunker being initiated into a covert black ops squad. Kalp was put under house arrest. I went from practicing how to use alien dining utensils to being taught how to shoot a gun, how to disassemble and clean it, how to pull a pin with my teeth, the best place to aim if you're trying to...to k-kill..."

She grimaced at the tremor in her own voice, swallowed the scalding tea and grimaced again at the heat of it. She pulled her lips inwards until they were a frustrated white knife-slice, her eyes bright and wet but her cheeks pale and dry.

The swell of motherly desperation surprised Evvie, but didn't. Its intensity, but not its existence. "Why you?"

Gwen coughed once and sipped more tea, slowly this time. "We knew them best. We're the *Specialists*. They thought we could predict their...*them*." She spat the word, ran a hand through her hair, and Evvie knew it was to disguise the way it was shaking, so she didn't look. "They *thought* we knew them best, but clearly...We heard about the Flashers, but we figured they were locational. Basil and I, we were assigned to figuring out how they worked—we'd recovered one from a...an assassination. It was too *easy*, the way that they knew we were coming, the way they toyed with our Specialists. We knew there had to be a mole, we *knew*. But...but we never thought that *Kalp*...After the second assassination...They kept Basil busy working on the Flasher. It was all he'd do. He wouldn't...he never came home. He stopped eating chicken. He just...he'd just *work*."

Gwen bit at her bottom lip, looked down at her cup, then back up to the surface of the table. "They came to our house, came to arrest him and one of the...Kalp was reaching for m-me and Aitken panicked and then..." She shook her head vigorously, scrubbed at her eyes with her sleeve again. "I'd gone home with a team to bring Kalp back to the Institute, to get his help with the device, but Aitken was already there, and he was...he was trying to...to run. And he..."

Her narrative got incoherent in her frustration and Evvie lost the thread of her timeline. Gwen stopped and cleared her throat.

"Basil had finished the Flasher. He was using it to triangulate the co-ordinates of the origin points, you know, trace them back? But it also tracked the movements of a single body through, uh, well...space, for lack of a better English word. Um, time-space, I guess is better. They called it *isck*. We traced another Flash building up. It was going to go off in, maybe another day, so Basil just decided to...go. The prototype wasn't *finished*, wasn't safe, but he was determined to try to get there—here—before the other person did, stop them, maybe. I talked him into waiting long enough to suit up, grab our gear...He wanted to find out who made Kalp do that to us. We thought we'd go somewhere but...but not some*when*. He had a theory, but we didn't confirm that it was temporal until...well, until I saw you screaming in the garden. The Flash we were monitoring—our device must have dropped us here at the same second as the pilot, even though we left...earlier." She pinched the bridge of her nose. "Time travel is...complicated."

That made Evvie's throat tighten and she tried to open it again with more tea. "So they're...they're coming back in time to...get rid of you?"

"The Specialists' personnel records would have been easy enough to liberate from any office in the Institute—we don't exactly keep our identities secret from each other."

"But why do this?"

"So we're not there when they go back." Gwen stopped, thought for a moment, chewing on her thumbnail. "That's sort of stupid, though, isn't it? I mean, if it's not me it'll just be someone else. And that means they must have something that keeps them free of the regular flow of time, something so that their memories aren't altered to account for the missing people. It's just not *clever.*"

Evvie watched the horror spread through Gwen's posture before the realization swelled into her face. "We'll just pop out of existence, one by one," she whispered softly and this time she didn't seem to be clamping down on the shakiness of her voice. "We'll just be *gone.* Maybe the Institute, hell, maybe *everyone.* And we won't just disappear because we won't ever have existed. No one will remember us and no one will know we're missing, because no one ever *met* us. The whole human race, maybe, just...just *poof.*"

Gwen shook once all over, convulsive and revolted, then went tense and white and blank-faced; Evvie thought for a panic-stricken moment that she was going into a seizure. Then Gwen reined herself back in and her unwanted military training took over, breaths slowing and regular again.

The weariness that was merely bone-deep before, now seemed to stretch all the way into Gwen's soul. The tenseness melted and with it seemed to go her rigid posture. She sagged back in her seat, tipped her head up and rested it against the back of the chair, throat bare in the moonlight that came through the window over the sink. There was a small purple hickey peeking out of the collar of her tee-shirt, mostly-faded, and Evvie tried very hard not to be shocked by it.

"How many friends have I lost? How many people have winked out of existence around me, how many people couldn't I save because I had no memory of them? What if I'm next?" Gwen raised her head and looked down the stairs at Basil's broad back, bent over a large piece of circuitry which he seemed to be stabbing repeatedly with a screwdriver. "God, what if *he* is?"

EVVIE LEFT Gwen to her thoughts and her misery.

She took her confusion, her worry, and her shuddering heart upstairs. She needed quiet, needed space to (fall apart) think. To process it.

Mark was already in the shower, washing off the sweat and grime and dirt of a day's worth of dusty work in the barn. The room held the faint hint of barnyard and next spring's harvest. His clothes were draped over the wicker chair in the corner. Evvie suspected that he had helped Basil and Gwen bury the spaceship: there were long dark streaks of soil that ran up the shins of the jeans. Keeping one ear open for Gwennie, Evvie tidied the bedroom, putting Mark's clothes into the laundry hamper, turning down the sheets. She refolded the laundry on the foot of the bed, put it all away, dusted the top of the dresser with a sock destined for the wash.

Anything to keep her hands busy and her brain occupied.

When she'd run out of things to do, she sat on the edge of the bed and waited. When Mark came out of the bathroom he was in a fresh tee-shirt and jeans. Neither of them wanted to drop into unconsciousness just yet.

Not with strangers (soldiers) in the house.

Not with this new world under their roof.

"How you feeling?" Mark asked, sitting beside her. He smelled like soap and cheap shampoo. Evvie locked her hand with his, grateful for the warmth and support and solidity of him, the blunt fingers, the rough bitten-down nails. He didn't seem ruffled at all, which Evvie knew was mostly just the stoic farmer act. Inside, he was churning just as much as she.

"I don't know anymore," Evvie admitted softly. "Aliens? Time travel?"

"It's a hell of a lot to swallow," Mark agreed.

Evvie licked her lips, debated telling Mark what she had learned.

She decided to share—she *needed* to. Whatever they spoke of would stay between them. Evvie felt like it was building, words like pressure behind that lump in her throat that could strangle her.

"Gwen talked about what happened," Evvie blurted.

Mark said, "Yeah?" There was a world of curiosity in that one syllable.

"Said it was nothing like those B-movies with the guys in rubber suits. That they were running. Needed help and shelter." She pressed her face into his shoulder, took a shaking breath. Then Evvie told him everything: about Gwen's team and the way Specialists were suddenly being assassinated, and their covert training, and the mole.

Evvie left out the parts about Gwen and Basil and Kalp's relationship, about same-gender marriages, about proper alien family units. If Evvie didn't talk about it, she wouldn't have to *deal*. But Mark's lazy drawl masked a keen mind. He had to have inferred at least as much from Gwen's sobbing confession on the back lawn as his wife had.

"Imagine that, Evvie," Mark said, bypassing the elephant sitting on the tips of each of their tongues. "Can you imagine waking up in the morning, seein' one of those things, all spaghetti limbs and lope shoulders and furry faces, walkin' its kid to catch the school bus at the end of the lane? An' it'll be *normal?*"

Evvie tried to envision it, a creature in a plaid shirt and rough worn jeans, all blue and furred and humanoid…or human-ish—or whatever reaching adjective was amateurishly employed to evoke a head, two arms, two legs, upright walking and emotive in the old pulp serials of her brother's youth. The sort of heavy-handed fantasy from which the plot of this wild day felt as if it'd been pilfered.

"One of 'those things' betrayed them," Evvie whispered. "That's why this is happening. I think…"

"Their…friend?" Mark asked, not comfortable with the concept.

What about VD? Evvie thought suddenly, absurdly. *Have they cured them in two thousand twelve? What if the aliens brought something new with them? What about that gay disease? All these fags, allowed to marry, allowed to take more than one lover…is that where the world is going?* "Wise up," Gwen said. *Like it's the dark ages.* She chewed her bottom lip for a second, tried to see it from Gwen's perspective. She'd grown up in a world where men could marry men, where women could marry women, where AIDS and gays and those sorts of things sounded…common. Here Evvie was reacting like her own mother when Evvie had told her that pre-marital sex was okay, and she had—

Oh.

Oh.

Mark narrowed his eyes at Evvie but said nothing. Evvie wrenched her mind back onto the conversation. "'Those things'," she repeated. "I just don't get it, I guess. I mean, the Specialists and everything, I understand that. But not the…not the assassinations. If they wanted to take over the planet or, or something like that, then why kill only the *Specialists*? We gave them our trust, opened our arms to them, and they…now they're doing *this*." She didn't have to explain what *this* meant, they both knew.

"I dunno," Mark said. "That don't seem right. Like Basil said." Mark pronounced it *Bay-zil*. "Why go to all that trouble? Especially if they knew that the Institute could follow them. They had to have known Basil had a Flasher doohickey. 'Less they don't know that it won't work?"

"I know," Evvie agreed.

"Like me pushin' that tractor into a pond and then hollerin' to people to come see. It don't do anything in the end but get you in trouble."

"I thought you said the McKinnion boys did that," Evvie said suspiciously. "And that they framed you."

Mark shifted in his jeans, which suddenly seemed to be too tight. He turned his head to stare at the baby monitor on the bedside table. "Hear that? Gonna go check on Gwennie," he said, and bolted out of the room.

The only sounds coming over the little speaker were Gwennie's soft, even breaths.

SLEEP WAS coming to no one tonight.

Evvie gave Mark a head start and some thinking room, then went back downstairs to fetch another bottle. Gwennie would be waking soon, hungry and soiled. Gwen was on her knees on the floor of the sub-basement, talking in low murmurs with Basil, handing him a tool occasionally. Basil made little head jerks, grunts of understanding, but his eyes never left the device in his hands. A little tip of a moist pink tongue poked out of the corner of his lips.

Evvie went over to the fridge, pulled out the bottle she had prepared before dinner, set it in the little pot of water they left on the stove for the purpose of heating it.

There was the rustling sound of clothing and the padding of socked feet across the kitchen floor. "Why aren't you asleep?" Gwen asked from over Evvie's shoulder.

Evvie felt a smile wanting to tug at her lips. "Why aren't you?"

"Nightmares," Gwen admitted straightforwardly, and something hitched at the back of her throat.

"Want to talk about it?" Evvie asked.

"Not particularly." Evvie heard rather than saw Gwen lean back against the counter across the kitchen from her. "You know, I've always wondered why you never planted anything in the dead patch above the strawberries."

Evvie chuckled. "I won't be able to rotor-till there without breaking the tines."

"But the grass will never grow back. High foreign metal content, maybe?" Evvie heard her snort, partially a laugh, partially hysteria. "In advance, I apologize for the stupid lie about the Europe scholarship. I should have thought of something better. You knew the whole time. I must have sounded like an *idiot*."

"I already forgive you," Evvie said. She was not surprised to realize that she meant it.

"And…and the fight too. The…the last thing you said to me was, 'I have something to tell you—', but I hung up. I cancelled my cell, moved away. And all you wanted to do was warn me about *this*." Gwen made another strange sound, gestured up at the house, at Evvie, at *this*. "I suddenly have so much more sympathy for Marty McFly."

Evvie turned off the element, put the bottle on the counter to cool a bit, and turned to face her. "Who?"

She shook her head. "Never mind." Her eyes went huge. "*That's* why you always laugh so hard at the breakfast scene!" She clapped her hands to the side of her head and said, "Ow. I think I just gave myself a mini-stroke thinking about it."

Evvie felt the smile trying to slide across her lips and let it come. "I can't understand half of what you say."

Gwen dropped her hands to her sides with a shrug. "Be thankful I'm not speaking in Welsh. I do that when I'm tired."

Evvie chuckled, and the exhalation of humour felt good (a relief).

"Tea!" Basil shouted from the sub-basement, his voice sudden and plaintive. "Teeeeaaaa! Get us more tea, love?"

"What'd your last servant die of?" Gwen shouted in return. The acerbity was still there, but now Evvie could see the affection underneath it.

"Answering back!"

"Har, har," Gwen deadpanned, even as she moved to the sink and began to wash one of the dirty mugs. "Damn Basil and his tea. I never drank this much tea before I...Oh!" Gwen said, standing up straight suddenly, craning her head around to look Evvie in the face. "In grade four, when I come home with a black eye, Annalise McNeil really *did* start it...and I didn't mean to rip my new jeans in grade seven, oh, and I totally hated that froufrou thing you wanted me to wear when I was the Fall Fair Queen and if you have any love for me at all, you'll burn it the minute Esther Boycott shows it to you."

Evvie sucked in a little breath. "You were the Fall Fair Queen?"

Gwen grinned. "Yeah. I was the first one they let wear jeans to the social."

"Why?"

She blinked, something just occurring to her, and lowered the sudsy mug. It clinked against the edge of the sink. Her grin turned mega-watt (real). "You accidentally set fire to the dress."

TRIPTYCH

EVVIE PADDED upstairs to give Gwennie her bottle and Gwen and Basil their privacy. Evvie wasn't quite sure what she expected the privacy to lead to. Surely they wouldn't make out in the basement, especially not with their respective exhaustion and the tenseness that the urgency of the situation brought. For all of their sitting and talking, they were still on a time limit.

Mark stayed upstairs to give Gwennie her feeding, needing something to anchor him, something solid and meaningful, something familiar, something to hold on to. For a while, Evvie sat in the rocking chair by the window and just watched. When the bottle was empty, Mark began to whisper soft, crooning things to Gwennie and Evvie felt a little like an interloper.

She took the empty bottle back downstairs to the kitchen, planning to wash it and refill it with formula. They always kept a prepared bottle or two in the door of the fridge. She had no intention of eavesdropping any further on Gwen and Basil, but the soft sound of the cassette player in the sub-basement breathing out a tinny rendition of Chicago's "Hard to Say I'm Sorry" piqued her interest enough for Evvie to stand at the sink with her ears open.

"Where did you find that?" Basil's voice murmured softly, above the tell-tale clinks of his mechanical debris.

Gwen's reply was just as soft. "Dad always kept his mix tapes in the cupboard under the TV."

"Mmm, this song makes me want to dance," Basil said.

Gwen's laugh was light, but melancholy. "You haven't danced since...hm."

"About time then, innit?"

The click of tools being set down into his little tin toolbox, the shuffle of socks against carpet, the soft *fap* of hands in hands. Palm to palm. No sound but their soft, deep breaths, the slow susurration of an intimate, slow sway. A long, low sigh.

"You never cried for him," Basil whispered, so low that Evvie almost didn't catch it. She let her hands rest gently on the edge of the counter, noticed absently that they were balled into white-knuckled fists.

"I'm not sad," Gwen said.

Basil chuckled again. Evvie could imagine his soft belly, warm and pillowing, bouncing slightly against hers. "You're a horrible liar. You cried for Lalonde, and Ogivly, and Derx. You even cried for Barnowski, and he used to drive you up the wall. You sat there and did the Ceremony of Mourning with their Aglunated. You and Kalp and...oh. Why won't you do it for him?"

"Why should I? The others lost their Aglunates. I only lost a traitor."

"What if he *wasn't*, Gwen?"

"Basil, *please*. I don't want to talk about it anymore."

"But, the *component*. It wasn't what I first thought it was. What if he—"

"*No.*"

Feet moving away from each other, the cassette suddenly snapped off. An angry crash of tools being hurled into the wall, and Basil's rough shout: "And you wonder why I don't sodding come home!"

Evvie took a step back, shoved her hands into her pockets, and gasped for the air that suddenly evacuated her lungs.

"We are seriously *not* having a domestic in my parents' basement!"

"Why not? Seems as good a place and time as any! At least we'll be talking about it!"

"I don't *want* to talk about it."

A sharp wail from above their heads put an abrupt end to the argument.

"What the *hell* is going on down there?" Mark called down the stairs, voice raised over Gwennie's misery.

"*Nothing*," Gwen called back, mutinous and petulant.

It was such a reflexive, daughter-like response, it actually made Evvie gasp. She'd be hearing that word in that tone again, no doubt.

When Gwen stormed up the short flight of stairs and towards the back of the house, Evvie shrank back into the shadows and hoped she wouldn't be noticed. Gwen was too preoccupied with her ire to see Evvie, and she was safe. Evvie heard the stomp of boots being jammed on feet, the crash of the screen door slamming against the cement wall of the mud room, and a frustrated litany of multi-lingual cussing that seemed to reach the stars.

THE OLD axiom was true, and the kettle was taking its sweet time.

It seemed an eternity passed, one long, endless night of muted, damp suffering before the little whistle cut through the thick air. Carefully, Evvie poured out two cups of soothing Earl Grey tea, let them steep, and carried them downstairs. Tea seemed to be the tool of comfort and confession tonight, and who was Evvie to break tradition? The house was turning into a Hemingway story.

"Time to take a break yet?" she asked softly, knowing that Basil had probably heard the kettle, heard her come down the stairs.

He sighed, rubbed his eyes with broad, calloused thumbs, and set down his screwdriver. "Yeah," he said. His eyes slid sideways to the new black scuff on the cream wall, and he winced. "Sorry."

"Nothing a little paint can't fix," Evvie assured, handing him one of the cups.

"Cheers."

"So how does it work?" she asked, nodding at the conglomeration of half-melted sleek black plastic and anachronistic chunky wires and metal shards. Something triangular and melted sat off to the side, obviously discarded but clearly something far beyond the scope of any kind of technology Evvie had ever seen before. The silverish thing from the ship's cockpit was now wired into the nest of technology that Basil had been attacking so vigorously all night.

Basil shrugged and tilted one corner of his mouth down. "I can't legally tell you. But, you know the transporters in 'Star Trek'?"

"Yes?"

"Nothing like that." He smirked.

Evvie returned it. "Cheeky."

She surveyed the collection of dirtied mugs peppering the carpet around him, including Gwennie's pink elephant sippy cup, and wondered if she should have fixed something stronger, like black coffee. Or a double of whiskey.

Basil seemed content though, holding the cup under his face, drinking in the warmth, and the steam, and the sweet, thin, spicy scent. He shuffled on his bum over to the couch and propped himself back against one of the arms. Evvie sat in the loveseat nearby and let him savour the tea, the silence, the moment of respite.

"Suppose you heard all that," he said, halfway through his cup.

"Hard to miss," Evvie answered, equally soothingly.

"She's wound up," he explained softly. "She's…she hasn't grieved. Any of it. It's not…healthy, issit? Doesn't help, me barricading myself in my lab as I do, but I have to…I *have* to *fix* this, before someone else loses their…"

"Aglunate?" Evvie tried warily, fumbling on the unfamiliar word.

He cut a calculating glance at her, but decided to let the evidence that Evvie had heard more than just the shouting part of the fight slide. "Someone is trying to wipe out the Institute. We've trained as best we can to defend ourselves, each other, but…I think they're going back in time, getting rid of those of us that they can't assassinate, perhaps the ones that took to the training better."

"Gwen is one of those?"

Basil nodded, mouth curled on the edge of the mug. His upper lip was smooth, as if no scruff had ever grown there, and Evvie was struck for a surreal moment by the gentleness, the kindness and intelligence that he radiated. Not exactly the most manly of men, but his shoulders were broad and his arms were (comforting) thick, his mind keen. Sheltering.

"So maybe they came back here to get rid of her that way." He touched the rim of the cup to the centre of his forehead, held it there, using the heat to soothe away what appeared to be a concentration-headache. He had been squinting at his little electrical components for hours. Too long. "Only it's a rather silly thing, innit? Time fixes wounds like that, seals 'em back up. People go missing, someone else will always step up, fill the role, so they achieve nothing. Nothing 'cept, you know…dead babies."

"I suppose I should be proud," Evvie said, allowing herself a light chuckle, trying to raise his spirits, trying to turn from a less morbid, less immediate subject. "My daughter is a strong woman."

"Stubborn," Basil corrected. "Belligerent, obstinate…God, really *mulish* when she puts her mind to something. Couldn't kill *her* unless she *wanted* t'be killed."

"You really do love her."

His grin was brilliant but brief, damp with strain and sorrow.

"And you loved Kalp, too?"

Again, the narrowed eyes, the quick and calculating gaze. "I loved Kalp just as much as I love Gwen," he said a mite forcefully. Like he'd had this argument many times before. He probably had. "Different but just as intense. People are capable of loving more than one person at a time."

"I'm not disputing that," Evvie said softly.

He swallowed his sharp retort, all the angry tension on his face falling away, rigid posture melting to a languid sprawl.

"You're one of the few, then," he said, just as soft.

"I don't see how it's my business, telling people where to fall in love," Evvie said tightly, because she was *wising up fast*. If she wanted to be able to accept, to love her daughter, she would have to also accept that this was how she chose to live her life and there was, clearly, *literally* nothing Evvie could do about it. "Though, I wonder about…" Evvie stopped. She looked down at her hands.

"Mixed breeding?" Basil supplied and he sounded like he'd had *this* argument before, too. "We're not genetically compatible, so don't worry about that. Any…" he trailed off, face scrunching up, and Evvie thought she saw him brush at his eye with his cuff. He pressed the heel of his hand against his temple, so it could have just been a gesture of frustration, of exhaustion. "Any child would have been mine and Gwen's, but Kalp…K-Kalp would h-have been…I'm sorry." Now he *was* crying. He wiped his wet cheeks on the arm of his tattered sleeve.

"You miss him."

"Hell, yes."

Silence.

Then, "Actually, I wondered about the wedding rings."

Basil looked up, the mottled flush back. "Uh, Kalp's people don't, and, uh, thin fingers…it kept slipping off. We just, uh, didn't bother."

"And Gwen's *sure* it was Kalp who…betrayed you?"

Basil set aside his tea, suddenly not interested in it anymore. He crooked his legs, wrapped his arms around them, rested a sharp chin on his knees. Alone.

For a moment he sat perfectly still. Then he reached into his jacket breast pocket, took out the round piece of palm-sized plastic/metal from the cockpit of the space ship, and began to flip it over the backs of his fingers and down his hand. Evvie had seen people juggle coins that way. The disc shone with the same out-of-this-world sheen as the little blackened lump by Basil's foot, though the colours were lighter, more pastel. This disc was human-made. Evvie had seen CDs like this on the news, but never so small.

After a minute of disc-flipping Basil answered her question: "The evidence seems to say so, but it's too…neat. Too perfect, yeah? Just one more Specialist out of the way. Occam's Razor—the simplest answer is probably the most correct, but the simplest answer makes them all seem so *daft*."

"But Kalp wasn't a Specialist," Evvie said, trying to understand it herself.

Basil made a small, frustrated sound in the back of his throat. "That's what I mean, innit? It makes no *sense*. They're not a stupid race. Kalp was too damn smart to…to get *caught* that easily. Unless…"

"Unless he was framed," Evvie said, voicing the thought that Basil seemed reluctant to put into (reality) words. "And Gwen's hurting too much to consider it. She needs someone to be angry with."

Basil nodded silently.

"Why kill Specialists? That's what I don't understand," she admitted. "What good would it do, getting rid of the people who were helping them adjust?"

Basil made the frustrated sound again. "We're just the tip of the iceberg, see? What happens below the water line, we don't know. They don't tell us. 'Help them,' we're told. 'Learn from them,' and 'teach them,' and now 'kill them.' Only they don't tell us why. They put Kalp under house arrest, like all of the Institute employees of his kind, so how did that bit of Flasher get in the house?"

"You could have—" Evvie tried to interrupt, but Basil shook his head sharply.

"I sure as hell didn't bring it home. I would have remembered that. But we were all so scared, so wound up, so strung out and our fingers are all on the triggers and just like that, here's the traitor? Fire at will? No." He picked up his tea again without looking, a long-ingrained habit. A comfort blanket in a mug. The small disc dropped to the carpet, forgotten.

"It's too perfect."

Basil smiled wryly against his mug, lips still on the rim. "Innit?"

"Gwen doesn't see it that way, does she, though?"

Evvie picked up the abandoned disc. It was lighter than she expected it would be, not at all metal, but more like holding a piece of hard feather; plastic but too smooth to be plastic. The future—Evvie was holding a piece of the future in her hands. It was more surreal, more believable, more...*futuristic* than a bloody gauze bandage. Evvie turned it side to side so the rainbow refracted in the surface skittered along the edges, then flipped it over to read the writing etched on the other side—*Raquel Winkelaar: Live From Montréal*.

"She's hurting. We've lost friends."

"And Kalp."

He sighed, heavily. "And Kalp." He counted off on his fingers: "A Linguist, a Pop Culture Specialist, an anthropologist, a security guard, a biologist, two of Kalp's colleagues...there's no connection. They're not even all human. All that's left is questions and grieving Aglunates."

Evvie frowned, something tickling the back of her mind. "Wait," she said. "*All* of them had Aglunates? Is it that...accepted, then?"

Basil frowned, shook his head. "Not really, no. Only the Specialists have formed proper Aglunates, because you know, we've known them longer, understand their culture. It's more accepted at the Institute, but it's gaining...well, people are getting used to the idea. You can't just disallow an entire part of someone's culture because it doesn't fit into your tidy world view. The rest of the planet will get there slowly."

The tickly something twitched again. "So, the Specialists being killed are all Aglunated."

"Yeah."

Basil reached out and plucked the disc from her hand. He read the label, then sneered. "This was, without a doubt, the worst night of my life, and only partially because it was such an awful concert. We all *hate* Raquel. It made Kalp's skin ache. He squeezed my arm hard enough to make bruises."

"His skin?" Right, yes, Gwen had said something about Kalp and the television, Kalp feeling with his skin, like...like a bat, maybe?

"Raquel in particular is horrible for them. She's got this synth thing in all her music that's all syncopated and grinding, and it just rubs the wrong way. Drives them loony. I haven't met one of 'em that can stand to be around her music without trying to scratch off their own fur. Physically *hurts* them."

Evvie frowned. "So why would the pilot of the ship have her album in the cockpit player?"

A beat.

All the colour slid off Basil's face, and he shot to his feet. "Why didn't I...*why?* And I'm supposed to be a genius! I see where Gwen gets it." He bent down, pecked a kiss to Evvie's cheek, and vanished up the stairs in a flurry of black uniform and flashing eyes.

His mug sat abandoned on the arm of the couch, a slow amber drop of cold tea sliding down the pristine white side until it bloomed against the fabric.

EVVIE FOLLOWED the sound of the screen door slamming back, feet pounding across turf, the shouting.

Gwen was sitting in the lowest branch of a gnarled apple tree on the edge of the property between the garden and the corn. Evvie wondered if this was going to be her favourite place to think while she grew up. Basil tugged her leg, pulling her to the ground, catching her against his chest.

"What the *hell* is wrong—"

"The pilot!"

"—with you, what? What pilot? Huh?"

72

Evvie slipped on her garden boots, folded her arms to fend off the chill night breeze, and crossed the dark lawn towards them.

Basil flashed an excited, white-toothed smile. "Jesus, Gwen, the *protesters*. You saw the riots when the first—when *our* Aglunate was government-sanctioned. It was *violent*. Those people were *determined*."

Gwen scowled. "What's that got to do with us? They were disbanded. Arrested!"

"All of them? Are you *sure?*" Basil said, eyes flicking over her face, searching for, hoping for some sort of realization, of understanding and acceptance, for some spark of emotion, for *anything*. "What I mean is…what if it's someone else? What if it's all humans? Someone using them—their technology—to sneak around the Institute? All of 'em not wanting us *mixing*."

"What? How do you—?"

Basil's mouth pulled up in the parody of a smile. "The pilot was listening to Raquel!" He cocked his head to the side, a *yes yes, you see?* expression on his face.

Gwen's eyes got wide. "He was human?"

Basil nodded. "I think. I mean, I didn't get a good look before you…it could have been a mask or, or plastic surgery maybe? Think about it—it's only human Specialists who've been Aglunated have been targeted, yeah?"

"What about Derx?"

"*With* Barnowski. Pias, too."

"What about…" she trailed off, swallowed once, "Kalp?"

By now Evvie was close enough to join the conversation. "He was a set up—a dummy," she said softly. "To get you to turn against your own teams. Get the Institute fighting itself. To kill the trust between our people and theirs."

Basil snapped his fingers, pointed at Evvie like a particularly bright student, and nodded. "Everyone on the bloody planet knew our bloody address, they could have *mailed* something and Aitken was just so keen…"

Gwen pressed her forehead against Basil's shoulder, and Evvie resisted the urge to reach out, to rub her back in soothing circles.

"*Oh*," Gwen whispered, voice weak and shaking. Her whole face turned a ghastly white and for a moment she appeared as if she was going to vomit. She swallowed heavily, hands suddenly shivering where she had them fisted into his tee-shirt.

Her knees went out from under her and for a second Evvie thought she'd fainted, but no, her daughter was stronger than that. She was just trembling too hard to remain upright. Basil held her up by winding his arms under hers, and looked with excited concern into her face.

"Gwen?"

"Yeah, yeah, I'm fine I...*fuck*."

Basil whispered quickly, excitedly into her ear. "Yeah? But it...it's perfect, innit? There are enough people who don't want them around. Enough *politics*. This is just one way to get the world's attention. Get their voices heard without causing any actual genocide."

"That's horrible," Evvie said. Misery and anger slid cold in her gut.

Basil snapped and pointed at Evvie again. "Of course, The Institute is the shining beacon of *integration*. Of accepting new ways. That's gotta go, too."

Gwen frowned, looked back up. Her cheeks were dry, and Basil's words on her stubbornness flooded back to Evvie. Gwen still refused to mourn for Kalp.

"They picked Kalp because of *us*. Because *we were*—"

"—*exactly*. So it was all—"

"—and they would have to target people we knew, people they thought were the worst offenders—"

"—like us, like Kalp—"

"—set him up and put him in a position to be murdered, without the onus being theirs, the *bastards*—"

Gwen and Basil stared, gap-mouthed, at each other for a moment.

Basil reached down, fingers shaking, and wound them around Gwen's hand tightly.

Gwen sniffed, her chin shaking. "I never cried for him," she said, eyes shining. "I *hated him* and I never, I never *cried*...he died reaching out for me and I couldn't...touch him."

Basil pulled her flush against his chest, buried his nose in the thready curls below her ear.

Gwen wept, and all Evvie could think was *finally, finally, finally.*

THEY RETURNED to the house, Basil buzzing with caffeine and new purpose. Gwen retreated to the master bedroom to have some time alone, her eyes red and puffy, her face blotched, exhaustion and weariness and grief pulling at her shoulders. Evvie felt, strangely, both hollow and filled. Too filled.

Mark left Gwen the room and went to go start the dawn milking.

Eventually Gwennie woke and fussed for breakfast, disturbing Gwen through the baby monitor. She stumbled out into the hall, bleary and looking no more rested than she had when she'd gone to lay down. Mark was still in the barn, so that left Evvie to juggle Gwennie and her bottle. Gwen was willing enough to help, and held her squirming self at the kitchen table, watching the red face, the chubby fingers, the bandage on her head.

Basil came up the stairs sometime after Gwennie settled. He had a piece of metal, roughly a box, cradled in his arms, three empty mugs clutched awkwardly in one hand and his strange flat, unbelievably small computer in the other one.

"Cheers," he said, when Evvie swooped in and took the mugs.

"Basil," Gwen said, looking up from where she was holding the bottle to her younger self's lips. "It has a big *red button.*"

"Yeah, I *know*," he said with the excited grin of a child with the best shiny new bike ever. He was practically vibrating with geeky (endearing) excitement. "Cool, innit?"

Now, if only Evvie could get him to wear tight jeans and ask for a second helping of apple pie. Evvie had no pie to offer, so instead she said, "Shower? Breakfast before you go?"

Gwen nodded, looking down at herself, sniffing surreptitiously. Then she said, "Ehg. Yes. Shower."

Basil wrinkled his nose. "Oh, yes please."

Evvie gestured at the stairs, then held out her arms for Gwennie. "I assume you know where the towels are?"

Gwen flashed Gareth's twinkling smile at her mother. It was real and it was a relief, and to Evvie it felt like it melted a burden (guilt) away. Gwennie changed hands with nothing more than a perturbed blink.

"I'll leave fresh clothes out on my bed," Evvie said after them as they walked up the stairs wearily, and tried very hard not to think about the fact that she could distinctly hear both sets of footfalls walk into the washroom together.

Evvie busied herself with dishes and laundry and Gwennie.

When they came back downstairs, Gwen was wearing the dark jeans and the bright teal sweater Evvie had laid out for her. She was shifting her shoulders around, grimacing. "Shoulder pads?" she asked, gesturing at them. "They're hideous."

"Lady Di wears shoulder pads," Evvie said, reaching out and adjusting them to sit properly.

Basil made an unflattering sound in the back of this throat. He was wearing his uniform pants, as none of Mark's were big enough. A clean, machine faded tee-shirt stretched across work-sculpted pecs, and he actually looked quite dependable. Evvie already knew that he worked unreasonable hours, but she wondered if he had a good benefits package.

Did he bring home flowers?

BREAKFAST WAS a rather subdued affair: runny scrambled eggs that Evvie couldn't cook properly because Basil had taken a piece out of the microwave without telling anyone, and toast that was slightly burnt for the same reason. The tea was hot because he'd had the good sense to leave the stove and kettle alone.

It had taken some convincing to get them to sit down for one last meal with the Piersons, and Evvie had a feeling that Gwen knew that she had ulterior motives. Motives that were harder to talk about than Evvie had assumed they would be. They sat there like a sixth diner in the corner, and hulked until she just couldn't take the tiptoeing around them any longer.

"I want to apologize," Evvie said.

Mark didn't look surprised, nor did Basil. Gwennie was calmly and with great dignity giving herself an egg facial, and Gwen didn't look up from her mug.

"I didn't mean to make you feel…" Evvie looked at Mark, trying to search for the correct word in his face. He found it in hers first.

"Unwelcome," Mark said softly.

Gwen put her mug down on the table and waited.

"I don't hate you," Evvie confessed. "You saved my baby's life. You're saving other people's lives. You are doing work that's helping people."

Gwen snorted, and said into her mug, "Rocks and hard places have nothing on this."

"I'm *proud* of you," Evvie said softly. Gwen jerked her eyes up, and they were wide and suspiciously wet. Evvie gave Gwen her biggest, warmest grin, the one that matched Gareth's. And Gwen's. "I want you to do what makes you happiest, even if I don't understand it. Even if I don't get half of what comes out of your mouth."

Gwen said nothing, ducked her head and butted it up against Basil's shoulder. He wrapped an arm around her shoulders, kissed her scar again, and went back to his eggs.

When the dishes were soaking in the sink and Mark was bouncing Gwennie on his knee, Evvie managed to talk them into one last cup of black, bitter coffee; nearly twenty-four hours without sleep had begun to tug at everyone's eyelids and she had given up on tea having enough kick to keep them all on their feet. Basil tapped away on his TV-notepad-computer and when Mark asked what he was doing, he said something like, "Detailed mission report. Best to do it as it's happening, then you don't forget anything."

And before Evvie wanted it to end, it was over. The kettle was empty, the day had fully dawned, and Gwen and Basil were cooing goodbyes to Gwennie in her highchair, shaking the Piersons' hands with grins and a soft, genial "so long" from Basil.

"What, 'so long'?" Mark repeated, startled. "That's it? No advice? Not gonna tell me which stocks to play?"

"Can't go changing the timeline," Basil said with a cheeky grin. "That's the Temporal Prime Directive, innit?"

"That's 'Star Trek,'" Mark crowed, triumphant. "I knew *that* one!"

Gwen punched Basil's arm again. Basil conceded and added: "I'll see you in twenty-nine years, maybe? Come for a proper family dinner, yeah? Uh, pay you back for the Betamax."

Evvie felt panic, surprising and sudden. "That's not... that's not enough!" she said without thinking. "I want to know...you have to..."

Gwen stopped, looked at her, expression a cross between amusement, puzzlement, and perhaps the slightest hint of anger. "What?"

"Just tell me...tell me *why*," Evvie asked, a little desperate. "Why can't you quit? Why don't you just walk away? Haven't you lost *enough*?"

Oh, that look of shock on Gwen's face. Of course Evvie knew what she had lost. Evvie was a mother. She may have been the product of a time before aliens and openness and the perfect slapshot, but she was not (obliviousbigotedhardhearted) stupid.

"I don't want to have this fight again," Gwen said softly. "I've already had it with you once."

"Well, it's the first time for me," Evvie said. "So explain it. Why does it have to be you? My Gwennie?" She gave in to temptation, reached out, cupped Gwen's cheeks in her palms. It was the first time Evvie had touched her. Her skin was soft, smooth, warm. And above all that, familiar. Evvie knew this face, this skin, had touched it before, caressed it, bathed it, soothed it.

This really was her baby.

The corners of Gwen's eyes crinkled with a soft, sad smile, and she turned her head to press a gentle kiss into her mother's palm. "You haven't called me that since I was fifteen."

"Why?" Evvie repeated miserably, not letting Gwen change the subject. "Answer me."

Gwen sighed, sort of shrugging all over at once. "Because...who else is there? If not me, then who?"

"Really?"

Gwen looked down at her feet. "Revenge, maybe?" And with a last, sad smile, she stepped back, took Basil's outstretched hand, squeezed his fingers once. "I hope that's enough of an answer."

"Call me," Evvie said, desperate. "Please, call me when you get back. I don't want to fight."

"I…yeah, okay."

Basil leaned over, murmured something soothing into her ear, kissed her cheek. Then he levelled one last calculating, quantifying stare at Evvie, as if she were some complex equation he could decipher by study alone.

With great deliberation, Basil depressed the red button on the surface of the device. There was a sudden flash of light so bright it left spots in Evvie and Mark's vision, the afterimage of two strange people dressed in their clothing imprinted against the inside of their eyelids.

When the images cleared and they opened their eyes, Basil and Gwen were gone. Evvie turned in a slow circle, but there was no trace of them anywhere, no evidence that they had even been here beyond the tampered-with technology and a trashcan filled with dirty, destroyed uniforms, a bloody onesie, and of course, Gwennie's cut. The scar.

And, winking in the fluorescent light of the basement, was a small lump of metal, curved and curled and strange, half hidden by the skirt of the sofa. It had the rainbow slick surface, same as the disc of music. It was *alien*.

Evvie looked at Mark. He was rubbing the corner of one eye with his blunt-tipped fingers. His lips curled up to match his wife's, small smiles of hysterical wonder.

"Did that just happen?" he asked.

Evvie nodded. "I think so. I'm pretty sure."

Mark nodded, too. Evvie looked down at her hands. They felt too empty. Mark picked up Gwennie; he must have felt the same, the strange void of knowing-but-not, the way that the whole world— the future—had shifted around them and left them feeling impotent and futile. Evvie walked down the stairs, slowly, and approached the small configuration of wires and casing and the future. She felt silly, reaching towards it with slow fingers, as if it was a dog that might snap if she was too nervous. It didn't, and she picked it up. It was lighter than she expected, and when she peered in through a gap in the side, it was filled mostly with air and a fine filigree of wires and plastic caps and bright green walls. There was a curved piece decending from the bottom, like a trigger, and several smooth round barrels and suddenly Evvie's stomach swooped down into her knees, because she was pretty sure she was holding a weapon.

Basil must have taken it out of his vest pocket to make himself comfortable, or to access a tool, and forgotten to put it back in. Gwen wouldn't have forgotten, but then Gwen was twice the soldier Basil had been.

Clutching it to her chest, Evvie went back upstairs and past Mark and Gwennie, who were doing a little dance together in the kitchen—Mark singing a sad but silly song about runny eggs—and into the little alcove off the mudroom that served as the farm's office.

Revenge, maybe? she heard Gwen say again in her mind. No, it wasn't enough of an answer. But it was all Evvie was going to get for the next thirty years.

Revenge.

Evvie wondered if (hoped) she got it. She dug a small cardboard box out of the back of the desk, emptied it of its blank envelopes, and tucked the weapon from the future into the bottom corner. She jammed the whole thing back into the only drawer on the whole desk that locked, turned the key, and for the first time since they'd bought the desk, removed the key from the lock. She hid the key under the base of the desk lamp.

She didn't exactly know why she didn't just throw the weapon into the trash and let it get carted away to the dump where it could never hurt anyone again. She just knew that she wasn't ready to let it go, just yet. That maybe she would need it to defend her family again, or to remind herself that Gwennie's scar really hadn't come from her falling down the stairs, or that she hadn't made this whole strange day up.

Evvie sat down at the desk, put her head in her hands and took a deep, hitching breath. She could do this. She would be fine. She would just wait. For the aliens, for the news, for the phone to ring.

Part II: Middle

HE HAS CHOSEN TO be a "he."

Humans use pronouns to distinguish between individuals of specific genders. They have two genders among his people as well, of course—almost every copulating species does—but they aren't as finicky about labelling them. They don't dwell on sexuality and gender performance on his world…or rather, they did not.

He has the reproductive organs of a male, or what the humans categorize as such, so he has decided that it is easiest to simply submit to the use of the aligned pronoun instead of insisting on the neutral.

Here, he must be careful to do and say the right things, the things that are associated with the performance of the male gender, which he has decided to embrace. It is often times confusing and yet one more thing he must constantly remember to do in order to avoid attracting the wrong sort of attention. Reminders to himself are so constantly buzzing within the confines of his skull that he marvels that he has enough automatic memory left over to continue to breathe the too-cool, over-oxygenated air of Earth. Odd, that there are some things that he cannot say or do, things he is not meant to enjoy, simply because of his biology. To pretend that he does not take as much pleasure in preparing meals as he does...did. To take up a sporting team to support.

Human faces are hard to read, but he's been assured that there are distinctive differences between the males and females: broader jaws, softer cheeks, longer lashes or fur on chins. He will learn to see these differences when he gets used to interpreting their eyebrows, the curl of flabby lips, the flat flashes of herbivore-like teeth. He will become accustomed, given enough time.

And he will have nothing but time with these people.

His race's faces are rarely so different from each other as to require gender pronouns; but everyone sounds and feels different. Each person is unique in the way they transmit their physicality, so each person is granted unique address: everyone is referred to by their name. A woman's smell is only distinguishable from men when she is seeking a Unit; no less attractive, but different all the same. Simply an evolutionary sexual signal, and no reason to refer to a body rather than to a brain.

To be addressed for his genitals, rather than his individual personality...it is another thing that he has to learn to become accustomed to; to accept.

They cannot go back.

"He" follows his guide up the corridor, lit with bulbs that make his skin hurt, glowing with a humming, audible brightness. His feet slip on the too-smooth floor, and he has to grip with the wide pads of his toes, feel the click of curving claw nails against the ridiculously shiny tiles, coated with too much polished wax. It is either that or suffer the dead feeling of deafness that he gets when he wears the shoes the Specialists have given him. This place, with its glaring whiteness and its stark right angles, is nothing like the buildings at home and everything is just all wrong.

He aches for what is gone with every broken fragment of himself.

He should feel lucky, he knows that. He has skills that the humans can use, there is something he can do to help, something that he can give to this new planet of theirs to make life a little better for everyone.

He can repay.

TRIPTYCH

It had been easy to say and think that when the Specialists met them. It had been easy to stand in the grassy field and stare at the too-blue sky and swivel his ears towards the diminutive, fat pink creature that had come to greet them, stumbling through the speech in the new language that was so foreign to all of them. The hordes of diminutive, fat, multicoloured creatures that shaded from pale peach to dark blackish brown, that stood behind the first. It had been easy to volunteer and easy to speak up about his expertise. Easy to step forward and say "me," just to get away from the stink of the ships, the crying children, the gazes starved for explanations and comfort and sunlight, the desperation clinging all around everyone in a dark cloud, the soot that no one could quite get out of their eyelashes, fearing to wash it away lest it was all that remained of a loved one.

It is different now, though, after so many lessons, so many months, after trying so hard and still being so…so anxious. So floundering. Now, now that he is walking through the…the…Institute, following the male—the man—who is leading him to his new position.

The life that is intended to be his.

Will be. But was not supposed to be.

A life that he is about to be given; given unearned.

He feels false; he feels like an actor who has stepped into another's role, unrehearsed and under-prepared, knowing the rudimentary plot but none of the dialogue, none of the vital gestures he is meant to parrot.

He reaches out and skims the wall of the corridor as he walks, feeling the smooth, glossy surface of the paper decoration and the vibrations beneath it; a thousand beings walking, talking, tapping, beating. Not alone, never alone.

A thousand beings, and he still aches to be touched.

He is lonely.

The guide stops, his all-colours-at-once military Institute security uniform rustling. He cannot read the man's face, does not know if that look means "kind" or if it means "angry." He does not much care, so he just turns his own face to the ground. He will probably never see this particular human again.

It is the people on the other side of the door he is worried about.

He rearranges his face into a smile. His Integration Specialist told him that he has the best smile in the class and it is a small, ridiculous thing to be prideful about. He holds the smile as the guide presses a button on a device by the wall. A low sound is relayed into the room, presumably a signal to tell them someone wishes to speak with them. He cannot read the sign on the door, the words are too long, even though the letters are familiar from months of intense study.

R-E-S-E-A....

Smile when you are introduced, his Integration Specialist had said. *A smile is a sign of pleasure.*

...R-C-H-L-A...

But she had never explained the difference between the pleasure at meeting a child and the pleasure at meeting the leader of a new planet. The pleasure, the terror, at meeting the team you will be working with for the foreseeable future.

...B-O-R-A...

He longs for the rigid hierarchy of the Greetings. He does not want to upset these people by failing to give them the pleasure they deserve, but he fears he just does not know how. He fears insulting them simply by existing.

Bigger is better, he has learned from his Popular Culture Specialist, *Pink is the new black, Mmm...Doughnuts, Oh My God They Killed Kenny, I See Dead People, It's Bigger On The Inside.*

He stretches his mouth until it aches.

...T-O-R-Y-#421

Raise your voice at the end of a phrase to make it a question. Lower it to make it a demand. Eye contact indicates trust.

So many little nuances, inflections and expression that he's had to memorize, had to learn to mold his facial muscles and mouth around. Humans spoke all over the register, high voices for excitement, loud for anger, but sometimes loud was for excitement as well. They were so *similar,* so many inflections were so alike that it took careful parsing of the expression to even begin to understand.

His guide presses the button again, and still there is no reply.

Perhaps they are ignoring the sound, or perhaps they are as nervous about meeting their new teammate as he is. The guide grows impatient and taps out something on the number panel by the door. The guide shields it with his hand so that Kalp cannot see, but he could have been at the other end of the corridor and still he would be able to reproduce the code simply by the pattern of vibrations washing across his forearm as the guide's fingers move.

But he is not concentrating on that. With his fingers pressed to the cool, opaque glass of the door, he can hear the occupants of the room talking, muffled by the barrier, in English and too rapidly to understand. Now he thinks that they merely have failed to notice the chime of the door signal. The conversation sounds intense. There are two voices; one low, therefore male, as he's learned, and one higher and therefore female.

In response to the guide's code, the door slides open. He snatches back his hand as the door tucks away smoothly into the wall. The talking stops. Hanging cylinders of light coloured wood are suspended just in front of the doorway to make a screen that prevents anyone from casually glancing into the room. It is decorated with green paint that creates a stylized, organic swirl of leaves and plants, naturally beautiful.

It reminds him sharply of the pattern that was on his workroom floor back home, and something inside him twists.

One of the humans—the woman—calls out, "Who is it?" in English. There is the muted clatter of tools being put down, ringing sharp against the skin of his torso, and the sudden buffeting shift of the air as someone moves quickly to their feet.

The guide calls out something littered with numbers and codes and designations and he is not listening to the guide, he is listening to *them*. He can hear their familiarity with each other in their movements, the way they echo. He can hear an exchanged glance and their footsteps in unison as they approach.

He straightens and checks that his smile is still in place.

The guide pushes aside a section of the clacking curtain of wood. They are all smaller than him, little, fragile looking people. They are pale and colourless, and like the guide, he can feel their hearts beating, a reassuring background patter on his skin which almost drowns out the abrasive throbbing of the overhead lights. Their shoulders are jagged and straight, unlike his, their limbs awkward, with only three easy-to-snap joints. They look like they shouldn't even be able to walk upright, their toes don't spread out far enough. And yet there they are, face to face with him, balancing.

The guide is introducing him now in English, but he does not know what to say, how to act, so he just keeps desperately smiling and mute. All those classes, all that studying and it is all for nothing, completely inaccessible in his apprehension.

The man starts to say something, but this human's words are too heavily accented for him to understand. He cannot even interpret the twist of the man's mouth and the ripple of the broad, strong muscles in his shoulder, and the sidelong glance he throws at the woman. The same something inside twists again, sharp and slightly panicked.

He *does not* know what that *means*.

She smacks the man in the arm, making both of them flinch, but then the woman steps forward to grasp his arms in the initial steps of the Greetings.

"Welcome," she says, in his own language, "My name is Go-win."

And even though her accent is so thick that she sounds like she came from the other continent (even that is gone, it is all gone now), he tightens his own grip on her fat, squishy arms in relief.

"I give thanks for your welcome and offer my name in pledge," he replies, comforted by familiarity and rote. "I am Kalp."

THE SOFTER lights of the laboratory—that was one of the long words on the door—hurt less. There are small incandescent lamps on each desk, burning a welcome in soft gold. These two humans prefer not to turn on the raucous fluorescent overheads, for which Kalp is profoundly grateful.

TRIPTYCH

The guide has since departed, leaving the humans alone with Kalp. There is an awkward first few moments, and then Kalp settles into a proffered chair and listens as they explain the gist of the project to which they are all assigned. It is to translate and create a working model of a design from a blueprint from Kalp's home world. Kalp cannot tell what it is from his initial glance, though he has an idea of what it may become. The humans have become blocked by some of the more technical and particular words present in the document and require the help of an engineer who is familiar with the specific jargon. That is Kalp.

But there are other things, smaller miscellaneous assignments that each must do for their superiors, that Kalp will eventually be given as well, and that is why, on the first day, Kalp's team whittles quickly down to two.

For someone who has spent so many long days learning, it is odd to be thrust so quickly into role of teacher again. Specialist Go-win, *Gwen,* whose name he has been practising silently over and over in his head in order to learn the proper pronunciation, has an assignment due. Those above her in hierarchy demand its completion without tardiness, and so Kalp is left alone in the room with Specialist Doctor Basil Grey, whose name is even harder—there is no "B" sound in Kalp's language, and he must push out his lips obscenely—and Kalp teaches him the first intimate steps of the Greeting alone.

The human is very eager to please, as eager as Kalp, and wishes to be able to perform the Greeting properly. Kalp is grateful, for the ritual puts him at ease on this planet that is so full of improvisation; but the human's mastery of Kalp's language is negligible, which makes the teaching difficult.

Specialist Doctor Basil Grey's accent is worse than Gwen's, his fingers are too short, too small, too pink to fit all the way around Kalp's bicep. His skin is too hot, too moist, too ridged with nearly invisible wrinkles, and covered with soft downy hair that feels simultaneously like a young child's and some strange creature's. But Specialist Doctor Basil Grey *is* a strange creature. Strange to Kalp. It makes Kalp's fur stand on end and his flesh recoil and his mouth stretch back with a smile that he holds onto desperately for fear of offending.

Kalp forgets to remember that he is in the same position in the hierarchy as Specialist Doctor Basil Grey. He wishes the Specialist Doctor had given him permission to use his name; four words is an awfully long string of syllables to address a person with.

Kalp spends the afternoon with his ears flattened all the way down.

AFTER THE first day of Institute Assignments has been completed, Derx is more boastful than ever.

Kalp says nothing because he is lower than Derx, and it is not his place to say. But he knows that some of what Derx says right now is incorrect, merely from just observing Gwen and Specialist Doctor Basil Grey today. Kalp endured Derx all the way to Earth, and it seems rather insufferably unfair that he and Derx have been assigned the same living quarters and employers after planetfall, as well. Kalp tucks his ears against his head in an effort to appear complacent, but to actually block out as much sound as possible. He burrows under the strange muffling layers of the blankets and 'duvets' filled with animal sheddings. He is for once thankful for their suffocating heat and the way the insulation dampens the world into blissful deafness.

Kalp drops into his unconscious cycle wishing he'd had the chance to clean the oils of the humans' skin from his arms. The large building in which all of his skilled people live has a disproportionate number of cleaning cubicles. He'd run out of time before the lights were removed.

Kalp could have easily found his way to and among the cubicles, as any of his kind can in the dark, but humans are easily frightened, slow to trust, night blind, and do not like surprises. For the sake of their small, pattering hearts, Kalp stays in the cot.

KALP RESUMES consciousness to the sound of Derx talking, accent broad and southern, and wonders rather uncharitably if Derx had ever actually stopped. If they are ever made unwelcome on this new world, Kalp does not doubt that it will be in part because of Derx's incessant blather.

"*To the moon, Alice…*" Kalp thinks and cannot help but take pleasure in the thought of someone striking Derx right in the "kisser."

Kalp sits up. The cot on which he sleeps—though given freely and with much sympathetic charity, for which they are all grateful—is too stiff, too long and thin, no good for curling up. He must sleep straight and narrow to prevent falling from the bed in the middle of the night and he is not used to that. Discomfort shoots across the base of his neck. He wishes Maru was here to press fingers under his skull, as Maru used to.

The cot is more comfortable than the hard-shelled pods back on the escape ship, but far less than the nest Kalp has left behind at…on…

Home.

Kalp touches the aching spot between his eyes and scrunches his nose—a gesture of self-frustration that he has already assimilated from the humans. His Cultural Etiquette Specialist used to make that gesture a lot.

The pads of his fingers still feel oily, and leave residue on the prickle of soft fur between his eye ridges.

Slipping from his cot carefully, certain not to turn his back to Derx or the other Higher Ranks whose cots were furthest from the drafty and noisy apertures of the doors and windows, Kalp makes his slow way towards the cleaning cubicle room.

"Kalp!" Derx calls out, and ever mindful of his rank, Kalp turns and lifts his palms to catch Derx's words. He cannot, however, prevent the wary droop of his ears. Kalp has never been very good at hiding his emotions; his ears reveal all. They always have.

"Your shoes," Derx says, pointing to the heavy deafening sheaths on the floor, lined up neatly side-by-side at the end of Kalp's cot. "Do not forget them today. It is offensive."

Kalp bends to retrieve them, snagging his nails carefully under the laces, then turns and retreats to the cubicles, away from Derx and his orders and the muffling cocoon of his duvet.

He wishes he could stay in bed for the next few solar cycles.

The poor, uncomfortable excuse for a proper nest is imminently more comforting than the inside of the ever-buzzing Institute office filled with the colourless, fragile human-things and their shifting smells and too-loud hearts and slick, leaking skin. Their strange words and their strange ways.

Kalp wants a real nest, *his* nest, and his Unit.

But Maru had been outside when the sky had first gone black and had never come back to their dwelling. Trus had been at the medic's awaiting test news and had been killed in the panicked trample and Kalp had been…

Lazing about in his nest, late into the morning.

Safe and saved.

Kalp drops the shoes outside of the cubicle, on the provided bench, and sheds his "pyjamas." He turns the water as cold as it goes. He steps in, for once alone in the cleaning room, and relishes the feel of the dirt and the smog and the oil and the guilty memory sliding off his skin.

OF COURSE, the first thing that the Gwen-human does is touch him.

She initiates the Greeting, a comfort and a sharp pain of memory all at once. This time Kalp's flesh does not try to crawl away from the stickiness her touch leaves behind. He is prepared for it now. Kalp has also brought disposable cleaning papers—"tissues"—with him today, so he does not mind as much. She can touch him now, and he will clean himself later.

He is terrified, however, that his new companions will be offended if they see him scrub away their residue. He determines to wait until both are occupied elsewhere before he uses the Kleenex. For all Kalp knows, maybe this expressive spreading of liquids is some sort of ritual scent-marking and they are paying him a compliment by rubbing their smell into his skin. Perhaps it is some sort of a biological imperative.

He wishes he could just *know.*

The twisting tension tightens. It is difficult to breathe.

He feels like he is living on the edge of a blade—one totter too far one way or another and he will fall. He will offend, he will be sent away, he will be worthless and alone and nothing. So Kalp watches, silently, desperately, waiting for knowledge to make itself clear to him, for things to slot into place, as they did when he did his schooling. He waits for the composite image to emerge from the components of the diagram.

The work day begins and Kalp settles into observation. He notices small things first, the habitual movements that the male makes with his hands and mouth, as if trying to coax understanding out of the air; the way the female keeps patting her hair down over her forehead. Specialist Doctor Basil Grey seems to touch Gwen often; fingertips at the back of her neck, a palm on her elbow, a brush of bare forearms, kind and claiming. Where is the pattern? Is he threatened by the proximity of another male? Is he staking breeding rights over Gwen or merely stating protection? Or is he just touching her because she is there and there is no inherent biological meaning in it? Are they gestures of friendship? Are his touches purposeful or instinctual?

But Gwen touches everything, lamps and desks and chairs, and Basil too. Does that mean the same as well?

There seems to be no rigidity to them, no code for Kalp to learn and read.

So much to know and so little *taught.*

But then Specialist Doctor Basil Grey touches Kalp in some of the same ways as he touched Gwen when he comes into the room that second morning, a soft hand on his wrist, a firm "handshake," a light touch on the shoulder of the kind that is shared between "pals." He uses only his given name today in the Greeting, giving Kalp permission to address and think of him as "Basil." He presses into Kalp's hands a slip of grubby cloth-paper, the sort that passes for currency.

"First task of Integration," Basil says cheerily, "is learning which lunch lady to flatter at the canteen, innit?" He talks slow and enunciates clearly. Gwen must have told him to speak so in order to make his words more easily understood, and Kalp is startled at the caring that the gesture shows on both their parts; Gwen for thinking of it, and Basil for following her advice.

Basil's mouth stretches, displaying his small white teeth in pleasure. This is a joke, Kalp is sure, but what sort he was unsure of. Slapstick? Sarcasm? Is Kalp meant to be the Straight Man or to reply? Panic surges. The tension twists tighter, and Kalp feels as if his air passage is closing.

Basil goes on: "Down the hall, take the second right, say it's for me and they'll know. Gwen wants coffee, black—bloody Canadian—and you get whatever you fancy. Cheers."

Kalp blinks. A desperate tightness presses at the back of his throat. These were things Kalp has never been taught! Coffee, black? Is not the steaming beverage brown? How does one fetch black coffee? Where does one find it? Take the second right to where, and how does one pick up a "right"? Who is bloody and do they need a medic? He understands the last command, at least.

He lifts a hand in the air and stretches his mouth wide and says "huzzah!" with what he hopes is the appropriate amount of enthusiasm, anxious to get this one little thing right, to prove that he is not stupid, that he is *useful*.

"Wha—?" Basil says, blue eyes going wide, the translucent lids dropping and lifting once.

Gwen starts to choke.

She makes a horrible hacking, swallowing, screaming sound, face going red in distress. She seals a hand over her mouth.

Kalp's ears shoot up in horror.

He's killed his teammate on his second day.

Gwen sucks at more air, straining, unable to take in enough. And she starts…

Singing?

It is a repeated trilling sound that ripples up Kalp's skin, leaving breathless wonder-pleasure in its wake. There are no distinguishable tones, though, no clear sustained sounds like the human-singing on the radio. Is she dying? Is this a knell?

And what will they do to Kalp when they find out? They will

execute him for killing her, surely, and he feels the pathetic burn in the back of his eyes that signals distress.

Basil makes the choking sound too, and then he is singing tonelessly as well.

"No, no!" Gwen splutters around gasping trills.

Kalp wonders if it is safe for her to be speaking when she is having such trouble breathing. Is there something he is meant to do? What if they *both* asphyxiate right here, by Kalp's shoes? But she goes on, proving that she is at least getting enough air to sustain sound:

"Not *cheer*, the imperative." Gwen splutters. "'Cheers.' It's local jargon for 'thank you.'"

She sucks more breath, apparently not having trouble retaining oxygen at all.

Realization breaks across him and the burn in his eyes gets worse. Shame. There is no relief in the revelation of this particular pattern. Kalp is thoroughly mortified. His ears sink again, pressing tight against the back of his neck.

What a *horrendous* mistake.

Basil begins to suffocate harder and Kalp takes a quick step towards him, feet almost slipping out from under him—he's forgotten the shoes, the careful way he must narrow his balance in them. He wraps the fingers of the hand not holding the money over Basil's shoulder and shakes him.

"Do not asphyxiate!" Kalp yelps, a little desperately.

Basil's face goes redder and he trills more.

Gently, Gwen grabs Kalp's wrist, her fat fingers pulling, and Kalp cannot help the flinch this time, the quick step backwards that sends the soles of the shoes slipping out from under him. Gravity, just as effective on this planet as his own, brings him crashing onto his back.

"Jeeze!" Basil says, cutting the trilling abruptly. "Kalp, mate, youallrigh'there?" Kalp does not understand the second half, it is too fast, and his head is reeling.

Gwen kneels down beside Kalp, and uses a gentle touch on the clothed part of his arm to prod him back up to a sitting position. She looks deeply at his face, her own a mask of pulled down eyebrows and down curled corners of her mouth—"anger"? No, "concern." She is worried for him. That is relieving to notice, at least.

"Are you hurt?" she asks, gently, slowly, and with far more kindness than Kalp is expecting. She is so sympathetic towards his many errors. Many of his own kind would not be as patient if she were making similar errors, were she the refugee on his world. Derx least of all.

The hot tight feeling in his throat gets worse, and this time it is shame. Shame for the way his society acts on his planet.

"I am," he says, struggling to speak English clearly around the closing lump. He touches the side of his face, and the grounding pressure slows and stops the reeling spin. "I am just...the shoes..." He makes a gesture that, on his world, means frustration but he is sure means absolutely nothing to these humans. So much he cannot *communicate* and it fills him with anger and despair.

Basil and Gwen's gaze move to the offending articles in tandem.

"Why on Earth are you even wearing them?" Gwen asks, and her tone holds puzzlement.

"I must. Otherwise, it is offensive," Kalp says softly, and manages to keep the bitterness at having to repeat Derx's words in check. The tightness is finally twisting so hard that his voice is coming out broken-sounding. They will hear his confusion, his distress, and that is even more mortifying than his mistake at the jargon for thanks.

He does not want them to see him unhappy.

And he is very unhappy.

"Bollocks," Basil says, straightening. "I don't care if you wear them."

"Me either," Gwen says. "Do what you like in this office, Kalp. It's yours, too."

Kalp licks his lips, ears twitching sideways.

"Truly?" he asks softly. He wheezes for air and his throat loosens. "As I like?"

"As you like," Gwen says. "Our status in this room is equal. Your rank matches ours."

Kalp lets forth a shaking breath of relief. Suddenly his lungs feel twice as large. The hot twisting winds down and sinks away, and the trembles in his ears and fingers cease. He shakes himself once, all over, to resettle the jagged lay of his fur, and proffers a wide, silly-feeling smile to indicate his relief at this statement.

"I will remove the shoes," he says.

Gwen smiles to match Kalp's, and he feels absurdly pleased that he is learning how to provoke a pleasure response from his co-workers. His head is light from the abrupt upswing in his mood.

"Oi, what did you mean about asphyxiating?" Basil asks, and he is speaking slowly and clearly once again. Now he remembers to enunciate, once the distress is passed. One buttock is perched on the edge of his desk. He already has a small tool and an electronic component back in his hands.

Kalp reaches down to untie the laces that hold the shoes onto his foot. He says, "You trilled. It sounded painful, like you could not get enough air."

"Trilled?" Gwen asks, lifting herself to her own feet. "What, you mean, laughing?"

"Laughing," Kalp repeats. "Yes, I have heard of laughter. You were laughing?"

"Yes," Gwen says, and makes a sort of small aborted trilling noise in illustration. "We were amused by your mistake."

"For which I am deeply, deeply sorry," Kalp says, kicking off the shoes and scrambling upright. He moves to bow his neck in the Apology, but Gwen's hand on his shoulder—still fat and fragile, but warm—stops him.

"Don't apologize," she says. "If one of us apologizes every time we make a cultural error, we'll be doing the Apology for hours a day. Let's just laugh at our errors together, okay?"

Kalp feels his mouth stretch again, but this time it is involuntary. Smiling.

"Okay," he agrees. "And now, I must purchase coffee and a...fancy?"

Basil snorts at the machine in his hands, and Gwen pats Kalp's elbow, the same tender guiding gesture he's seen Basil use on her, and turns him towards the door. "We'll go to the cafeteria together."

Her palm is still oily, but Kalp appreciates the acceptance inherent in the gesture, even if Gwen is not aware that she has done it. Perhaps, Kalp thinks, he does not mind being scent-marked by Gwen, after all.

Not if it means she worries for him like this.

KALP HAS a sore neck.

It is left over from lying on the cot, surely, but it also comes from stooping low to bend over Basil's blueprints. Kalp longs for a taller table, but would not presume to ask for one. How then could Gwen and Basil read from it, if it was tall enough for Kalp?

Attempting to be subtle, Kalp raises his fingers slowly and presses the back of his own skull, applying pressure to two little knobs. Right below the skin are knots of nerve endings and hormone centres that help regulate the flow of chemicals that keep his body functioning correctly. Though he knows it will not last much beyond a few moments, he feels temporary relief from the release of the enzymes produced by the pocket of chemicals there. He lets out a long breath.

"Whatcher sighingova?" Basil asks, forgetting to be articulate, to scrub out his argot.

Kalp snaps his eyes open. "I beg your pardon?" he asks, careful to use the politest form of requesting clarification he knows.

"You sighed," Basil repeats, conscientious this time of his speed and word use. He is leaning on the brace of his hands, elbows locked backwards in a pose that makes Kalp's arms sore just witnessing it. These humans seem so stiff and angular, until he witnesses them doing things like this, turning their arms around in their sockets, or the way they pivot on the balls of their feet when they wish to move fast, seeming to ignore the existence of their own toes. He has seen contortionists performing on television.

Kalp does not know this word, "sigh," and pulls his eyebrows down to indicate so. That, at least, is one facial expression their species share.

Basil huffs out a breath, repeating what Kalp did earlier. "That's called a 'sigh.'" He does it again and clarity washes through the air. Then Basil touches the back of his own neck in the same place Kalp had touched his. "Why?" he asks.

Gwen, who is leaning over a pad of paper upon which she had been scribbling translations as Kalp made them, looks up in interest.

"I have pain," Kalp says, deciding not to lie. If he explains what the problem is, perhaps they can correct it. At the least, conversing will allow for the excuse of the momentary drop in productivity. Breaks are often very informative in this office, even the unofficial ones where they must stay inside and cannot venture forth for refreshment.

Kalp has learned—and taught—more about their differing cultures during these small conversations than in all the classes he has attended. At least, it feels that way.

"Pain?" Gwen repeats. "Your neck is sore? Or is it a headache?"

"Both," Kalp admits.

She sets down her writing instrument. It threatens to roll off the table's surface, but stops at the edge. "Is it from doing the translations? We can take a break. Or are you thirsty? I always get a headache when I'm dehydrated."

"The translations do not pain me," Kalp says, trying to explain carefully that it is not work that is hurting him. He wants to be clear on that. He does not want work taken away from him; it is the last thing that is keeping him sane, from dwelling too long and too often on the tormenting past. From the loneliness. "Though I will require water soon."

"Could use a cuppa myself," Basil says with a bob of his head that indicates affirmation, though his words are once again puzzling and Kalp is unsure with what Basil is agreeing. Kalp decides that it will take especially long to learn how to communicate with this particular human.

"You can *always* go for a cuppa," Gwen chides, and this is humour Kalp knows, has seen before on the television. She is being derogatory but with a smile and a pleasant tone—teasing. "So what's causing the pain, Kalp?" Gwen asks, using his name directly.

Kalp likes the way his name feels across his skin when she says it.

"These arrangements…" Kalp hesitates. Would admitting the truth about the work environment be considered impolite? Gwen and Basil are both waiting, faces open and patient. Kalp once again decides on truth over safe words, over the mask of politesse; it has not failed him thus far. "They are not comfortable."

Basil's eyes narrow, and run up and down Kalp's body once, then flick to run similarly over the table, the note pads, the blueprints; assessing with his engineer's mind. He grins suddenly and presses the thumb and the middle finger of his left hand together and then draws the middle finger down swiftly into his palm, producing a sharp fleshy clicking sound that makes Kalp's whole scalp shiver.

"Ah ha," Basil says. "Table's too low."

"Oh crap," Gwen adds, consternation crossing her features. "I should have thought of that. I'm sorry, Kalp."

"Do not trouble yourself—" Kalp starts, falling back unconsciously into humble speech, ears folding. But Basil is already across the room, snatching the chair on wheels out from under his own desk.

He flicks a catch on the side and the spindle under the seat hisses out air and rises until it is as high as it will go, which is still low enough to fit under the drafting table.

"There you are," Basil says with a flourish. "Should be the right height now."

Kalp hesitates. It is an extremely generous offer, to share one's stature-seat with a co-worker. A true gesture of equality. He wonders if Basil is aware of how awed Kalp feels.

"Sit, sit!" Basil says, flapping his hands impatiently.

Kalp makes another smile of pleasure, toes curling as he feels the breeze from Basil's impatient gesture ruffle the fur on his face. Kalp sits. Basil touches the catch again and the spindle sinks a bit under Kalp's weight. Basil reaches under the seat, playing with the handle and tugging and adjusting the altitude until it becomes the perfect height for Kalp to tuck his legs under the draft table, yet still see the documents without having to hunch over. Basil's fingers slide against the nape of Kalp's neck in passing as he makes adjustments, wonderfully hot, and Kalp resists the urge to lean back into the touch.

The continual and steady stream of consideration and generosity coming from Kalp's partners is truly overwhelming, and Kalp sees now why Earth took them in so readily. They seem to see these acts as natural, obvious. Here, kindness is a right, not a privilege to be earned.

Perhaps there is something to be said for loose hierarchies.

Basil smacks his palms together, making the same sharp fleshy sound the clicking fingers did, only on a larger scale. "So, tea for me, coffee for Gwen—requests, Kalp?"

The snap of flesh on flesh makes Kalp shiver once more, and he likes the way his name sounds when Basil says it, too.

"Water, please," Kalp says.

Basil snorts. "Just water? You'll see—I give it a week before you're a tea drinker." He waves at the air, sketching a form of salutation, and walks out the door. The wooden cylinders in the curtain click together soothingly as they settle back into place.

"We can take a break now," Gwen says, walking over to her own desk and writing something down on a different piece of paper.

"What do you write?" Kalp asks, taking her comment as an invitation to conversation. He has not had the opportunity, really, to have a free and open-ended dialogue with a human yet, and this is the part of his work that he is most looking forward to. He arches his back in an effort to relieve the ache from hunching forward, revelling in the muscle-releasing click his spine makes in response.

"Hm? Oh, memo. Uh—a reminder to myself," she clarifies when he makes the face of confusion to indicate his puzzlement at yet another new piece of vocabulary. She clicks the end of her writing utensil repeatedly, making the tip from which the ink emerges vanish and reappear at a constant rate. Kalp has noticed that Gwen almost always has something in her hands—a pen she flips through her fingers, a cup whose handle she strokes. She taps her chin, picks at her lips, runs her fingers through her hair. He hears every movement, and it is constant, a throbbing wash over his body, and she feels just so alive. Alive and active in ways that none of his kind have been in what feels like lifetimes. "I have to remember to order you your own desk and chair at the right height."

"You would—" Kalp begins but Gwen stops him with a smile and a wagging finger.

"Equal status, Kalp," she says. A soft reminder, but seriously delivered.

He does not finish his sentence. Instead he basks in the warmth of this feeling of…welcome. He moves his head to the side to look at the door, to see if Basil has returned yet, and a sharp pain slices up the side of his neck. He grimaces.

"You okay?" Gwen asks.

Kalp knows that "okay" is universal Earth jargon for everything from "feeling well" to "pleasant," "delicious" to "good."

"I am not okay," he admits, still fighting the impulsive urge to be polite and tell smart words instead of the truth.

"Your neck, still?"

"Yes."

Gwen moves back to his side. "What brought this on?"

She is close and the rhythmic patter of her heart is soothing. "Where I sleep, it is very hard," Kalp says.

"Ah—bed cramps," Gwen says with another one of those affirmative head bobs that she and Basil seem fond of. "And what does pressing your fingers there do?"

"There is a chemical," Kalp explains, turning his head and shoulders together, carefully, to look up at her so as to avoid another sharp pain. "It is in our bodies. It makes us feel good. Over stimulating the painful area forces the body to release the chemical to counteract the pain. It also helps to work the tension from the muscles affected."

"Endorphins," Gwen says. "We have them too. May I?"

Before Kalp can ascertain what Gwen is asking permission for now, her fingers are on the back of his neck, warm and moist and pressing carefully in the same spot he had been. Then she moves her strong thumbs in small circles along the connective tissues of his neck, and Kalp nearly weeps with relief.

He slumps forward, giving her hands better access to the back of his neck, not caring that this means that she could easily slit his throat or strangle him in this pose. She is his teammate and she is showing great caring and trust in providing this relief. It is only fair that he shows the same.

Besides, it feels fantastic.

Basil comes in then, his hands full of containers of liquid, and stops just past the wood curtain. "Oi!" he says, sounding very annoyed. Kalp flinches away from Gwen's wonderful hands and cowers, ears flat back.

Kalp has already deduced that Basil is, if not currently, planning to be mated with Gwen. Kalp fears that the therapeutic touching has damaged his fledgling camaraderie with the human man. Basil has been touching Gwen a lot, and to catch Gwen touching Kalp in a similar manner...will Basil take this as a challenge? Kalp knows so little about human mating rituals; will he and Basil have to fight?

"I apologize—" he starts, but Gwen is trilling again. Laughing.

Basil's anger, it seems, is not real. This is another joke.

Kalp "sighs" in relief.

"If Kalp gets a massage, I want one, too," Basil says, coming forward to divest himself of the beverages. Two are in paper cylinders, and he hands one to Gwen and keeps one for himself. Kalp assumes the clear plastic cylinder filled with water is for him.

"Later," Gwen promises and blinks, somehow, with only one eye.

It is some sort of communication method, a physical gesture that Kalp does not understand. There is more silent conversation that occurs with meaningful muscle spasms in the face, but it is a conversation with a code that Kalp is not privy to. Feeling as if they have forgotten his presence entirely, Kalp decides not to interrupt.

He opens his bottle and drinks.

When the silent conversation is complete, Gwen and Basil return to their positions at the table, and they all three resume work. At the end of the day, Kalp's neck is still sore, but less than before, and he feels the warm glow of belonging settling under his skin. He still longs for a chance at the cleaning cubicle, but the humans' secretions are somehow less offensive today.

Gwen touches his shoulder in parting, as she and Basil head in one direction across the Institute's parking lot towards the conveyance that they share. Kalp goes in the other, to the larger one that his kind takes back to their building.

There is a smile on Kalp's face and he does not remember putting it there.

BACK AT the Sleeping Place, Kalp returns to his cot from the cleaning cubicles with water droplets still clinging to his fur. He misses the soft sponges and the meagre buckets of water that his own people use, but the "shower" is soothing in its own way, the water sluicing cool across his bare skin, a blissful pitter patter down his flesh. He drops his shoes under his bed and nudges them out of sight with his toes. He is very pleased to remember that he does not have to wear them ever again, at least, not to work. He has been given permission from equal-status teammates, and even Derx cannot order him to wear them now.

Let Derx and the other High Statuses scrambling for acceptance half-deafen themselves for it. Kalp is accepted already. His team regards him with affection and is concerned for his well-being and comfort. To them, this is more vital than his proper Integration, and Kalp feels a little surge of pleasure at the thought that learning to be accepted by Earthlings may not be as taxing as he'd originally feared.

Kalp is aware that his pride is perhaps ill-founded and too quick. Today, after all, was his first real full day at "the office," and perhaps they were acting especially nice because of the novelty of his presence. Kalp fears that this might be the case, but he is fairly certain that it is not. Gwen and Basil are just as easy with him as with each other, and their mutual affection seems natural and unforced.

They are simply kind people.

And truthfully, after so many months in the escape ship, followed by hours, weeks in military installations and medical centres, and then still more months in classrooms and teaching halls interspersed with so many stuffy, formal functions and welcome parties, after having lost…

After. Just after.

Well, Kalp is understandably a bit skin-starved. Just to be touched, touched with purpose and warmth, even if it is with moist, scent-marking hands, is a little bit of a wonder.

He lies down on his cot. The time when the lights are removed is far off yet—Kalp has not yet gone down to the other building for his evening repast—but he feels languorous and revels in the silence of having the Sleeping Place almost entirely to himself. He stretches his hands far above his head, touching the wall behind him, and stretches his toes as far as they will go in the other direction, and lays indecently sprawled in his clean clothing, enjoying the closest thing to silence that the electricity-laced walls can offer.

The sounds from the park around them—the chitter and flap of the native fauna, the flying animals that so astounded Kalp when he first saw them—is rather soothing. It cancels out the zip in the wires, and Kalp decides that he likes birds. Their quick little hearts and their hollow bones and their flittering wings wash excitement across his body, so he lies still and enjoys it. He inhales and exhales slowly and deliberately, holding onto the oxygen. He practices his "sighs."

The moment of respite is broken by an exclamation in the corner closest to the door. When Kalp came in, there was a knot of Lower Statuses sitting on a cot, peering intently at some form of Earth literature. Kalp did not so much ignore them—he is not as arrogant as Derx—as leave them to their own pursuits. They had all returned earlier than he; they are younger and as such are attending the local "University," which keeps shorter hours in deference to the extra work the young ones must complete at home.

Kalp likes that word: university. A city in which the universe is found. Or founded.

The others who had returned from the Institute that afternoon with Kalp have gone their own way, seeking a meal or entertainment, or things that Kalp did not long for. So he had parted ways with them to take advantage of the relative privacy of the cleaning cubicles and to think.

Only, he cannot think now, because the young ones are shouting.

"It is on the outside!" says one, and his companions gesture for him to keep his voice low and respectful. Were Kalp not in the room, they surely would not care. The speaker's voice drops to barely a whisper, but Kalp swivels an ear in their direction, intrigued. Besides, it is nice to hear his own language after so many hours struggling to find the correct words in English.

"Only when—" another starts, but stops. "Oh, no, there it is before. That's...rather revolting."

"Well, no one says *you* must perform intercourse with any."

Now Kalp sits up.

"What are you reading?" he asks, and they all immediately turn to him, raise their palms and drop their ears. The literature lays spread open on the cover of the cot.

Kalp stands. He is concerned about their overt interest in copulation because he is older, because he is an adult and they are not...yes, he is only interested out of concern. Kalp almost believes his own lie. In truth, he is just as intrigued as the young ones about the mechanics of human reproduction. It is not a topic that has been openly discussed in any of his classrooms to date.

Do they, like his people, engage in the act for pleasure as well as to conceive? From the looks of the glossy, thin book lying open on the bed, it seems they do. They also, like his kind, produce pornography in order to stimulate sexual pleasure in a reader.

Do they have orgasms? he wonders. *Are they capable?*

Kalp walks over and looks down at the book, and the young ones' fingers all tremble.

"Oh, do stop," he says and they drop their hands as one. "I am not here to chastise you—in honesty, I am as curious as you. From where did you obtain this book?"

One of the young ones, whose name Kalp does not know, says, "My classmate. I think she...the term is 'crushes me.'"

Kalp touches his nose. "Sounds unpleasant."

"No, it is slang. It means 'to wish to have intercourse with.'"

Yes, Kalp is very familiar with the problems of Earth jargon. He avoids the instinctual nervous gesture of tugging on his ear at the memory of "cheers," and instead puts his hands on his hips, mimicking the pose of stern, concerned parent he has seen the humans use.

"And she gave you this book in order that you would be informed in the manner in which this is accomplished?"

The young one nods like a human.

"Do you intend to follow through?"

The young one lifts his shoulders and drops them again, a shrug. Kalp thinks he is bad for picking up the humans' gesture tics, but the young ones are worse. The humans' physical communication methods are starting to overshadow his own people's, and Kalp wonders if he should be concerned about preserving his native culture. Well, there are others whose first concern is that, anthropologists and the like from both races. Let them worry. Kalp will do as he feels comfortable doing; he will do what is needed to be understood.

"I thought perhaps I would investigate it first," the young one admits.

"We are not genetically compatible," Kalp reminds them, "so there is no danger of impregnation, but they have different sexually transmitted diseases. Use prophylactics," he adds in deference to his elder status. Parents and adults are meant to be sources of opinionated imperatives.

But the curiosity is pulling hard, and Kalp cannot take his eyes from the book, from the page that it fell open on. "May I take this?" he requests. He could demand it, but Kalp has never been one to demand anything. Few people do follow the old strictures of the hierarchy—even at home they were nothing more than a way to shuffle the world into logical organization. It is only the arrogant ones like Derx that *demand*.

The young ones seem unhappy at the loss of the literature, and Kalp promises, "I shall return it when I have finished my perusal."

They share a glance and agree, uncomfortable with denying a Higher Status at any rate, and disperse to go play a game of "hoops" with the human soldiers who live in a Sleeping Place of their own on the far side of the park.

Kalp picks up the book and, feeling ridiculously salacious, returns to his cot with it. He opens it to the first page, skipping the graphic photographs in favour of reading the accompanying text, practicing his English first, building his vocabulary. It is an exercise in maturity and self restraint. It also builds a slow, anxious, but delicious sort of anticipation. As he reads, he tries very hard not to envision the faces of Maru and Trus.

When he finally does allow his eyes to turn to the images, he somehow cannot imagine that under their clothing Gwen and Basil look like that, glistening pink and splayed out and vulnerable.

KALP IS having an understandably hard time concentrating on work.

He is in Basil's chair again, because the desk and chair that Gwen requisitioned have not yet arrived. He is supposed to be concentrating on the schematics before him, but all he can seem to look at is the small shadow of flesh at the top of Basil's chest. His top shirt button has worked loose and the vee of lightly furred skin is far more intriguing than it ought to be. Kalp looks at Gwen, busy laying out an assortment of delicacies that she apparently baked the night before, arranging them temptingly on the edge of her desk. She too has her top button undone, but he can only see the dip in her collar bones, and no further.

Discreetly, Kalp undoes his own top button. It seems the done thing.

He wonders at the fashion trend that makes a whole pairing of fasteners obsolete, when they are obviously there to be fastened, but then he puts that thought aside. He has seen stranger on his own world.

Kalp had finished looking at the pornographic book before anyone else returned to the Sleeping Place, and, as promised, left it on the younger one's cot. He spent the rest of the evening, however, thinking about Maru and Trus and how much he misses his family. He misses frantic, heated intercourse for no other reason than for the sheer pleasure of revelling in each other's bodies, in the sweetly gasping responses and arousing little sounds. He misses comfortable quiet domestic compatibility. He misses performing kind gestures for no other reason than to evoke pleasure in another. He misses cherishing and being cherished. He misses falling asleep wrapped in his nest and around his Aglunated.

He only allowed himself the usual mourning period; he could not stand to dwell any more than that. It had just been so fast, all of it, and sometimes it still feels like it never happened, that he may wake up any moment, rise up out of his unconscious phase and find it all to have been an illusion of the mind while he slept. Maru and Trus will be there, and the sky will be the soft green of his childhood.

He performed the Ceremony and still feels incomplete—not that he had been alone in performing it on the refugee ships.

Their mutual loss is what is holding those who are left together.

Some had escaped with family—parents, siblings, children—some with Aglunates, some with whole Units. And some, like Kalp, utterly and absolutely alone. Kalp has no one.

Kalp is widowed and touch-starved and, yes, he admits it, empty-feeling. He feels left behind, like maybe he really did die with Maru in the smoke field or Trus in the panic, and he is not on Earth, placed among—between—two of these strange, squishy creatures and trying vainly to adapt. To Integrate.

And humans *are* squishy. Perhaps solely because they are nearly sixty percent water, they leak, ooze, secrete, and shed all over the place. It is a wonder that they do not leave puddles in their wake. While fornicating, the blood inside them flows all down in men and all up in women. Women make natural lubrication, but men do not, and yes, as the young ones found so revolting, all of the men's sexual organs are at all times on the outside of the body.

Kalp has to make an effort not to stare at the area of Basil's pants that hide his genitalia as the human passes by in front of the drafting table to fetch more tea. Beyond a small tell-tale wrinkle, he looks perfectly flat in front, like Gwen and Kalp himself. Do men tuck themselves into contraptions to flatten their crotches, Kalp wonders, just as women tuck their fully inflated breasts into lingerie to buoy them up, to enhance their visibility and put their fertility on display?

Kalp will not deny that "bras" are flattering, and add to the attractiveness of a woman, but it is strange to him that their breasts are inflated at all times, and not just when they are prepared to create and nourish a child. It is a strange evolutionary signal and Kalp is eager to investigate medical literature to further understand it. For the same reason he wonders why the penis and the precious sacs in which seminal fluid is created are placed in such an unprotected area. Kalp's genitalia are safely tucked under his rib cage, where no stray jarring or accidental injury could endanger his chances of procreating. It seems only logical.

Kalp is roaming amongst his thoughts when Gwen moves to stand before him and wave her hand in front of his eyes. The gentle buffet of sound that the movement creates brings Kalp back to the present. He fears Gwen will be angry with his distractedness, the way he has ceased to work, but she is smiling.

"Earth to Kalp," she says. "Where were you?"

Kalp has heard this idiom before. He replies, "I was lost in thought," and says nothing about the nature of his thoughts.

"About what?"

Kalp lowers his head and feels his ears droop. Gwen can read his body language well enough, it seems, not to press the issue. Instead she proffers a clear plastic container filled with delicious smelling sweets.

"These are called brownies. Have you had chocolate before?"

Kalp has, and says as much, but the first tender bite makes him wonder if he had been lied to originally. The "candy bar" that he had eaten several months ago was nothing at all like this. *This* is fantastic. Kalp's pleasure pleases Gwen, and she grins.

"I figured you'd like them," she says. "I thought, if you have endorphins, you'd have to love the rush that chocolate gives."

Kalp is too busy licking the last morsels of the treat from his lips, trying not to look like he is sizing up the rest of the shallow dish.

"Have another," Gwen says, "but don't eat too many too soon. The sugar will make you sick."

Kalp takes another, says, carefully, "Cheers," and stuffs it with rather less grace than usual into his mouth, licking around his teeth to make sure he has chased down every last delicious molecule.

Gwen's eyes go shiny and bright and Kalp is not sure if she is more pleased about his reaction to the brownies, or that he has managed to utilize his jargon lesson from yesterday so effectively.

Basil sweeps back into the office with a cup of tea, a cup of coffee, and a bottle of water. He sets all three down on the draft table, seemingly unconcerned about the ring of moisture the condensation from the water bottle causes on the thin paper, and dives in for a handful of brownies of his own.

"Chocolate!" he crows, cramming two into his mouth at once, chewing lustily.

"Hey you," Gwen says with a smile, pulling the container away from his grabbing hands too late. "These are for Kalp. You ate your half last night."

"I only had batter," Basil protests. His speech is still slower, but Kalp is slowly becoming accustomed to the pattern of his cadence and today Basil's words are easier to decipher, even if they are muffled by the detritus of food between his cheeks.

"Exactly," Gwen says.

Basil opens his eyes very wide and makes his lower lip protrude, and Kalp stops. He watches Gwen's reaction to this strange new expression.

"Don't beg," Gwen scolds, but she is still smiling.

Ah, so this arrangement of the features is "pleading." Kalp memorizes this dutifully and wonders if he can make his own mouth into that shape. He doubts his lower lip is plump enough, but perhaps he will try later when he is before the mirrors in the lavatory. If this is the expression he must make to earn more brownies, he is certainly willing to practice.

Gwen sighs—another term from yesterday—and holds out the box for Basil. Kalp does not begrudge the human man more of the brownies; they truly are excellent and Kalp believes that in the spirit of good will and mutual cooperation, he can sacrifice a few to Basil's good humour.

But then Gwen does something Kalp did not expect. Right before Basil's fingers close on a brownie, she tugs the dish out from under his fingers. She smiles at him, but the expression is different, wider and yet more narrow, and with a jolting stab of revelation, Kalp realizes he has seen this face before, too.

This is "sly." This is the "invitation" face the woman in the pornography was making at the man.

Like the man in the book, Basil obligingly takes a step into her personal space and presses his mouth against Gwen's. There is chocolate at the corner of his lips and Gwen's wet pink tongue darts out to lick it away.

Kalp stands abruptly.

If they are in the opening phases of sexual intercourse, Kalp feels that for decency's sake, he must leave them to it privately. He is no prude, but Kalp feels intercourse should only be witnessed by those in the Unit involved. He also fears his own physical reaction to the deed. His own genitalia, once engorged, would be very visible. He fears either that they will be disgusted by the physical manifestation of his arousal, or angered that he was aroused at all.

And after reading that pornography, Kalp does not doubt that he will become aroused.

He turns to walk towards the door, but Basil calls out to him, "Oi, mate, where you headed?"

Kalp stops, because it would be inconsiderate of him to depart without explanation, especially after so direct a request. "I will make myself absent for a time," Kalp says. "So you may…finish."

"Finish what?" Gwen asks, and the puzzlement in her voice forces Kalp to look over his shoulder at the two, just so he can gauge her reaction.

They are no longer entwined. Gwen is at her desk and Basil at his, the brownies temptingly unguarded in the middle of the draft table.

"Were you not just initiating intercourse?" Kalp asks, for clarification.

When they choke and turn red and trill, this time Kalp knows it is laughter and is not alarmed. He is mildly annoyed that they are once more laughing at his mistake, but he is more eager for them to cease laughing so that he may discover what they find amusing.

"It was just a kiss," Gwen says. "It could lead to…to intercourse. But, uh…not in this office."

"Anymore," Basil adds under his breath and Gwen's face flushes pink, again like the woman from the pornography.

Is she shamed or aroused? Kalp wonders.

Still, this is a revelation that Kalp must muse over in solitude. "I require the lavatory," he says, and it is the first outright lie he has told a human since Earth-fall. Were he feeling less conflicted about other things, he may have felt guilty for the deception. As it is, he is merely anxious to depart the office.

Basil waves him permission and Kalp goes.

Kalp retreats into one of the small metal cubicles and puts the lid down on the commode and curls himself into a ball and thinks.

Basil and Gwen are, if not a Unit, at least committed sexual partners.

Kalp knew that they were comfortable with each other, with each other's proximity and bodies, but he had not suspected that they currently engaged in intercourse. Or rather, he *had* suspected, but suspicion and confirmation are two very different things, and Kalp cannot help but feel mildly surprised. He tugs his ears nervously—the images behind his eyes grow more vivid. The woman and man in the pornography suddenly wear the faces of his teammates and it is too intriguing to be professional.

A sudden, lurching thought occurs to Kalp.

They touch him the very same way.

No one has initiated something so intimate as a kiss yet, but perhaps that is due merely to shyness. Basil and Gwen each touch Kalp with the same casual affection that they touch each other. They had displayed their sexual initiations before him today, and unless Kalp missed the meaning of their exchange regarding the brownies, then they had been discussing intercourse that had been performed the evening prior. Intercourse that had involved Kalp's brownies. In front of Kalp. And Basil keeps referring to Kalp as "mate."

Most importantly, Kalp is a widower.

Here are two humans, already well on their way to being Aglunated, and him alone, who had volunteered to do whatever it takes to gain the human's trust. What if he had misunderstood the question about volunteering? It was entirely possible—when the Specialists had come to them, Kalp's grasp of English had been shaky at best.

Kalp could have agreed to anything without being sure of the particulars of the arrangement. It is not an unknown occurrence, even on his own world. Mistakes in comprehension are sometimes made.

What if what Kalp thought was a working relationship is actually a symbolic marriage? Has Kalp been purposefully placed into an Aglunate composed of humans and himself, as a political gesture?

For a brief moment, Kalp rages.

How dare! Kalp still aches for his lost Aglunates, he is not ready to retake others, especially so soon and especially a pair of leaking humans! He will not be used as a political tool, his own emotions rendered invalid. It is not fair and it is supremely undemocratic. Yet Gwen and Basil are kind, and Kalp really is willing to do whatever is necessary to ensure that his people stay welcome on Earth. There is nowhere else they can go. The bonded pair of humans the Institute selected for Kalp could be worse.

It may not be so big a hardship, Kalp hopes tentatively, to be bonded to two people who are so thoughtful. Already he is very fond of them. Their generosity and kindness has impressed him, made them endearing. It makes him want to do something kind for them; like making brownies, or sharing a status-seat. He wishes there was something he could give, but he left his home with so little and everything he owns now is meagre and was donated. The thought touches the place inside where he still aches for Maru and Trus, but this time it does not hurt as much. Perhaps, he muses, spreading his palm flat, his fingers wide against his chest, the step towards intimacy and domesticity would not be as shockingly difficult as he fears.

Perhaps, just perhaps, this is exactly the thing he needs to help make the pain of abandonment fade.

For many long moments, Kalp remains in the commode's cubicle, fingers tugging at his ears, thinking. He conjures up Maru's and Trus' faces and scents—they had been trying for a child, he and Maru and Trus. Any offspring generated from two would have been considered the product and pride of three. A Unit of four is the idyll on his world.

TRIPTYCH

Kalp had been looking forward to offspring.

He had wanted very much to be a father. He had been anticipating lazy sunny afternoons with a picture book; evenings in the kitchen, the small one reaching up to thieve a sweet before the evening's repast has finished cooking; teaching the child everything that Maru and Trus could not, the things that he knew only from his own parents. All the things his mothers and father taught him.

Now he will never know the child he had so envisioned. Not one of his own, not unless he enters into another Aglunate of his own people, and there are so few of them, they are so scattered…But here, he has been offered a place—symbolic, surely, but it appears as if Gwen and Basil are willing to take a step beyond the symbolic, to make it a true Aglunate, if he is willing to participate. The resultant offspring will not be his own, but Kalp thinks he would not mind helping to raise theirs. He will care for it, he knows, as if it were his own, pink and fragile or not. He could be that child's father, too, and teach it everything that Maru and Trus would have, everything his own mothers and father taught him, could have the lazy afternoons with the picture books, even if they would be in English, could have the sneaked sweeties.

Yes, Kalp decides. He will do this.

For his people. For their future on Earth. For Gwen and Basil, and for, perhaps, the child he may be father to. For his own happiness.

He can try.

Choice made, Kalp emerges from the cubicle, washes his hands to ensure no cross contamination of bacteria, and returns to the office. It is quiet when he enters, Gwen and Basil each sheepishly bent over paperwork at their desks. Basil has retrieved a second chair from somewhere. Both of their cheeks flare red briefly, fetching and signalling shame all at once.

Kalp, taking the cue of silence, walks over to the drafting table and sits, and works over his own translations quietly until the mid-afternoon repast.

THE ONLY item in this whole marriage that confuses Kalp is the domicile arrangements. If he and his teammates are meant to be an Aglunate, then why does Kalp not reside with them in their own home? Do Units not live under the same roof, here? But he has seen on television that they do, at least in the unrealistic perfection of the fantasy world that Kalp knows television represents.

Perhaps Gwen and Basil merely do not feel that it is necessary. But Kalp surprises himself by realizing that he wishes it was. He is equally surprised to realize that he may not even mind living with the secreting humans. As the Aglunation *is* purely symbolic, he need not even keep a room with them; indeed, many households on his world kept a spare nest in case one of the three was feeling unwell or just a specific two were attempting to conceive. Kalp would be happy to sleep elsewhere if only it meant...

Meant not going back to the Sleeping Place.

Kalp feels ungrateful. He is given a room in which to sleep, clothing to wear, food to eat, a place to clean himself, all for free. But he does not like it.

Every afternoon, at the completion of the work day, Kalp has returned to the Sleeping Place and neither Gwen nor Basil has made a move to redirect Kalp to their own shared home. Perhaps, he thinks, they are attempting to create an offspring and do not wish Kalp to be in their home at that time. Kalp is not sure about his own reaction to this—he is relieved in part, because according to the pornography, human intercourse is very rough and involves an extreme amount of bodily fluid. Kalp has just gotten used to their oily scent-marking. He is not sure he could handle full fornication.

But he is also somewhat disappointed, for as messy as it seems, the humans do appear to be having fun, and Kalp would like to try it. He misses intercourse. Self-pleasure is fine, but it is rare when he is alone enough to engage in it, and it is not as satisfying.

Perhaps they are merely allowing him time to become accustomed to their arrangement before they commit to it fully, and Kalp finds he likes this line of reasoning best of all. He is not a stupid man. He is aware that he is probably deceiving himself, but he cannot find it in himself to argue. It is a more likely possibility that Basil and Gwen would prefer to keep their Aglunation in the symbolic, at least where intimacies with Kalp are concerned. He cannot say he blames them. He must be as strange to them as they are to him.

Comfort is comfort, and he will take what comfort he can, all alone on an alien planet.

At night, he imagines what it may be like, between Gwen and Basil, pressing his mouth awkwardly against theirs when they are touching so intimately, feeling that burst of warm affection between three that he scarce hopes to experience again. When he drops into his unconscious phase, even Derx's droning cannot divest him of his quiet, hopeful joy.

BEFORE LUNCH on the third day, Kalp notices the slice of white, puffed scar tissue on Gwen's forehead. It is slightly startling—his own people develop scars, of course; anything with skin does—but unless the scars are very serious, their colouring and fur often disguise the disfiguring marks. Therefore, presenting or showing scars to another is rare and strange and intimate.

Yet here is Gwen's scar, white and clean, starting just above her eyebrow and arching back along her scalp, hidden by the swept-sideways way that she has styled her hair.

He only sees it because she has become exasperated with her hair hanging in her eyes as she tries to write, and has secured it to the side with, of all things, a little silver paperclip.

It serves to remind him again of just how terribly naked these creatures are.

Poor colouring for camouflage; fragile, thin skin; fat, slow limbs; reproductive organs open to any attack; no easy method of seeing or hearing behind them. How had they become the dominant species of this planet?

The development of speech and opposable digits, Kalp supposes, just as it was among his people.

Kalp watches Gwen fiddle with her hair for a moment, patting it down over the scar, smoothing it out to hide the pale line, then frustratedly shoving it back behind her ear or into the paperclip in an effort to get it out of the way of her sightline. She repeats the process several times before Kalp realizes that the first part of the three-step dance of tucking, untucking, and patting of hair, is unconscious. She is constantly trying to hide her deformity and does not even know she is doing so.

Kalp wonders how she got the scar.

It is thin and clean, as if it could have come from a blade or a very particular fall. He hopes one day Gwen will trust him enough to tell him.

The other distraction of the day is that Kalp's new desk has still not come in.

He does not want to make a nuisance of himself, but he cannot concentrate on his work for the pain that spreads all down his back. Surely, he must not be the only one of his people who is suffering the ill effects of human-style beds, but to whom could he complain? They are lucky enough that have been given hospitality; to ask more will invite ill feelings.

Yet he cannot even take his mind off the pain long enough to consider that Basil and Gwen are both now wearing shirts that are tight across their chests and expose the bare skin of their arms. The weather has changed and it is growing ever warmer and more humid. In an effort to leak less, they have opted to wear less clothing. Practical, from a logistics point of view, but ever so distracting.

Or, it would be, if Kalp could manage to sit up straight.

He is seriously considering requesting a pain blocking medication. Kalp was informed upon his entry to the Institute that medicines based on his own people's dwindling supply of pharmaceuticals had been created in mass quantities and were available for his consumption. He only need request them. He has not yet, but he thinks that if he can take a muscle relaxer, then he may just be able to unwind enough to keep the tension from returning, and concentrate on his duties.

He is wary of the medicine, however. Not because he seriously believes that the humans would poison him intentionally, but that they may do so accidentally. There is still much about the other that each species does not understand—as Kalp had already proved with his verbal errors and Gwen and Basil had proved with their casual touching.

Mistakes do happen.

"Your back's hurting again, innit?" Basil asks, putting a vessel of tea down beside Kalp's arm. The engineering schematics are now artfully marked all over with rings of moisture stains, but they do not impede Kalp's ability to read them, nor Gwen's to translate, nor Basil's to build, so no one minds. Kalp notes that this tea smells of flora—another herbal blend that Basil has decided Kalp should test.

He has, apparently, wagered money with Gwen on whether Kalp will indeed begin to drink tea by the week's end, and is doing his best to keep from losing. So far, Kalp has yet to find a blend of the beverage appealing to his palate. They are all too sweet, which Basil finds a hilarious notion, because Gwen calls them all too bitter.

Kalp performs the head bob of affirmation. "The cots," he says, choosing his words carefully, not wanting to sound ungrateful, "are not as we usually sleep."

"How do you usually sleep?" Gwen asks, abandoning her notepad. She is always as eager as he is to set aside the drudgery of their prescribed tasks to converse about cultural differences and similarities. Her fingers are stained with ink, as they always are. At first Kalp found this unintentional habit slightly revolting, dirty, but now that he understands that it is the inevitable side effect of her scholarship, he finds it rather endearing.

"At home, we built nests." The stick and mud berths of the flying animals are also called "nests" in English, and Kalp sees their confusion. "Not as birds do. We like soft things. Many many pillows, pushed together and confined by walls. Piles of soft blankets. We sleep curled up."

"Mm," Gwen says. "Sounds heavenly."

"Sounds like a recipe for high chiropractic bills," Basil shoots back. "Humans need firm spine support."

"We are more...fluid," Kalp explains, struggling over a suitable adjective. The only ones he knows that are close to the appropriate descriptors are used to describe the flow of water, and he is not liquid. "Your cots are too firm. It is like..." He trails off, failing to find a suitable simile.

"Like if we slept on the floor," Gwen says. "It's too hard."

"Yes. And narrow."

"Narrow?" Basil repeats. "Waitaminute—hard and narrow, and you said 'cots,' yeah?"

Gwen catches on to Basil's line of logic, but Kalp still does not know the workings of their minds well enough to guess what they are thinking. "Kalp, where are they putting you up?"

Kalp is surprised by this question. "You do not know?"

Both humans shake their heads from side to side, the gesture for the negative.

"In the Sleeping Place," Kalp says.

"Sleeping Place?"

"A large building, on the same base as the military. There is a large room with a high ceiling and many cots lined up, and cleaning cubicles in the common bathing room."

"You're in the *barracks?*" Gwen says, aghast. Kalp does not know this term, but he assumes it is the English word for where he is living. "That's awful!"

"Gwen, maybe they want to make sure that nobody disturbs them—"

"Or maybe they want to keep them under surveillance!" Gwen's blood has rushed up to her face, pressing against the underside of her skin. Kalp knows this expression, though he's never seen it in person before. This is "fury."

"Gwen you don't know—" Basil begins, hands held out, palms up. It is shockingly similar to Kalp's own people's gesture of pleading.

"The hell I don't!" she snaps back, cutting off his words. "They said that they were living in all due comfort! I was expecting motels at the least. Something with mattresses!"

"I have meals," Kalp insists. "I have clothing and access to clean water, and a place on which to sleep. What more do I need?"

"Comfort!" Gwen yells. Her rage washes against Kalp's skin and he fights the urge to curl up and deafen as much of his body as he can, protect it against her wild heartbeat and furious, grating tone. But he knows that she does not direct her anger at him, so he sits still and lets the emotion run its course. "A semblance of home! They at least owe you privacy!"

"Perhaps for monetary reasons—"

"Bullshit! It's the U.N.! They have the cash!"

Basil now has his hands on Gwen's shoulders. He is staring intently into her eyes. "Gwen," he says, and his voice is firm but soothing. "Calm down."

"I will not 'calm down'! This is an outrage! This is—"

"—look at Kalp."

Gwen stops and looks at him. Kalp is doing his utmost best to endure the screaming volume of her displeasure, but it hurts his skin and he has doubled himself over, finger pads digging into the bottom of the chair, ears flattened against the back of his neck.

The room blessedly silent, Kalp ventures a look back up.

Gwen is leaking again.

Water is running out of her eyes. She looks very angry still, but also contrite. "I'm sorry," she says.

"No apologies," Kalp starts, uncurling himself muscle by muscle, skin still ringing from the loudness of her fury. "We agreed."

"No, no, really," Gwen insists. "I shouldn't have lost my temper and I shouldn't have hurt you. It was very irresponsible of me." She bends her wet face down and performs The Apology. It is messy and moist and hasty and amateurish and the most amazing thing Kalp has ever seen. This human angry not because of him, but *for* him, and apologizing for it anyway.

"I am okay," Kalp insists. "There is no lasting effect. Except…that you are leaking on me."

Gwen trills, a soft little chuckle and turns out of the comforting embrace to fetch Kleenex from the multicoloured box on her desk. She mops at her face. Basil stands in place and fidgets, digging at the mechanical grease under his fingernails, and waits. It is a small relief to note that it seems that males all over the universe, no matter what species, have no idea what to do with an upset female. Kalp feels just as agitated as Basil, and they share an ironic look.

Finally, Gwen turns back around. The cosmetic paint that she often wears around her eyes is smudged under her lids and her face is red in patches and Kalp thinks that she is very beautiful, for a human. Perhaps it is the way her cheeks are flushed, or the way her eyes glimmer with leftover salt water, or the way biting her lips has made them redder, plumper.

Kalp knows it is not just himself, because Basil is staring transfixed as well.

Gwen slaps her palms together, rubs them briskly, and then retrieves her light animal-hide coat from the back of her chair. She swings it over her shoulder, thrusting her arms into the sleeves with determination. It is a signal of intended departure.

"Uh," Basil says, snapping to attention. "Where we going?"

"To get Kalp's things," Gwen says.

Kalp stands up now, too. "I beg your pardon?"

"We," she says, gesturing with a single finger between Basil and herself, "have a spare bedroom. You," and here she points at Kalp, though he was sure he had been taught that indicating a person with a single digit was disrespectful, "require somewhere better to live than a drafty, noisy, barrack."

Basil looks alarmed. "Can we talk about this?" He reaches out, grabs Gwen's arm in a manner that is not as affectionate as Kalp is accustomed to, and drags her out of what Basil assumes is earshot.

It is not, not quite—Kalp can still make out the low patter, the mood of the tone, if not the actual words themselves. But Basil is speaking too rapidly for Kalp to understand what he is saying, even if he could hear complete phrases, decipher them.

The stabbing shock that accompanies the apparent need for this discussion is distracting Kalp anyway. It is clear now that Basil and Gwen never initially intended for Kalp to join their household. His assumptions about their relationship were erroneous, and for reasons that Kalp does not wish to explore, it hurts.

Gwen seems to win the skirmish. Basil dons his own outer wear and they all three depart the office. For the first time when they reach the parking lot, Kalp turns to the right to follow Gwen and Basil to their conveyance, instead of left to the place where the bus picks him up and drops him off every day.

Basil's automobile is not as shiny and clean as the ones Kalp has seen on the television, but it will be the first one that Kalp has ever entered and he is excited for the opportunity all the same. He focuses on the sensations of the trip rather than the motivations for it, because he is nervous enough as it is, without considering that his whole life is changing again. And that maybe, ensconced in their household, Gwen and Basil will still come to care for him as strongly as he hopes.

When they arrive at the military compound shortly thereafter, they each flash their identification cards to the soldier at the gate, and are let in with a smile and a wave. Kalp directs them to the correct building. Basil goes in one direction to speak to the human in charge of residence arrangements—to "harangue," Gwen calls it, and Kalp guesses the definition of the word when he hears Basil's raised voice echoing across the open spaces between the low concrete buildings of the base—and Kalp takes Gwen in the opposite direction and shows her into the Sleeping Place. It is neat and tidy, just the way they all leave it each morning, but Gwen looks distressed all the same.

"Where do you sleep?" she asks.

Kalp leads her to a bed almost exactly in the middle of the room. It is indistinguishable from the others, except that there are a pair of shoes peeking out from under the sheet that hangs down to cut the draft under the cots.

"This is it?" she asks. "Not very luxurious."

Kalp has a trunk under the cot. There is clothing in it, all labelled carefully on the inside with the English version of his written name. He has enough, and the cleaners whose duties it is to attend to the bathing rooms and commodes and floors take them away for laundry once a week. His sheets are fresh and clean, and the meals they provide are nutritious and hot. He is tempted to say again that, despite the discomfort of the cot, all of his basic needs are being met and he is content.

But Kalp can see what Gwen is upset about—his basic needs should not *just* be met, he should be comfortable. But this is a planet where a small percentage of the population owns a large percentage of the land and wealth. Changes are coming to make certain that everyone's level of life is elevated from "survival" to "enjoyment," but the process is slow, even Kalp knows that. He is grateful to have been given as much as he has, especially when there are so many others with less.

Basil storms in, head held high in triumph, and drops down onto Kalp's cot with a smug grin. He immediately jumps back up. "God, this is where you sleep? It's…awful. These sheets are awful, the mattress is awful, it's…this is just—"

"Awful?" Kalp supplies.

"Awful," Basil agrees. "Let's get out of here, eh?"

Gwen and Basil share the weight of Kalp's trunk between them, and Kalp is left to gather up his shoes and a small box of the only things he managed to bring with him when he'd fled—a rendered image of his Aglunates, another of his three parents, a neck accessory that he happened to have had on that morning, and a small wooden toy that is half finished, that he'd had in his pockets, meant to have been a gift for the child that he and Maru and Trus had been trying so hard to produce.

KALP PUTS his shoes down on the tiled floor of the small foyer and dutifully says, "Honey, I have arrived." He looks down, fingers splayed, waiting for the small quadruped that ought to be greeting him. He is looking forward to the experience of petting a cat. He has been informed that his own fur is not dissimilar and he is intrigued.

"It's 'honey, I'm home,'" Basil corrects, pushing past Kalp. He kicks his shoes in the general direction of the hall closet and bundles himself—laptop case, BlackBerry, coat, file box, blueprint tube and all—up the stairs at the end of the hallway.

The trunk is still on the front step.

Gwen removes her shoes at a more sedate pace. "Why are you standing like that?" she asks, and the question is not spoken with the anger face or tone. She has the "curious" tone, her head cocked to the side in a way that indicates interest.

"Your cat," Kalp says. "I must stroke it before I enter your dwelling, must I not?"

Gwen smiles, one of those large, genuine flashes of small flat teeth that Kalp is beginning to associate with real pleasure, and laughs. Kalp straightens and tries to lean into the rippling sound without looking desperate for its touch.

Kalp loves Gwen's laugh. It is so *good*.

"We don't have a cat," Gwen says. "And you don't have to say 'honey, I'm home' every time you walk in the front door, either. That's another of those television stereotypes."

Kalp had learned about television stereotypes today while watching "Diff'rent Strokes" in the canteen at the Institute.

There is muted banging from upstairs, and by the vibrations that skitter down the walls and waft from the open air above the staircase, it feels as if Basil is pushing around furniture.

Kalp turns to head up the stairs, curious, but Gwen catches his elbow and leads him instead back to the front step. Together they move the trunk into the hallway beyond the entry, leaving it at the foot of the stairs where it will be easily accessible but not impede progress. Once that is finished, she walks him through a door with a rounded top, into the kitchen. Kalp pauses just outside it, staring at the photograph of Basil and Gwen standing before some large round mechanical contraption that has been built beside a wide river. Beyond the river, through the spindles of the wheel, is a stately building.

"What is this?" Kalp asks, tapping the glass that protects the photograph. "This machine."

"Hm?" Gwen pops her head back around the corner to see what he is referring to. "Oh, that's the Eye of London. It's a Ferris wheel. You, uh, see these pods? You pay for a ticket and you can go up and around and come back down."

"And what is the purpose of a Ferris wheel?"

Gwen shrugs. "For fun. To look. I like getting up in the sky, as close to the clouds as possible. Basil does it because he likes to look at the city all laid out like toys. He likes the shapes of the buildings and streets."

"When may I utilize the Eye of London?" Kalp asks. He is filled with hope that Gwen will say tonight, but knows it is a juvenile desire. They all have one more work day before the week-end, the two day rest holiday, and therefore they must be responsible and stay inside the domicile today and take appropriate rest.

Gwen considers his question. "How about we go into London on Saturday? Go up in the Eye, take you shopping, get 'proper fish and chips' for Basil?"

Saturday is not today. Today is Thursday. But Kalp keeps the disappointment hidden. He is lucky enough to be going at all, and he cheers himself with the thought that the anticipation will just make it more enjoyable.

However, Kalp is unsure why he would need to go shopping—the Institute has provided him with food and clothing to this point, and Gwen and Basil have now provided shelter. He has very little currency accumulated from the last few days of work, and he has yet to receive his pay packet. Even if Kalp felt that he required something, he has no tender with which to purchase it.

He would very much like to ride the Ferris wheel, however, so he does not object.

Gwen returns to the kitchen and this time Kalp follows her all the way into the narrow, bright room. Late afternoon sunlight is entering through the large window above the washing station, a soothing happy wave of sleepy vibrations.

She retrieves a small glass vessel from a cabinet and fills it with cold water from the faucet. She passes it over to him, and then pours another for herself.

"This is the kitchen," she says. "Everything in it is fair game. That means you can eat whatever food you find, however you'd like to eat it, at any time. Do you understand? No starving under my roof."

Kalp smiles. He finds the more he does it, the easier and more instinctual it becomes.

"Basil and I usually have coffee and tea in the morning. We'll make enough for you too, if you indicate that you want it. There's bagels and fruit, yogurt, eggs…whatever you want in the morning before we leave, have. We exit the house at eight o'clock sharp—it's our only morning rule. We can't be late."

"I understand," Kalp says, with the affirmative head bob. "There are many people who are eager to replace you should you prove to fail in your duties, so you must instead prove dependable."

Gwen blinks once, and she seems to be surprised that Kalp understands the situation that thoroughly. "Uh, yeah," she agrees.

"I will not be late," Kalp promises. "I do not wish to see you replaced. I am too fond of your company."

There. He's admitted it.

It is thrilling.

Gwen's response is a soft, tender smile. "We're fond of you too, Kalp."

He considers trying to kiss her now, and hesitates because he is not sure how quickly humans move to physical intimacy after such declarations. He has never done it before, is not sure how to start. Before he can work up the gumption, the banging upstairs stops. Gwen sets aside her empty glass and brushes past Kalp towards the stairs. Kalp lingers in the kitchen for a moment, enjoying the fading sensation of her hot skin against his bare arm, and then sets down his own glass vessel and follows.

They cross a room that has a table and four chairs—why four? There are only two residents of the domicile; perhaps in anticipation of offspring?—and then another room that has a long animal hide sofa facing a ridiculously large television mounted on the wall, a fireplace to the right of it and glass doors that open into a small, walled garden to the left. Yet all the furniture belongs together, like a pack of ill-matched but nonetheless companionable friends. Kalp is fascinated by the fireplace. He has seen them on television, but like the car, never experienced it first hand. He thinks he'd like to try roasting marshmallows. On the same wall as the fireplace are the stairs, and Gwen is already halfway up them.

Kalp follows at a slower pace, placing his toes carefully on the narrow steps. They are just large enough for a human foot, clearly not designed for one shaped like his own. He will need to remember to go slowly every time. It would be embarrassing to tumble down them. Perhaps even dangerous.

At the head of the stairs there are four doors, two on the left and two on the right. From the feel of the water standing in the pipes, it appears as if the bathing room and commode are on the far right, above the kitchen. The door on the far left is closed, but from the strength of the combined scents of Basil and Gwen, he guesses that particular room is their own sleeping chamber.

Kalp does not know what is closest on the right—that door too is closed—but he makes a wager with himself that it is a linen closet. The door to the left directly beside him is also closed, but he can hear Gwen and Basil inside, so he pushes it open.

The bed frame has been disassembled and stacked in a temporary fashion against the wall. One of the mattresses is on the floor, and the other, the firmest one with many springs, is on its side against the wall beside the frame. The horizontal mattress is piled with every pillow that Basil must have been able to find, and every blanket as well. Kalp now also makes a wager with himself that the linen closet is empty. There is a small low table beside the makeshift nest with a tiny, vibrating light whose wattage does not make Kalp wince, and a chest of drawers, and an empty place just the right size for his trunk.

Kalp has no words.

Their easy generosity has already shocked him to the core several times over, but this, this is far more than Kalp had ever expected from anyone who are not his Aglunates.

He shuffles forward across the soft carpet that muffles the sounds from the wires under the floor, and wraps his arms around both of them, across their shoulders, and squeezes carefully. He knows it is called a "hug." He likes this too, the feeling of their arms around him, their hot hands against his sore back, their heartbeats a syncopated rhythm against his ears.

"Cheers," he says, because he cannot think of anything that will express his gratitude better.

KALP MUST still share the bathing room, but now it is only with two instead of thirty. It is a luxury he never expected to have again, especially when Gwen introduces him to the wondrous joy of bubble baths.

To be wholly surrounded by water, the noisy world quieted, the only sound his own breathing...It is miraculous. He has to be careful not to drop into his unconscious phase while in the soothing hot bath, or he could drown. But Gwen showed him a trick with the inflatable bath pillow, so he is not too concerned.

The domicile that Gwen and Basil share is squeezed into a row of identical looking houses on a street. Kalp is glad for the numbers on the outside by the doors, or he would not know which house to enter, and it would be unpleasant to accidentally startle a neighbour by mistake. The walls are thick and solid, so he can barely feel the movements of the humans who live next door. Only when they walk or talk especially loud do their vibrations carry through, or if they're standing right next to the adjoining wall.

The domicile itself is much more active than Kalp expected—water sloshes through the dish-washer in the kitchen and through the laundry machine in the basement. Both chug in a surprisingly harmonious rhythm so it is not irritating. There is electricity in the walls here, too, but not as much as in the Institute or the Sleeping Place, so it too is quieter. But there are microwaves and coffee makers, digital clocks, computers, video game systems, and the car, and each of them has their distinct sound and feel. It is overwhelming now, and Kalp hopes that it will soon dull itself down to background noise when he becomes used to it.

Downstairs, Gwen and Basil are talking. Kalp's ears are still out of the water, so he can hear the soft murmur of their voices, but he cannot make out the words. He is content to let the cadence of their speech and heartbeats wash over him, ripple along the surface of his ears, the exposed top of his skull. They are comforting.

They sound like home.

Kalp can smell something too—there's a rhythmic *chop chop* coming from the kitchen and Kalp assumes this combined with the appealing scent means somebody is preparing a meal. According to television, stereotypically it ought to be Gwen, but Basil confirmed that they share the domestic chores more evenly than is tradition. They clean together, and make domicile repairs together. Kalp will be expected to help, and he is pleased to. He's eager to try the vacuum.

Kalp also longs to make the dishes that he used to enjoy on his planet. He does not think that he will be able to get all the right ingredients, but he suspects improvisation will not be too difficult. He will make enough for all three of them, and will hope that Gwen and Basil like it. Kalp enjoys Earth food too, of course, and he has not had a complaint about it yet, but it is not the same.

Kalp stays in the bath long enough for the water to cool. It is not uncomfortable, but he feels he has relaxed enough. The bath has achieved its purpose, and the tight knots of muscle that were making his back ache so ferociously have melted away. He exits the bathtub carefully so as not to puddle water on the tile floor, and pulls out the drain plug. The towel they have left for him is warm and thick and fuzzy. It feels very nice against his damp skin, much better than the thin serviceable towels provided at the Sleeping Place.

Kalp hopes that the others of his people find such caring co-workers to move in with as well. There had been talk of transferring from the Sleeping Place to houses and apartments scattered across cities, as soon as everyone has accumulated enough currency to purchase or rent them. It will take a long time for everyone to earn enough money, however. Kalp is acutely aware of how lucky he is.

He dresses in fresh clothing and leaves the damp towel on the rack in the bathing room to dry, and pads slowly down the narrow stairs. When he reaches the bottom, he sees that the table has been laid out with eating utensils, and that one of the four matching chairs has been altered. The chair is now shorter—someone has sawed off several centimetres of the legs. Kalp's knees will be tucked up awkwardly, but this means that he will be at the appropriate height for the table. A small hand saw is now resting on the mantel of the fireplace and the spindly bottoms of the chair are waiting to be put to another use in the dented copper bin beside the hearth.

Again, he is touched by the simple gestures of thoughtfulness that these humans display. He is even more determined to be the creator of tomorrow night's meal as a way of expressing his gratitude. He will broach the topic of purchasing suitable food items tonight during the repast.

THE NEXT morning they are summoned immediately upon entering the Institute to the office of "the boss."

Word has gotten around about Basil and Gwen's "stunt"; not all the Specialists are pleased that they have absconded Kalp from the Sleeping Place. Conversely, some are thrilled. Kalp is called before a panel of Specialists and explains very ardently that he is very happy to live with Gwen and Basil. He also explains that there is nothing in particular that is wrong with the Sleeping place (Gwen cuts in and sharply describes the torment of the cots), only that it was not very home-like.

The three of them are verbally reprimanded for failing to follow proper channels of hierarchy and for a moment, Kalp is terrified that they will all have their employment terminated. Instead the very dark, very elderly human in charge of the panel sucks on his moustache and shakes his head a little and says, "All right then. Have fun. Now shove off, I have six more hearings today and I want to go up to my cottage before the sunset. Ta."

Either in celebration or to avoid any further confrontations with co-workers while the topic is still in debate, the three of them depart the Institute at the lunch hour and inform the receptionist in the lobby of their intention to not return to work again until the following Monday. They stop at a small store that specializes

J.M. FREY

in frothy coffee confections and pre-packaged sandwiches and take them across the street to a green space.

They sit on the grass. Kalp enjoys the tickle of the verdant foliage against his bare feet and the sunlight on his face. Basil grumbles and applies a thick protective cream to his pale skin to avoid sun damage. He offers it to Gwen and she politely declines. Basil tackles Gwen to the ground playfully, wrestling her until he has her pinned beneath his strong thighs, her hands trapped against her legs, and slathers her face with the cream against her half-hearted protests.

He offers some to Kalp, but Kalp's fur is protection enough and he does not relish the thought of how oily the cream looks. He half hopes Basil will tackle him, too, but is not disappointed when Basil does not. Thus far, there seems to be no indication that the humans are aware of his physical regard.

They drink their cold coffee and eat their cold sandwiches. Kalp discovers that he does not like lettuce, and picks it out of the melange between the bread. This does not offend Gwen or Basil—they explain that many humans have food preferences as well, and so disliking lettuce, while perhaps rare, is not unheard of. Kalp is relieved. He worries less and less everyday about offending his teammates, but he still worries all the same.

There are many birds in the park, and several of them very bold. Basil rips a piece of his bread off the top of his sandwich and tosses it at his feet. Immediately the birds swarm, cooing and flapping, and Kalp is amazed at the tussle that goes on for a single scrap of bread. He eats most of his own sandwich but retains a portion to feed to the pigeons.

There are also several human mothers or fathers nearby with their offspring. Catching sight of the first, Kalp is unable to breathe for a moment. A *child*. He aches, deep down, remembering how strongly he and his Aglunates had been hoping for one of their own. It hurts to see this perfect little being, so far away from his ruined planet, safe and happy and completely unaware of the horrors that had happened a galaxy away. This child must be very young. Perhaps it had not even taken its first breath when Kalp's Aglunates had taken their last.

His eyes burn in sorrow and Kalp turns away, covering them.

"Kalp?" Gwen asks, and her voice is soft and filled with concern. Kalp forces himself to look up, to fake a smile, but she can see that it is fake.

"The child," he says. "I...it hurts me."

Basil frowns. He balls up the empty wrapper of his sandwich and keeps pressing at it with his fingers nervously. "Hurts you how?"

"You would say...'my heart breaks.'"

Gwen sucks in a little gasp of breath and her eyes become wet again. "Oh my God, Kalp—we never asked. I feel like such a *heel*. Did you lose anyone? Stupid, obviously you did, I just meant...I mean, we didn't *ask*."

To lose is an euphemism for *die*.

Kalp shakes his head. "My parents. Maru and Trus...my Aglunates. We were merely hoping for a child."

Gwen snakes out a hand and wraps it around Kalp's. He notes with strange detachment that he no longer recoils from the feel of the secretions of her skin and the almost invisible swirl of wrinkles on the tips. He only takes pleasure in the warmth and intent of her touch.

"I'm sorry," she says softly.

Kalp knows that this is not an Apology. Kalp has heard these words uttered in this way many times since coming to Earth. They are an expression of condolence. Basil pats his arm on the other side, and it feels good to be between them, to feel the warmth of their skin, the patter of their hearts, and know that he is protected and is precious.

Kalp looks back up at the child. Kalp cannot tell if it is male or female—it is clothed in the generic denim pants and tee-shirt that all humans seem to wear. It is so small it cannot propel itself and requires its mother to hold onto its hands to remain upright.

The mother is staring at him, eyes wide. Kalp supposes she has never seen one of his people in the flesh before. She does not look scared, but she seems wary. The child is oblivious, pointing and trilling at the antics of the pigeons.

"I have an idea," Gwen says. She pulls the last of the bread out of Kalp's hand and tugs him to his feet. She goes over to the woman and Kalp trails behind at a suitable distance.

Gwen introduces herself to the woman, and Kalp notes that she leaves off her job title. Interesting. She offers the child the bread, breaking it up into small pieces and handing them to him one at a time. She breaks off three in succession and the child dutifully tosses them at the birds. The pigeons swarm and the child laughs.

"This is Kalp," Gwen explains to the mother. "He's never seen a human baby before. Can he give your son bread?"

Kalp makes a note to himself to ask Gwen how she knew the child was male.

The woman nods. Kalp crouches beside the child and peers into its—his—face. He is not scared of Kalp. He peers back, blinking, then reaches out and pats Kalp's cheek. His hand is even wetter, even fatter and more fragile than any other human hand, and it breaks Kalp's heart a little more. He reaches out and returns the gesture, running his finger pads across the plump cheek, over the fine, smooth hair, being very careful not to scratch with his nails.

"He is very handsome," Kalp says truthfully to the mother.

She smiles.

There is a *whiirrrr-click* and Kalp recognizes that sound. Still image-recording devices—cameras—have been present at every event Kalp has attended on Earth. So, he does not have to turn around to know that Basil has removed a camera from his briefcase and is taking this opportunity to capture what Kalp is sure will be a future favoured memory. Kalp wonders if Basil will mount it on the wall beside the kitchen. He hopes so. He would very much like to be part of that house. That home. When he walks through the domicile, he can see Gwen and Basil in each room. Kalp wants someone to be able to see himself there, too.

Kalp takes the bread from Gwen and breaks off small pieces for the boy. He throws them jubilantly. Kalp joins in. The pigeons coo and click and get closer and closer, until the boy kicks up a foot in a dance of elation, and they all scatter.

When the bread is all gone, the mother picks up her son and walks away, smiling. She raises her son's arm for him, mimicking the parting salute by shaking it gently. The boy is laughing.

Kalp feels like perhaps he should be laughing too.

Lunch finished and their trash tucked into the provided receptacles, they make their way back to the car.

BASIL IS very excited about the prospect of Kalp's cooking.

Basil is usually excited about any and all food in general, but the thought of getting to eat alien food prepared by an alien himself has him eager and wound up. He rushes up and down the aisles of the chain grocery store searching for viable substitute ingredients, reading nutritional guides, and snubbing the lettuce table in the produce department.

Kalp is rather more distressed, because the green things are too green and the red things are not red enough and none of the herbs smell correct. He wants this meal to be perfect, but he cannot find what he needs. The floor of the supermarket is waxed to a shine, and Kalp cannot seem to grip it well enough to keep from sliding around corners and into shelves. It is mortifying and frustrating and Kalp is hating every second of it.

After a quick consultation over a bin of sweets that Basil has surreptitiously dipped his hand into, they pay for the three vegetables that were suitable and pile back into the car.

"I am sorry," Kalp says, miserably, his toes sore. He is riding in the passenger seat this time, and even the breeze from the open windows and the motion of the vehicle are not enough to cheer him.

"Not your fault," Gwen says. "I'm not a fan of big box stores anyway. We know another place."

This "other place" is a small outdoor market tucked away in an ancient square at the centre of the village in which they live. As Basil parks the car, he points out the church that was built in 1407, the meeting hall across the square, the pattern in the coloured cobblestones. He is clearly proud of his cultural heritage.

Kalp asks Gwen where she was born and whether they might visit her home village, and her answer is more complicated. She tells him about deportation ships and horse theft, of a country called Whales and another called Kanada. Kalp gathers she is from the opposite side of the planet, which explains why her accent is so much flatter than the other humans around here. For a while Basil and Gwen playfully fight about the relative merits of Hockey and Football ("real footy, not the sissy-boy crap with padding"), and Kalp is not quite sure which either is, but they sound like sorts of war games.

She does not invite him to go visit her nation with her. Basil senses his disappointment and holds Kalp back for a moment while Gwen goes to investigate a stand filled with soft bright scarves.

"Gwen had a really horrid row with her mum," he says quietly. "She doesn't talk to her no more, yeah?"

Kalp comprehends. He is unsure how he feels about the news. He understands the slang word "row," that it is a very heated argument. He had rows with his mothers and father when he was young. All offspring do. But he also wants to shake Gwen and yell at her, tell her to talk to her mother before a disaster strikes Earth, too. Before it is too late. Kalp's family died while he had no regrets, and he is lucky. He would be unhappy if Gwen remained miserable about her mother, and then something horrible happened.

It is also partially selfish, and he can admit that to himself. He wants to see Kanada. He wants to travel to the other side of the planet and see long flat prairies and pointy mountains and the curved waterfall that is famous for simply existing. He wants to see them with Gwen.

He wants to hear people talk in the same flat cadence that Gwen does and know it as her own, as her accent, her marker of home.

Basil rubs Kalp's shoulder in a comforting, friendly way, and tentatively, Kalp raises his hand and returns the gesture. Basil accepts the touch, seems to enjoy it as much as Kalp does, so Kalp leaves his hand there as Basil leads him over to the side of the square with the food stalls.

Basil tells Kalp about his own family—the torment of being the youngest son with two elder sisters, his mother's rotten culinary skills, his absent father—while they crush and sniff herbs between their fingers. These sprouts are far more fragrant than the ones in the commercial market, though they are not as visually appealing. Kalp wonders at the inanity of cultivating the visual quality of an herb over its ability to add flavour when all one is going to do is chop it up for the purpose of *adding* flavour anyway.

They purchase great handfuls of several different plants, including one that smells like it may produce a beverage Kalp used to enjoy at home, and the woman behind the stall gives them their package wrapped in yesterday's newspaper. Kalp finds it quaint. The next vendor is selling fruits—big red apples and purple figs and green fuzzy little things that Basil tells him are kiwis and come from the bottom of Earth—but the vendor is not pleased with Kalp's presence.

He makes a sharp gesture that Kalp does not understand. Basil, however, *does* understand it and becomes immediately enraged. He shouts, quickly and in a baser language filled with cusses and slang. The fierce anger flowing from both human men hurts.

It almost comes to fisticuffs. Kalp has hold of Basil's arms as best he can, his long fingers wrapped around to restrain the furious human. Gwen comes rushing to their aid and to Kalp's surprise, is even more vocal in her reprimand of the vendor than Basil, though she helps Kalp keep Basil's fists in check. Kalp supposes that her vocabulary of impolite words is even more extensive than Basil's because she says several things he does not understand (but nonetheless perceives the meaning), and then she speaks in an entirely different language: *"Cer i grafu! Y sais afiach!"*

The vendor's reaction is to turn entirely white, then entirely red. Another vendor must come and restrain the first and Kalp presses his ears against the back of his neck, eyes darting to the growing crowd, searching for escape points.

This day really is not going well.

The sharp bark of an angry man breaks up the crowd and they scatter away like the pigeons in the park. This man is wearing the uniform of the local constabulary and Kalp's whole posture sinks. They are going to be arrested and thrown into jail for this disturbance!

But the police man does not yell at his team, he yells at the vendor.

He calls the vendor "bigoted" and "slanderous" and tells him to pack up his cart and go home. Kalp is sure that the vendor cannot afford to be closed for business on a fine sunny afternoon, and he supposes that is his punishment for starting the altercation.

The vendor packs, muttering more obscenities under his breath.

The police officer sends a few sharp words to his team, as well, and Kalp dutifully bends his head and lifts his palms to catch the reprimand.

Bemused, the police officer then shakes Kalp's hand, apologizes for the "display" of the argument, welcomes him to Earth, and strolls away. Kalp is confused. Basil is still puffing through his nose, cheeks mottled and red, and Gwen's hands keep balling up and flexing alternately on her hips.

"Finish your shopping, dear," says the woman from the herb cart. She comes over and pats Kalp's arm affectionately. "Go on. Don't take nothin' old Rudy says seriously. He's always off on 'those Pakies' and the 'dirty blacks,' huh! As if he weren't the boy of immigrants himself. Go on now—there's a new girl opened down the end of the row I think you'll fancy."

"Thank you," Kalp says, and he can see that Basil's breathing has evened out. Kalp is relieved. Basil's heart has been pattering too fast and it is making Kalp anxious.

This time, Kalp takes the initiative and tugs on Gwen's hand. His other hand has the now-crushed herb packet. Kalp leads them to the cart at the end of the row, and Basil follows. Before he is within five feet of the cart, Kalp knows what it holds. He stops at its lip, staring down at the assortment of produce with wide, burning eyes.

It is all food from his world.

Some of it is smaller and tougher looking. Some of the fruits are a bit misshapen, some are not vibrant enough, but some are bigger and brighter and fatter than Kalp has ever seen them grow. The woman—barely an adult, Kalp thinks—grins hugely at him.

"Was 'opin you'd come my way," she says. "See anythin' familiar?"

Kalp is overjoyed!

"Where did you acquire the seeds?"

"One o' yer people was a botanist—snatched thousands of 'em from her labs. She's working with my Pa. Got us the best hothouse in the county."

Kalp's eyes burn anew to hear that so much flora has survived.

Kalp wants one of everything. He wants all of it! But Gwen has only meted out a small amount of tender, enough to buy the required ingredients for one meal. He points out what he'd like, squeezing and sniffing and grinning back at the vendor. For every one he purchases, she gives two for free. He is as flattered by her generosity as he ever has been with any human's.

Basil keeps up a steady stream of inquiries, asking what that is, and this, and what does it taste like, and how is it prepared, and can you eat it raw, and can he try one of these right now? Kalp selects the ripest of a small red fruit his people call the *osap* and the vendor washes it with her bottled water and Basil goes into raptures eating it on the spot. Gwen demands a bite, and is equally as pleased.

The vendor is happy, because now other shoppers are crowding around. Where the strangeness of foods from other worlds at first kept them away, now they are drawn by Kalp's ability to explain what it is and how everything is used, by the novelty of the experience, and by Basil's ringing endorsements.

Soon the vendor is too busy dropping produce into cloth bags and collecting tender to converse with them, but Kalp is happy to have helped her become prosperous. This is an excellent way to pay her back for her generosity. Kalp, Gwen, and Basil turn to go, and the vendor stops them with a shout:

"Oi!" she says. "You stop by after closin' next Friday, mebe, we'll talk. Mebe I'll take you up to Pa's farm, eh? You can give 'im tips?"

Kalp bobs his head in the affirmative. He would very much like to see the farm. Kalp is no grower of plants, no cultivator of land, but he has been on farms on his own planet as a child and would like to compare.

Their last stop is at a vendor's cart laden with animal carcasses. Kalp's front teeth are sharp, an evolutionary throwback from carnivore ancestors, and he is eager to peruse the wares. He cannot find exactly what he is looking for, but settles on something called "venison," which he hopes tastes close enough.

All the way back to the car, Basil keeps trying to dip his hands into the sack filled with produce to snatch another *osap*, and Kalp gamely keeps the purchases elevated far above Basil's sneaking arms. Kalp's reach greatly exceeds Basil's.

Kalp tries out his first laugh, and it seems to be well received.

THEY PACK the few leftovers that the dinner meal produces into more plastic containers. These go into a cloth sack, and Basil adds a small loaf of crusty bread, some plastic bottles of juice, and a plastic bag of Gwen's brownies.

Basil calls it a "picnic lunch" for tomorrow's trip to London. After dinner, Basil must adjourn to the office space in his bedroom to complete tasks that must be finished for Monday, and Kalp stands beside Gwen at the sink and carefully dries the dishes and utensils and drinking vessels that she hands him. He learns the lay of the kitchen in putting them away, where each object goes, what is in the cabinets and under the stove and above the refrigerator.

Kalp feels that the meal was not his best attempt, but he is proud of the results considering his limitations. Basil's distended tummy and the soft smile on Gwen's face seem to underscore this achievement.

Gwen is still staring at the dissipating soap bubbles in the grey water when she speaks. She has been opening and shutting her mouth, drawing breath and sighing for the past ten minutes. Kalp is guessing that she has something important that she wants to say and is working up towards vocalizing it. He remains quiet and waits.

Finally she says, "How do you feel about what happened today?"

Kalp is not completely surprised by this inquiry. He carefully arranges the drying towel on its rack on the handle of the stove and formulates his answer. "You and Basil were far more upset than I."

"What that man said and did was inexcusable," Gwen says, and she is weary from her own anger. "And unfortunately, common. For such a bloody enlightened race of people we're still a big group of back-stabbing bigots."

"Not you and Basil."

"No," Gwen allows, and takes her bottom lip between her teeth, biting lightly. Kalp is uncertain about the significance of this gesture, but finds it strangely endearing.

"Then I am unconcerned," Kalp says, pulling his attention back to the conversation. "Would he have attacked me physically?"

"Probably not," Gwen says. "Men like that are all hot air."

The idiom is unfamiliar, but Kalp supposes he understands the meaning all the same. "Are there any who would seek to harm me?"

"Of course there are!" Gwen says. She still does not turn around. "Fuckers with baseball bats and tasers…did you know there was a riot last week in Dallas?"

This is not new information—Kalp has been warned that there are those on Earth who are not pleased with his people's presence. Then again, they are also displeased with the presence of other humans whose skin or moral or spiritual or sexual values do not match their own, so Kalp supposes there is no pleasing everyone. Even among his own people there used to be dissent between the citizens of the different continents. That dissent has fizzled in the wake of the disaster, and they have become one race rather than different nationalities. He hopes Earth's nationalities will follow suit soon enough, without the impetus of a similarly horrifying tragedy.

"I am capable of defending myself," Kalp says. He chooses not to click his nails or bare his teeth to indicate so. He is sure Gwen is more than adequately aware of them. "In the mean time, I will not fear walking in the open street. Some people are unpleasant. But most are not. I enjoyed the child in the park today."

Gwen is staring at her water-shrivelled fingertips.

He reaches out and touches the back of Gwen's neck, a possessive, caring gesture that he has seen Basil perform. It is very intimate, according to the pornography book, and Kalp's fingers tremble as he does it.

Gwen jerks out from under his touch, startled.

"I'm sorry," Kalp says softly. His fingers are hot.

Gwen reaches up, rubs the back of her neck. Her eyes are wide and her pupils open. Her mouth is wet. Kalp wants to try to kiss her, but he fears that this is an inopportune time.

Instead, he turns to the stove and puts on the kettle. Basil lost the wager to produce a tea Kalp found palatable, but Kalp needs something for his hands to do, to distract his mind, and he feels it would be a caring gesture to bring Basil some of the soothing beverage right now.

Gwen walks out of the room without saying anything.

When the kettle whistles, indicating that the water is boiled, Kalp pours out one tea and adds milk, one instant coffee, black, and pours the remainder of the water over a sprig of herbs that he had kept separate from dinner for that very purpose. Basil will be disappointed to learn that Kalp does indeed enjoy tea, just not Earth tea.

He delivers each cup quietly—one to Basil's desk, one to Gwen in the courtyard garden, and he returns to the kitchen with his own.

Carefully, he sets to work separating the seeds he had saved from the fruits and vegetables into plastic bags. He uses a fragrant black writing utensil to label them. He plans to purchase potting soil and little tin buckets, like the herb garden in the neighbour's courtyard, to grow his own *osap* and *shric* and tomatoes.

THE STRESS of yesterday and the discomfort of the incident in the kitchen seem forgotten in the bustle of trying to get out the door the next morning. Kalp feels wonderful—his nest is perfect and the ache in his back has vanished. He is conscious first, so he boils the kettle and starts the coffee maker gurgling, and then goes back upstairs to clean himself and change out of his pyjamas. While he is walking past Gwen and Basil's door, he hears Basil saying "wakey wakey, Sleeping Beauty."

Gwen mutters, the sound muffled by the pillow Kalp imagines her face to be mashed into.

"Oh no," Basil says in response to her, "if I let you sleep until the alarm goes off you'll be a grouch all day. Up. Kalp's already used up all the hot water."

Kalp would be alarmed at his own rudeness for depleting the supply, if he did not already know that this is one of Basil's favourite phrases for teasing.

He also understands now what Gwen meant by "shopping." When he opens his chest of drawers, Kalp realizes that he owns no civilian attire. The only clothing Kalp owns is meant for work, so in the end, he is wearing a pair of Basil's blue jeans. They are far too short in the leg and Gwen says they look like clam-diggers. It takes Basil's explanation around a mouthful of eggs at breakfast to understand what Gwen means. Kalp is also wearing one of Basil's seemingly endless supply of tee-shirts with intentionally humourous phrases printed across the chest. This one says *Obey Gravity! It's the Law!*

Basil wanted to put him in a tee-shirt that had one arrow pointing at his face with the label *The Man*, and another pointing towards where his genitalia would be were he human and the label *The Legend*. Gwen had looked at Kalp in it, giggled, and vetoed it.

"Besides," she had added as Basil herded Kalp back up the stairs to change again, "the arrow isn't even pointing to the right place!"

Basil had turned pale and pushed him back into the bedroom.

Kalp cannot help the little thrill of joy at the memory. Gwen, at least, has studied enough of his kind's anatomy to know where all the pertinent parts are; perhaps, like him, she has also read pornography for the sake of study.

Kalp is consuming a pot of kiwi yogurt—he is unsure that he likes the taste of the grainy green fruit and is glad that they did not buy any at the market yesterday—and watching Gwen pack, unpack, repack, and reunpack a vinyl shoulder bag. "Hat, keys, sunglasses, chapstick, sunblock, oh, Basil, hand out," she says. Basil does not stop shovelling food. He merely switches his fork to his other hand and holds up his free palm obligingly. Gwen squirts some of the oily cream into it, and he rubs it all over his face as he's chewing.

Kalp loses his appetite for the similarly-textured yogurt.

He abandons it on the table and fetches an apple instead, crunching through the red skin to the soft white flesh below, trying to keep the juices out of his chin fur. Kalp is not even finished eating the apple before he is hastily ushered out the door to the car. They drive to the train station. It takes forty minutes, during which Gwen slathers herself with the sunblock cream and tries to remember if she locked the front door (she did, Kalp watched her do it), and fusses about counting out enough tender to pay for train tickets.

Kalp will receive his first pay packet next Friday. He feels guilty for being unable to contribute to the excursion—Units share—but Gwen assures him that he can pay next time, and that puts his conscience at ease. By the time Basil has parked the car, Kalp has consumed the entirety of the apple ("what, core and all?" Gwen notes, aghast) and has to duck to enter the train station. It is an old building and its ceilings are low. Generations ago, Basil explains, humans used to be shorter.

They buy three tickets and the station master is unsure whether to laugh or scream at Kalp's stooped countenance. Kalp does not let the man's discomfort affect him, and soon they are back out in the open air of the platform, waiting for the train to arrive. Kalp has also never been on a train before. He wonders what life will be like when he's run out of things to do for the first time, and hopes that the day when that occurs is far, far off.

There is a family with two little boys who look even more difficult to tell apart than usual—"twins," Basil calls them, a litter of two—beside them on the platform. At first the boys are terrified of Kalp, and Kalp, who hovers very high above them, does not blame them. He crouches low to the ground to remove some of his looming impressiveness, and says, "This is my first excursion on a locomotive."

The mere mention of a train is enough to get both boys, who are each clutching small plastic models of a blue steam engine with a smiling face on the front, excited.

"What, never?" one asks, and then both are off, chattering so excitedly about this rail line and that engine, that their fear of Kalp vanishes entirely. Kalp cannot understand all that they say—their accents differ again from Basil's and Gwen's, and they speak far too rapidly, but the enthusiasm is infectious and Kalp finds that he does not care.

Kalp thinks that if all children react to him as favourably as the ones he's met thus far, men like Rudy will eventually become obsolete as people outgrow their bigotry. It is a comforting notion.

When they enter the train, the family heads towards the front so the boys may watch the driver, and Basil, Gwen, and Kalp find a group of four seats facing each other in a relatively unoccupied car near the back. Gwen sits opposite Basil and Kalp and drops the carry bag filled with lunch and other necessary items into the seat next to her.

"You're good with kids," she says. She kicks off her sandals and lifts her feet, and puts them in Basil's lap. It is shockingly intimate and sends a thrill up Kalp's spine. "You would have made a good dad."

Kalp smiles. He anticipates the hot twist of pain that should accompany the thought of his Aglunates and what they were denied, but is surprised to note that it has mellowed slightly.

He supposes that the Earth idiom is true, and time eventually does heal all wounds.

KALP DOES not like the Eye of London.

It is beautiful to the sight, but the grinding clanks of the machinery in motion and the bobbing sway of the glass-ensconced pods make his heart beat too fast and his breathing ratchet up. If he had the skin for it, he knows he would be as flushed as Basil when he is angry. Only this is fear.

Kalp sits on the bench in the exact middle of the glass pod and pushes the pads of his fingers together in an effort to keep from tugging on his ears in distress. Kalp can hear the small hissing breeze that is slithering in through the rivets and joints, the surging gasp of electricity sparking over wires, and it is *unnatural* to be so high up and supported by a few small creaking bolts.

Gwen calls his reaction a panic attack.

Basil calls it agoraphobia, claustrophobia, acrophobia, and a sensible mistrust of potentially shoddy workmanship.

"It's just twenty minutes," Gwen says, and points to her wristwatch, "and look, see, we've done seven already. Just a little bit more and we're off. There's a trooper."

Basil huffs and comes back from the window and sits so close to Kalp that Kalp can feel the warmth of his body all along his side, from knee to shoulder. It is a comforting, grounding distraction and Kalp welcomes it. He closes his eyes and concentrates on the sounds Basil's body makes when it is pressed right against Kalp's sensitive skin.

The other humans in the pod with them keep their eyes resolutely aimed on the distractions outside. Kalp suspects this is due to Gwen's sweeping glare, and this he appreciates as well.

The truth is, the glass pod reminds Kalp too strongly of the escape shuttles that he had been crammed into—the segmented hive-like compartments that had been jammed to dangerous capacity with the weeping, the wailing, the ash-coated, and bleeding, and for some, the dead and dying.

Kalp remembers the one in the coffin-like sleeping pod beside him. The face was half gone when the other person had thrown themself into it. The person was bloody down all one side. They had groped blindly and called for people who did not come, and Kalp had grabbed the upraised hand and held it, just to make it *stop*. To make the other person *shut up*. He felt the death, heard the heart stop beating and the skin stop throbbing and he had to break the dead fingers to get them off of his. He had barely freed himself before another came and threw the corpse carelessly to the floor, where those who hadn't been quick enough to claim a pod were huddled, and took its place.

Kalp's stomach churns and the yogurt of the morning seems intent on rebellion.

He breathes deeply over and over again through his nose and calls out to Gwen and pulls her close to his other side to block out the hissing breeze that is pushing in through minuscule gaps between steel and glass and sounds exactly like a child screaming.

Gwen and Basil wrap their arms around Kalp, trying to cover off as much of his skin as they can with their fat, awkward limbs and he is too busy trying not to be sick to marvel at the familiarity of it.

He is here now. He is on Earth, surrounded by healthy humans, on a conveyance of amusement. He is not in space, surrounded by shrieks and corpses, on a conveyance of despair.

When the pod shivers to its slowing stop, Kalp is the first off and none of the other passengers begrudge him this position. He walks swiftly to the bottom of the ramp, as the signage requests he do, turns into a small grove-like area made up of large potted flora, and empties the contents of his stomach at the base of one.

Some small part of his brain that is not occupied with the retching wonders if his unique stomach acids will harm the plant.

Gwen is there when he is finished, handing him an already opened bottle of water with which to rinse the sour taste from his teeth, and something called "gum" which is sharply refreshing and is not meant for swallowing. It disguises the scent and flavour of sick and he is happy for it.

Basil comes around the corner a moment later, tucking the black animal hide fold in which he keeps his currency back into his pocket. In his hand is a cardboard frame with a glossy photograph. In the photograph, Kalp is standing beside Basil, his long arm reaching over Basil's shoulders to rest on Gwen's. All three are standing before the great machine, in the same position as Basil and Gwen's photograph on the kitchen wall.

In the photograph, Kalp has mastered his smile, Basil looks bemused, and Gwen is grinning. It is a "before" shot.

"This is not an accurate reflection of our experience," Kalp says, peering over Basil's shoulder to investigate the image.

"No," Basil agrees. "But it'll make for a good story one day, wonnit?"

THEY STOP for their lunch of leftovers after that, sitting on a bench facing the water on the Riverwalk Quay. Kalp is not very hungry, but he nibbles at the bread to help settle the last of the roiling discomfort in his stomach. Gwen makes Basil leave enough food for Kalp to eat later, and Basil once more performs the expression of begging—wide, wet eyes, jutting lower lip—but this time Gwen is resolute. Kalp does not feel that he will be eating any time soon, and rather than see Basil hungry, he gives his permission. Basil consumes the remainder happily, though Gwen smacks his arm when he dips his chin to lick the dish clean.

They walk to Gabriel's Wharf next. By the time they arrive, Kalp's heart has returned to its normal rhythm and his ears are back up, swivelling to catch the sounds of the busy market. It is like the open square in their home town, but on a far more massive scale. Someone is playing a stringed instrument at the corner, and people are throwing him coins in approval. There are so many carts displaying so many different kinds of wares that Kalp does not know where to begin. They try on hats and sunglasses, poke through piles of second hand books, and Kalp purchases a long sleeved, long-hemmed white shirt of a gauzy material called "linen." It is delicately embroidered all around the scooping collar and the hem of the sleeves with bright red and yellow and green thread fashioned to resemble birds. Basil calls him a "hippie" in it, but Kalp adores the shirt, adores the birds. He strips off the quirky tee-shirt, folding it into Gwen's carry bag, and dons his new shirt immediately.

The vendor is so pleased he asks to have photographs taken with Kalp for advertisement. Kalp is not adverse to the notion, and poses gamely. Soon, however, there is a whole flock of tourists taking Kalp's picture. This was not anticipated and is slightly uncomfortable. He smiles for what must be ten minutes, and sometimes there are people who shove their way through the crowd to stand beside him, to be captured with him, without first requesting permission.

He does not want to offend by walking away, but he is no longer enjoying himself. There is a very large difference between one photo as a favour and many simply because people have him cornered. When his smile starts to flag, Gwen grabs him by the hand, thanks the humans for their attention, and pulls him away. Kalp is more than happy to go.

He did not dislike the experience, but it was wearying. He now pities those of his kind who are the military and governmental leaders, who now work in high profile positions with the Earth governments and must endure such photography sessions often.

Kalp is very happy to not be famous.

When they complete their shopping, they are just in time to make a walking tour of the National Theatre, so they double back for that. Kalp is intrigued by the counterweight pulley system that raises and lowers set pieces, but they are not allowed to touch them. Basil mentions that there is a community theatre playhouse where they live that is always bothering Basil to be a technician, and maybe he can get Kalp in to do volunteer work on weekends. After the completion of the tour, they walk all the way to the end of the quay on the Thames. It is nearing the dinner hour and Basil is nagging for a pint. They stop in a pub with an outdoor patio so they can "people watch."

Kalp has sampled beer before, and wine, and champagne. There were many parties when he first made Earth-fall, and at the time he had been hurt and angry by the celebrations. He knew he should have been celebrating his survival, the survival of his race and culture, and the new-forged friendship with the humans, but all he could think about was that they had not buried their dead. There were neglected bodies, just lying on the streets, in homes, in offices, floating jettisoned through space, and here they were making small talk and sampling delicacies and consuming psychotropic beverages.

Never mind that, rationally, Kalp knew there were no streets and homes and offices left; that the whole planet had cracked apart and disintegrated into particles so small they could be inhaled. It still felt *wrong*.

Kalp associates beer and wine and champagne with this sense of wrongness, so he allows Gwen to order him a drink that does not taste like those. She finds something called a Strawberry Daiquiri on the menu, which comes out in a tall round vessel with a paper umbrella, violently pink with a swirl of nearly phosphorescent green. It tastes like tart *osap* and Kalp is pleased. Gwen has a glass of red wine and Basil a pint of Guinness, and the manager of the pub sends out a waiter with a camera. If Kalp and his friends will not mind posing for a photograph to go behind the bar, the waiter says, their drinks and whatever food they order will be free.

Friends. Until now Kalp has thought of Gwen and Basil as teammates, co-workers, potential Aglunates, but never as "friends." He likes it.

But Kalp is also starting to resent this form of generosity—it appears harmless, but it is, in truth, selfish. It is not generosity like Gwen and Basil opening their home to him and asking for nothing more than his fair share of domestic duty. It is utilizing Kalp in order to procure more business. Kalp is sure that the shirt vendor and the pub owner will pull in far more revenue simply by displaying Kalp's photograph than the amount they lose in compensating his purchases.

He thinks about denying the server his photograph, but also understands that if he says no, then they will have to uproot and move to a different pub because the owner here will be resentful. And even still he will probably be asked for his permission again for a photograph at the new pub. Kalp sighs and agrees and puts on his best smile for it.

When the waiter goes away, Kalp says, "I do not wish to pose for any more photographs."

"Thank God," says Basil. "I'm sick to death of them."

Gwen grins, genuinely this time, not the fake and careful smile she had used for the picture, and sips her drink. Because the owner has promised them free meals and because Kalp is feeling bitterly used, they each order a full meal from the expensive part of the menu, and a dessert to accompany it. When each meal arrives—steak tartare, lobster, and roast veal; chocolate cake, an ice cream sundae, and key lime pie—they push their plates together into the middle of the table to sample each dish. It is another of the marvellously intimate things that Kalp's people would never have done were they not of one Aglunate, and it gives Kalp hope.

He is desperately fond of both of these humans.

He hopes they are growing as fond of him.

He knows he is behaving as an abandoned stray animal might—slavishly devoted to whoever rescues him first, no matter how kind or cruel they may be—but he cannot help it. It has been so long since Kalp has been shown such simple, honest kindness. Had he a tail, he is sure it would be wagging.

Gwen tries to steal Basil's last piece of chocolate cake, which is by far the best dessert on the table, and Basil grabs the hand that holds the fork and tries to aim it back towards his own mouth. They struggle above the plates, laughing, both of their cheeks pink with mild exertion and alcohol. Kalp is feeling pleasantly warm himself, all his joints loose after his second daiquiri, and slightly daring.

He leans forward, snakes out his tongue, and snatches the last moist morsel of dessert out from between them. Basil and Gwen both stare with dropped jaws. Basil bursts into a flurry of trilling laugher, and Gwen follows suit, but there is something different in her narrowed eyes.

She touches the back of her neck, and Kalp looks down at his hands and says nothing, chewing contentedly.

AFTER DINNER they go to a mall with a store especially for tall men and Kalp purchases an armful of blue jeans and khaki trousers and some more loose shirts with buttons up the front that are similar to the one he is wearing with the bird adornments.

Gwen calls them hideous, touristy Hawaiian shirts, but Kalp enjoys the smooth texture of the fabric, the large hook-beaked birds, and the busy, bold colours, and Gwen's protests are overthrown.

The day has tired Kalp more than he has expected, the alcohol still weighting his limbs, and on the train ride home the steady chug of the engine and the soothing heartbeats of his companions lulls him down into his unconscious phase. He sleeps for nigh on two hours.

He wakes a few moments before their stop to the gentle whispered conversation between Gwen and Basil and out of respect, does not listen to their buzzing words. The car ride back to the house is equally peaceful, music provided by Basil's BlackBerry plugged into the vehicle's sound system. It is the only sound above heartbeats and engine and lazy breaths. The playlist is all mellow music from a human who pretended to be from outer space to sell records. Kalp likes the irony that he is sitting on Earth listening to it. The music is simple and straightforward, yet the melodies are complex and the voice is emotive. He enjoys it far more than the techno or R&B music he has heard, with its painfully relentless bass lines and electronically generated noise.

He finds there is a lot about Earth that he either really enjoys or really does not enjoy, all his experiences classified by the strict polarity of fond and longing memory. He has to think hard to remember if there was anything back home that he strongly did not enjoy. Perhaps there was, but nostalgia paints his memories with the veneer of perfection, and he cannot distinguish between pleasure and non-pleasure now.

When they arrive at the house, Basil takes all the shopping in his arms, except Kalp's, so Kalp takes his own and Gwen's carry bag. She strides forward with the keys and opens the front door. They move together into the foyer in the same easy silence. Gwen bids them both good night with a pat on the arm for Kalp, and a kiss on the cheek for Basil. She heads up the stairs. Basil drops the shopping on the sofa, still in its bags, yawns, and bids Kalp pleasant dreams as well. He follows Gwen, his eyelids droopy but his gaze intent on something Kalp cannot see in the empty air before him.

Kalp considers following them up the stairs and sleeping too, but after his fortuitous nap on the train he is not tired. Instead he decides to pull all of the shopping out of its bags and fold it nicely on the kitchen table to make certain the garments will not wrinkle. He retrieves the innocuous London Eye photograph and perches it on the mantle. Then he goes into the kitchen, and, as quietly as possible, cleans the dishes from the morning's hasty breakfast and the clear carry bins that lunch had occupied. He stacks them carefully in the dish rack so they will not fall. He is just rubbing his hands dry on the tea towel when he hears the first thumping creak.

It sounds as if someone is moving the furniture again, and he swivels one ear towards upstairs. Gwen and Basil are in their room, and their heart beats are worryingly fast. Their bodies sound the same as they do when they are angry, the rushing blood, the zapping nerve endings, the labouring lungs, but there is no shouting. Neither are they vocalizing, outside of some soft sighs and grunts, and there is the repetitive rippling feel against his skin of flesh slapping against flesh.

They are fighting.

Kalp knew that they were volatile species, quick to anger, but he never considered that partnered humans might physically beat each other like this; at least, not Gwen and Basil. Alarmed, Kalp runs up the stairs as quickly as he is able and rushes to their door at the far end of the upstairs hallway. Without announcing himself—for fear that it would cause one or the other of them more harm—he throws back the door.

Basil has Gwen pinned to the bed, his hands pushing hard on her shoulders. Gwen is trying to throw him off by grasping his padded hips with her knees but appears to be unsuccessful. Basil rocks against her once, hard, and then stops, looking back over his shoulder at Kalp, blue eyes wide and startled.

Kalp starts forward to wrench Basil off of Gwen, to demand that they settle their differences like civilized people with words, when he sees that Basil's penis is erect and both of them are without clothing.

Kalp stops and cannot help but stare.

They are performing intercourse.

They...are actually performing it. Logically Kalp knows humans pleasure each other for the sheer sake of orgasms. But to actually *witness*...They are leaking and disgusting and yet...

The pornography literature did not describe how it would *sound,* but Kalp now feels horrendously incompetent for not guessing what the sighs and slaps meant before this.

"I am...I am so sorry," he says, walking backwards towards the gaping door even though every fibre of his being would like nothing more than to strip off his own clothing and lay beside them.

He has not been invited and it is rude to include oneself without invitation.

Gwen scrambles for the blanket and wraps it quickly around both of them.

"I heard," Kalp starts, and stops to swallow. He can feel his own genitalia sliding out of their pouch in interest and he is very thankful that his clothing is loose today. "I thought you were fighting," he explains, and he is aware how pathetic the excuse sounds now. "I will go."

He backs out of the room because—and it is selfish—he wants to see as much of their nakedness as he can before he departs, even if their faces have gone white and their eyes and mouths round. Kalp shuts the door quietly.

He stands in the hall with his forehead pressed against the wall for a moment, forcing his flesh to be distracted by the feel of electricity and movement in the house, instead of other things.

Then, when his body is settled and calm once more, he flees to the little walled garden out back and stands among Gwen's potted plants, and stares up at the moon.

Somewhere, out there, in the dust of the cosmos, is what is left of Maru and Trus.

And Kalp is here, on this planet, alone, breathing the cool night air deeply and shaking in the aftermath of denied arousal.

THINGS ARE uncomfortable in the house the next morning, and Kalp cannot help but wonder if they will rescind their offer of the guest room and send him back to the Sleeping Place. He would not blame them if he did. He knows that on Earth interrupting people in coitus is considered the height of ill manners. The television situational comedies have taught him that, if little else really useful.

He sleeps fitfully on the sofa, snatching brief strings of moments of unconsciousness, not daring to go back upstairs. He watches the sun rise quietly. When it has dawned fully, he fetches his breakfast quickly and silently from the kitchen and goes back out to the garden. He sits on the rough, humble garden bench and crunches his way morosely through an apple and watches the birds. His only comfort today seems to be the birds, and he reflects on his joyed and oblivious state of this time yesterday.

Well, no. This time yesterday he was trying not to be sick in the humans' amusement contraption.

Still. Naïve.

That seems to be his defining state of being lately. He wishes desperately that it were otherwise, that he could somehow transform back into the sure, knowledgeable, steady person that he used to be. Before. Employed, meaningful, loved. He remembers being that person—staid and reliable—but he cannot puzzle out how to become him again. It is humiliating and frustrating.

Inside the house, through the thin pane of cheap glass that separates Kalp from Gwen and Basil, he can hear them talking. There is no shouting, no angry—or aroused—patter of beating hearts. Kalp can feel the electricity surging gently in a regulated rhythm into the coffee maker, can hear the kinetic energy of the water boiling on the kettle on the stove. When both machines complete their duties, Kalp can hear the pouring of hot beverages and the clink of spoons against ceramic drinking vessels. He pulls an apple seed out from between his teeth and pokes it down into the dark soil of a pot holding a sad little sprig of a tree.

He is surprised when the glass wall is slid to the side and Basil and Gwen join him in the garden. Basil is carrying a chair from the dining room, which he sets down opposite Kalp, and Gwen unfolds a worn stool that was leaning against the fence. They settle into their respective seats, fingers wrapped around steaming mugs.

"Look," Basil says slowly. "We wanted to apologize."

Kalp sits up straight. "You?" he says. "But it was I who—"

Gwen cuts him off. "We should have...I don't know, told you not to come in, or something. Put a sock on the doorknob. It was perfectly reasonable for you to think that we were fighting, you don't know anything about—"

"But I do!" Kalp insists, trying to cut the explanation short, both out of desperation to avoid the embarrassment of the retelling, and to keep himself from appearing ignorant; even more naïve. "I have read a pornography."

Neither Gwen nor Basil seem to know what to say to that.

Gwen settles on "Oh," and turns bright red in embarrassment.

Basil clears his throat, takes a sip of tea and says, "What, just one?"

Gwen smacks his arm, a comfortable and predictable response. Kalp feels his nervousness swing down, but that just makes him anxious again because he knows that he should not revel in this, this easy familiarity, because it is about to end. This is no longer his, but he cannot help basking in the glow of what is left of his friendship with his co-workers, to soak up whatever he can before they exclude him.

Kalp taps his fingers together and screws up his courage. It is better to pain himself now, quickly rather than allow it to drag out and cause even more suffering. "I will pack my trunk today," he says. "And send for a taxicab."

"What?" Basil asks, "Why? You don't want to leave, do you? Because of…us? We don't make you…I mean, that didn't freak you out, did it?"

Kalp tugs on his ears. He cannot decide how to answer that. He chooses not to. Instead he says, "*You* must wish me gone."

"No!" Basil says. "No, no no! It was all just…well, that stuff happens when people live together. Admittedly, usually roommates know what a closed door and a squeaking bed means, but, uh, now you do so you can just…I don't know, now you know and you won't do it again and we'll be a bit more careful and…yeah," Basil winds down lamely. His cheeks are now the same shade as Gwen's.

Kalp licks his lips while he thinks, scrubbing away the last of the apple's juices, and asks, carefully, "Then you do not wish to send me away for witnessing your act of intercourse?"

"Oi, a little louder," Basil hisses, but counters his own imperative by speaking softly. "We're outside and there are nosy neighbours."

"But the answer is no," Gwen adds in the same hissing whisper.

Kalp is torn. He is relieved that they do not wish to send him away. But they also have not invited him to join them. He is suspended in a limbo of confusion—do they or do they not want him? Surely, now that he has witnessed, things cannot go back to simple platonic cohabitation.

Can it?

Is that what is done here?

Apparently it is, because that seems to end the conversation and the conflict, at least for Basil and Gwen. They all move back into the kitchen. Kalp is not hungry, his mind still reeling from the revelation that they would like him to remain a fixture in their domicile, but Basil makes an omelette for everyone. Slowly, as they recap yesterday's adventures and discuss the small banal tasks that require their attention today, the uneasiness leeches from the room, leaving all three with the same comfortable atmosphere of the night before.

Kalp is unaccountably pleased.

MONDAY DAWNS grey and wet, and they must brave the heaviest downpour of precipitation Kalp has ever experienced on Earth to get from the parking lot to the Institute building. Basil alarms Kalp with tales of the season when all the precipitation will be frozen, and Gwen alarms him further by reminiscing a time in her native nation when, in her childhood, the piles of the crystallized water were higher than her own small head.

Kalp thinks that it is very irresponsible for Gwen's parents to allow her out into such a dangerous environment alone when she was so very small, and so easily crushed. Human parents seem to allow their offspring into all sorts of potentially fatal situations, with little regard for danger. Skateboarding, mock fighting, allowing an alien to feed the pigeons with them. Such things were unheard of on Kalp's world.

When they enter the office, it is to see that Kalp's desk has finally arrived. They adjust the height of the legs to suit Kalp's need and push it up against the end of Basil's and Gwen's to form a rough triangle. Now they are able to converse in comfort while working.

They toil steadily through the day, their "stunt" of the week before already forgotten by the other Specialists in the wake of an ever-expanding world of wonders to translate, rebuild, theorize, and understand. Kalp enjoys his work acting as a go-between for Gwen's translations of the blueprint schematics and Basil's attempts to make a working scale model. Kalp finally sees what they're building when Basil screws two pieces together—it is a solar energy converter that is several times more efficient than the ones the humans currently use, and probably far more inexpensive to construct. Mass production of this item could drastically reduce current pollutants on Earth, and Kalp takes a moment to bask in the notion that he truly *is* doing something to contribute to his new home. The planet and the people.

Monday evening brings the joy of take-away pizza and the frustration of trying to make his fingers move quickly on a video game controller made for much smaller hands. Tuesday they skive off working on the solar panel once Basil has finished constructing the scale model. They spend the rest of the afternoon at the Institute watching "Star Wars" on Basil's ridiculously oversized computer monitor with a bag of the microwave popcorn that Gwen keeps in her desk drawer for just these sorts of days.

Basil holds something mechanical in his hand, tweaking this, poking that, holding pieces up to the screen of his BlackBerry, examining them against patterns on the device. The impossibly tiny screwdrivers appear and disappear out of and back into the case on Basil's desk as he works in the thin bluish light of the computer monitor and the handheld. Kalp thought the work on the model was complete, and Basil confirms it. When Kalp asks what the man is making, Basil only grins, quick and sharp, and calls it a surprise. When they play with the video games later that night, Kalp finds that the small controller with its impossible, tiny buttons, has been replaced with a larger, more Kalp-friendly version.

The rest of the week is more of the same. On Wednesday night, Gwen produces a small bottle of purple lacquer, and Kalp watches in fascination as she coats the small blunt claw-nails on her toes with the shiny liquid. When it hardens it sparkles and makes the skin around it look pale and delicate and even more attractive. He realizes that it looks similar to the flush of blood under the nails that signals mating. It is another cosmetic trick that females use to make themselves look more aroused, more physically attractive, like the donning of red lip paint that mimics the engorging of the genitals.

The signal seems to work on Basil. In the middle of the night, Basil wakes in the room next to Kalp's and his motion, as it always does, wakes Kalp too. Kalp waits for Basil to climb from his bed, relieve himself, and return to sleep, but Basil does not. He makes a noise and then Gwen wakes and makes a similar noise and Kalp realizes that they are staying true to their word and only having intercourse when they think he is asleep.

Only, the frenetic motion of their bodies and blood would have wakened him anyway, even if he had not already been conscious. Intercourse cannot be performed while laying still. He cannot help but find the wash of tender motion arousing and this time when his genitals distend and slide into the open, he does not work to hold them back. He feels guilty for using his friends in this manner, in featuring them in his own private pornographic imaginings, but he feels such an aching fondness for both—their squishy skin, their oblivious generosity, their acceptance—that he cannot help but want to be a part of their intimacies as well.

He masturbates to the sound of them entangled together and finishes with them. Satisfied and perhaps less tense than he has been in months, Kalp cleans himself off and drops back down into his unconscious phase.

It is only when he wakes the next morning, still feeling the positive effects of last night's release, that he realizes how very on edge he's been for so long. He comes downstairs and participates in breakfast and is surprised to find that without his input whatsoever, his mouth has seemed to mould itself into the shape of a smile, and it cannot be undone.

On Thursday they fight.

It is an inane domestic quibble, the likes of which he has had many times over with Maru and Trus, and it is comforting to discover that sexual partners all over the galaxy still get angry at each other for little habits that they cannot control. Gwen is at both of them for urinating with the commode seat up and then leaving it there after they have finished. Instead of being abashed, Kalp takes this as one more sign that he is being pulled ever more closely into the radius of this relationship, and resolves to remember to return the seat to its proper position when he has finished, even though the males now outnumber the females in the household and it seems an exercise in futility.

On Friday, Kalp receives his first pay packet. He divides it up carefully and pays Gwen and Basil back for the food and clothing they have purchased for him, and adds twice that again to pay for the electricity, water, and heat he has used in the house. They protest that they are not charging him rent and he agrees—he is only paying for what he has consumed. They grumble good-naturedly and take the tender. Units share.

Kalp requests that they return to the outdoor market so that he might speak to the vendor girl as promised and gather ingredients for another meal of his own making. Rudy the bigot averts his eyes when they arrive and Rudy's lips turn white, he is pressing them together so hard to prevent unwelcome words. Kalp does not wish another confrontation, so he copies the man's expression and passes by in silence. Basil is excited about the *osap* and this time they buy a whole tray from the cart. Kalp buys the required produce for dinner and speaks to the girl and they arrange a farm tour for the weekend after next, and then all three return home to prepare for the evening's repast.

For several weeks, they work this way. Kalp makes dinner on Fridays and they go sightseeing on Saturdays, and in between they work and clean the house, eat and do the dishes, sleep and, in the case of Gwen and Basil, have intercourse. Sometimes Kalp watches television all day Sunday, and sometimes he plays video games with Basil. Sometimes Gwen lets him help her paint her toenails, and one memorable occasion, they paint his.

On the news, there are reports of large gatherings of people who object to Kalp's kind interacting with the humans. Gwen calls it "stuff and nonsense" and Basil calls it "tosh," but Kalp notices that on the days that these people are out in the major cities, including London, the three of them stay in and play board games. One night, Kalp accompanies Basil only to a sports themed pub and Basil's friends, all male, challenge Kalp to a game of billiards. Kalp is an engineer, is familiar with force and angle and trajectory, and he repays the men for all the money he has won in their wager by buying them Strawberry Daiquiris, his favoured alcoholic beverage.

The first week of the month of October is far more chilly than Kalp expects. He has been warned that the tilt of the Earth's axis renders the seasons extreme on the poles away from the equator, but the temperature never varied as hugely on his world as it does here, so he assumed Basil was using hyperbole in his descriptions again. Now he is not so sure.

Once more, Kalp marvels that these fragile humans have survived long enough to become the dominant species on this planet, when they must struggle against such a varied climate and yet never evolved any particular physical traits in order to help fend off cold beyond the useful opposable thumb. There also seems to be very little in the way of physical traits that differentiate between cold-climate dwellers and warm-climate dwellers—as one travels further north the humans become squatter, rounder in order retain more body heat, and grow more and more colourless. Beyond that, they are exactly the same as their southerly neighbours.

On the crisp mornings, Kalp crawls reluctantly out of his nest, thinking that perhaps he will have to "suck it up" as Gwen puts it, and begin to wear socks and shoes just for the sake of keeping the chill off. He is reaching for a sweater when he hears an ugly, retching sound coming from the bathroom.

This is the fourth morning in a row that Gwen has been ill, and Kalp has already expressed his concern. She has refused to attend a medic, so there is little Kalp can do. He merely walks into the bathroom as she flushes the commode, and fetches a glass of water from the tap for her, as he has done every day since the first morning.

"Cheers," she says, and swishes her mouth out, and spits into the sink. Kalp takes the empty glass from her hand and sets it on the counter. She reaches up and clutches his fingers. "Don't tell Basil," she begs. "Let me figure this out first."

Kalp agrees to keep her secret, though he cannot understand why she wants him to. Basil must surely know that she is ill. If he does not, then he should be informed as he is sleeping next to Gwen and would be the next to catch the virus. She must see a doctor.

Kalp knows it is irrational, of course, but as much as he thinks that Gwen is foolish for not seeking medical attention, he cannot help the tight grip of fear and remembered agony at the thought of Trus, alone, in a medical office. Without him.

It is ridiculous—there is no danger to Earth approaching on the horizon, but then, Kalp thought there was no danger in letting Trus go to the clinic alone on that day.

Gwen sits on the edge of the tub and puts her head in her hands and cries, and Kalp, though he does not want to catch the sickness, does want to comfort her. He weighs the risk and considers it worth it. Besides, if he catches the illness too, then at least Gwen would not be at the doctor's clinic alone, and that thought motivates him to lift his arms. He wraps her in his embrace. She leaks hot water onto his neck and that seems to make her feel better, at least, so he does not mind that he is going to have to change his shirt when they are done.

Over the next few days, Kalp dutifully says nothing about the illness, even though it persists. Neither he nor Basil, thankfully, seem to have caught it, though. In an effort to lighten the damp mood in the house caused by Gwen's exhaustion and Kalp's worry, Kalp suggests that they obtain a pet. It would be amusing, he explains, to add another being to the mix, and he has not yet had the opportunity to experience a domesticated animal personally.

Gwen smiles ruefully at his description about adding another, and rubs her stomach.

In the end they agree and leave Kalp with an entire zoology encyclopaedia, pulled dusty and forgotten from the back of some tall shelf, to choose from.

It is Gwen who is surprised that Kalp wants chickens. Basil seems to think there is nothing strange about it at all. Kalp likes birds, but he wants ones that cannot fly away from him. "They stink," Gwen protests.

"But, fresh eggs!" Basil rebuts.

Gwen mutters something about Basil and the shine of being a real farmer rubbing off quickly, but concedes as long as the little beasts stay outside. Kalp and Basil build a tiny shed for them to winter in safety, and they paint it blue and add the words "Police Box" to the outside in order to render it similar to the spacecraft in their mutually favourite children's television program. They have yet to perfect a sensor system so that when a chicken enters, or exits, it makes the recognizable "vrop vrop" sound, but they are working on it.

They get three birds. They start out small and fuzzy and yellow, and grow very quickly. In weeks they are nearly adults. On Sundays Kalp sits in the sofa beside the fireplace and stares out at them as they peck in jerky staccato. When the weather is nice he sits outside beside them on the fold down stool, and the rhythm of their tapping is like hail on his face.

The chickens like him, he is convinced. He dutifully cleans out their blue box daily to keep the stink of their refuse from bothering the neighbours. It is not suitable for spreading on his potted plants, he learns through research, so it is instead put in its own refuse bin on the kerb. The chickens are very accustomed to his physical presence as a result; they stand on his foot if he puts seed there. They allow him to touch their necks gently. Even though their feathery flapping sometimes keeps him from dropping into his unconscious phase (still carefully regulated to the 31.76 Earth hour cycle), they soothe him in other ways.

He likes the way they do not move smoothly, still for a long moment as if they are thinking about it, before stabbing down and back up. That reminds him strongly of Basil, chewing on the stylus of his BlackBerry, working out a problem. There would be no sound for the longest time, until suddenly Basil reaches out, and tweaks precisely the right thing. No hesitation.

The black chicken catches the swing of Kalp's arm through the window as he moves to sit closer and settles in to watch them. She jumps, looking as though she might bolt, staring at him warily through the glass, all alert and round, glassy eyes. With a twitch, she is cocking her head, realizing he is no threat, and with that comes curiosity. She cocks her head to the other side, pauses for a beat, then goes back to her methodical pecking.

They make low, constant noises, like the neighbour's TV when she tries to hide the silence made by the non-presence of her dead family.

By late November, Gwen's illness fades and Kalp is sore with relief. She still begs Kalp to say nothing of its existence to Basil and still he complies, wondering if this will cause a rift when the truth does emerge, as it inevitably must do. Kalp quashes the urge to lean down and kiss her when she begs up into his face, and it is harder to do every time.

Her lips look very soft.

THE DAY that the frozen precipitation first falls, they move the chickens into the basement where it will be warmer for them. Again Gwen protests, and again Basil puts his engineering abilities to work, and devises a sort of ventilation system that keeps the air upstairs fresh and chicken-scent free, and the birds downstairs warm and well-aired. The chickens are put into a pen beside the laundry machine with old paper on the floor to make it easy to clean up their droppings. Gwen avoids the basement now, because she fears getting ill again from the chickens. Kalp is unsure how a chicken could cause human illness—he has heard of the avian flu of the decade previous, but everyone is inoculated against that now.

Basil must learn to do the clothes washing, and on one memorable occasion, turns everyone's white garments bright pink by dint of a stray red pair of panties.

That night there is a party. It is the first one that Kalp is actively looking forward to. The others after his Earth-fall were miserable, tight affairs. He is anticipating this party because it is the first that he will be attending not as a pitied refugee, but as a valued co-worker. Basil helps Kalp purchase a suitable suit, and they spend hours in the store to make certain to match the tie very carefully to the shade of Kalp's eyes.

Basil helps him wrangle the material into the correct form of knot, looking frankly stunning in his own suit. Kalp's touches have been growing more steadily intimate, and he has been going slowly, as one does when taming a wild creature. As he has, carefully and patiently, tamed the chickens; he is making sure Basil is comfortable with one level of intimacy before moving onto the next. It is a slow dance, but Kalp is enjoying the leisurely pace of the seduction.

He has not made as much progress with Gwen, due to her illness and now her strange new irritability. Basil says that she is "bitchy" because she dislikes the winter holiday season. It reminds her of the chasm between herself and her parents. Kalp thinks that Basil is being ridiculously oblivious—it is clear that it is the illness that has made Gwen unhappy. She seems, however, to be content to let Kalp sit very close to her on the sofa and rest his head against hers when she falls asleep against him. Once she pulled his long padded fingers across her stomach. He felt a flutter there, like bird's wings, but inside. He does not know what it was—her bowels or her stomach or her heart skipping a beat because his touch was warm—but he hopes she will let him do it again.

Kalp reaches out and boldly ruffles Basil's hair. Before he finishes tying the necktie knot, Basil closes his eyes and leans his cheek into Kalp's touch.

For a moment he stays very still, breathing softly through his nose. Kalp leans down and brushes the side of one velvety ear against Basil's forehead.

Basil starts backwards, and his eyes are wide and blue and confused. "I—" he says, and stops, licks his lips, and huffs out the rest of the breath he had taken for speaking, unsure what to say.

Kalp is satisfied with this one small step, does not want to push too far, too soon, so gives Basil an opportunity to make his excuses: "You have not completed my tie," he says.

Basil jumps at the offered out, the distraction. He hastily finished the process, until the swatch of fabric is laying smooth and flat down Kalp's shirt front. Basil slowly runs his palm down the tie, hot against Kalp's chest, deliberate. Then he snatches his hand away and turns and leaves Kalp alone in his room.

Kalp listens as Basil makes his way to the bedroom, calling for

Gwen. But Gwen is not in there. Kalp heard her throw her clothing onto the floor with a huff of extreme frustration and go into the washroom ten minutes ago. She urinated, and now she is just sitting on the commode, waiting for something. She has not flushed.

"Gwen?" Basil asks. He emerges from his bedroom at the same time Kalp emerges from his own. Basil's cheeks go bright red. Kalp finds even that attractive now, as he knows that it signifies the exertion that intercourse requires or the rumination on such activities. Kalp nods towards the bathroom and Basil frowns. In his hand is the sleek black dress that Gwen was meant to have been donning.

"Gwen?" Basil asks again, tapping on the door with his knuckles to indicate his desire for entry. When she does not answer, he pushes open the door, and Kalp crowds in behind him, worried. Gwen has never not answered before.

The door swings inwards and reveals Gwen in her pyjamas, sitting very still on the lid of the commode, a white plastic stick clutched between shaking hands. The stick must be symbolic—it means nothing to Kalp, but Basil seems powerfully affected.

Basil drops the dress to the floor of the bathroom in shock.

"I'm sorry," Gwen whispers in the tone that is used for consolation. "I hoped I was just…I thought it was the flu. But my dress doesn't fit any more."

She gestures at the small bulge in her middle. It is so infinitesimal that had Kalp not been looking, he would not have seen it.

"Holy shit," Basil says, and his face and lips have gone totally white. He is shaking and Kalp puts out a hand, spreads the pads of his fingers along the bottom of Basil's back, fearing that Basil will faint. "Holy *shit.*"

"I do not understand," Kalp admits. "Is Gwen gravely ill? Are you dying, Gwen?"

Gwen chuckles, but it is a watery weak sort of laugh that conveys no real humour.

"Pretty much the opposite," she says. "I'm pregnant."

Basil does faint then, and Kalp is too shocked himself to catch him.

TRIPTYCH

THEY ARE late for the party because Gwen has to choose a different dress, and Basil must be waked without spilling water on his expensive suit. Kalp is smiling and cannot stop. He has tried and it hurts too much to be not smiling.

They are going to have offspring.

His Unit is having a child!

Gwen is driving, her party dress hiked up and puddled around her thighs to allow for the operation of the vehicle. Basil usually drives. Tonight he cannot because Basil will not release the pregnancy test. He returned to the bathroom upon waking and seized it and investigated its readout, and has not let go of it since. The skin around his eyes and mouth is very tight and white, and he has said nothing. He has allowed Gwen and Kalp to herd him into the car, but he has not said a word.

Gwen keeps shooting concerned looks at his face, and when they finally arrive at the Institute—decked festively in red and green lights—Gwen parks, shuts off the car, and, still gripping the steering wheel and staring straight ahead, asks, "Are you angry?"

Kalp blinks and his smile slides away.

How could Basil possibly be *angry*? This is wonderful, joyous, fantastic news! This is news worthy of the celebration of the evening.

Perhaps Gwen fears Basil will be angry because she hid her illness—the first signs of pregnancy in humans, Kalp learned—from Basil; perhaps she fears that Basil will be concerned because they are not married; perhaps Basil will leave because they had not agreed to have the baby together first. Kalp loves Basil very much but if Basil leaves Gwen alone and pregnant, Kalp will be very angry at Basil. Kalp of course will stay and care for the offspring—it will be his son or daughter instead of Basil's.

But he hopes it will be "with" rather than "instead of."

Basil turns his head so slowly and stiffly that it appears as if he is some sort of child's toy, his neck a ball joint swivel. He licks his lips once, and takes a small breath.

Before he even speaks, Gwen flinches.

"I," Basil says slowly, fingers opening and closing on the pregnancy test. The cramped interior of the vehicle smells faintly of urine. "I'm gonna be a daddy."

He grins now, wide and white, and Kalp sighs and slumps back against the back seat, relieved.

Gwen yelps in joy, and Gwen and Basil lean towards each other to press their mouths together. It smears Gwen's red lip paint all over Basil, and makes Kalp's chest ache. He wants to kiss them, too.

He settles with placing one hand on the top of each fuzzy human head and smiling wide. They turn to him and he leans forward tentatively, pursing his lips and pressing one small, nervous kiss on each cheek.

"You're gonna be an uncle, Kalp!" Basil says.

Kalp would prefer to be the father, too, but uncle sounds just perfect for right now.

Gwen repairs her lip paint with the reflection in the rearview mirror, and then they go inside the building, Gwen's arms threaded through theirs, one on each side in grand presentation, to keep them all from slipping on the ice. Kalp is wearing shoes today, because he has already had his toe-pads freeze to the parking lot once and is not eager to repeat the experience.

Inside, the music is steady and calm in deference to the employees of the Institute from Kalp's world. Basil is relieved. He has never been a fan of the harsh loud music that is popular currently. They shed their thick outerwear and pass it to a woman who takes it away and leaves them with a claim ticket. Kalp sends his shoes with her, too.

The canteen is decorated to approximate a sort of classy eating establishment, with balloons and bright red starburst flowers on each cloth-draped table. Kalp, Gwen, and Basil purposefully take seats at a table on the far side of the room from Derx and his human friends, Barnowski and Edgar, all three of them loud and offensively self-congratulating. Kalp was astonished to discover that there were not one but *three* people in the universe like Derx. Of course, all three like nothing more than the sound of their own voices, and to be told that they are clever, and so every conversation between them sounds more like three separate monologues.

As long as they are happy—and Derx's attention is therefore elsewhere—Kalp is happy for them.

Another team sits at the table with them, these three all human, and congratulate Gwen enthusiastically when Basil all but shouts their good news into the din of the candle-lit room. Kalp knows the name of only Agent Aitken, a female with interesting blonde hair that frizzes out like a curled light flare. She is reservedly polite to Kalp, and he thinks that she is perhaps afraid of him. There are still those, even at the Institute, who have very little contact with his kind. He would be the same, had he not been placed with Gwen and Basil, he thinks.

They eat, and Gwen avoids the fish and alcohol for the sake of the child growing within her, and Kalp makes the expression of pleading to be allowed to touch her soft round stomach again, now that he knows what the thrilling flutter had been last month.

Kalp can hear the baby with his fingertips—the small pattering heart is strong and steady, and he tells her so. Gwen's eyelashes dot with moisture and she is very pleased to hear it.

Basil scrubs a hand through his hair, and shoots to his feet. "Come dance with me, Mummy." He extends a hand to Gwen, "I'm antsy."

Gwen graciously accepts his hand, uses it to pull herself to her feet, and follows him onto the dance floor. There are several other couples out there, holding each other close and swaying artfully to the rhythm of the music. Some are made up of same gendered humans, some of opposite genders. It is beautiful and surreal and heart-wrenching.

To Kalp, they all look incomplete. Torn apart.

They only dance in twos and it looks *wrong*.

Only widows dance as couples.

Kalp can see the pain he feels reflected in the expressions of his people all over the room. Even Derx's ears are pulled back against his head, a sure sign of distress. This is simply something with which they cannot cope. Kalp's eyes get hot in sorrow. It reminds him too much of all the death that they have had to endure, and he knows the same reminder is in the minds of everyone else.

Seeing Basil and Gwen, smiles wide and faces shining, as just two, *hurts* Kalp deep down in the same place it had hurt him when he lost Maru and Trus. He feels like he is dead, like he is the one who ought to be absent, like he is the one who was killed on his home world and not his other Unit. He feels invisible; like a ghost.

Kalp waits for someone, *any*one to take the floor and complete any of the pairs, but no one moves, either out of distress or out of fear of offending the humans.

Offending them.

Stuff and nonsense, Kalp thinks, and the words echo in his head in Gwen's voice. They are here to be Integrated, yes, but they are also here to live their lives and retain their own culture, and if the humans have an issue with a proper three person Unit, then they have no business working at the Institute.

Kalp stands, and all the eyes and ears of his people swivel in his direction. Derx makes a gesture that demands Kalp return to his seat, but Kalp commits the horrid sin of ignoring the Higher Status and walks across the dance floor. He comes up beside Gwen and Basil, and they step apart from each other. "Wanna take the happy mummy for a spin?" Basil asks, offering Gwen's hand to Kalp.

"No," Kalp says, firmly.

Basil frowns, his normal crooked expression of puzzlement endearing. "Wanna take me?"

Kalp doubts that Basil is aware of the innuendo that peppers his question, so answers it on the non-sexual level. "No," he says, though he would gladly say the opposite in another, more private setting.

Gwen's eyes narrow, and Kalp thinks she understands immediately what Kalp is about to do.

Kalp leans down and rubs his cheek—and the scent pouch behind his jaw hinge—first along Basil's neck, then Gwen's. Gwen gasps and lifts her hand to the quickly drying wet patch of scent chemical. She knows what this means. Basil does not. Derx's ears shoot upwards, and he is *furious*, and it makes Kalp cruelly content to feel Derx's extreme displeasure. Agent Aitken gets up from the table and departs.

"Did you just—?" Gwen asks. But she does not finish her sentence. Kalp suspects it is because she fears his answer.

"Just dance with me," Kalp says. "Just dance, for now."

"For now," Gwen agrees, nodding once. Her tone and expression says that there will be conversation later. A long, long conversation, possibly filled with shouting. Kalp will do everything he can to make sure her agitation does not harm the child. Her body vibrates anger.

"What just happened?" Basil asks, accepting Kalp's hand on his shoulder, guiding him in a slow circle in a parody of the sort of dance that is used to announce a new Aglunated Unit. Basil leans into the warmth of Kalp's body so naturally, Kalp wonders if he knows his posture has betrayed his feelings.

All over the room, Kalp's people's ears jump up and they whistle shrilly between their teeth in congratulations. Kalp just hopes that this "stunt" works out as well as the last one.

THEY DEPART after two more dances. One is with just Basil, who is flushed and nervous, his palms secreting copiously; he finally realizes what has happened and seems torn between mortification, fury, and interest. The other is with just Gwen, who performs the motions of the ritual dance out of respect for Kalp's people's traditions, and the many many eyes of the rapt spectators around them, but says nothing.

The car ride home is tense and silent, but this time Kalp does not allow his nervousness to consume him. The car pulls to a juttering halt in the drive. Gwen slams into the house, stomping up the stairs to her bedroom. Kalp can hear her stripping off her fancy dress and putting on her house clothing. Basil sits down in the dining area, undoing his tie and the top two buttons of his expensive shirt in a daze.

Kalp suspects that Basil must be rather shocked—to find out that he is to be a father in one evening is quite excitement enough, but to then also be informed that Kalp has what essentially amounts to proposed marriage to both him and Gwen, in public no less…it must be very hard to process.

Kalp undoes his own tie, glad to be rid of the mild choking sensation of the garment, and goes into the kitchen to put on the kettle. Basil's ears catch the familiar sounds of Kalp's motions and he lifts his voice and says, "No, no, something stronger."

Kalp returns to the dining area with two glasses of Basil's whiskey and one glass of water for Gwen—if she should deign to descend the stairs and join them. He and Basil sip at the whiskey in thoughtful silence, and Kalp fancies he can actually hear Basil's mind thinking very quickly, and very hard. *Why us?* is practically written across the human's forehead.

After a long, long time, Gwen finally comes down the stairs. She is breathing calmly and her heart rate has returned to normal. Basil and Kalp are each on their third glassful.

"Why didn't you say something?" she asks. They are the first words anyone has spoken in hours.

Kalp lifts and drops his shoulders, a gesture he has learned means that one is unsure of how to answer. He adds, "I have tried for many months to convey my affection."

Gwen touches the back of her neck, guiltily. Basil touches his cheek. They both catch each other's movements, and flush.

"It is not cheating," Kalp says hastily. He has seen many a film on Earth whose protagonist goes through emotional torment because he or she has added a third, either intentionally or not, into the romantic relationship. Humans seem extremely concerned about proprietary rights over each other's bodies and pleasure, and Kalp strives to assure them that it is still a monogamous relationship, simply with one extra person added. "It does not make you gay, either," he directs to Basil. There are an inordinate amount of films about that, too.

"But why us?" Basil asks. "I mean, why me? Why Gwen?"

"You have been kind to me," Kalp says simply. To him, it is that simple, but humans always look for more answers, more reasons, more excuses and explanations. "I enjoy your company."

"But we were just being *nice*," Basil insists, but it is phrased as a question. Kalp knew he would ask it. "It was just the...the right thing to do."

Kalp takes breath to speak but Gwen beats him to it.

"But that's it, isn't it?" she says. "The fact that we were just...nice. Nobody was being nice to you, were they?"

Kalp droops his ears a bit. "Yes," he admits. "At first it was...blind affection. But I see how happy you make each other and I would like to be made that happy. To *make* you that happy. I enjoy your company and you enjoy mine. We work well together and we care for each other. I am aroused by your physical shapes. Why should we not become an Aglunated Unit?"

"You've got a dick, for one!" Basil spits, but looks immediately contrite at his inability to control the disconnect between his mouth and brain.

"Technically speaking," Kalp chides softly, unhurt by Basil's drunken outburst, "I am not male. Nor am I technically female, by your standards. Our procreation process is far more complicated, which is why we are biologically incompatible with humans."

Basil looks confused again. "Well, then how can we—?"

"Biologically," Kalp repeats, "But not sexually. I have read pornography—more than one, now," he adds hastily, anticipating a repetition of Basil's previous comment. "I am aware of how to pleasure a human body. And I can easily teach you mine."

Basil looks faintly green.

Gwen's mouth is a thin line.

Kalp does not let that deter him. He is confident. All he has to do is convince them, and they will see the logic of the arrangement. They will see how hard he adores them. They will be able to overcome the strangeness of his body, his genitalia, and learn to find it appealing, just as he has for them. They will learn to...to care for him deeply, as he has, to care beyond what pleasure the body can offer and to the pleasures that comfort and company can give.

"What if we don't want to?" Gwen asks, and the words are like a stinging slap across Kalp's face. "Have you considered that?"

Kalp takes a deep breath. He must stay calm. He must be rational and *explain* or there will be no chance. "I...have," he admits. "But I desperately hope that you hold the same affection for me as I do for you."

Basil and Gwen exchange a glance, filled with meaning that Kalp has always wished he could decode. He thinks perhaps he is getting closer to understanding.

"Just try," Kalp pleads, and he is surprised at how fraught his own voice sounds. "Please let me show you how much your generosity and acceptance has meant to me."

"This isn't payback," Gwen states, lifting a finger, and it is not a question. "You're not going to do this because you feel obligated to."

Kalp cannot help but tug his ear and make the self-depreciating chuckle sound. "I first thought it was."

"Come again?" Basil asks, reaching again for the whiskey bottle.

If they do have intercourse tonight, which is Kalp's favoured outcome of this discussion but the least statistically likely, he hopes that the alcohol does not impede Basil's ability to attain an erection. The whiskey may have instead the positive effect of loosening his inhibitions, though, so Kalp does not stop him.

"When they first placed me on your team, and you invited me into your home—I thought we had been made a Unit for the sake of…Integration." He shakes his head ruefully at his own naiveté. "I realized, of course, that we were not, but the hope remained that you would accept me."

"But why threes?" Basil asks. "I mean, if it still only takes two to tango…"

"Mostly, it is for the sake of the parent who gives birth to the offspring," Kalp says, turning his eyes to Gwen. "One leaves the home to earn a wage, one remains to care for the birth parent and the offspring, and one gives birth and recovers. Sometimes, though rarely, more than one parent is pregnant or has a small child simultaneously."

Another meaning-filled glance passes between Gwen and Basil.

At the end of it, Basil shrugs and Gwen echoes it.

"Okay," Gwen says. "Okay—we'll try it. Just…just *try* it. But, but if we don't think it's working…"

"I understand," Kalp says, and has to refrain from leaping up from his chair and yelling in joy. "I can transfer teams, I can move…if I must."

He lowers his head and looks up, through the lowered whiskers of his eyes, at Basil's cheeks, noting the spotted red that surges to the surface at the coy invitation. Kalp has learned that expression, that mode of tilting his head and gazing just so, from one of the other pornographies, and he is pleased to see that it is an effective signal, even on his face. "What... what would you like to do first?" Already he can feel his genitalia sliding into the cool air of the dining room in happy anticipation.

"Dunno," Basil mutters. "Only been in a threesome once."

Gwen smacks his arm and the easy familiarity of the gesture breaks the uncomfortable tension of the conversation. Basil stands carefully, with the deliberate motions of a man trying very hard to be more sober than he really is. He walks over to Kalp's side, and looks down at him.

"Oh, fuck it," Basil says.

He grabs Kalp's ears and drags his head up and presses his hot mouth directly over Kalp's.

It is Kalp's first kiss.

It is everything Kalp hopes for.

It is wet and hot and the soft slick slide of tongues is breathlessly exhilarating in ways that Kalp had not expected. Basil's hands are fisted in his shirt now, demanding and controlling the angle and depth that he can manoeuvre. He is trying to prove something, prove that he is not scared of Kalp or scared of himself and this strange want, Kalp is not sure. Kalp tilts his head back and lets his mouth fall open a bit more and lets Basil take everything he wants. Anything he wants.

The kiss slows. It becomes tender a way that Kalp has never seen in the pornographies he has watched. Basil licks into Kalp's mouth, running his tongue against Kalp's, over the roof of his mouth, and across his teeth.

Then he jerks back sharply and claps his hands over his mouth.

"Damnit," he says, the words muffled by his fingers. A small drop of blood slides through a crack between them and down the stairway of his knuckles.

"Basil?" Gwen asks. She is still sitting on the chair, and her cheeks have gone a delectable shade of red. She is breathing hard, as if she has been the one exerting herself physically. The effects of kisses seem to be communicable. Interesting.

"Fangs," Basil says again and grimaces as more blood drops out from between clenched fingers.

"Is it bad?" Gwen is already getting up out of her chair, reaching for the tissue box that lives on the side table by the end of the sofa.

Kalp reaches up and takes Basil's hands and Basil tries to wave him off. Kalp persists and manages to convince Basil to open his mouth and stick out his tongue.

It is not bad. The bleeding is slowing already. A surface scrape.

Kalp gets a sudden saddening flash of knowledge: his people were not made for kissing. Basil frowns and goes into the kitchen to rinse out his mouth—it is not a deep gash, but Basil will be avoiding curry for the next few weeks. Kalp lets go.

"I'lb do it bettah nexzt time," Basil swears before cupping a hand under his chin to keep the blood splatters off the carpet.

The carnivore in Kalp licks the last of Basil's blood off his teeth and likes it. He will not tell the humans, though. He does not want to freak out his Unit and he knows from surreptitious research on the internet that bloodplay is a sexual fetish that not many people indulge in. Asking them to participate in a threesome polygamous relationship with an extra-terrestrial is probably as far as they are willing to stretch their sexual proclivities for this particular moment.

Gwen comes back to stand beside Kalp. "Idiot," she mutters and whether she is talking about Basil and his mouth, Kalp and his intentions, or herself, Kalp is unsure. She reaches out slowly, runs one hand over the soft velvety fur of his ear, down his cheek. She leans down, and presses her lips, warm and dry, against his. Her kiss is softer, gentler. There is no invasive tongue, no pushy puckers. Hers is a whisper and, Kalp is slightly disappointed to note, tentative.

He realizes now how communicative a single kiss can be, how much can be said with the push of mouths and the hot pant of moist breath.

Basil wounded and drunk, Gwen uncertain and tired, they retire to Kalp's bedroom.

"For sleep," Gwen says as they each strip down into their sleep wear. "*Just* sleep." Kalp plans on wearing no clothing to bed, as always, but then re-dons a pair of boxer shorts when he notices that Basil and Gwen have retained their undergarments. Gwen removes her bra but adds a tee-shirt from Kalp's dresser, and it is thrillingly intimate. Her breasts are not the ballooned, pale globes that the women in the pornographies sport, stiff and extending out from their chests in an immoveable way. They are low and slightly pendulous, tipped in stiff brown and smattered all along the swell with the same dark brown skin discolorations as decorate the bridge of her nose, the tops of her cheeks. Gwen does not seem to mind that Kalp is looking.

Basil is watching too, his lips closed shut firmly to keep his new injury protected, pulled down in the sides in a frown. Basil makes an aborted and slightly desperate gesture at his penis. It is mostly engorged, poking at the inside of the boxer shorts, the purple-red head visible and weeping.

"Oh, for!" Gwen says and rolls her eyes.

Basil makes the begging face.

Gwen cuts a glance towards Kalp, suddenly nervous again. Her heart beat speeds, an exhilarating patter against Kalp's skin, and her forehead and underarms bead with perspiration.

"May I…?" Kalp asks, and he must stop halfway through the sentence to swallow heavily and clear his throat. He wants to growl, to emit the lust-filled rumbling purr that signals to his mates that he is ready to begin intercourse, but sounds too much like a wild animal for a human's bedroom. "Please," he tries again. "May I watch?"

Basil's eyes widen and his pupils blow wide and he hisses, "Fuck, Gwen, please? *Ow.*"

Gwen rolls her eyes again, and watches carefully as Kalp moves to lean against the corner, out of touching range. Kalp folds his legs under him and waits.

Gwen, moving carefully to give her belly ample time to adjust to a new position, guides Basil down onto the cushions on his back, kneels down between his legs, and carefully, slowly, slides his penis out of the slit in the front of the boxer shorts. She glances up at Kalp and her eyes are twinkling, her lips curled up in a smirk and Kalp's own pulse quickens when he realizes that she is *teasing* him.

Gwen blows a soft breath over the head of Basil's penis, and Basil arches under her touch, heels digging into the blankets. Kalp licks his lips and sits forward, eyes wide and determined to see, to understand, everything. Gwen opens her mouth and licks up the bottom of Basil's shaft, and Basil moans in pleasure, and Kalp thinks it is the most intimate, the most beautiful moment he has ever seen on Earth, *ever*.

IN THE morning, Basil's mouth is tender and he sips his tea slowly, gazing forlornly at the pot sitting between the hobs on the stove. He is leaning against the cupboards, half-full mug clasped like a lifeline between curling fingers. By this time of the morning, he's usually finished that pot and is boiling another to pour into his carry-mug and take in the car.

He whines and he moans and he generally makes a big fuss that he had been really looking forward to "real" sex last night and did not get any at all. Gwen scoffs and makes a point of saying that for someone who "got a blowjob" he was being pretty pissy.

"I should have gotten sex," Basil mutters, though it is more like, "I ssssould habe goeen seksh," because his tongue is still heavy and fat, sitting at the bottom of his mouth where it hurts the least.

"Stop complaining," Gwen says. Kalp cannot tell if this is more teasing or if she's serious. Her face is strangely unreadable today.

"A man has two lovers, he should have twice as much sex," Basil points out. "Laws of…physics or sommat, innit?"

Gwen leans over from where she's washing the breakfast dishes and kisses him firmly on the mouth. He yelps, and she pulls back, smirking. "There, see? Hurts too much."

"I can do more than just use my tongue!" Basil protests.

Gwen's expression turns positively wicked.

Basil blinks, and then his expression changes to match hers.

Kalp is fairly certain that they've forgotten that he's in the room, and that if Basil's tongue had been up for it, and their morning schedule allowed, there would have been a lot less clothing on them and more on the floor right now.

Kalp—who has been standing on the other side of Gwen, watching—reaches out and runs his fingerpads over her hair, down her cheek to settle gently on her neck, an echo of the motion she made last night. He watches the goosebumps jump into existence all over her skin.

"Kiss me instead," he says.

Gwen turns her head obligingly and does. When Kalp tries to repeat what Basil did to him on her, licking at the seam of her lips to request entrance, she hesitates before she lets him in.

Once she does, though, the kiss immediately turns dirty. Kalp is just as good with his tongue as Basil, and he is determined to prove it. He wants one of those wicked glances turned his way.

When he pulls back, Gwen's mouth is bruised and red, and her eyes have fluttered shut. Her hands, still covered in water and little clouds of dish soap bubbles, are curled against the side of the stainless steel sink. Her chest is bobbing, her lungs filling and deflating at a rapid pace that makes her breasts bounce in a way that Kalp finds extremely arousing.

Kalp looks up at Basil, whose own eyes are wide, pupils large and very black. His cheeks are red and his mouth hangs open a fraction.

Then Basil blinks several times in a row, coming back to himself. He licks his lips, frowns, and says.

"That is totally, totally unfair, innit?"

Kalp smirks, trying to copy the dirty look, and Basil blinks again. It seems to be working.

Gwen clears her throat and opens her eyes and touches her bottom lip with the back of her soapy hand.

"Uh," she says. "Um. Wow."

Basil makes a little whining sound, and if Kalp did not know any better, he would say that Basil was about five seconds away from throwing a full blown temper tantrum. As it is, he stomps his foot like a child, and says, "Totally, totally unfair!"

WHATEVER RELUCTANCE Gwen had about engaging in physical pleasures before, it seems to dissolve in the heat of anticipation.

The day at work is long, longer than Kalp remembers it being. He repeatedly looks up at the clock, wondering how it is possible that time seems to have slowed itself to an almost infinitesimal crawl. He thinks that maybe he should bring up this concern with someone, that perhaps an experiment elsewhere in the building has somehow gone awry and affected perception of the present, until he sees Gwen and Basil each glancing at the clock with the same sort of intense longing.

When the end of the day comes, they rush their ritual goodbyes to the other Specialists, pile into the car, and have just enough presence of mind to swing through the drive-thru of the nearest hamburger restaurant. The paper bag, already spotting over with grease stains, is left to get cold on the kitchen table. They are barely up the stairs, heading for Kalp's nest—fits three better, nothing to fall off of—before somehow Basil's hands are on Kalp's buttons and Kalp's tongue is back in Gwen's mouth and Gwen's fingers are on Basil's fly.

There is a moment when Basil has to stop to stare at Kalp's naked body, to investigate and touch Kalp's genitalia. Gwen strokes and fondles, and Basil shows Kalp how useful tongues really are when it comes to women. There is another moment when Basil fumbles for a prophylactic, scrambles to his feet and runs into the other bedroom for it, before crowing and coming back empty handed because he realises that Gwen is already pregnant and therefore no condom is necessary.

Basil throws himself joyously back onto the pile of pillows and blankets. He buries his face in the crook of Gwen's neck and begins to suck there, leaving behind a livid red mark when he disengages. Gwen's eyes have rolled back into her head, glassy, and she is fumbling for Kalp's hand. She twines their fingers and pushes his palm against the entrance to her body, slick and hot. Kalp lowers his head to peer at the folds of flesh, and carefully, minding his nails, strokes the pad of one finger into Gwen.

She arches from the bed with a stifled little cry, and Basil seizes the opportunity to wiggle under her, to lift her up without disrupting Kalp's view or ability to touch, and engage their bodies fully. Kalp releases Gwen's hand and runs his fingers around where they now join, and Gwen and Basil jerk together, both letting out little puffs of strained breath.

Then, with Kalp laying on his stomach so he can watch and touch and flick out his tongue with ease, they begin intercourse in earnest.

SEVERAL HOURS later, the cold hamburgers are most likely so congealed as to be beyond salvageable. Or edible. Kalp thinks of them only briefly, forgotten on the table downstairs, when a particular shift in the airflow in the house brings the sickly greasy scent to his nose for a second.

Gwen has a goofy smile on her face—rather, what Basil terms "goofy." Kalp takes this to mean that she is well sated and happy. They are lying in bed, speaking idly of food, of the work they are putting off, of what Basil's family might do for the coming holiday. They speak of housework yet to be done, the little plumbing and carpentry projects that Gwen has placed upon Basil's "Honey Do" list. (They must take at least five minutes explaining the humour of the title of this list—Kalp attempts a laugh of his own once he understands. Gwen reaches over and pats his back, fearing that he is the one choking this time. Kalp decides that his experiments with laughter are exponentially less successful than the ones with smiles, and perhaps it is time to abandon that particular attempt at human non-verbal communication.)

Kalp knows that they will not rise. Despite their lists of chores and tasks and bodily requirements, they will not spoil this moment.

Basil lies between Gwen and Kalp, his legs spread shamelessly wide and his own smile equally goofy, if not more. Gwen is tucked up against his side, still panting, all of her limbs slotted in around his, twined in a way that Kalp believed that a human's stiff, inflexible elbows and knees ought to have prevented.

Kalp himself is as equally entwined, and Basil keeps pushing the small of his own back downwards against the mattress, seeking the firm flexibility of the hand that Kalp has pressed there. Gwen is stroking the soft, downy fur at the end of Kalp's nose with the very tip of her pink finger, the rounded and carefully maintained nail. Kalp lets forth the tummy-rumbling purr that he's been holding back all evening, unable to control the comfortable automatic auditory response any longer.

Basil starts, and then laughs, turning his face into Kalp's throat, seeking out the vibrations of his vocal chords with one prickling soft cheek. Gwen and Basil's bodies are still flushed red, their foreheads wet with perspiration.

Kalp still finds the slightly oily moisture unpleasant against his own skin, but for the pleasure it signifies, he is willing to endure it for a few hours. At any rate, he will soon have a shower. Perhaps, like in the pornography video that Basil believes he has hidden adequately in the basement workshop, they will the three of them shower together. Kalp thinks that would be wonderful, the slow slide of hands and tongues pulsing in sharp counter rhythm with the whooshing slosh of water through the pipes, the hot dragging touches pulling the staccato beat of the water droplets into a delicious dance across Kalp's skin.

Kalp's genitalia are growing engorged again, and Basil chuckles to feel it press against his hip. Gwen runs her free hand down Kalp's neck, pressing hard all along his flank until she can wrap her fat little fingers around him and relieve the lust. Basil watches with parted pink lips and takes himself in hand, matching Gwen's speed and twisting wrist with his own. Basil and Kalp miraculously reach their orgasm together.

"Now you?" Basil murmurs, but Gwen shakes her head.

"Now bathroom," she says instead and works at disentangling herself.

This time Kalp initiates the playful wrestling, pulling and tugging at Gwen until she is sprawled across both of them, laughing uproariously as Kalp and Basil tickle her mercilessly.

"No, no!" she shouts. "The pregnant lady has to pee!"

Basil and Kalp take pity on Gwen and let her scramble away. The goofy smile that Basil sports grows wider and he sighs happily. Kalp turns his own cheek against Basil's shoulder, shyly rubbing his scent sacs along the tendon of Basil's neck. The liquid evaporates away quickly in the chill evening air and Basil shivers.

"Daddy, Papa, Father…" Basil says softly. "Boy or a girl, do you think, Kalp?"

Kalp scrunches his shoulders and finds it more difficult than he anticipated trying to shrug while lying down. Basil understands his meaning, however.

"No, I don't much care either," Basil admits. "Just healthy and happy's enough, innit?"

Kalp hears the flush of the toilet, the rush of water from the sink and then, unexpectedly, the sudden patter of the shower. Oh.

Kalp tries not to be disappointed. Maybe Basil will still want to share.

Basil closes his eyes, his lids heavy. Kalp has never felt particularly exhausted at the conclusion of intercourse, but he has been given to understand through the observation of many situational comedies and "chick flicks" that human males do tend towards requiring a quick restorative sleep. Kalp lies back upon his nest and allows Basil his rest, settling one of the cool sheets over his naked body in case he wakes cold.

When he looks back up, Gwen has returned to the room. She is clad in her house coat, a tattered but cosy looking maroon terrycloth that makes her hot-water dappled cheeks appear all the redder. She is standing in the doorway, frowning.

"Gwen?" Kalp asks softly. He raises a hand, invitation. Gwen shakes her head, sucking her lips inward and biting on the bottom one.

She turns away and Kalp follows the sound of her footsteps on the stairs. Gwen goes into the kitchen and puts on the kettle.

Kalp debates with himself. Should he go downstairs to speak with her, or was this deliberate separation an attempt at a few moments of privacy? He believes that Gwen may be upset, but for what reason he is unsure. Perhaps she is confused or conflicted.

Gwen has just experienced her first sexual encounter with one of Kalp's kind. Perhaps she is shaken or experiencing delayed revulsion. Perhaps she is worried for her relationship with Basil, or the health of the child she carries. Perhaps she is just not sleepy.

Kalp waits until he feels the whistle of the kettle, the clink of a spoon against the side of a cup, before he carefully extracts himself from the nest. He dons his own house robe—left hanging on the back of his door—and pads quietly down the stairs.

He pauses at the bottom, craning his head around the railing to watch Gwen. Her elbow is on the table, her chin in her hand. She is staring into the back patio, watching birds or the black sky or the flutter of a stark white moth beating with futility against the glass, leaving a smear of wing powder against the transparent surface.

Kalp smells an herbal tea, sharp and fresh and slightly sweet. Kalp recognizes the scent as peppermint chamomile, one of the blends Basil had purchased in his quest to win his bet over Kalp's palate.

Gwen prefers strong black coffee. Kalp is puzzled.

Gwen does not turn to look at Kalp, but she says, out loud, "How do you feel?"

Kalp flicks an ear, unsure how to respond. Even on his world, partners did not always say what they meant, and sometimes answers were the starting points of arguments that he had no idea had begun until they were shouting.

"I am very happy," he says. It seems a safe enough response to settle upon. "May I partake of the tea?"

Gwen waves acquiescence at the pot, and waits in silence for Kalp to fetch a clean mug off of the sink-side drying rack and sit in his chair beside her. "You don't like this stuff."

"Nor you," Kalp says, picking up the disgusting hamburger sack and tossing it in the general direction of the kitchen counter. It lands in the sink. "However," he adds, when he turns back around, watching Gwen's eyebrows settle back down, "I do believe tonight is a night for trying new things?"

Gwen smiles, and Kalp feels slightly more relieved. It is a small and gentle and somewhat sad smile. It does not make her cheeks puff out or her eyes sparkle. Perhaps Kalp is not *too* relieved then, but a little at least. Yes, that.

"Are you happy, Gwen?"

Gwen looks away, down at her teacup. She sips, then grimaces. "I hate this stuff."

"Why drink it?"

"It's good for me. For the baby. No caffeine. No more coffee for me until the little brat is weaned."

"I understand. It is a sacrifice to protect another."

"Yeah."

"Gwen. Have you…?" Kalp stops. He is not certain how to ask. Or if he wants to. He begins again. "Gwen, have you performed intercourse with me only because it made Basil happy?"

"What?" It is an automatic objection, with no real thought behind it. Kalp waits for her to process what he's asked. The silence lasts as long as it takes for Gwen to blink three times and swallow once. "I…" she says, and then stops.

Kalp tries again. "Are you happy?"

Gwen peers down into the bottom of her cup, looking, Kalp thinks, for answers to this question imprinted into the cheap porcelain. He knows there are none there, and waits again. This is an important question. The answer must not be rushed or forced or influenced.

"Why us?" Gwen says instead, trading question for question. Kalp wonders if Gwen knows that he finds this answer as difficult to verbalize as she must herself with her own.

"Are you so undeserving?" Kalp asks. He hopes that it is both answer enough to her question, and a question that may aid in forming her answer.

Gwen's hand rubs her stomach again. "No," she says. "Maybe?"

Kalp wonders, for just a moment, if he is pathetic; if he is so desperate for affection and approval that he is willing to steal it away from someone else, someone gentle and wonderful and sweet, someone who has opened her home and her heart to him and has demanded nothing in return. Gwen and Basil had given Kalp everything they possibly can—hospitality, friendship, compassion without demands for explanation, and in return Kalp had asked for the one thing they possessed that they had not offered up, the one thing that he perhaps had no right to, the one thing that was their own.

"I care for you deeply," Kalp said slowly, "but if this makes you unhappy…"

"It's not like we can go back," Gwen interrupts. "Not to things the way they were."

"But, you had to have known…" Kalp says, then stops, staring into his own cooling tea. No, no answers there, just as he suspected. "Is this such a hardship?" He feels his ears pressing against the back of his neck and cannot seem to make them rise again.

Ah. Yes. He is scared.

Scared she will say yes. That she has changed her mind.

"It's not a…a fucking hardship," Gwen says. There is fire in her words, but not in her voice. That is small and tired. "It's just…hard. That's all. It's hard. And there's no one to…to help. Nobody else who understands what we…*this* is."

"There is me," Kalp says with as much warmth as he is able to muster. Not an iota of it is fake. "There is Basil."

"Yeah," Gwen says, but Kalp understands that it isn't them that she is thinking about. Kalp can guess at who Gwen means. Kalp's own relationships were often made easier to fathom with the advice of his parents. He takes a breath.

"Your parents must be very sad," Kalp says softly. "Do they not mourn your removal from their affection? Will they not wish to meet their grandch—?"

Gwen rises to her feet and leaves the room before Kalp can finish the question. He supposes that is reply enough.

IN THE morning, Kalp finds Gwen laying in the bathtub. The door to the bathroom is slightly open and no one answers to his knock. He wants to relieve himself, but seeing Gwen's wrinkled feet hanging over the edge is enough to panic Kalp into forgetting about his bladder for a moment.

Surely Gwen wouldn't…

The soles are pointed at him, soft and vulnerable.

"Gwen?" he says.

"Hm?" She lifts herself out of the water. She is wearing a pair of wireless ear buds. Ah, the MP3 player is laying on the top of the toilet tank. "Kalp. Did you want the bathroom?"

"Yes," he admits. Then, "No. You did not answer when I knocked."

She touches her earbud. "I was trying to relax." One hand drops to her belly.

"Does the child pain you?" Kalp asks. "I could perform a muscle relaxation rub?"

"No. No, the kid's too small for that, now," Gwen says. She rubs one palm over the little bump. "I just…had trouble sleeping."

Kalp closes the lid of the toilet and sits. He looks down through the murky water at Gwen. Once, there had been bubbles in the tub, but they have all popped, leaving only a thin film that makes human's skin soft, though it always makes his fur matted.

Kalp bends down, does something he's never tried before. He kisses the soft, calloused parts of her clean feet. Gwen does not pull away, as Kalp fears she might have done as early as last night, and he takes it for a good sign.

Kalp reaches out slowly, and brushes her damp hair off of her forehead. He runs a finger pad over her scar. It is the most intimate place on her body that he knows. He leans forward and kisses that, too. She closes her eyes, squeezing them hard, and a sob escapes. Kalp is startled. The tears that run between her lashes and over her cheeks are fat. They roll more than fall.

"I had a dream," Gwen says. She is crying so hard her shoulders are knocking against the side of the tub. "I had a dream that I drowned the baby. I don't know what it means."

"No, no," Kalp says. He sheds his house robe and crawls into the tub beside her, wrapping his arms around and around her shoulders. The water is barely above room temperature. Kalp wonders how long she's been in the bathroom. "No, Gwen. It will be well. The baby, and you, and Basil. It will all be well."

"And you," Gwen says, turning her face into his neck, digging her fingers into his fur, hard and desperate. "You too, okay?"

This is the okay that means "well."

"Me, too," Kalp agrees, and rubs the scent sac behind his jaw hinge across her own jaw, then leans down and leaves a smear of scent above her belly button, just where the baby pokes out of the water. "Me, too."

THE NEXT few months fly by in a flurry of pleasurable interaction. At first they tiptoe around one another, a complicated dance of three that Kalp has known before, but that is entirely new and strange to the humans. Slowly Basil and Gwen's former tight choreography, the quick one-two, becomes a waltz.

It is not easy, at first. It causes strain. It causes poor sleep and queasy stomachs and the consumption of far too much alcohol on the part of Basil, and the wish to consume far too much alcohol on the part of Gwen. But like any difficult matter, it becomes easier with practice. Easier with every affectionate pat, with every sticky night, with every shared trip and car ride and household chore. With practice, they become a newborn Unit, shaky on just-birthed legs, but confident and curious. Willing, *wanting*, to survive.

Nothing that is worth having comes without practice.

They move around one another in the morning, dropping kisses and reminders, teasing and nagging, trading clothes and barbs. Dinners are made, dishes washed, shopping done. They stand together in the little back garden in a thunderstorm, fingers wrapped in fingers wrapped in fingers. The world smells of wet pavement and fat earth worms. The sky rips open with light. Basil tells stories about a childhood spent fearing the thunder; Gwen speaks of the great awe-inspiring bolts of electric fire that danced over the cornstalks of her youth; Kalp paints the sky above their heads green with the stories of another that was far away, and a long time ago.

Now, Gwen has two men to rub her sore feet. Basil has four hands on his tense shoulders. Kalp has twenty blunt fingers to brush the tangles out of the fur at the base of his back, where he cannot reach.

They fight. They scream. They throw sofa pillows, and video game controllers, and sharpened words. All loved ones fight. But the fighters also love. They apologize and they work through the worry and the tension and they find newer, better ways to slot together.

Kalp does not think of Maru and Trus so often any more. No, that is not true. He sees them daily in Basil and Gwen, but now it does not *hurt*.

Gwen's stomach gets rounder, more distended, and they must be careful when they perform intercourse in order not to make her uncomfortable. Kalp's intercourse with Gwen is soft and tender, and with Basil it is fierce and strong, and when it is all three together it is a miracle. They cook and clean and work and sleep as they did before, only now when they make love, Kalp is in the bed with them. Basil continues to come to bed late, slipping between the sheets after finally abandoning his projects, his mound of electronic guts that he has been sifting through for the last few days on the dining room table. Basil lets in what feels like all the chilly air in the house at the same time. It annoys both Kalp and Gwen.

And when Kalp cooks on Friday nights, he makes enough for four.

One white, crisp afternoon so cold it is fit for nothing but snuggling on the sofa and drinking uncanny amounts of hot tea and chocolate, Kalp curls his fingers around Gwen's belly and presses the flats of his ears against the sides and his left cheek just under her breast and he tells the baby a story.

"In a place that is not here," he starts. Kalp's parents had told it like this. All parents did, where he was from. They started their stories differently on the other continent, but neither was better than the other. It was just a preference. Tradition.

"In a place that is not here," Kalp repeats, because the start is the most important part and bears repeating, "There was Vren."

"Who's Vren?" Basil asks, sinking into the sofa on the other side of Gwen, clutching his mug of tea like a lifeline, like he always does.

"Shut up," Gwen says.

"Vren was tall," Kalp said. "And his eyes were very yellow."

"Is that usual?" Basil asked. "Yellow eyes, I mean? Or is it a…a, yunno, a signifier. A symbol?"

Gwen elbows him. "Shut up, Baz."

Kalp does not lift his head. The story is for the baby, not Basil, and Basil's questions will wait for later.

"Vren had long strong arms and a long strong body and a long strong mind."

"How can a mind be long?" Basil asks. A glare from Gwen and Kalp both makes him roll his eyes. "Yeah, yeah, shut up Basil," he says.

"Vren was not wealthy. He was not High Status. He was not renowned for any particular trade. He was, however, completely and devotedly happy, and in those days, that was rare."

"Why rare? Yes, yes, shut up Basil, I gettit."

"Vren pitied all those who were not as happy as he, and so he set out to find a way to ensure that all people everywhere had the pleasure they deserved. He walked for many cycles, hardly pausing to drop into his unconscious phase, and when he ceased walking, he found himself in a small town where everyone's ears drooped all day."

Here Kalp shifts his head to the other side of Gwen's tummy, so Basil can hear better.

"He raised his hands to catch their words and asked, 'Why are you sad?'" Kalp recites, raising his voice into a light falsetto, the timbre of the heroes of all his childhood stories.

Basil snorts tea up his nose and has to pull a tissue from the box on the side table to keep it from leaking down his face.

"We are sad," Kalp continues, this time in the lowered voice of the distraught, "because there is never any time for intercourse."

This time Basil howls and has to put the mug down to keep from splashing Gwen and the back of Kalp's head.

"Sorry, sorry," he says, the tissue clamped firmly over his face. "Go on."

Kalp twitches his ears in amusement, then lays them flat again. He knows now that mentioning intercourse around human males always causes some sort of strange gleeful, immature reaction. It is such a bizarre form of prudery.

"Vren, who had always been very sufficient at self-pleasure, nonetheless could understand the villagers' problem. He asked them, 'Why do you have no time?' and they replied, 'Because the males must support the females after they have given birth and the females must attend the child, and those who have no Aglunate are not satisfied with self-pleasure but dread the hardship that will come of Aglunation.'"

Kalp breaks his own narrative to look up at Gwen and Basil. "That was before prophylactics and medicines to prevent pregnancy," he clarifies.

"Oh, of course," Basil allows, shoulders still shaking with suppressed mirth.

"'That is a hardship to be sure,' Vren admitted. He looked at the harried mothers and he looked at the sex-starved fathers and he looked at the lonely singles and he counted. When he finished counting the people, he saw that there were exactly the same number of singles as there were couples. Deftly, he manoeuvred those with no Aglunates to stand besides the Mothers and Fathers and Children. 'There,' he said. 'Now you are three. You may have intercourse with one another. One may go to earn your keep, and one may raise the children, and the other may care for you all. You will split your work evenly, and you will split your intercourse evenly, and you may be happy.'"

Kalp smiles.

"So some Aglunates were made of two females and one male, and some of two males and one female, but all loved each other and there was enough intercourse and enough affection for all, and from that moment on, no others were ever so happy as that village. Eventually, the wisdom of Vren's edict filtered throughout the world, and everyone agreed that Aglunates were meant to be in threes." He rubs his fingers along Gwen's stomach, revels in the butterfly flutter in response. "And fours."

Kalp sits up.

"What, that's it?" Basil asks.

"Did Vren have a Unit?" Gwen asks.

Kalp shakes his head. "No, Vren did not. It is what you would call an epic, The Deeds of Vren, but none end so happily as that, and so are not so fit for unborn ears."

"Is it true?" Basil asks, ever the empirical scientist.

Kalp performs the shrugging motion. "Does it truly matter if it is?"

"No, don't suppose," Basil allows.

"We call those myths," Gwen says. "Histories that are fantasy."

"Myths," Kalp repeats, committing the new word to memory.

He wonders if one day someone will be telling myths about him, The Deeds of Kalp, the First-Aglunated of Earth.

KALP'S CLAIMING Gwen and Basil for his Unit at the holiday celebration seems to act as tacit permission, and three other Aglunated Units form within the Institute within the season. It should be surprising to Kalp that Derx is among one, but Derx always seemed to be about single-minded selfish pleasure, so it is not.

But, as with all joy, Kalp is beginning to learn, comes sorrow.

Word gets to the media and press of Earth about the union between Kalp, Gwen, and Basil—a mixed-race Aglunate and polygamous marriage that makes several religious factions and parental rights groups absolutely furious. Kalp tries to point out to the first microphone shoved at his face, on their own door step, that they have not undergone the actual bonding ceremony yet, but Basil says "Not helping!" and drags him away from the camera as Gwen protects her belly and says, "No comment, no comment!" over and over again.

They stay home from work for a week, hiding behind locked doors and drawn blinds. Basil has taken apart three different radios and their components have begun to vanish into a device that Basil takes pains to keep from the view of Kalp. They let the chickens out afternoons, so they may have some fresh air, and they must feed the chickens through a small gap in the patio doors. For three days the papers carry an absurd image of Kalp's hand throwing bird seed into the back garden.

Finally the police and the government manage to draw up suitable penalties for the reporters who hound the little house they share. Several are arrested, all are charged, and the reporters leave them alone, at least in person. The shirt vendor in Gabriel's Wharf and the pub owner in London both sell their photographs of the trio to "gossip rags" for an obscene amount of money, but the people of their own village rally around the Unit and keep their lips sealed, and block the news vans deliberately with their own cars at intersections.

The mayor pulls several prominent citizens together and the town holds a baby shower-cum-congratulations party to show their support of their local heroes. It is in the same small square that the Friday market occurs in and in gratitude, Kalp buys up whole flats of *osaps* and turns them into Daiquiris for the occasion.

In an effort to curtail the pressure from the press, the Institute oh-so-gently suggests that Basil and Kalp make an honest woman of pregnant Gwen, and both marry her already. They decide on a quick and informal Aglunating ceremony, to honour Kalp's contribution, and it is attended only by Institute employees and one conscientiously chosen team of a reporter and photographer. There is a splashy yet tasteful spread in the London and New York Times filled with full-page colour photographs and a quick write up about the history of Aglunation and triad families. Personal information is completely omitted, though it does not stop the lower rags from speculating.

The British love their tabloids, and Basil's mother calls the day after the article is published to say that she is making a scrapbook. Basil groans at the phone.

Scandal sells papers, and once they are Aglunated and their humble speeches to the press have been recorded and run, Kalp's Unit is no longer scandalous. Kalp learns the words "husband" and "wife" and rather likes the connotations of ownership that are implied by them.

The world moves on to other, more sinful people. Anti-Integration protests move to Moscow, where a human and an alien have professed to trying to get pregnant together via in vitro. Basil or Gwen or Kalp's faces periodically reappear in the tabloid news when someone with a camera phone catches them canoodling in public, but otherwise the fanfare dies.

On those rare spotlight days, Basil spends hours on the

telephone with his mother and sisters, reassuring them of his personal happiness and safety. In every conversation, Basil promises to visit his family with his Unit, once the media circus dies. Later, he promises. Always later.

Kalp eagerly anticipates later's arrival.

Gwen always looks miserable when Basil hangs up, but walks out of the room when Kalp suggests she call her own parents; that they probably worry for her.

Kalp wishes his parents were here.

He thinks—he's sure—they would be happy for him.

Besides the ever diminishing picket lines at work filled with angry people waving rude signs at their car every morning, things start to go back to normal. It is now March and the world has ceased to be white, for which Kalp is immensely glad. Now he can forego shoes again. There are three more months before the baby is born, and Gwen is determined to continue to live normally until she absolutely cannot. She refuses a lighter workload, or the Institute's offer to telecommute, and comes in every morning same as ever, only waddling a bit more now and taking far more frequent trips to the toilet.

Kalp teaches Basil, lesson by lesson, how to massage Gwen's feet and back in a way that relieves the pressure that the extra weight of the child adds, by demonstrating on Basil first. This usually leads to more intercourse, and Basil does not seem to mind. Kalp certainly does not. Basil tries to repay Kalp in kind and slowly gets better at the massaging technique, the more he practices.

Kalp slowly learns about human bodies, about the different ways to press Basil into ecstasy, to rub Gwen into sighs, about little nubs of flesh, about orifices, lubrication, preparation and pouncing, and about what fits where. He is surprised at first that human men have no pleasure orifice near their genitalia, but approves of the biological compromise that is the evolution of a prostate.

Eventually the progression of her pregnancy means that Gwen cannot participate in intercourse as often any more. She complains of discomfort and aches and concern for the child, but enjoys the massages and professes that she is "just fine with watching." Basil and Kalp are fine with it too.

As a gift for Basil's natal day celebration in late March, Gwen surprises everyone with tickets to see a live concert by an artist named Raquel Winkelaar. Kalp has never heard of her, and neither has Basil. Basil suspects that Gwen was given them by a press agent who wishes to cash in on their lingering celebrity, but she neither confirms nor denies the accusation. She smiles and calls them a surprise from a co-worker and nothing more.

Kalp caught Gwen conversing in quiet tones with Agent Aitken yesterday afternoon in the cafeteria. He has a fairly good idea from whom Gwen received the tickets.

Gwen is not so heavy now that she cannot manoeuvre herself into the concert hall under her own power, so she does not see why they cannot go. They do not know what kind of music it will be and agree not to look the artist up in order not to spoil the surprise. However, the concert is being held in a very posh symphony hall in London, so the men don the same suits they'd worn to the holiday party in December and Gwen wiggles into a red sheath dress that accommodates her stomach and makes her look surprisingly delectable.

They are late for the opening act as a result.

They sneak in as the curtains close to allow for an unseen equipment change. If the press *was* lying in wait, the hour at which they arrive seems to have sent them packing. March is still too chilly to wait around outside of a concert hall on chance for a few blurred, and now illegal, photographs.

It is not until they're seated in the auditorium and the first screeching wail of an overpowered electric guitar rips into the air that the three of them realize with horror that this is an *electronica show*. The curtains swoosh open to reveal a flashing metallic set refracting screamingly bright neon lights. Kalp claps his ears to the side of this head and whimpers. All of his fur stands on end and he can feel his skin rippling in an effort to *get away get away get away*.

Kalp cannot hear anything but the painful screech of the

throbbing bass line, the grinding wail of the syncopated counter rhythm. He tries to stand, to flee. He feels his feet go out from under him, the gratefully familiar throb of Basil's hands under his armpits, hauling him up the aisle towards the doors and away from the massive speakers. He wraps his fingers around Basil's arm and squeezes too tight. Gwen is right beside him, trying to use her body to get between Kalp and the speakers, shrieking at the humans who have surged into the aisles to dance. She yells at them to move, to get out of the way. The concert goers are impeding their progress.

When they finally reach the parking lot, Basil and Kalp collapse onto a median mounded with soft, wet grass. Cold ground water seeps into Kalp's pants and stains them. Basil wraps his body around Kalp's, his chest against Kalp's, his arms heavy, his thigh thrown over Kalp's hip a familiar, grounding weight against the agony that rips through him. Gwen fumbles herself to her knees, rubbing her hands down Kalp's over-sensitized skin on his head and ears and neck over and over, trying to smooth out his fur, to soothe his jarring discomfort.

Had he the ocular glands for it, Kalp is sure he would be crying. Oh, it *hurts*.

And then, suddenly, it hurts a different way. There is a sharp pain in the back of his head. Basil's body is suddenly ripped away and he can just barely hear Basil shouting over the ringing after-pain that still ripples all over his body. He reaches blindly for Gwen, but she is gone, too.

There is another sharp pain in Kalp's stomach, and then his face. He feels one of his teeth break and slam into the back of his mouth.

Someone is *kicking* Kalp.

"Fucking freak!" a voice shouts, right beside his ear and Kalp *howls* when the hard heel of a boot grinds into his fingers.

Now he can hear Basil shouting, threats and promises and horrible, horrible swear words.

Then he grunts, and there is a slapping sound and the cracking of breaking bones and someone is shouting "Fucking faggot, fucking faggot!" over and over again.

And Gwen…Gwen is begging. "No, please," she says, and Kalp cannot see for the dark blood that is now running into his eyes, but he can hear her sobbing, her own yelps as she too is struck. Kalp is appalled. Who would strike an expectant mother? It is inhumane, monstrous! "It's Basil's, it's not his, *please!*"

"Get her!" screams the same harsh voice that called Kalp names. "Get the freak baby!"

And Gwen screams, so high and so desperate that Kalp balls his hands up and bares his fangs and throws himself in the direction of the sound. He meets a body, hard and male and *not Unit,* he can tell by the smell and feel, and he rears back, snarling and snapping his teeth as the punk tries to kick Kalp off.

"You will not harm her!" Kalp says and sinks his sharp teeth into the tender skin under the punk's ear and rips.

Something hard—a baseball bat, perhaps, Kalp thinks—strikes him repeatedly in the back of the head, but Kalp does not let go. Consciousness slips away, and Gwen is still screaming.

Kalp still does not let go.

WHEN KALP wakes, he knows much time has passed. He is slightly surprised to have awakened at all. His hand aches, and he looks down to see it encased in bandages. His head aches too, a spinning nauseous pain in the back, where it is supported carefully by a stirrup that is keeping it from touching anything. A quick probe with his tongue reveals a broken gap where his front tooth used to be, and there is a sharp discomfort in his stomach. Even his skin is still tender from the horrible music.

He does not remember a lot past the first screeching wail of the guitar, but he does remember the taste of blood in his mouth, the surging fury, and Gwen's screams.

Gwen!

Kalp tries to sit up. The agony brought on by the movement rips a soft cry from his throat.

"Kalp?"

It is Basil's voice. The restraint on Kalp's head, pushing his ears flat, keeps him from being able to turn to the side to find the man from which the voice originates. Kalp tries not to panic, but he wants to *see* his husband. Thankfully, Basil limps into Kalp's field of view, leaning heavily on a cane. Perhaps Basil is just as desperate to look into Kalp's eyes as he is into Basil's. The skin around one eye is florid and swollen, the same colours as Kalp's favourite Hawaiian shirt. The eye itself is flooded with blood, all the white gone that entirely human, too-vibrant red. There are stitches sprinkled beside his eyebrow. Kalp doubts that the resulting scar would be very visible, not like Gwen's.

Basil smiles and it is thin, like it hurts too much to mobilize so many muscles in his face.

"Where...?" Kalp tries, but it hurts too much to get much more breath than that, and his mouth is gummy and dry.

"Don't talk," Basil says. He hobbles around the foot of the bed to the side. He pulls a chair up beside the metal rail, just inside Kalp's field of vision, and drops himself carefully into it. He lays aside the cane so it does not clatter, and picks up a small cup of water from the bedside and holds it to Kalp's lips.

Grateful, Kalp sips softly, knows that if he imbibes too fast it will only make him ill in this condition. The fuzzy, gummy feeling is washed away.

"We're in the hospital," Basil says, answering Kalp's question as he sips. "The cops came, someone called them on their mobile, thank God, but not before..." He stops and tips the glass again.

When Kalp has had enough water, he says, "Gwen?"

Basil goes white.

Kalp swallows heavily and feels his stomach roil despite how much care he took with the water.

No.

No, Kalp does not believe it. He will not be widowed a *third* time. He refuses.

Basil hisses out between his teeth. "She's...alive," he says, as if the term is something he needs to debate. "She's still asleep but they think she'll wake up…soon. She's, I mean…*she's* pretty much fine— there's some bad bruises, some, um, road burn, but they really only went after, uh…there was some surgery, to fix all the damage they caused inside, and *Gwen's* fine…ex-except for…but not…" His eyes get wet and he reaches out blindly, wrapping his fingers around Kalp's arm. Kalp bends his good fingers back and grasps Basil's hand, as comforting as he can be when he is this immobile.

"The baby?" Kalp asks. Not because he wants to, but because he has to; he has to *know*…

Basil shakes his head once, slowly.

Kalp's eyes burn.

Basil buries his face in the hospital sheets covering Kalp's side, hands threaded in utter despair on the back of his head. Kalp wraps his good arm around Basil's shoulders and rubs in small circles. Basil cries so hard it sounds as if his soul is being wrung out into each tear.

WHEN GWEN wakes two days later, the hospital staff moves the three of them into a private room. They do this to keep the grieving family together, and safe from the press. It also allows them to use fewer security guards.

Gwen is inconsolable. The damage inside of her is irreparable, the doctors explain. It is a wonder that she did not bleed out on the asphalt.

For Gwen, there will be no second child.

Basil weeps and Kalp holds him, his eyes burning, and Gwen… stares at the wall and says nothing.

She only responds to the touches of her Aglunates, communicates in curt head gestures, and refuses food until the nurses threaten to strap her to the bed and force sustenance on her via intravenous tubes. Gwen is not best pleased by the threat, so she eats her Jell-o morosely and drinks the orange juice. That satisfies the nurses for now.

Gwen might not take being held down again very well, and everyone knows it.

Kalp is relieved that it does not come to strong measures, though he is worried for the state of Gwen's mind. She has not, he thinks, cried for her dead child yet, and that scares him more than her silence and fasting.

Worry burns like a hot stone in the bottom of Kalp's stomach, in the back of his throat, and he spends every moment of every day fairly sure that he is about to puke.

Three days pass in this manner, and every time Kalp awakens from his unconscious phase he is more exhausted than he was going into it.

Every time Gwen turns down food, the nurses tell her that she's lost a lot of blood and that she needs to get up her strength, and it makes Basil flinch. Kalp thinks it is utterly cruel of them to keep reminding Gwen of what she has *lost,* and finally says so in a very loud and perhaps less than civil manner. The nurses, who up until now have treated him like some sort of exotic teddy bear, get round-eyed in horror and flee. When they return to bring the required meal a few hours later, they look ashamed.

Good.

The nurses seem to have forgotten that his kind come equipped with a mouth full of very sharp teeth and fingers tipped with dark, strong nails. He has reminded them.

Kalp thinks, uncharitably, very early one sleepless morning, that if his kind had come in their full force, they could have just *taken* the Earth as their new home, instead of begging for a place among its cruel multitudes. Their weapons had not been particularly advanced, but they had been different enough to perhaps have afforded them the advantage.

Kalp regrets the thought instantly. He loves his Aglunates and would not have seen these fragile, wet creatures burst like a ripe fruit under the cruel heels of his world's ruthless dictators. No, there are some things that Kalp is glad have passed away.

More days and nights blur together, and Kalp is unsure how many have passed, how many sunrises and sunsets he has missed, how many times he has looked at Gwen or Basil and looked away only to find that the quality of light outside of the window has shifted dramatically.

TRIPTYCH

The police come and go and come and go. They take fingerprints and statements and more statements and more fingerprints. They take DNA samples, and fibers, and hairs. There is security footage, they explain, of the inside of the concert hall and of the parking lot. The same someone who called the police on their mobile then began to film it with the phone's camera. It is a very clear video and the evidence is obvious.

What Kalp cannot understand is why this person chose to hold up a phone instead of choosing to try to save a child's life.

Basil calls it Genovese Syndrome, and the Bystander Effect.

Kalp calls it cowardice.

No charges are being laid against Kalp's family, even though the man that Kalp bit did not survive his wounds. It was self defence, the police say. The others have been incarcerated and will stay in jail for the rest of their natural lives. They are charged with willful first degree murder in the case of the baby, and attempted murder for the rest of them. The crime is so well known, so closely followed, and the evidence so clear cut, that it bypasses the usual tedious waits of the legal system and goes almost immediately before a judge. Out of deference for their horrible loss, none of the Unit are forced to attend the circus of a trial, and Kalp and Basil are able to give their accounts via webcamera from the hospital room. Gwen still is not speaking.

But the press are not so forgiving.

Kalp has committed murder, they say. He ripped out the throat of a boy high from a concert. He is dangerous. He is an animal. None of them deign to mention that he was attacked first, that he was protecting his wife and their child. There is such a backlash that the Institute has to tighten security protocols and a police escort is required to accompany Kalp's Unit home when they are all well enough to take care of themselves, and each other.

Things in the house are quiet. The atmosphere is damp with sorrow.

Gwen spends a very long time saying nothing. Basil talks for hours on the phone with his mother. Kalp lies in his nest and wishes he could cry. All three of them sit together in a small huddle on the sofa and watch the chickens in the garden through the patio glass door.

WHEN GWEN finally speaks, it is a week later, and the first word she says is "Gareth."

She is sitting on the sofa, staring out the window.

Basil drops the teacup he was clutching and rushes to sit on the edge of the hearth and clasp Gwen's hands between his own. Kalp comes inside from where he had been sweeping out the chicken coop.

"Gareth?" Basil repeats, clearly begging for more, for explanation.

Kalp fears that this word will be the only one that Gwen speaks, but no, she takes a breath and goes on.

"My Uncle Gareth—I wanted to name the—" she stops speaking abruptly, throat closing up, and she sucks in a hitching, shuddering breath. Tears, fat and hot, drop over her eyelashes and roll down white cheeks, and Kalp slips over the back of the sofa to cradle and rock her against his chest.

Basil climbs up onto the other side and kisses up her scar and down her cheeks and over her lips, hands around her arms, her shoulders, her waist, murmuring, "Yes, yes, Gareth, it's a good name. We'll name him that."

Kalp wonders how you can name the dead.

IT IS only later, when Basil calls the hospital to tell the doctor their deceased son's name—Gareth Trus Grey—that Kalp understands the symbolic ritual of naming the child. Doing so makes it—him—a person. With its status so altered, the survivors are free to finally mourn the boy properly.

Fifteen generations of Greys have been buried in the same cemetery in Salisbury Chipping, so they journey under the cover of night to evade the press. The drive into the city is long and wearisome. Dressed in matching sombre black, they meet the tiny white casket in the garden of ended lives, and lay to rest the body of their baby.

Kalp wants desperately to howl up at the moon, to fall to his knees and perform the Ceremony of Mourning, but they are trying to avoid attention. He must be silent and calm, and he thinks that Gwen's pain is still too raw to be able to witness his own breakdown.

For Gwen, Kalp must be strong. For Basil, he must retain his composure.

He will perform the Ceremony alone, later, in the closed safety of his own nest.

They cover the too-small box with fresh soil, lay a strip of verdant sod down to erase the ugly scour in the turf, and two large-muscled men with tears dotting their lashes struggle a stately grey stone into place above where the baby's head would be.

Side by side by side, the stones along the row read name after name, date after date, Grey after Grey, ending with "Gareth Trus Grey; never born."

"It's supposed to be me, next," Basil says, patting the top of the stone, the sharp slap of his palm ringing out across the still night, startling some birds out of sleep and into the sky. "That's my grandpa, my da, and I'm supposed to be the one here. Not…not him."

Gwen turns in his arms and howls.

The sound is muffled in Basil's neck.

SEVERAL WEEKS pass, and slowly the reporters slink back into the shadows. There is no story to be got out of such deep mourning, and even the most ruthless of paparazzi seem to have misgivings about mining the death of an infant.

Eventually, Gwen and Basil have to return to work.

Kalp is asked by the Institute to stay home. It is not an order, not exactly, but it might as well be. They fear it will not be safe enough for him to come out, not yet, and a security guard who is much better at Guitar Hero VI than Kalp is—especially with his new hand injury—stays to keep him company. The guard is Agent Aitken, the quiet, intimidating woman with enthusiastically curling hair and a stern mouth with which she alternately smiles or glowers. Kalp makes a pact with himself to never anger her.

It is also the day that Derx is shot between the eyes.

Kalp learns about it from the news first: a fatal shooting at the favoured restaurant of the employees who shun the canteen of the Institute. High powered bullets came through the plate glass window, sprinkling the diners around the tragic trio with shrapnel that sent nine more to the hospital. The reporters announce that there were two shot. One is dead, and one is en route to the hospital, in dangerous condition. A third bullet is furrowed in the back of one of the stoves, having travelled miraculously through the back wall of the dining room and into the kitchen without hitting a single body.

Kalp imagines it to be Gwen and Basil for an hour, before the news releases Barnowski's and Derx's names. Oh! If only Derx had not been such a snob, or if he had not been so against simple cafeteria fare…

Everyone from the Institute is sent home early, and Kalp is waiting at the door to usher Gwen and Basil in when they manage to force their car past the knot of reporters that has sprouted on the street outside of their house. Aitken shoves people away and yells things until the crowd disperses.

They lock the doors and draw the blinds.

Kalp feels like his life is spiralling down, slipping through his control, and he cannot quite get a grip on it, no matter how hard he squeezes. That night they perform intercourse again for the first time since the concert—they mark the date by the concert and not by whatever else happened the same evening—and it is frantic, desperate, clinging and gasping into mouths and holding each other tight enough to leave lurid marks behind; tight enough to prove that they are all still alive.

Nobody leaves the house the next morning, and the Institute does not call them to demand that they attend work. The whole building is shut down for the day, out of respect for Derx's death. Every section, except the secret police brigade. They are out searching for the murderer.

This time, Kalp does puke. He spends all morning by the toilet and for an absurd second fears that he might be pregnant. But it is just fear and horror and too much loss for a body to handle, too much shock to go through. He drinks ginger tea after ginger tea, brought to him by a worried Basil, until his stomach is settled but his hands are shaking. Gwen stands in the shower with him, helps get the sick out of his fur, and off his snout, and he kisses her scar, kneels down and kisses her flaccid belly over and over and over.

On the second day, there is no news on the killer, but only the humans are allowed to come into work, for fear of someone else being shot. Basil and Gwen leave reluctantly, and Kalp passes the day feeding his chickens and trying to beat his own high score on the video game machine and emailing answers to the questions Basil asks via his BlackBerry. They are strange questions, questions that are far more theoretical than Basil has ever asked before, and Kalp isn't sure how to answer many of them.

Kalp is only an engineer, not a quantum physicist.

Basil comes home with a thick, glossy black briefcase with a no-nonsense lock under the handle, and when Kalp asks if this is what Basil was asking him about all day, and could he see it, Basil turns pale and shakes his head and goes to put the thing away in the safe under his desk.

They are informed that night that an Earth-style funeral is being planned for Derx, once the coroner has completed his investigation. A more formal Ceremony of Mourning will follow, and Kalp mentally prepares himself, writes notes about what he has to teach Gwen and Basil, what they must do and say. They have to be there. As his Aglunates, it's only proper. Then maybe they will go to the other cemetery, to the other grave, and repeat it there, a private circle for just three. Three pairs of arms can make a circle easily around a little grave.

On the third day of Kalp's confinement—and he realizes now that this is what it is—a fox steals into the garden and attacks his chickens. Two flee into the hen house safely, but the third's wing is broken and one of its legs chewed and there is a series of long gashes that bleed freely from its head to its ribs. Kalp chases away the fox with an angry snarl, and a flash of bigger, sharper fangs, but it is too late. The chicken is dying.

Kalp is distraught. He does not know what to do. He cannot seem to contain his anguish. It is just a chicken, Kalp knows, and it is ridiculous to wail so and carry on for a mere chicken. But he cannot help it. He tugs at his ears and makes the high keening sound of sorrow until the security guard that is staying with him in the house calls Gwen in a panic. She and Basil leave work early and come home. Basil speeds illegally, because they get to the house much faster than they ought to, and Gwen tells Kalp that there is nothing to be done for his feathered pet. There are only two choices—it dies slowly, suffering, or she can break its neck and kill it quickly.

Kalp agrees to let her end its suffering, and covers his face with his hands. The revolting snap makes Kalp retch, and the texture of the little death makes his skin feel dirty. Would Gwen break his neck, he wonders, if he asked? He hurts so much he can hardly stand it.

He needs a distraction, so together he and Gwen strip the chicken's carcass, removing the few still-beautiful wing feathers (which Kalp wants to keep as mementos), taking out its innards. Gwen says they should eat the chicken, it would be a waste not to, and besides, it may help Kalp come to terms with its death. She admits that this is the same thing her father told her when her pet piglet got snared in a barbed wire fence when she was a child. There is a discussion about accepting the death of a beloved pet. Kalp tentatively broaches the topic of her family again, but she will not say anything more.

Basil resolutely stays in the dining room with his paperwork and the mysterious contents of the locked black briefcase until the chicken no longer resembles a chicken, and instead looks like food.

Since Gareth, Basil can no longer look at a mass of raw flesh without vomiting violently.

They eat the chicken dinner in silence, and retire to their now-shared bed. They only sleep, everyone too emotionally wrought to do anything more than lay in the dark and clutch each other's hands.

On the fourth day, Barnowski dies in hospital. He succumbs to the wounds he sustained trying to get between Derx and the sniper. The coroner must process his body too, and they push back the funeral to bury the lovers together. Edgar, understandably, quits the Institute.

So do seven others.

On the fifth day, Kalp receives a small package in the post addressed to himself.

Who on Earth, quite literally, would send *Kalp* a package?

Kalp sets it on the top of his chest of drawers, too agitated to open it now. He cannot quite decipher the words that the letters spell out on the box; he sees the address at which he lives, and the address from which it came, but it is just a string of numbers – RR#3, Cnty. Rd. 1475, ON., and the word CA-NA-DA. He says it out loud: "*Sanada.*" He does not know what a canada is or where it may be, or why all those numbers are 'ON' it, and in a pique of annoyance at his own meagre abilities, even after so many months of study and immersion, he abandons the package.

He is too fraught with frustration and curling worry to deal with what probably amounts to hate mail from someone who did enough research, read enough newspaper articles, watched enough special interest television programs, to find him. Whatever is inside the slim paper-wrapped box, he is fairly certain that he will not like it.

He should discard it immediately, he knows. Possibly it is even dangerous, a threat. But there is something powerful about finally receiving mail of his very own, and so he will keep the package— just, never open it. It seems an overly emotional choice, but Kalp is as satisfied with this compromise as he ever will be, and he puts it from his mind.

He tries to calm down in a hot bath. It works for a little while, but then the lack of emotion-distracting sound gives his mind too much time to wander, and he imagines Basil and Gwen at the restaurant where Barnowski and Derx...

He goes down to the basement of the house to howl, so as not to startle the security guard who is in the garden, hand-feeding the remaining two chickens. They seem sad to have lost their companion and will not eat unless it is from the palm of someone's hand.

By the time his Unit returns home, he has succeeded in forgetting about the package entirely. The three of them do not sleep in his nest as often anymore, so he rarely has occasion to enter his own room. When he does, it is with a purpose distracting his mind: to fetch clothing or towels, or drop more paperwork onto the top of the dresser. Gwen and Basil rarely sleep at the same time, trading off turns in their old bed. Kalp, unable to face the thought of a nest devoid of his loves, often naps during the day on the sofa or in their bed.

There is one horrible argument, shouted and glared across the dining room table, between Gwen and Basil about the hours Basil has started to keep, about how he is never home, that all he does is work on the accursed *thing* that is in the locked black case—and Kalp curls his ears down and says nothing and just watches the way their shoulders shake and their chins wobble, listens to the way they deliberately prick at one another with hurtful accusations, and wishes he could do something, that he could just *say* something to fix it all, to make it all the way it was before the concert.

For the next week, Gwen and Basil are told that they must attend work early. They are not allowed to inform Kalp why, and return home pale and drawn, sore and miserable. They begin to wear earpieces every day, even at night, in bed. The pieces are quiet. They only chirp occasionally. When they do, Basil or Gwen, whoever was signalled, excuses themselves from the room that everyone is in—kitchen, living room, basement—and goes outside to speak, where the wall and the wires and the world keep Kalp from overhearing. Kalp knows that he should not be hurt that they are not allowed to have their conversations where he can hear, but he does not blame them.

He blames the Institute.

He blames them for the poor food in their cafeteria that drove Barnowski, Edgar and Derx to seek a meal elsewhere. He blames them for driving up hype about "the aliens" with their secrecy and military alliances. He blames them for not handling his own marriage more gracefully in the face of the press. He blames them for not stifling the growing flames of anger and hatred among the protesting humans. He blames them for driving this wedge of silence and growing mistrust between him and his Aglunates.

Sometimes, when he is feeling the most abandoned, he blames the Institute for ever introducing him to Gwen and Basil at all.

He blames himself for volunteering.

He blames himself for not going to attend the medic with Trus, for not going shopping in the market with Maru.

He blames himself for sleeping late the day the sky turned black.

THE DOUBLE funeral is on Friday morning.

Kalp sits in the pews of Barnowski's Catholic church and holds his weeping Aglunates, and wishes that he could cry to alleviate the burning pressure in his own eyes. The weather is unfairly pleasant when they, as a congregation, move into the adjacent cemetery. They deposit the caskets in their places, Derx's name on the headstone beside Barnowski's, under the selfish, unblinking eyes of the paparazzi cameras kept at a distance by the low cemetery walls.

All of the Aglunated Units move to the basement of the church, graciously offered by the priest. Kalp learns that this is rare, that the religious leaders of this world do not often tend to allow other rituals of other cultures to occur in their own basements, and Kalp is grateful for the exception. For all their talk of tolerance and peace, the humans have a disturbing habit of being segregated and opinioned. It is an unfair assessment, for there was racism and exclusionary behaviour on his planet, too, just as Kalp assumes there is among the less-sentient fauna of this planet or any other. But he cannot seem to recall the bad through the haze of nostalgia any more.

The Aglunates sit in a circle big enough to metaphorically accommodate the corpses of the deceased, if they had been there, and perform the Ceremony of Mourning.

It is the first one Kalp has attended in the last two years, since the disaster. He had very much hoped to be done with this rite forever.

Kalp knows full well that he should have been performing the Ceremony of Welcoming today, instead.

He should have been celebrating the birth of his child.

They return to their house at sunset, weary and weak. Kalp falls into his unconscious phase on the sofa while watching the chickens, and wakes in the dark to the sound of a chirruping ear piece. Basil answers and turns even whiter as he listens. Kalp can hear every word from the other end, and this time he does not bother to be polite and tune it out: "Lalonde tried to push Pias out of the way and…the bullet went straight through. We lost both of them. I'm sorry, Doctor Grey, I know you and Lalonde were close."

"I haven't worked with her in years," Basil says softly. "Not since we finished the Array." But there are already tears dotting his eyelashes. He scrubs at his eyes and pulls his fingers away wet, staring at the moisture as if startled to learn that he still has any tears left to cry. Humans are sometimes bizarrely unaware of their own bodily functions.

"We need you to come in, Doctor."

"I can't. Gwen will need—"

"This is not a request, Doctor Grey," the voice says sternly. "We found another one of the…devices. We think it was the shooter's. We're still not sure what it does and…well, you need to come in."

Basil sighs, every bone weary, his posture drooped and his forehead pressed against the wall. He scrubs his face with his hands.

"Fine," he says. "Yes. I'll leave in an hour."

"Now, Doctor."

Basil screws up his mouth, frowns and says, "Yes, yes. Now."

He clicks off.

Kalp is sitting up on the sofa, and Basil turns to look right at him. Like he knew the whole time that Kalp was awake. And is not sorry Kalp listened in on a clearly top secret conversation. But Basil does not tell Kalp that Pias is dead, either.

Kalp did not know Pias, but he feels that he deserves the right to be told all the same.

"When Gwen gets back from the chippy, tell her I'm sorry, I got called in."

"Yes," Kalp says. Does Basil know that Kalp heard everything, and that's why he's not bothering to relay anything about Lalonde and Pias? Or is he flatly not allowed? Is this Basil's way of getting around the rules?

Maybe.

Kalp's still not sure whether he should be hurt by this, or not.

"Tell Gwen I…" he trails off and stares at his hands. "I'll be back when I'm back."

"Yes," Kalp says softly. He lies back down and pretends to go back into unconsciousness while Basil gathers up his briefcase and BlackBerry, and walks out the front door.

Kalp desperately hopes that Basil will walk back in it.

The package.

It is only now, brought on by the thin-strung silence that permeates the dark, strained atmosphere of the house, that Kalp remembers that someone sent him a package. He feels immediately guilty. What if it had been a warning about Pias?

He goes upstairs and retrieves it from the back of the top of his chest of drawers. It has almost fallen down the crack in the back, covered in the very beginnings of a thin layer of dust and several magazines which Kalp has read from cover to cover to alleviate boredom during his confinement.

He sits in his nest, noting that the sheets smell stale and need to be washed—maybe he will do it tomorrow—and tears the paper wrapping open carefully with his nails.

There is a single sheet of paper inside the box, folded many times over to fit inside and inscribed in even, machine-generated hand to disguise its origin. It is indeed addressed to him. It reads:

> *Dearest Kalp;*
> *You do not yet know me, but you are known to me.*
> *You must listen very seriously to what I say. Your future depends on it. You will be next to be killed otherwise.*
> *Do not go to the Institute. Go into hiding. Depart.*
> *If you wish to live, you will do these things immediately. There will be more assassinations. You are involved.*
> *There are those who watch you constantly. Things will be changed. There can be no mixing, now.*
> *I will call you here when you have fled.*
> *--E*

There is an address under the signature, and Kalp doesn't recognize it any more than he had the sender's address. He knows it is in London, for it says as much, but nothing else. Kalp sets down the letter, hands shaking. Then he turns to the box. It is stuffed with fluffy white fibers which cradle a small lump of burnt metal. Kalp does not recognize it, but he pulls it from its nest all the same. He revises his assessment—it is not a single lump but some sort of electronic or mechanical component that has been fused together by the heat of what appears to have been some sort of flash explosion. Kalp turns on his drafter's mind, and can find the wiring and nodes in the mess of what's left. Possibly it is even still workable, though what it is meant to do or how he is supposed to use it, Kalp cannot guess.

It is mostly triangular, with melted pockmarks and holes burned straight through it. It is made from an alloy from his world, and it looks vaguely like a gun, a piece of some wire sticking out to resemble a trigger, a cylindrical intake that could double as a barrel, but Kalp knows that it is not. They did not have guns on his world; at least, not like the kind that the humans carry.

It is, for all intents and purposes, useless.

He sets it back into its nest of protective fiber, and wonders what the intended message of the lump of metal is. The letter is a threat—could this be a piece of a symbolic object from Kalp's world, one that was destroyed to provoke a reaction? Maybe it is meant to be an illustrative example of what they are going to do to Kalp if he doesn't depart as ordered.

Kalp suddenly wishes he'd paid better attention to the attacks in Moscow, the riots in Dallas, the protests in Toronto and Washington.

Then he wishes that it really *was* a gun, because he feels so vulnerable here. Alone with only Aitken to protect him. Just one human against…this. All of *this*.

Next, the letter said.

He is next.

He will die next, and everyone in the world knows where Kalp lives now.

Depart, the letter says.

No mixing. End your relationship and go. Or die.

The front door opens and shuts, and Kalp huddles down into his nest, terrified. The assassin has found him already. He has lost a week, by failing to open the package. He debates the merits of trying to go out the window, but the security guard is still watching the house, and Kalp is not stupid. He knows the guard woman is there to keep Kalp in as much as she is there to keep others out.

Footsteps come towards Kalp, and if he was not so terrified, he would be able to make out the heartbeat over the sound of his own pattering system. When the door opens, it is just Gwen carrying greasy newspaper cones filled with fish and chips.

Kalp sighs.

Then he feels ridiculous.

He shoves the letter and the package under his mattress and goes to relieve her of her burden. He tells her that Basil has departed and does not know when he will return. Basil has taken the black briefcase with him. It is locked, but Kalp knows at least a little bit about what Basil is hiding within it. He can hear the electricity, the whine of the dying batteries, the yelping jump of the poorly repaired circuits of some device inside the box.

Kalp and Gwen watch a film on the television and eat their fish and chips. Basil's goes cold on the coffee table.

Kalp thinks he will return to his own nest tonight. He needs time alone to contemplate what he should do next, to whom he should speak. But before he gets up to depart, there is another chirrup from Gwen's ear piece.

Before Gwen can even turn it on, Kalp knows.

This time it is Ogilvy and Vius. Ogilvy had a child from her first union, and the little girl is in the hospital, being treated for severe shock. She saw it happen. They are calling around to everyone who worked on the same floor, trying to decipher who the child's father is, so they might locate him. Gwen was not close with Ogilvy, so she has no answers for the caller. The caller bids her good night, and then tells her to stay with Kalp and keep a wary eye.

Gwen nods, and clicks off. Then she goes up into her bedroom and comes back downstairs with a pistol strapped to her thigh. Kalp feels his tongue go dry.

Kalp has never seen Gwen carrying a weapon before and it frightens him. He tries to kiss her, to gain reassurance that it is not he that she is arming herself against, but she refuses him. When they decide to share a pot of tea and watch the chickens, she sits with the gun on the far side of her body from him, where he could not possibly make a stealthy grab at it.

This hurts more than anything else she has done.

Gwen no longer trusts Kalp, not because of something that Kalp has done, but because someone else has told her not to.

Basil does not come home that night. Kalp waits and waits for the phone to ring or for Gwen's ear piece to click to life. He waits for someone to tell them that Basil is dead. No such call comes, but Kalp loses a whole night of sleep anticipating it nonetheless. By the time the sun rises, his eyes are heavy and his body feels slow and stupid from lack of rest.

In the morning, Agent Aitken returns, relieves the night guard, and sits quietly on the sofa. Nobody plays video games.

Gwen goes to work early and Kalp sits in his room and reads the letter over and over again, trying to screw up the courage to sneak out of the house and flee. He turns the lump of metal and wiring over and over between his fingers, as if he would learn the sender's intent by osmosis. He does not know where the address leads, but maybe he can figure it out once he is away. They have cut internet access to the house, so there is no way he could use the online mapping function and search engines to decipher the intended meeting location. Worse, Kalp cannot even gain access to his email to ensure that Basil is well.

It is a tedious, knife-edge afternoon. Every sigh, every squawk, every sound of something dropping or every puffing automobile bang outside makes Kalp's ears shoot up and his lips curl off his teeth. His anxiety is making Aitken more and more nervous, and her nerves are jangling across his. The chickens' pecking no longer feels like hail, but bullets across his face. He wishes they would just stop moving.

TRIPTYCH

When night falls, Gwen and Basil are still not home. They do not answer his phone calls to the office, and the night security guard refuses to try to gain contact for him. Kalp scrolls through the television news channels obsessively, trying to find any indication if there has been another shooting, or where the object he was sent is from. As far as he is able to ascertain, there has not been a shooting or an explosion, but would it be broadcast now? There seem to be so many secrets, so much dishonesty. The Institute has probably dropped a blanket of silence over everything.

He wishes he could just *ask* and get answers. But nobody will listen.

The night passes and the day comes and still nobody will talk to him, and his Unit still does not come home, and a sense of foreboding builds in Kalp's chest, hot and twisting and awful.

Something terrible is coming and he must get out of its path.

The letter has made its demands clear enough. If he wants to live, he must depart, but he fears the security guard will surely shoot him if he tries to go. Gwen and Basil will be angry if they return home and he is gone, but Kalp thinks maybe once he has fled, once he has found where he must go, he can call here, leave a message with the answering service or on the machine, tell them about the package. And they will be safe, that is the most important thing.

They will *all* be safer if he goes.

Maybe he can simply leave the letter and the object behind for them to find. There is not much information in it, and Kalp has already read it so many times that he has the threat memorized. He could tear away the bottom of the page, keep the address for himself.

He loves his Aglunates.

He will find a way to leave them word, and when the assassin is caught, they will reunite. He must go.

Plan made, Kalp rips the bottom of the letter off and carefully places the slip of paper in his pocket. He lays the remainder of the letter out carefully on the dining room table, where it is sure to be seen immediately upon walking into the house, and puts the triangular metal lump on top of it to keep it weighted down.

He wants them to know why he has fled. Perhaps then, when they

213

have read it, when Basil has had the chance to decipher the meaning of the metal object—as Kalp has no doubt that Basil will—they will not come after him with guns, but protection.

Kalp wonders if the rendezvous location will be a trap, but decides to worry about escape first, and then try to decide whether to meet his correspondent or not.

The letter is vague—purposefully so, Kalp suspects, in case it is intercepted—and Kalp is still unsure about whether the writer really is foe, or if they are friend. Either way, he cannot stay in this house. He will be killed if he does, and worse still, like Barnowski and Lalonde and Ogilvy, Gwen or Basil may be killed along with him.

Kalp takes two apples, and all of the cash currency in the house that he can find. He feels guilty for taking from Gwen's purse without first asking permission, but Units share and he can pay her back once they are together again. Aitken is outside on the street, doing a sweep of the neighbouring houses and gardens, and Kalp knows he has about ten minutes before she returns, if no one else arrives here to draw her attention back to the house before that time is up.

The fingers of his injured hand have not regained their full strength and mobility yet, but Kalp thinks that if he stands carefully on the chicken coop roof, he can boost himself over the garden wall and into the neighbour's courtyard. From there he can scale the next garden wall, and then the next, slipping between rose bushes and barbeques and patio sets until he is at the end of the street.

Kalp knows which way London is, and if he moves fast and stays low, he thinks he can follow the train tracks all the way there. Once in the bustling city, he could lose himself in a crowd and…

Kalp has forgotten for a moment that he is not on his home planet, and this realization settles with a startling bump. He is in a place where he *cannot* get lost in the crowd. He stands head and shoulders above everyone else, his skin and fur too colourful to miss. They will be looking for him, too.

No, no public places. Sewers, maybe? Or catacombs, until he can find a library with the internet freely accessible, somewhere he can sneak into after closing to determine where the address is leading him. Never mind that Kalp has no idea how to break into buildings. He is an engineer. He is pretty sure he can figure out how to use a crowbar. The vibrations of the electricity in the walls are tell-tale enough that he thinks that he may be able to hack the tiny computer lock pads with which some of the doors on Earth are equipped.

He wraps his fingers around the latch of the patio door and depresses it quietly. The slow, sad roll of the door seems to scream along his skin. It seems abnormally, incomparably loud. Aitken surely must have heard it, must hear his pounding heart and nervous breaths, he is certain, for they are so loud in his own ears. He stands still, waits for the sound of heavy boot-tread footfalls, of shouted orders to "freeze!", and marvels when they do not come.

Softly he takes a step into the courtyard, toes splayed wide so the pads are near silent on the stones, arched to keep his nails from clicking. A wide step and he is on the grass. Its tickle gives him no pleasure right now.

Another step and he is over at the wall, his hands raised and gripping the top when one of the chickens sticks a curious head out of the blue box. It cocks it first in one direction, then the other. Kalp goes still and watches the bird, hoping that it will love him enough to withdraw and let him go in peace.

But no, he has trained his pets too well.

The chicken sees Kalp and associates him with food. She waddles down her ramp, flaps around the corner and over to him and squawks loudly, demanding the seed she expects to be in his palms.

"No, no," Kalp hisses. He drops to his knees, tries to pinch the sharp orange beak shut with his fingers, and gets a particularly painful nip in response. He chokes off his own involuntary yelp and closes his fingers around the neck of the bird.

It squawks again, this time a high and terrified sound.

Kalp cannot bring himself to tighten his grip.

There has been too much death in his life, and he does not wish to add this innocent animal to the list.

Instead he shoves the chicken, protesting loudly, back into the coop and pulls the mesh wire door closed. He straightens up and that's when he hears the click of Aitken's pistol coming off of safety.

"Back in the house, freak," Aitken says.

"Please," he says, without turning around, eyes still on the chicken coop. "I was…" he hesitates, ears pulling flatter against the back of his neck. "Only…the chickens, you see, I was…"

"You were on top of the coop. You were trying to go over the wall."

"I…" He cannot lie. He is so weary of lies. "Yes," he says, then: "Please. I have to go."

"No," says a voice, and it is not Aitken's.

When Kalp turns, it is Gwen who stands in the living room, between the mantelpiece and the large sofa, with her gun aimed at his head. Aitken is behind the dining room table, aiming across one upraised shoulder, keeping Gwen out of her line of sight. But Aitken's eyes are on the metal lump on the table, and they are white around the edges.

It takes a second to decipher the utter terror on Aitken's face, but then Kalp realizes: *Aitken has seen this object before.*

Kalp swings his gaze to Gwen, to see if she too knows it, if this is something of which the Institute is aware, but Gwen's face is closed off. Kalp searches for the woman he loves in that face, the woman who held him and kissed him, who cleaned the sick off his fur and who let him be the father of her child, who opened her home and family to him. Who has lost so much.

All he can find is the loss.

Three others in black are standing behind her with their pistols raised as well. Gwen is in black, too. She has her hair pulled back, under a blank black ball cap, and she wears a tactical vest Kalp knows is lined with Kevlar. She looks alien, more unknowable and surreal than any human that Kalp has ever met, because this is the same body but not the same *person* inside of it. The world dips and swivels under his feet, and Kalp thinks it is because of the shock of seeing Gwen dressed thus, though it may also be from the lack of sleep and the hormones coursing through his blood to keep him alert in this time of danger.

"Gwen, please," Kalp says softly. "The letter…"

Gwen's eyes flick to the letter, sitting partially refolded on the table. Her hand never wavers. She scans it and frowns.

"Who is E?"

"I don't know. It is a threat, Gwen."

"It's correspondence! It's *orders*," Aitken shouts, and her lips are curled in a sneer that seems triumphant to Kalp. It is terrifying.

"No," Kalp says quickly. "I am not part of anything. This was just sent to me."

"Where are you supposed to meet?"

"I don't know—the address is strange." He pulls it slowly out of his pocket and tosses it at Gwen's feet. The paper flutters to the carpet like a wounded bird. She looks down, but the gun still doesn't move.

"That looks just like a safe house address," Aitken says. "He's not supposed to have access to anything."

"I do not!" Kalp insists.

Aitken sneers. "Traitor."

"No!"

"Shut up!" Gwen growls. "If it's what you say, then why didn't you tell me about this?"

A hot surge of bitterness wells against the inside of his chest.

"Why did you not tell me about Pias and Lalonde? Ogilvy and Vius?" Kalp counters, aware that anger will do nothing to help his situation now but unable to hold back the petty accusation. "You do not *trust* me anymore Gwen."

"No," Gwen says, "That's not true."

"You do not love me."

"That's not true!"

Gwen's hands are shaking now, and her eyes are wet, and that heartbeat Kalp is so very fond of is racing so fast he fears for Gwen's health. For a moment he worries for the baby, but then he remembers and his whole innards sink. No baby. And now, no Gwen.

Gone.

"Please," Kalp pleads softly, hands held out, up, to prove they are empty. "Please believe me. It is not me. How could it be me?"

From outside, Kalp hears a car arrive in the front drive and stop, the engine clicking to a cease. The car door opens and closes, a soft metallic *whump*, then there are thick-soled, booted feet coming up the driveway.

Basil comes in the front door. Kalp can hear him, his well-loved heartbeat, the zinging zap of his keen mind. He too is dressed in black, and he is holding the locked black case in his hand. He stops just inside the door, gobsmacked. The BlackBerry that was tucked under his elbow is released in his shock, and it falls to the tiled entry floor, the back cover snapping off, the battery skittering away and into the kitchen.

"Basil!" Kalp begs. "*Please.*"

Basil looks surprised by all the guns. "What, Gwen? What's going on, I thought you said—"

"I've done nothing!" Kalp says. "I swear to you. I love you, and I—"

"Don't you *lie to me!*" Gwen shrieks and everyone around her blinks, but otherwise does not move. Kalp winces at the shrillness. "Is it you, Kalp? Are you killing these people? Are you doing it?"

"No, no, I've said I swear. I just received the letter, it is not me." He lifts his hands, reaches towards his lover's face. "Gwen," he says softly, pleading. "*Gwen…*" He takes a step forward, and then he hears the gunshot.

It is flat and surprisingly loud in the small space.

It sounds nothing at all like the gunshots in the films that Basil likes.

He hears Basil scream, and Gwen scream, and then he is on the floor and he does not know how he got there. The back of his head hurts. His chest hurts more.

This, Kalp thinks, *this is unfair.* Has he not suffered enough in this lifetime?

Suddenly his whole torso burns, radiating heat and agony like a small star. When Kalp tries to take a breath, all he hears is a gurgling sound and he gets a mouthful of blood. Kalp guesses that no, apparently he has not suffered enough.

But like his beautiful black chicken, someone has finally put him out of his misery.

He feels Basil's hand on his cheek and he turns his face into it.

He doesn't want to close his eyes, but there is blackness all the same.

He reaches out for Gwen, and she is not there.

Part III: After

BASIL PERCIVAL GREY HAD been given two things by his father.

The first was his admittedly horrendous name, which had earned him more than his fair share of scorn in the school playground and the rough teasing of his two older sisters. The name had made Basil defiant from the beginning. It had made him snappish and standoffish in school. Combined with his higher-than-average intelligence and his smug acknowledgement of his superiority to his classmates, Basil had grown up into a right proper snot.

The second thing that Basil's father had given him was imagination. When it seemed that Basil's loud self-importance and brash isolationist tendencies might nurture him into a serial killer or vicious bully, Richard Grey had taken his son aside and handed him H.G. Wells' *The War of The Worlds*. Basil was stunned and shamed and torn.

Stunned that such intellectual and scientific literature existed, full of stories about people like Basil—smart and keen on science and useful in the saving of worlds. Shamed, because Basil knew that if life out there did exist, then perhaps his own petty behaviour would not be very impressive to any docile or benign visitors that arrived and interacted with him (as they inevitably would, Basil being the pinnacle of intelligence on Earth in these limited childhood fantasies). Torn, because he wanted to be someone worth meeting, but was unsure where the first step on that journey should fall.

Humbled, Basil quickly moved on to Asimov and Shelley. He returned to the comics magazines that he'd scorned in school, and found that they had matured with him and now portrayed at least a lingering pseudo science. Suddenly the petty territorial squabbles of the playground seemed so inconsequential. So…childish.

Basil and Richard spent long afternoons repairing hobby radios and telling each other stories of the sorts of wonders the future would hold: the technology, the people, the exotic places they would visit on Venus and the moon. Basil quickly found his penchant for verboseness, and the cares of the persecuted schoolyard victim fell by the wayside. All that mattered were the stories, heard, read or told, and afternoons working on the radios with his father.

Not long after that, Richard Grey died in a tunnel accident that could have been prevented had there been an advanced enough communications system in his mine. Basil turned that vast and fantastic imagination onto science. The hobby of tinkering with radios became an all-out obsession with building a better telephone, a faster electric wire, a clearer radio signal. Aliens and spaceships and beings from other worlds still held a place in Basil's heart, but as he forged forward his imagination and creativity were harnessed into technological advancement.

Basil had lost a father, but retained his lifelong love of the fantastic.

He rose quickly to the top of his classes, and in university had a penchant for leaping to strange and strangely workable theories before most of his classmates even understood the questions they were being asked to solve. He had a reputation for figuring things out in the most eccentric and science-fiction way possible—an observation which was meant to be an insult, but which he took as a compliment every time.

And then the Institute had come knocking on his door.

All of which had somehow, in some strange and circular way, led him *here*. Here and *now*, to the place where all of it, everything, came together and defined his life in ways that Basil could never have imagined. In ways that *mattered*.

Or, used to matter, at any rate.

Basil tried very hard to feel guilty.

He closed his eyes and stuck out his tongue and concentrated.

Nope.

It just wasn't happening. A glance to the side told him that Gwen wasn't feeling particularly repentant either.

Court martialling, firing, whatever; the Institute could terminate or redirect their careers as much as they wanted, could lock them both up until the end of forever. He still wouldn't feel bad for what he'd done.

The thought that they might not be imprisoned in the same jail only caused a light surge of concern in Basil. He'd sort of run out of his life allotment of panic, pretty early into his first few assignments with the Institute.

There was really very little that could cause Basil to panic now, not after the aliens had first arrived. Not after the realm of science fiction that he had so enjoyed in his youth had suddenly come to inhabit the reality of social fact. Once you'd seen spaceships descending slowly, limping through the haze to hover just under the cloudbanks, not very much could get you wound up—unless it was meeting one of those aliens, and, heh, marrying it.

Hm, well. Yes, Basil supposed he got himself *worked up* often enough, but that was sheer social pressure and a very strong sense of self-preservation, and was in no way at all like real, actual animal panic. Yes.

Of course, the panic-denial did not change the irrefutable fact that Specialist Gwen Pierson and Doctor Basil Grey had gone back in time, saved Gwennie's life, and figured who and where the people who were assassinating their co-workers were.

Which, by the way, had been completely fucking *cool*.

Well, and by that, Basil also meant *terrifying* and *horrible* and *awesome*, but the latter in the extended biblical sense of the word and by no means as the playmates of his youth had crowed while imitating animated martial-arts-performing amphibians. Cool.

He tapped his toes against the leg of the bench, grimaced at the hollow ring it produced, and stopped. Gwen had already glared at him enough for that particular offence today, but he couldn't help it. He was hopped up on too much of Evvie Pierson's tea and not enough sleep and the glittering glory of knowing that once again he was *right* and his peers were *wrong wrong wrong*. Time travel *was* possible. Ha!

Through his body flowed the pounding, addictive adrenaline rush that came on the heels of an invaluable breakthrough or an amazing discovery. It was a rush that had borne him through countless hours of gruelling graduate lab work in his younger days, and through the pig-headed politics of the PhD programs he'd waded through before the divine hand of the United Nations Specialist Program had plucked him up out of the riotous and unwashed masses of computer geeks.

Basil's knee jittered of its own volition. It had been at least forty minutes since Gwen had given up and stopped telling him to quit biting his nails. His shoulder didn't hurt any more, but it was stiff. If he were anywhere but here, he might have asked Gwen to rub the soreness away. Instead he put a hand down on his knee and tried to calm down.

But he couldn't help it. He was *anxious,* eager even, to get back to the research lab. He had left a program running to triangulate the data he'd coaxed out of the first Flasher before he and Gwen had ducked out of the lab—soldiers on both sides of the door—on the pretence of needing a pee. They'd snuck into the armoury with the newly minted Flasher secreted in his pocket (the old one he'd been dissecting in order to reverse engineer the new was left as a decoy, temptingly visible on the drafting table, nestled in the open black briefcase), and had serendipitously taken off for twenty-nine years ago.

Now they were, well, *now,* and he and Gwen had the *who* and a pretty educated guess at the *why*; it was just the *where* that was missing, and that was so close that Basil could practically taste it, mingling with the aftertaste of Evvie Pierson's excellent-if-undercooked breakfast.

Unfortunately, getting to his office was going to pose a bit more of a challenge than Basil thought he could surmount at the moment. Seeing as, of course, he and Gwen were locked in the brig.

Yeah, oops.

Court martial for going against direct orders to, as Agent Shelley had so crudely put it when he had found them kitting each other out in the armoury, "not activate that goddamned thing, Grey, or I fucking swear I'll—no, don't you da—"

Basil assumed that there had been a "—re," but by the time Agent Shelley might have uttered it, Basil had been standing next to Gwen on an autumn-crisp lawn, watching a baby about to get its throat slit open.

The stark cruelty of the intended butchery had frozen him in his tracks, mortified. But not so, Gwen. For once, Basil blessed the Institute and its goddamned covert ops training. She had raised the P90 and fired a head shot without any hesitation. And then, of course, things had gotten *weird*.

And now they were locked up and waiting for their boss to arrive to berate them, and possibly lay formal charges, but possibly also to actually listen to what they had to say.

Gwen reached out and twined her fingers, soft like always but with strange new trigger calluses, around his.

"I don't..." she said, and she sucked in a breath and stopped. Basil looked straight ahead, out of the bars of the cell, because that's where she was looking. By some silent pact they had agreed not to try to read the expressions on each other's faces. Instead, he squeezed her hand.

"I can't remember," she finally confessed.

Basil felt his own breath hitch. He knew, without her having to articulate the entirety of it, what she meant. "Me either," he said. "There are no gaps where people could...people should *be*, but that doesn't..."

He stopped, because the rest of the sentence, the rest of the *thought* was plainly the most horrifying thing he'd ever been forced to contemplate. Even compared to the thought that back in that house that was theirs, there was a brown-purple stain on the cream carpet that he would never want to clean out.

The back of his eyes burned for a second and he blinked hard. No, no. No tears, not now, he was so *done* with crying now, thank you very much. He was pretty sure he'd done more tear-shedding in the past year than he had in his entire long childhood of using them to manipulate his mother and shame his older sisters.

Against the back of his eyelids, Basil watched a parade of clips from sci-fi's greatest hits: white-garbed pacifists in saucer-shaped vessels, futures where "us" peacefully and prosperously interacted with "them"; intermingled were the tolerance commercials and the press conferences about cooperation and harmony with which the Institute had bombarded the world's media. It was all so attractive and, Basil feared, impossible.

His childhood had lied to him.

Gwen's long breaths got short, and there was a single tell-tale sob that she choked back with more detached efficiency than Basil ever remembered her having before…Before Kalp, before Gareth, before an entire sentient species had been near-exterminated and limped to Earth begging for help. Somehow, all of the wonderful experiences that had filled Basil up and out, made him *more* than he had been before, had made her *less*. Restrained and cut off and quiet.

"I feel like someone's died," Gwen admitted, and her words were damp with sorrow. "Maybe no one has, but I feel like, maybe…I feel like I should be in mourning, anyway. For more people than…than just him. I'm so…*sick* of death."

Basil wrapped his free arm around her shoulders, hauled her in close and kissed the thin, long-healed scar that arched across her forehead. Kalp had once called it beautiful, because among his people the display of scars from under the fur had been very, very personal. He kissed the scar a second time.

Squeezing her fingers again was the closest he could come just now to agreeing with her out loud. Her sweater smelled like the farm, and the ugly shoulder pads were a comfortable pillow on which to rest his chin. But the sweater was a relic of Gwen's childhood and that made Basil's heart thump up into his throat every time he contemplated what it meant. Time travel. For real.

Basil tried very hard not to think about what might have happened if it had been his own childhood they had arrived in, rather than hers. Gwen had no illusions that Basil was a geek, but to have been seen by his wife as he was when he was sixteen...spotted, in a swag tee-shirt from a comic book convention that was two sizes too big and hadn't been washed in a week, sitting in his room alone, watching something ridiculous with leather bustiers and pointy eared warriors slamming at each other with foam props and cheesy dialogue. It wasn't until grad school that the forced time sharing a lab had taught him how to rein in his more obsessive monologues and learn to enjoy his pursuits in a more moderate manner. He'd had a few girlfriends, made some acquaintances, made some rivals in the advanced engineering departments, and ran a tabletop roleplaying game on Friday afternoons in the common lounge. Meeting Gwen had been accidental, though providing the filthy little poem for translation had been a calculated attempt at sparking lust in her in return.

This whole getting married thing hadn't remotely been Basil's goal. But here he was.

Married, and in the brig. Sort of.

In jail, but not in trouble...married, but a widower.

Basil turned his head, breathed in the lingering tickle of Evvie's floral shampoo on Gwen's hair, and said, "Hey, so, what would you have thought if you'd caught me as a kid being a nerd. What would you have..."

He stopped, smiling. Gwen had fallen asleep. Or was, at least, affecting sleep convincingly enough that Basil couldn't tell the difference.

After a long, drawn out passage of time characterized by Basil's best go at absolute stillness, he sighed and laid his cheek back against her shoulder. He fell asleep leaning into her space, chilly and alone. Gwen was gone to the world, her own emotional upheaval wringing from her body all the energy, and perhaps desire, to remain aware.

But Basil kept waking up. Every time he closed his weighted eyelids, all he could see was Gwen as she was now, laid out on that deadening green grass of the Pierson farm, blue eyes staring upwards blankly, face white and bloodless, her head cut open in a neat, red line. He saw

Kalp, purplish blood burbling from the gunshot wound like a fount, maroon in the soft light of the side-table lamp, mouth hanging open, black tongue lolling. Basil gasped and shivered, and couldn't seem to be able to swallow without it tasting like vomit. Eventually he gave it up as a lost effort, sat up, wrapped his fingers one around another, and resisted the urge to sit on them. Gwen slumped into his warmth.

Someone he loved very much was…gone. And wouldn't be coming back. Again. Basil pressed the heels of his hands just under his eyebrows.

His eyes felt puffy and gritty and he wanted to wash his face, lay down in a real bed, take a pill to make him sleep without dreams, make him forget everything he'd seen and lost. Just for a little while.

There was a muted beep. The guard by the door answered his ear piece, frowned, then turned his back on the cage of prisoners to unlock the door. Basil straightened and dislodged Gwen gently, which snapped her back into full military alertness. The door swung open.

Framed by the light in the hallway and looking furiously resplendent in his anger, was Director Addis. His fine chocolate suit was rumpled and what little tightly curled white hair he had left was rocketing upwards like a broken sofa spring.

Director Addis did not look like a happy man. As if to underscore Basil's assessment, he said, "I am not a happy man."

Gwen and Basil exchanged a glance but otherwise stayed silent. Gwen disentangled her fingers from Basil's and smoothed down the front of her sweater, her face carefully masking over into that blank soldier stare that Basil still hated so much, more now that he knew what rollicking turmoil it confined.

"Tell me," Addis snarled, stomping across the room with more echoing force than his slick dress shoes should have been able to provide. The soldier locked the door behind him.

"Tell me," Addis repeated, his splendidly smooth South African accent growing jagged in his anger. "*Why* do I have two of my own Specialists in the brig for defying orders, breaking into the Institute Armoury, stealing weapons, and manufacturing non-sanctioned technological devices that they claim make people *travel in time?*"

"So you read our debriefing statement, then?" Basil asked, and couldn't keep the cheeky tone out of his voice. The statement had been agonizingly and deliberately vague. It consisted of just forty-five words:

We were trying to triangulate the origin location of the Flashers when we detected an anomaly that could only have been another Flash. I set our Flasher to arrive at the same location. We ended up in 1983. We killed an assassin and returned here.

Basil, who had always been accused of biting verboseness, had been perversely pleased with his tantalizing brevity.

Addis said nothing, so Basil asked, "Going to let us out so we can go take care of my triangulation program?"

"The program ended six hours ago," Addis snapped. "Agent Shelley is reviewing the results now. We've already called MI5 *and* Scotland Yard. They're sending down a forensics team and a veritable platoon of SWAT guys as we speak."

Startled, Basil looked at his watch. Huh, it was twelve hours off, then. Forward.

Well, that was a bit of an unforeseen side effect of travel in the fourth dimension. He would have to write a paper on it, or something. Not that the U.N. would let him publish it, say, *ever.*

Addis ran his hands over his mostly bald pate, encouraging the frizzing curls into an even taller display of frustration. "I don't know what to do with you two. You *snuck out* of your own lab, for God's sake, and stole two automatic assault rifles! How am I supposed to handle that in front of the Board? I understand how the loss of your Aglunated could spur feelings—"

"We know where there's evidence that could put these fuckwits away for life," Gwen cut in. She had not moved from the bench in the cell, hadn't immediately sprung to her feet like Basil had when the director had stormed in, hadn't grabbed the bars and blurted.

She had just sat there. Waited for the director to tell Basil off and get out all his frustration and anger, his professional humiliation.

Now she said again: "We know." The tidbit of vital information dangled between the three of them like a particularly tempting carrot.

The director sighed, wrapped his own hands around the bars like he was the one imprisoned, and rested his high dark forehead against the cool poles. He let out a soft and surprisingly vitriolic string of cuss words filled with more impropriety than Basil thought such a proper man would have known.

Addis sighed again, and asked his shoes, "What do you want?"

"All charges dropped," Basil said, immediately.

"And we'll be the only ones going to fetch this evidence," Gwen added.

Addis winced.

"Let us go alone, or I won't tell you," Gwen said again, and her voice was eerily monotone. "You'll need it to put these assholes away for the rest of their miserable, small little lives," she reminded him.

"Gwen—" Basil said, at the same time the director looked up and said, "But—"

"There's no danger," Gwen whispered, and that hard, military look was gone. She looked human again, and vulnerable, and miserable. She looked like a woman who'd fought viciously with her mother, who had hated a dead lover unjustly, who had buried her child.

She looked like *herself.*

"It's just...it was my..." Gwen tried to say, and then stopped.

Basil cleared his throat. "It's personal."

The Director frowned. "Doctor Grey, I still can't—"

"*Very* personal," Basil said with a particularly emphatic eyebrow wiggle.

Addis stared at them for a long moment. Basil felt his stomach tighten, worried that he had just made things worse. Finally Addis narrowed his eyes and shook his head once.

"Fine, yes, okay," the Director huffed, and gestured for the guard to unlock the cell door. "But we nail these guys first. Then you go get the evidence. Our first priority is to make our people *safe.*"

"Oh, yes," Gwen said, and rose and walked out of the cell.

"Debriefing with security in ten, then." The other man's dark eyes narrowed. He blew out hard through his nose. "You're a shrew, Pierson," he said to Gwen. "But you're good. I need to know what you're bringing me back."

"An aircraft," Basil said. "And its pilot."

"Mint condition and unharmed?" Addis requested. His tone held hope but his gaze was resigned.

Gwen smiled. "Absolutely not."

Basil stopped just outside of the cell door to pat Addis on the shoulder and added, "Also? I'll need that Flasher back. And can you get someone to bring me my wallet of tools and the bag of electronic components that were in the back pocket of my tac vest? Cheers."

Addis scowled and didn't answer, but as Basil broke into a trot to catch up with Gwen, already out the door of the holding room, he saw Addis poke his head into the hall and wave a junior specialist over. Good.

They were led by the guard first to cold, industrial change rooms. They were handed new clothes and given a few moments of privacy to wash up and prepare for the debriefing that was about to follow. Gwen said nothing, changing and splashing water from the sinks on her face and under her armpits with brisk efficiency. Right now, she was the soldier the Institute had taught her to be. The brief glimpse of hurting woman Basil had seen in the cell was hiding again, waiting; the empathic daughter was just a memory.

Basil felt sort of foolish washing up in a sink, though he piled a big marshmallow of foaming soap into his hand and thoroughly scrubbed the corners of his eyes and along the rough scrape of his stubbly beard. It felt fantastic.

Following her lead, Basil changed quickly; clean, new shorts straight from the cellophane packaging, crisp new uniform trousers, new socks, a new shirt. His old clothing he deliberately and viciously crammed into tiny balls and punched into the already full wastepaper bin. It was satisfying to see the bloody, dirty pants vanish under the mounds of wet paper towel.

When he looked up, Gwen was watching with wide eyes.

"My father's tee-shirt," she said.

Of course she'd want it.

Basil felt stupid. He reached back into the bin, pulled out the shirt, shook the paper towel detritus off it, and folded it neatly. He placed in on the top of the pile of Gwen's carefully folded borrowed clothing—the teal sweater with the hideous shoulder pads, the tight high-waisted jeans.

Her eyes were slightly glassy, her pupils wide, her gaze locked onto nothing in the middle distance, her mind in the past.

"At least I won't owe Mark a shirt as well as a new Betamax," Basil said, inching up behind her. Gwen was no wispy starlet, and for that Basil loved her. He circled those wonderful hips, that waist that was thick with muscle, the soft little spot under the belly button he adored so much. There was a still-healing line of white flesh, firm under his fingertips, that ran across her tummy—proof that he'd almost had a son, once.

They'd all been strong enough to get through that, but only because they had each other. How would Basil get through this? When the soldiering and the debriefing and the technological tampering was over, when it was just him and Gwen alone in a small dark room, how would he...? He shook his head. Later. He'd think about it later. Right now, he could just hold on.

Gwen made a sound, and it took Basil a second to figure out exactly what it was meant to be. Her laugh was so flat—yet at the same time, so genuine—that it hurt to hear it. He pressed his forehead against the back of her neck as she made that terrible mirthless sound, sucking in her warmth along with the air he gulped desperately, trying to absorb her temporary amusement to fend off his surging sorrow.

In control. Right.

Kalp was dead.

It hurt to hear it only between his ears, so he said it out loud: "Kalp is dead."

It had only been about fifty hours since Kalp had denied anything to do with the letter on the dining room table and Aitken had panicked. Basil wasn't even sure that he really *knew* that it happened, even though he'd already cried a lot, even though he'd been in mourning since before Kalp hit the ground.

Like an equation too dense for him to decipher, it just hadn't *sunk in*.

Gwen turned around and kissed him hard on the mouth. "Yes, he is," she said, and then they went to the meeting to tell everyone in the debriefing room why.

AS THEY took their seats, the same junior specialist that Addis had waved down placed a tray in front of Gwen and Basil—sandwiches, cups and a pitcher of water, and the components and tools Basil had requested. Excellent. Addis may not have liked their methods, but he seemed to be perfectly cognizant that the best way to catch the bad guys was to trust them.

The room around them filled slowly with people who looked like lawyers, boardroom suits, someone who looked disappointingly like a psychotherapist, and of course, their peers—Agent Shelley and his special ops squad. Lastly, Agent Aitken slid in to the seat furthest away. She wouldn't meet their eyes.

Gwen picked at her sandwich but Basil dug in, alternating hands in order to have one free at all times to get at the small circuit boards inside the sleek, half-melted shell of the Flasher they'd used to get to 1983. He had an idea, but he wanted to make sure it would work before he told anyone, even Gwen, about it. Gwen glanced over, recognized the ruined Flasher, and jumped to the erroneous conclusion that Basil had hoped she would: that he was trying to *repair* the Flasher and not remake it. Gwen turned away again, back to glaring poisonous daggers at the top of Aitken's bowed head.

"Well?" Shelley said, when everyone was assembled.

Gwen cut a glance at Basil. "Go ahead," he said, a piece of lettuce catching on his lower lip. "Busy here. Besides, you know how much of it you want shared."

So Gwen stood up and told them.

As she narrated the last thirty hours—carefully edited to exclude the fact that the child they had rescued had been *herself*—the room was silent, disbelieving. Nobody asked for proof, but nobody quite believed either, and then someone in Shelley's squad said, "Does this change tomorrow?"

Basil looked up from his work, eyebrows drawn down. The crumb of some already-forgotten piece of bread crust fell from his chin. "Tomorrow?" he asked. A sense of mild dread pushed at the back of his throat. "What happens tomorrow?"

Shelley scowled at the agent, and it was clear that somebody had been telling tales out of school.

Gwen put her hands on her hips, and Basil knew that she understood the relevancy of the verbal slip just as well as he; something was planned, something that they were not supposed to know about, something that they were being shut out of purposefully, probably because of Kalp.

"Agent Shelley," she said. There was no patience in her voice. She was already slightly hoarse from speaking so long, and she sounded very, very fed up.

Tiredness and impotent frustration scratched against the underside of Basil's skin; he could only guess how irritated Gwen must be.

Some sort of nobility or soldier's guilt (probably relating to the fact that he'd been the one who assigned Aitken as Kalp's personal guard to begin with) tugged at Shelley's expression. Something within him quickly won, but Basil wasn't sure which side it was until Shelley spat, "Fine."

Shelley tossed a lurid red folder into the space of table in front of them, and Basil shoved away the empty sandwich tray to peer over Gwen's arm as she flipped back the cover. The first page was a slightly blurry aerial shot of some sort of down-on-its-luck factory and yard. Basil wondered if it was once filled with fresh-cut lumber or piles of shining roof tiles or corrugated metal shipping containers of tinned food. He supposed he would never know; all it was filled with now were some rusting piles of scrap metal and litter. The walls of the building were graphitized in a lurid yellow that Basil could see in the photo, painting bold splashes on the brick, but the angle and clarity robbed the words of readability.

"What's this?" Basil asked.

"Tomorrow's target," Gwen answered for Shelley. The head of ops gave a quick nod. "You've found the circle assassinating our people?"

Shelley snorted. "It's amazing how many people believe the urban legend that the traffic cameras aren't actually on or monitored. The last guy was careless. But," and here he paused and looked up and directly at Basil, "it wasn't until we went to search your lab after you two took off that we could find the final destination. We had him on traffic cameras all through London, but once he hit the countryside he was gone. We knew the direction he was *headed*—the Flasher residue gave us the location."

Basil felt himself colour, at once pleased that the program he'd written had worked and furious that they had gone in and hacked his personal computer. *Well, of course that's what they were going to do*, he chided himself. *You were missing. Besides, everyone on base is a paranoid bastard, lately.*

Gwen flipped the page. The next one was filled with military speak written with so many dense abbreviations and code words that Basil could barely follow it. Gwen's eyes skimmed over it and she nodded to herself, apparently approving of the plan that Basil couldn't even decipher.

"And for the non-grunts in the room, that translates to...?" Basil asked, looking up, exasperated.

Aitken's eyes flashed angry for a moment, then she went back to scowling at her own red folder. Shelley told them about the warehouse in a rural, half-dead community just outside of the metropolis, and the report that had gone to both the British government and local constabulary in the wake of the warehouse's discovery. The military had been called into service, asking for a squad of Institute Special Ops soldiers and a van-full of geeks to help them take the place out. The sooner, the better, which was why this meeting had originally been convened with Shelley and his corps in the first place: they were waiting for the head of the military squad to come in and debrief them. Gwen and Basil's presence—return—had just been convenient timing.

The operation was set for ten-fifteen in the morning.

"And you're not coming," Shelley added, closing his folder with a note of finality, his ink-black eyebrows squiggling down into a look of determination that Basil had seen quite frequently back when Shelley was helping him build the Array. Determined and bossy.

A hot flash of anger pressed at Basil's sternum, but was dampened almost immediately with sleepiness and mental exhaustion. He looked down at his nearly complete device and sighed. The fun had gone out of tinkering with anything months and months ago—after Gareth, if he was going to be honest with himself.

Work, work, work, and all of it just leading to…what? Not much of anything but more killing, more violence, more pain. Disgusted, Basil pushed his screwdriver away. He had joined the Institute to *make* things, damnit—alien toys and better technological solutions and bridges between cultures, not for black ops raids and ways to track down people like animals.

No, no, these assassins, these bigoted assholes were not "people." They had killed Kalp.

Basil picked up his screwdriver and went back to work.

"Excuse me?" Gwen said.

Basil felt all the little hairs on the back of his neck and arms stand upright. Uh-oh.

Gwen licked her lips. "Because we broke the rules but came back with a crap load of valuable intel, or because you're embarrassed that we gave you the slip when you were supposed to be watching us?"

Shelley went red around the ears and glowered. "You're fatigued," he finally answered, eyes cutting around the room to the tight gazes of all of the other agents. Basil's stomach tightened. Really, Gwen needed to stop picking battles in front of her co-workers. "You're mourning."

Basil cleared his throat. All eyes turned to him. "By which you mean that you don't want us there because we're 'too emotionally involved to be objective.'" The splotch of colour crept inwards across Shelley's cheekbones, flagging over his nose. "Which is exactly why you need us. We know things you don't."

Shelley snarled a "Dismissed!" at them, and Gwen and Basil had no choice but to obey it. Of course, they took their sweet sauntering time while they collected up their files and tools and trays, to make it very clear that they had no respect for his authority even if they still had to obey.

Aitken reached out to help Basil pile all of his mechanical bits onto his discarded lunch tray. One piece, something burnt and melted beyond any use, he thought, might have rolled onto the ground, but when Aitken bent down after it, she came up empty handed.

"I need more sleep," Basil decided.

Gwen left the room first, head high and face closed. Basil shut the door behind him. They exchanged a glance. In unison they turned towards Addis' office, and Basil smiled.

He reached out, ran his fingers down the inside of Gwen's wrist and tangled his fingers with hers. "I totally love you, sometimes."

"Only sometimes?" Gwen echoed with a snort. "I'm losing my touch."

But it was good to hold Gwen like this again and he would not let her make light of his very real need for a connection right now. Basil tugged her to a stop in the hallway and folded her close and kissed her forehead gently. Gwen wound down a bit, her shoulders descending from around her ears. The hyped-up adrenaline shivered across her skin as her anger dissipated and her weariness weighted on her back. Basil knew exactly how she felt. The urgency of the debriefing and the rush of finding out about the sting operation could only do so much to fight off the pull of sleep and grief.

They reached Addis' office suite and didn't bother to knock. His assistant stood to berate them, took one look at their faces and sank down into her chair silently. Basil let Gwen go towards the inner office first, deploying her like a weapon, a calculated strike. Gwen, blessedly stubborn Gwen, pulled up her shoulders and straightened them and stormed in, slammed her hands down on the desk and then pointed to the scar on her own forehead.

Director Addis jerked backwards, eyes white all around his irises, startled. He dropped a mug of coffee into his lap and winced. Basil flinched in masculine sympathy. Ouch.

"They did this to me," Gwen said very, very calmly when she was sure Addis' attention had been drawn to her scar. Basil stood in the door, leaning against the jamb. He watched and tried not to grin.

He knew that tone, that look, and knew from experience that Addis would eventually have no choice but to capitulate. "We went back and found me, there. A baby me. That's where we went, okay?" Basil was only slightly shocked by her method of admission; he knew that Gwen was saving that particular tidbit only for the most potent blackmail. Apparently, she felt strongly enough about being a part of tomorrow's mission to lay it out now. "I've been waiting twenty-nine years for the payback. I will be a part of the squad whether you authorize it or not."

Addis sighed.

"Also?" Basil added, and held up the small cell phone that he'd been tinkering with since their return. "Mobile Flasher Tracker." Addis' eyes sparkled. "But it's encrypted, innit." The sparkle faded.

"This is blackmail," Addis pointed out. Which...*duh*.

Gwen smiled, but her tone stayed grim. "Is it working?"

"Officially? No," Addis said. "I know you two are way too involved and I don't even know everything that's happened. Unofficially?" He looked down at his folded hands, clenched and dark against the slick surface of his creamy leather blotter. "My wife was killed by a drunk driver. Report to Agent Shelley tomorrow morning, Specialists. Get some sleep. Good night."

THEY COULDN'T bear to go home.

They were told that Specialist Wood had taken their chickens to live in her own back garden for a few days. A service had been called to clean the blood out of the carpets, and someone had packed up all of Kalp's personal belongings, probably as evidence. The house was safe to return to, now; no grim souvenirs remained.

But they still couldn't go.

Kalp was...Basil didn't ask where Kalp was. Probably the Institute morgue. Basil didn't know if the Institute had a morgue; but it had to, right? The Institute had performed autopsies on Ogilvy and Lalonde and Barnowski, so surely there was a morgue.

Somewhere.

He hated thinking about it, about Kalp far below his feet, quiet and cold and…not moving. Downstairs somewhere. Alone. Not sleeping. Just…just *not*. Basil curled up in a ball in his borrowed bed in the building's private suite—reserved for visiting dignitaries and officials, usually, but put at their disposal—and tried very hard not to think about it. About, about *anything*.

The adjoining bathroom door opened and Gwen padded out, naked save for the water droplets that still clung to the back of her bowed shoulders, the steam that followed from the shower, the faint drifting scent of a cloying floral shampoo. Gwen snapped the bedside lamp off, sinking the room into complete darkness, and pulled back the covers. A blast of cold air crept along Basil's spine, licked the bottoms of his toes, but then Gwen was there, shower-warm and damp. She tucked herself against him in silent misery, hooked her chin over his shoulder and said into his ear, with minty breath, "We should bury him beside Gareth."

Basil nodded and squeezed her as close as he possibly could and replied, "You should call your mother."

Gwen didn't react as if she'd heard, except for a quick tightening of the skin right between her eyebrows.

Seized by the notion, Basil said, "C'mon, it's the right thing. Right now." He steered her first out of the bed, then into clothing, then out into the hallways, then into their office.

The whole room had been tossed, probably in an effort to figure out where they had disappeared to. Basil snorted; it wasn't like even *he* had really believed that they would reappear where they had.

Basil ignored the minefield of scattered beads from their torn privacy curtain, clicking and sliding under the soles of their boots; he ignored that the contents of the drawers had been dumped all over the drafting table; he even ignored that his computer was off and he *knew* that he'd left it on before they departed.

What he couldn't abide was that Kalp's chair was lying on its side, futile and helpless as an overturned turtle, and looking just as sad. Basil paused and lifted it carefully upright, set it down gently on its feet as if it really were a living thing. He ran his palm across the backrest once, searching for...he wasn't sure. Residue? Body heat? A fine dusting of turquoise hair?

The chair offered him nothing.

The hollow thing inside Basil echoed once, a low pang in the place where Kalp used to be. Where he still was, sort of, but not... filling the space any more. There, but not there *enough*.

Basil looked up. Gwen was already sitting on her own pilfered desk, watching him quietly with sad eyes. Then she turned to the phone. She picked up and dialled.

Basil moved around the chair, giving it a ridiculous and yet respectful distance, as if the ghost of Kalp was really sitting in it and Basil didn't want to rudely bump his knee.

He'd give anything to be able to accidentally bump Kalp's knee right now.

Looking up at Gwen, hesitating before she dialled the last and fateful digit, Basil amended that thought. *Almost* anything.

Gwen held the receiver tight against the side of her face. Her knuckles were white. Basil longed to reach out and brush his fingers across them, remind her to relax. Instead he slid one arm around her shoulders, kissed the dusting of white hairs that clustered around the puffy end of her scar.

He was close enough that he could hear it when the phone began ringing on the other side of the planet.

There was a muffled click and then a voice that he knew, oh, so well, said: "Piersons, Evvie speaking."

Gwen sucked in a breath, sharp and a little scared sounding. A little *young* sounding, and Basil could hear it now; the pain that the rift between them caused, the child that Gwen had been when she'd shut her mother out of her life forever.

"M-mom?" Gwen said. Her grip strangled the handset.

"Hi, baby," Evvie said. "I'm so, so sorry about Kalp. I wish I'd met him."

Gwen sucked in another breath and heaved it out again in a wrenching sob that Basil could tell surprised them both.

"Come get your space ship, baby," Evvie said, so softly that Basil almost didn't catch it. "Come home."

"Yeah, Mom," Gwen whispered and turned her face against Basil's neck. "Soon."

"See you soon," Basil echoed, and took the handset from Gwen. He hung it up and wrapped his arms around her.

They sat that way until Basil's ass went numb.

He stood, punching his sleeping butt in an effort to bring back sensation, and Gwen turned away, pretending she wasn't scrubbing ferociously at her cheeks so nobody could see the salt stains there on the way back to their room. They returned through the lesser-used hallways, Gwen leading the way; Basil followed and didn't comment on this deliberate choice.

When they got back, there was a note on the door. Agent Wood had come by. She wanted to tell them that she'd transferred the chickens and their strange blue coop into the Institute's courtyard that evening, thought Gwen and Basil would be comforted by the sight of their pets.

Gwen and Basil stood together in the private room, Gwen's back pressed firmly against his front, her arms clasped backwards across his waist, his like bands around her shoulders. They stared out the window at the chickens two floors below them, fuzzy little fluffballs down in the Institute's courtyard.

They were no comfort at all.

A yawning ache swallowed everything underneath Basil's skin and even Gwen's touch felt too cold.

The chickens pecked at the grass that had gone to seed between the cobble stones, looking lopsided and lonely now that they were just two.

"AGENT PIERSON, report!" came the staticky hiss over the headset. Basil had to resist the urge to tap his own earpiece and demand a response of his own from Gwen.

Being the smart bloke left behind in the surveillance van *sucked*.

It reeked of B.O. and gun oil and overheating electrical doodads. The air conditioning had quit before they'd even gotten past bloody

Whitechapel, and being cooped up in a small space filled with whirring computers and twenty geeks and grunts had been no picnic. Basil had envied Gwen and Shelley and the rest of the Agents over in the military transport wagon, luxuriating in the cool breeze of a functioning fan.

Basil sat back in his chair in the far corner of the van. There were five different screens arranged in an alcove of computer banks around him, each with their own interface keys and ports. One was a radar that tracked all of their GPS tagged ops and military combatants, one was a sort of Google-Earth-on-steroids meant to work in tandem with the first, and one was for Basil's necessary split second calculations and computations just in case he detected some Flasher activity while en route. One was devoted to the computer chatter between the different units of the operation, and the last was an early warning system for the initiation of a Flash, should one of the targets choose to try to escape in that manner. So far, that station had been silent. On the console beside that screen, the cellular phone that had been altered into a Mobile Flasher Tracker lay waiting, a funny little dog spinning in circles on the screen saver, ready to jump into action to point its user to the centre of the temporal phenomenon.

Basil clenched his fists on his knees and stopped breathing, waiting for Gwen's response. After long minutes, she replied with an urgent, "I have an unlocked door. Going in…"

Basil sighed in relief.

"No," came the order from Colonel Wright, the mission leader from the military side. "Wait for the army. I'm sending them around to your position now."

Wright was two computer banks down from Basil, standing with purpose in the very middle of the surveillance van, frowning with a practiced air of paternal gravity at the screens, beret at a jaunty angle. Basil thought that all he lacked was a pipe, and had passed several long minutes imagining what type the colonel might prefer.

"But sir, I can hear them retreating," Gwen protested, and Basil felt his gut clench. Gwen was going to ignore the order, Gwen was going to barrel in and get shot and Basil was going to have to go to *another* funeral, another fucking *double* funeral with chillingly quiet caskets perched side by side. He was going to be left alone, the last one, just like Kalp had been after Maru and Trus. Basil would shrivel up if Gwen—

"No. That's an order."

On the other side of the radio, Gwen sighed. "Yes sir," she said, and went quiet.

Basil knew that tone, that little huff. Gwen had settled down for a good pout and Basil had never been so fucking grateful for her moodiness before in his goddamn life.

After a few tense seconds, a soldier reported that they had taken up position with Agent Pierson and would send her back to the van on Wright's order. Basil let out a long hiss of breath between his teeth, his lungs aching with relief—that was it, then. The army was going to take care of the arresting-and-shooting part and Gwen could stop skulking about and come back to where it was safe.

Colonel Wright surveyed the lay of his soldiers according to their GPS trackers. He waited half a second, frowned at a few shifting dots, scanned the heat cameras pointed at the buildings and snapped. "No time to wait for Pierson, it has to be now." He lifted his hand to his earpiece and said, simply and without any special inflection, "Okay, boys and girls. Give 'er."

Basil blinked—that was it?

No grand speeches, no kingly encouragement, no Shakespeare quotations? Basil decided that he needed to stop taking fantasy epics and police procedurals so seriously.

In the distance, Basil heard the first shout, the first loud, sharp pop of a flashbang round meant to stun the assassins into immobility; then, the quiet prolonged wheeze of a canister of tear gas emptying. He wasn't sure if the sound was leaking in over the headset or if it was coming from outside of the van.

He swallowed hard and tried to look calmer than he felt. His hands were shaking. Jesus, Gwen wasn't back yet. Gwen was *out there*.

"Agents, disengage when it is safe and return to base camp," came Wright's next command. Shelley and twenty out of his twenty-two agents barked confirmations of retreat.

Gwen, of course, was not one of them. Basil had not been able to keep track of who the other one had been, too absorbed in straining his focus to catch Gwen's reply. There was a pregnant pause, and then Wright lifted his hand to his earpiece again.

"Pierson, Aitken," Wright snapped, "the rest of the Agents have started reporting in. Get your asses back. You are not trained for intense combat!"

Aitken grunted that she would comply as soon as it was clear enough for her to run. Gwen said nothing. Basil made a harsh sound in the back of his throat, his whole body stiffening up, waiting for—fearing—that fatal, familiar cry, the sharp rapport of automatic rifle fire that could cut it short.

God, he really, *really* needed to watch fewer action movies. Geez.

A familiar voice by the mouth of the van caught his attention. Basil looked up as Agent Shelley, sweaty from his exertions, his palms and the side of his left arm covered with a fine white layer of gravel dust, bent his head to speak in low tones with the tactical commander seated by the doorway. Then Shelley moved away swiftly to the other transportation wagon.

The first cough of gunfire rang out. Shelley froze and threw up his hands instinctively, protecting his head. The reserve soldiers shoved him and all the other Agents that Basil could see through the narrow van opening to the ground.

Basil's heart shot straight into the back of his throat, expanding, blocking all hope of breath. His chest screamed for want of air, his eyes burned, teeth clenched. "No, no," he moaned.

The interior of the van, already sweltering beyond comfort, came alive. The air crackled and suddenly everyone was straining over the computer screens, yapping into their ear pieces and relaying orders. It was chaotic, made Basil's whole body shiver with claustrophobia. He pocketed the Flasher Tracker. Squeezing behind the ridiculously cramped chairs, sucking in his gut, he slalomed around personnel, feet feeling like they weighed a brick's worth each. He dashed for the door, for the open air, diving around the chairs and the flailing limbs. When he burst out into the world, the cool air slapped him in the face and turned each pearlescent rivulet of sweat arching over his forehead and down his nose into a splash of ice.

Another soldier shoved him back against the van, and the bumper jammed painfully against his ass. Basil clamped down on the automatic 'oof!' that wanted to jump out of his throat.

He grimaced, and the soldier shot him a glare and Basil raised his hands. *Not going anywhere, I get the idea,* he said with his expression, and the soldier nodded once and moved away to the far side of the van, towards the sound of the skirmish. The other Agents found their feet and dashed for the relative safety of their own van, parked around a low stone wall by the street.

Basil sat back on the bumper, ignoring the throb of a building bruise on his butt cheeks, and dragged the sleeve of his shirt across his eyes and over his forehead. He looked around, desperately. The Agents were loitering by the transportation wagon, tense, hands on the grips of the pistols in their thigh holsters or wrapped tightly around their P90s, tracking the progress of the fight over the earpieces, waiting for the order to reengage if necessary. Basil blocked it all out, white noise until he could catch Gwen's voice.

No word from her came, and Basil's neck got tighter. He tugged impotently at the zipper of his jacket, only to realize that it was undone all the way to his navel, exposing the broad black swatch of his tee-shirt, and not done up all the way to his Adam's Apple like he'd thought.

He was scared, and he wasn't afraid to admit it.

A familiar nipped cry arched over the sound of gunfire and Basil whirled towards it.

"Gwen." He started around the corner, heedless, unthinking, knowing only that he had to get to her *now.* He didn't pause to check that he had a gun, or even that he was wearing a tactical vest—which he wasn't.

Only the swift clap of a hand on one shoulder kept Basil from foolishly plummeting around the protective cover of the vans and into the fray. Shelley yanked him off balance, forcing Basil to sway back, to stop. Basil was surprised—the other Agent must have nearly vaulted over the stone wall to stop Basil that quickly. Either that or Basil's sense of time was getting thrown all out of whack by the adrenaline surging through his system.

I told you so, Shelley's face said, mouth a hard line of disapproval. *Too involved.*

"Gwen's hurt," Basil shouted, and because he had nothing better to do with them, frustrated and useless, he wrung his hands.

Shelley looked up, over Basil's shoulder and his eyes widened.

Basil blanched. "What?"

Shelley jerked his chin, and Basil followed the direction in time to see a pair of white-suited military paramedics dragging Gwen past the surveillance van, past the transportation wagon, and to the ambulance waiting on the far side of the warehouse's low brick gates. Basil had been warmed and worried by the ambulance's presence; foresight was marvellous, but it left a horrified and cold feeling in the gut of his stomach that they had been *expecting* people to get hurt.

By the time Basil had finished his sprint over to her, Gwen was conscious and seated on the rear fender of the ambulance, staring morosely at her empty hands. There were paramedics and latex gloves and someone shining a penlight in Gwen's eyes, which she didn't appreciate, if her scowl was anything to go by.

"Gwen, you *stupid...*" Basil started, but was too happy to see her alive, swelling gash above her eyebrow and all. "Are you trying to *prove something?*"

She blinked at him fuzzily for a moment. Then she groaned.

"Did that just happen?" she asked.

"Yes," Basil said. "I think so. What's 'that'?"

Gwen grimaced in lieu of a smile. The paramedic had just applied a gauze full of bright yellow iodine. Served her right!

"I think someone tried to brain me with a blackjack," she confessed. "I saw Aitken when I fell. I guess she scared him off."

"I...really? A blackjack?" Basil stopped, all the anger on pause. "That's sort of...Wow. Old fashioned."

"But classic."

"Kinda cool?"

"I wholeheartedly agree."

Their eyes met, gazes connecting over shared humour and worry, wry smiles twisting across their lips. Under the paramedic's swift hands, Gwen looked relieved. She also looked vulnerable. Tired.

But alive.

Basil sighed.

"So that's it, issit. All over, then?" he asked, hands jammed in his pockets, leaning one shoulder against the shining white metal. It was sunwarmed against his shirt, the heat seeping pleasantly into his pores. His ass started throbbing again at the angle, but he ignored it. He wasn't about to speak up and end up with his pants around his ankles in front of half of the Specialist Agents as a paramedic checked him over, too.

"Looks like," Gwen said and tried not to flinch as butterfly bandages were applied to her temple to hold the gash shut.

The paramedic slapped some fresh gauze into her hand and said, "Apply pressure for now." It was a testament to how weary and heartsick Gwen was that she readily obeyed.

Someone in the distance shouted, "All clear!"

Basil felt every sick and twisting nerve in his body abruptly and without warning unravel into gratified noodle-ness. He slumped against the side of the ambulance. The adrenaline that had kept him tense and alert rushed out of him, and for a startling second Basil feared that he was going to puke as it washed away, leaving him shaky and dizzy. He swallowed heavily and it passed. Gwen stood and began walking in the direction of the nearest warehouse.

"Now wait!" Basil said, pushing off from the ambulance and following right on her heels. "I think there's been enough fearless heroics for say, like, ever! Time to leave all this to the professional grunts, innit?"

"I have to see, Basil," she said. "I need to see what they were doing in there."

Basil wanted to protest, but truth be told, he was eaten up with curiosity, himself. Rubbing the spot at the bridge of his nose, just as Kalp used to do, Basil followed her into the building, ducking under the yellow ribbon of warning tape that a pair of dead-eyed forensics experts were erecting around them.

The door opened straight into a long, low-roofed hall with exposed iron girders in various states of decay and defacement, a ringing cement floor, and row upon row of crude wooden work tables and chairs of every shape and variety. They looked like they were pilfered from kitchens, junk shops, cafeterias, anywhere that someone could get their hands on a seat.

The number of rows—ten, maybe, possibly even twenty, made the queasiness push against Basil's sternum again. No, surely they can't have had *that many* people working on this project. No, no, it had to have been just a few guys, all their stuff laid out.

Basil refused to believe that there were enough bigoted fucks to fill all of those chairs.

The next thing Basil noticed was the smell; if he thought the B.O. in the surveillance van was bad, this was a hundred times worse—blood, loosened bowels, and the coppery reek of fireworks and splattered brains that Basil remembered all too vividly from the garden behind the Pierson house. The floor was littered with at least six corpses in various states of dismemberment. P90 automatic rifles did a lot of damage to vulnerable human organs and limbs, and the military hadn't been quite as careful at taking the prisoners alive as perhaps their orders had stated they should.

They too were parents, adults, people with wives and husbands and lovers, kids, maybe. They had been just as outraged as the Agents by the horrors imposed by these terrorists on those left behind, even if their hatred hadn't been quite so personal, so connected, as it was for the Institute's employees.

"Put a pedophile in prison," Basil whispered to himself. He forced his eyes away from the gore and onto the tech and plans scattered along the work benches attached to the nearest wall. "Give a widow a gun…"

Gwen had gone over to stare down at the jumble. She was shaking, the hand holding her gauze to her forehead shivering so violently that Basil feared she was going to rip the butterfly closures clean off her skin. Her eyes were narrowed and glassy with hate.

This workbench in particular was filled with alien tech: solar panels and engine pods and all manner of devices that had been stripped down and torn apart. A shock thrilled over Basil's skin as he recognized a smeared blob of fake fur and gears that resolved itself into one of the latex masks with motorized jaw hinges. Some were helmets with faces on them like the one worn by the pilot who had tried to kill Gwennie. Some looked like they allowed for enough vision and flexibility, enough close-skin mobility, that a sniper with his cheek pressed against a barrel would still have a perfect shot.

Doctor Zhang and his crew were already inside, tagging and dusting, busy with a camera and body bags further towards the centre of the filthy cement floor. Basil studiously ignored them, his stomach still slightly flip-floppy. Instead he watched quietly as Gwen lifted one of the half-finished masks off of a work table.

"Muppets!" Gwen snarled hatefully, finally dropping the gauze away from her forehead. The revealed skin was an angry pink. Basil couldn't help but think that she was going to have a wicked lovely scar along her eyebrow to match the one above it. Already the skin around her eye was starting to purple—it would be one heck of a shiner, too.

"Gwen?"

"We were fooled by goddamn Muppets!" She kicked one of the animatronic helmets across the warehouse. It skittered sickeningly along the bare concrete, looking nothing so much as a decapitated head when it splashed through a wide trail of drying blood. Basil couldn't decide if he wanted to giggle or vomit.

Someone had gone to a lot of trouble to frame Kalp and his people. But *this* far? It was almost too much—it was almost ludicrous. At least now those same someones were going to pay for it. From the brief glimpse in the direction of Doctor Zhang's team, Basil guessed a lot of them already had. The Institute was vicious about protecting and avenging their own, and Basil was sure that lot of reports written tonight would contain the words "fire fight" and "accidental" and "intended to capture alive."

Basil wondered how many had been rounded up into the final vehicle of their little motorcade, the armoured prisoner transport. He hoped *that* air conditioner was broken, too. *Oh, yes,* Basil thought with the closest thing to glee that he could manage while still so emotionally raw.

Basil swept his gaze over the mechanical detrius littered along the work benches. The spread of devices was tempting for only a moment, before he remembered that all these marvellous little gadgets had been invented for the sole purpose of killing those he loved. It was all evidence, and it was pretty damning. This warehouse held everything they'd need to put the surviving terrorists away forever.

Well, almost everything.

The spaceship was still at the Piersons' farm.

That would be the final piece of evidence required for the inevitable upcoming trial. There would have to be some way to carbon date it—to prove that the machine had been built now-ish before it went then-ish. That morning he had handed over the full contents of the black briefcase; the Flasher Basil had reverse-engineered and wrangled into existence with the lump of circuits and metal that Kalp had left them on the dining room table. The second one he had rigged out of 1980s technology and the remains of the ship's Flasher were under lock and key, officially and permanently off limits. They couldn't go back and get the 1980s version of the ship. They would have to fetch the now-version if they wanted the ship at all.

Time travel was dangerous, and it was over. Basil had already made certain that the technology couldn't be copied. He had never written down any blueprints or notes of his own, had purposefully handed over the Flashers sabotaged, and had created a computer virus to slowly worm through the Institute's database and eat up any information about the Flashers any time another safe house was raided and information transferred in.

Just as well. He had no desire to do any more time travelling, especially if there was any chance that next place they ended up could be in *his* childhood. The grandfather paradox temporal theory was all well and good, but Basil didn't want to test the idea that it would be physically impossible for him to accidentally kill or influence his younger self, all the same. He'd gone through enough gut-flipping panic when Evvie Pierson had handed him baby Gwennie.

Basil wrenched his mind off of that surreal moment and sidled over to the table where the Flashers had clearly been studied. Picking up a few pieces, he turned them over in his hands, using the appearance of studying the technology to "accidentally" roll the notes up and drop them into a filthy pool of dust and gore. "Oops, clumsy me," he said, taking a deliberate step into the middle of the puddle and crushing the fragile blue paper a few times, just to be sure.

Something caught his eye. Nestled in the middle of a jumble of discarded nuts and circuits was a small, perfectly triangular casing with a narrow halo of wires and ports feathering from the cap of a tube. He picked it up, watched the vivid dark rainbows that marked it as not having originated on Earth dance across the surface, and snapped it open along the hinge. The inside was familiar, but he couldn't quite...ah-ha! If he just imagined it melted, half destroyed in the crash of a spaceship into a strawberry patch then, yes, he recognized it very well. It was part of the triggering mechanism for the Flashers that the assassins had been using. He had used one of these very same components to get them back to the present, and one that was in even worse condition to get them to 1983.

One that he had found on the table in his own dining room. The world around Basil skittered to stop for a brief second, going still and meaningless as his brain lanced through the problem that had been eating at him since that horrible day in their house: *why did Kalp have a Flasher Trigger?* It begged the question: Who sent it to him, and why? Did they expect Kalp could have used it to build his own Flasher? And if so, did that mean that the letter had come from somebody trying to help Kalp escape from the Institute, or to convince him to use it to flee after having assassinated someone?

He knew now that Kalp would never have sided with the assassins, but that didn't mean that the sender of the component and the letter did.

Uncertain about what this meant for the investigation, Basil surreptitiously pocketed the trigger and continued to rifle through the rest of the mechanical debris on the worktable with a renewed urgency. Nothing else jumped out at him.

Basil was willing to bet his life that they would never meet the person who invented the Flashers; nobody would own to it at least, and Basil took vicious, hopeful pleasure in imagining that the creator had been the pilot whom Gwen had shot in the face.

He held no hope for retrieving the corpse buried in the corn field in a condition pristine enough for the courts to do anything beyond verifying whether the body had once been human. Basil remembered the long awkward fingers that had grabbed baby Gwennie, the way the tips hadn't moved or flexed, the way that its feet weren't quite right, and hated that he'd been duped by latex gloves and the unnatural stillness of death.

Of course, he hadn't examined the corpse closely after Gwen had blown off its head; it was a *headless corpse.* They just dragged it out and got rid of it and tried not to look. Basil tried not to think that somewhere, right then, somebody might have been doing the same to the man he loved. *Had* loved. Still did.

"Here comes trouble," Gwen said under her breath.

Basil looked up and followed her line of sight—oops, Director Addis, storming in the door and puffing with displeasure.

"Grey, Pierson," he snapped before either of them had a chance to offer an excuse for defence. "I'd have you both very harshly disciplined for failing to follow orders *again* if it wasn't for the fact that you always seem to bring me something worthwhile when you go on these damned little constitutionals of yours. What have you found?"

Gwen pointed to the heads. Addis went as pale as a man with his complexion could go, turning a sort of strange mossy grey.

"Right. Okay. But, seriously, never again. It's as if you *want* a punishment."

"I don't know," Gwen said with a shrug, "I could use a bit of punishment, me. Suspension at home, maybe? Barred from the Institute for a…month or two, say?"

Addis spluttered.

Basil grinned, catching on. "Just long enough for one more… constitutional, sir."

Addis narrowed his eyes.

Gwen held up her hand, palm out, like a Girl Scout. "Last one, sir. I swear. For a little evidence retrieval."

The director nodded curtly and threw up his hands. "Get it all sorted out with requisitions, I don't want to hear about it. You just bring me back that evidence."

Basil grinned and nodded in return and then Addis was gone, off to harangue someone else with his flashing black eyes and great brown brow of disapproval.

Over, Basil thought, and let forth a great sigh. For the second time today he felt all of the tension slide out of his posture and he leaned back against the work bench, rubbing his temples with his knuckles to dispel the headache that was building behind his eyes. *Thank God, that's it, it's finally—*

And then the Mobile Flasher Tracker vibrated in Basil's pocket.

For a second, everything froze. Basil felt his breath block up his throat, felt his heart twitch into stillness, his limbs swing to a halt. And the device in his pocket vibrated rhythmically, insistently, the way the heavy dinosaur footfalls vibrated in "Jurassic Park."

But…but no. No. he thought, straightening slowly. *We've got them. All of them. They said "all clear." Right?*

It vibrated again, a low chittering of the casing, the swooshy hiss of the fabric of his pockets being forced into motion. Gwen's head swivelled toward him and her eyes narrowed on his pocket.

He pulled the device out, staring at it with such intensity that when it vibrated again, he was so startled that he nearly dropped the thing. Gwen stared down at the device as if it were a slimy, three headed hydra. Her lips went white.

"No," Basil hissed. "Someone's got one, and they're warming it up."

"Shit," she said. "We missed one."

She glanced at the map on the screen, looked up and around the warehouse to get her bearings, and then she was off, a shot of streaking black against the dust-dull concrete floor and the dowdy red brick, weaving around the forensics teams and banging out of a small, rusty door that might have once been the warehouse's lunch break exit. Basil resisted the urge to shout her name, to try to rein her in. He would have better luck calling down Halley's Comet. Instead he just sprinted out the door after her.

None of the other Agents looked up as he passed, too intent on their own work. Once outside, Basil realized that he had completely lost sight of Gwen.

He turned in a circle, looked down at the insistent red triangle that was flickering on the Tracker's screen, and hesitated.

"*Basil,*" hissed his ear-mounted radio and Basil jumped. "Can you hear me?"

"Gwen?" he asked, tapping his ear piece on. "How the hell…where are you?" He looked around, peering into the deep shadows thrown off by the sharpness of the various out buildings of the warehouse. There was nobody out this way but himself, nobody to see or overhear.

He turned his head anyway, cupped his hand over the mic.

"Gwen, you're supposed to be broadcasting on all channels, not using our team frequency."

"Basil, you need to come here."

It was getting hotter, the clouds scudding away from the sun as if they were also suffering from its too-intense glare, and a heavy damp heat was swiftly dropping over the warehouse's yard, eerily still and thick. The calls and curses of the angered Agents and Ops men and women floated over the charnel house that had been the assassins' last refuge, and she wanted him to follow her into that mess? His spine prickled with cold apprehension.

Oh, no, no. Basil was a scientist. He was supposed to stay in front of screens and white boards. He knew that now. Suddenly yearning for the pungent interior of the surveillance van, he was torn between his overwhelming but carefully honed instinct of cowardice, and the desire to make sure that the woman he loved, the only lover he had left, didn't go and get herself accidentally shot by one of their own guys.

He dithered, feeling stupidly like a child presented with two washrooms but no way to tell which was for men or for women, desperate to use a toilet yet scared to make the wrong choice.

"Basil, get your ass out here. *Now.* There's…I found…Basil, *please.*" Her voice took on a plaintive tone that Basil hadn't heard since before their Gareth had died. That made up his mind. Worry punched into Basil's chest. Gwen never said please, not like *that*.

"Fine, okay," he hissed. "Turn on your GPS."

He fumbled for the PDA in his vest pocket and switched it on. As soon as he'd logged into the tracking system, he saw Gwen's bright red dot flashing. She was alone—or at least, there were no other tracked agents around her—in a shed on the other side of the tomb of a warehouse. Basil cursed. Of course Gwen would be the only person to head in the opposite direction as soon as she'd been dismissed back to base camp.

Basil went around to the other side of the wall, looked around to make sure he wasn't being followed, then shot across a disturbingly empty stretch of crumbling parking lot to the rusted silver shed. They had dismissed this shed upon first evaluation of the compound as holding nothing but garden tools, but it sounded as if Gwen had found something infinitely more interesting.

Basil resisted the urge to stop and look around to check for telltale flashes of spotting scopes in the sunlight, and instead poured on more speed.

He was wheezing by the time he got there, heart pounding in the back of his mouth. The door had been left hanging open, and Basil had enough presence of mind to pause before rushing in. He looked around the corner.

He needn't have bothered.

There was nobody here but Gwen.

She was standing with her back against the wall, staring in disbelief at the hulking great mass of metal that filled the rest of the shed.

"Is that…?" Basil began, then stopped, throat closing up around the confirmation.

Gwen nodded. Then she shook her head uncertainly. "I think so?"

Basil reached out, touched the wickedly pointed nose of the aircraft, followed the flare into the saucerish wings. Up close like this, he could see where the paint didn't match, where the alloy of the metal gave way to rivets and steel disguised by painted-on designs. It had been salvaged and put back together piecemeal with whatever the builders could find, or steal, mixing Earth and alien technology and disguising it poorly with a slap of paint in approximately the right places.

Yet from far away, it would look identical to an official scout ship. Basil knew this for a fact. He *remembered*. His stomach flipped and something sour pressed against the base of his throat.

"Was it this one?" Basil asked, swallowing heavily, dropping his voice into a whisper for no reason save that it felt wrong to ask this out loud, to vocalize it. "Can you tell?"

Gwen shook her head. She had to swallow once before speaking, too. "It was so crushed up that I didn't...I thought the only modifications were in the cockpit. But this means they stole more than one of the ships from the Institute or somewhere and fixed them up. They must have been planning for months. I just don't *understand*."

Basil came around beside her, sparing only a glance at the parchment frailty of the skin on her face, the deep hollows under her eyes. She looked haunted. She looked as if she was remembering this ship, not from three days ago when they had travelled in time, but from the first time she had seen it, before she could talk.

Basil didn't resist the urge to press the dry palm of his hand against her hot cheek. She was pale, but her skin burned hot with her anger, her confusion. She turned her face into his touch. He wanted her to kiss the base of his thumb, like she usually did when they were sharing an intimate moment like this, but she didn't. Still the soldier, as long as she had the vest on.

He turned away, climbed up the ladder rungs welded awkwardly up the ship's sleek body and pressed his face against the window of the cockpit. There, on the seat, was an old fashioned mini disc player. Basil had a very good guess at what album they'd find inside it.

He dropped down to the dusty, rat-crap strewn floor of the shed. The force made the dust billow up, bringing with it the gagging scent of vermin and gasoline. He tried not to breathe too deeply. "I think there's just this one."

"But," Gwen said, then stopped and licked her lips and said again, "but we already shot one down."

"No, we *will* shoot one down," Basil said, and now he could feel it, the surge of adrenaline that was the preface to discovery, the soaring glee at being *right*. "This one." He tapped the nose. A low metallic chime rang through the shed, and he grinned.

Gwen's face went even more ashen and her mouth thinned into a knife slice. She pulled her gun from her hip holster and levelled it on the ship.

"No, Gwen," Basil said hastily, his joy cracking apart in the face of the reality of what this discovery meant. "What if the bullets ricochet? I…I'll get under the hood! Gimme a sec."

Reluctantly, Gwen reholstered. Basil got down on his knees, gagging at the closer odour of stale machine oil and old feces, and peered under the nose of the craft. There wasn't really a "hood" to these things so much as a hatch-door that let a mechanic stick his head and shoulders up into the guts of the ship.

He raised his hands, his shoulders too broad for an opening made for an entirely different species, and began tracing the wires back to their metal origins, trying to figure out how to do the most amount of damage that would be the least repairable in the shortest amount of time.

It was easy to pull this wire, yes, put it over here, yes, okay, and re-secure a piece upside down so when the ship…oh yes, like that!

He was so focussed on the multi-coloured strands and the clumsy patches the workers had engineered that he had no warning. He heard Gwen's sharp cry—déjà vu!—felt the tug on his ankle that yanked him out of the ship and smacked the back of his head off the floor. Then he was staring at the barrel of a paradoxically wide-mouthed pistol. Or, no, the barrel was normal circumference. It was just that Basil's head was swirling from the hit and the gun was really, disturbingly close to his face.

Basil tried to bring his hands up, but the woman in the tight teal flight suit kicked them back down. She had a helmet under her other arm, the animatronic face on the thing nauseatingly familiar.

So was her own.

Basil tried to keep the look of dumb surprise out of his expression, but he was sure it was a losing battle.

"Agent Aitken," he said softly, by way of greeting.

She inclined her head slightly, like a magnanimous Hollywood villain. Impotent, the gun aimed between his eyes, he lay still on the ground and shook with fury. She looked to the side and Basil followed her gaze, found Gwen crumpled against the wall. Fear twisted his guts until he saw that her chest was still rising and falling, still alive, thank God. The gash in her temple was oozing blood again and a goose egg was already forming.

"She's a hard one to keep down," Aitken said. Lying beside Gwen was a bloodied asp.

Basil shook his head. Then he wished he hadn't. Blackness swirled at the corner of his vision, bulbous and thick like the lava in the lamp he'd had on his bedside table as a child.

"But you're one of *us*," Basil protested, blinking hard to keep conscious. "You're Institute!"

"I was!" Aitken snapped. "I believed in what we were doing. Until...until you two *twisted it*, made it *wrong*."

"It's Integration! Jesus, Aitken, it's what we were hired to *do.*"

"*No!*"

The shout echoed through the shed, bouncing painfully against the metal walls and back at Basil's already throbbing head. He winced.

"No," Aitken snarled again, her voice dropping low. "No, they were supposed to become like *us*. They were supposed to be made *right*. We weren't supposed to be like them. It's wrong. And you two are to blame for everything, for all of it, for all those disgusting lemmings following you into Aglunation! It's perverted!"

"You xenophobic asshole," Basil snarled and Aitken's finger tensed on the trigger. But she was smiling. And she didn't fire. And Basil had to know. "You're the mole, then. And you didn't warn your compatriots about today."

"I needed the distraction." Aitken smiled. "Something to cover the noise that this thing is going to make, keep the Institute and their nosy little devices busy." She patted the nose of the ship affectionately and then brought the heel of her modified boot down hard on the

Flasher tracker that had fallen out of Basil's pocket. It crunched hard, and Basil winced again.

"But they died!" Basil protested.

Aitken's lips curled up further and for the first time Basil caught the glaze-eyed expression of complete belief in what she was saying, the zealot's fever. "For the greater good," she said, and it sounded like a recitation. "All to help me with this, the only important mission."

Basil seethed. "So you shot Kalp on purpose. Did you plant the letter in our house, too, you fucking traitor? Did that trigger come from one of your Flashers?"

Aitken laughed and kicked out. The sole of her boot connected hard with the side of Basil's cheek and he was rolled onto his side with the strength of it, seeing sudden stars. Basil curled up to protect his head, but no further blows came. Carefully, he peered out from between his elbows. Blood ran into his eyes. It stung.

"It wasn't me," Aitken said gently, as if she was talking to a particularly stupid child. "I have no idea who sent it. It was fortuitous, though."

"Fortui—!" Basil was too furious to finish the word. He spluttered.

"And now…" Aitken said, and one handed, slipped the alien head on over her own, hiding a blade of a smile behind an animatronic snout and fake fangs. She reached into a zippered pocket of her flight suit and there was another altered cellular phone, a red progression bar sliding inexorably from one side of the screen to the other. Warming up. She pulled something else out of her pocket—a Flasher trigger. The one that Basil had dropped in the conference room yesterday. She snapped it in place against the back of the cell phone and the progression bar on the screen started flickering urgently.

But why would she need Basil's Flasher trigger when there had been one right on the workshop table?

Oh, no, of course! *That* was why Aitken had been trying to get into the warehouse, and hadn't retreated when Wright had given the order. She had been trying for the new Flasher trigger just in case. She had the burnt out, half melted one she had stolen from Basil, and it looked like it might survive at least one or two more trips, but Basil couldn't blame her for wanting another, more reliable component.

But then, where did the newer one that Basil had found in the cockpit come from?

And then suddenly Basil *understood*.

Basil took a deep breath to ground his spinning head, reached into his pocket while her eyes were on securing the trigger to her Flasher, and flicked the trigger in his hand at Aitken. She ducked and it pinged off the back of the seat and skittered into the cockpit, where he assumed the crash would jam it into the console. Exactly where he had found it three days ago.

"Missed me," Aitken gloated. "Just for that, I think I'm going to do you two perverted little shits first." She sneered, and the mouth of the fake head moved with her words, and eerie ghosting that just looked *wrong*. "Gwen first, though, I think. Just so you can have the agony of watching her fade from existence."

"It won't be like that," Basil wheezed from the floor.

It wouldn't, actually. If Gwen was erased from history, it wouldn't be as if Basil would be able to watch her vanish beside him, like a ghost in an old sci-fi flick. No, the world would just rewrite itself, instantly, and Basil would suddenly and without knowing, without remembering, be somewhere else, doing something else, and Gwen would have never existed.

But this scenario wasn't actually going to play out like that. Basil meant that, too, but he was fairly sure that Aitken didn't understand.

Aitken lifted her Flasher, and Basil recognized that, too. He'd spent a whole night fixing it, once. "Funny thing, serendipity. Trying to figure out their transportation technology, we accidentally invented a time machine. We're going to use their technology to make sure that the perverts like you who welcomed them—*fucked them*—were never born." Basil felt his eyes widen. "Oh yeah, *Doctor Basil Grey*. I'm going to take great fucking pleasure in killing your mother while you're still inside her. Then just think of the kind of reception those *freaks* will get when they show up, especially when they're already in the books for murders that are thirty years old."

Bile roiled against Basil's Adam's apple, but he kept his mouth shut. He didn't want to give this *psychopath* any reason to shoot right now and be done with him instead. It would be an irony, a bloody cop-out on the part of whatever sci-fi author had been writing the last few surreal months of his life.

Aitken chuckled. It looked wrong, parodied by the mechanical mouth. Everything was all wrong.

"Pussy," she snarled at Basil. When he didn't lash out or fight back, she stepped over him.

Basil could have grabbed her foot, dragged her to the ground, wrestled with her on the reeking floor, maybe even managed to wrest the gun away and take that final deadly shot.

Instead he said, "Leave her alone. Please."

Aitken scoffed without even turning her eyes back to him, without loosing her grip on her gun. "Why should I?"

"Because it's the right thing to do," Basil said. "Because nobody deserves…not for just loving—"

"You sure as fuck do!" Aitken snarled and her voice rang once again through the metal hanger, beating against the side of Basil's abused temples and his already-puffing ear.

Basil closed his eyes and said nothing else. There was no point in provoking her any further. One stray bullet could finish either him or Gwen. One ricochet and it could be over. No, better to let the asshole go. Because she wasn't going to succeed. Because she was still going to die. Basil had wondered why a few bullets from a P-90 could have taken down that ship, and he now knew that it was because the ship had already been sabotaged.

Gwen was going to get Aitken between the eyes in five minutes, three days, and twenty-nine years ago.

Aitken mounted the steps and heaved herself into the cockpit. She connected the Flasher to a twisted cord of wires that Basil had already ripped one sleeve on, trying to disconnect them from the scrunched metal of the ruined dash. A snap of a switch and Raquel Winkelaar's hideous excuse for music slammed into the air around them. The engine whined to life.

Basil's heart collided against his throat in time with the syncopated backbeat.

For an instant he was back in that parking lot with the punks and the baseball bats. He could hear Gwen's anguished shriek in the piercing riff of the electric guitar, Kalp's furious roar in the thumping drums. Basil swallowed heavily, closed his eyes, pushed that memory, that horror back and down, away.

"Any last words, doc?"

"Yeah. I know how this is going to end," Basil said softly.

Aitken laughed. "Oh yeah? And how does this end, Doctor Specialist Basil fucking Grey?"

Basil lifted his empty hand, formed his thumb and index finger into a child's mimic of a gun. "Bang," he said softly. Aitken blinked. "Try not to look too surprised this time, though," Basil cautioned, giving voice to his earlier thought. "It's a pretty stupid face to die in."

She flipped him the bird, closed the clear hood, then jammed her hand down on the Flasher.

The ship disappeared. The bright light, the loud noise that Basil had expected, none of it happened. Just a quiet sucking pop where the air rushed into the vacuum.

Gone.

He dropped his arm, a circular and horrible déjà vu prickling under his skin.

"Bang," he said again, staring at his hand.

NEXT

BASIL WATCHED THE HOUSE blossom into view around the bend in the road, fancied he could see it emerging up from the curvature of the Earth, before he saw the name on the red-flagged mailbox.

He didn't have to read the name—faded brown from too-hot summers and biting winters, peeling away stubbornly from the corrugated tin—to know where he was. He recognized the solid two-storey sand-coloured brick edifice, the gingerbread porch and matching gables, the tenacious clinging ivy, the victory garden that was half the length of the front lawn, dark and rich.

Perhaps the vegetable garden was a bit smaller, now that the one who tended it was older, now that there were only two mouths to feed; perhaps the trees were slightly bigger; perhaps there was an empty dog hutch leaning lonely against the side of the porch stairs; perhaps the ruts on the laneway were a bit better defined, less filled with tire-crushed weeds, deeper grooves.

But nothing about the *feel* had changed.

It wasn't as if he could ever forget this particular house.

"Where it all ended," he whispered, chin propped on a palm, leaning his head out of the window to scent the fine late autumn air like a mutt. There were late apples and goldenrod on the breeze, and he sneezed into the crook of his sleeve.

"Or where it all started," Gwen muttered under her breath in response, eyes never leaving the narrow laneway she turned onto and set the U-haul truck crawling up. Either pot holes or reluctance had her tapping the gas lightly, and Basil wasn't about to put voice to his guess as to which it was.

"Depending on which side of it you're on, innit?" Basil agreed, calling to mind Evvie and Mark Pierson, young, newly married, parents of an infant barely old enough to chew—the woman Basil would one day love.

The woman who had...almost had...his son.

For them, the Piersons, for that baby Gwennie, it had been the beginning. The time and place where the whole world had gone utterly and completely wrong for twenty-four hours.

Would they, Basil wondered, feel the same sort of gale-force relief that Basil did? Now that the assassins had been stopped, the mole found and knowingly eliminated, the dead mourned? Or would they feel terror, confusion, having lived nearly thirty years knowing exactly what was to come and then suddenly knowing...nothing?

"Depending," Gwen echoed, and her knuckles on the oversized steering wheel were white.

Basil abandoned the window, the gently scented early morning breeze, and scooted across the seat. He leaned over the gear-shift and pecked a soft, dry kiss to her cheek.

"I'm here," he said.

"Here," she repeated, and the truck shivered to a hesitant stop, crunching the gravel under the tires, beside the gracefully age-drooped doors of the largest barn.

Yes, we are, Basil thought.

IN THE back of the rental truck, they had shovels and cheap disposable coveralls, a tarpaulin, a half-constructed wooden crate and lots of foam peanuts, a pair of overnight bags with changes of clothes, the clothing they had borrowed thirty years ago, and the letter of permission from the Institute to oversee this particular mission alone.

They had flown into Pearson International airport on Institute-provided fake visas, landed in Toronto and rented a truck, bought the gear at a hardware store on the outskirts of the metropolis, and driven all night. Gwen had insisted on doing all of the driving. Basil had never driven on the right side of the road, and so didn't contest. He was fairly certain he wasn't in the mood to die in a horrible multi-car pileup on the highway, especially after he had survived...well, everything he had survived.

It would be ridiculous, first off.

Dawn had come and gone, and so had more Tim Horton's drive-thrus than Basil would ever care to see again. Gwen couldn't get enough of the Iced Capps, said that they tasted of home, but he was so sick of cheap workman's tea that he almost wept at the memory of Evvie Pierson's well stocked pantry. He felt caffeinated and exhausted all at once and was simultaneously ready to lay down for sleep and jitter through the walls between space and time.

Time, he thought, marvelling at the strange place his jet-lagged brain wanted to go. It was always worse when you went backwards across the globe. He wondered how feasible it would be to demand that the Institute only send him forward from now on. London Heathrow to Moscow, Moscow to Tokyo Narita, Narita to Honolulu, Honolulu to Vancouver, Vancouver to Toronto. Sure, he could do that.

He was pretty finished with this whole backwards-in-time thing.

And after what Gwen and Basil had been through in the past few weeks, the Institute owed him one; owed him at least that flight. Boy, did it ever.

Thank God the momentary sky-high blip in fuel surtax flight prices from a few years ago had vanished when the Institute had reverse engineered and then mass-manufactured the first hydrogen engines to fit in 747s. He could at least *afford* to take the ridiculous route if he ever felt the need to indulge in it.

Sliding down off of the high rental truck seat, Basil had half expected to get mobbed by some suitably scruffy mutt, but nothing save the crisp air and the low-level throb of laconic possibility, the shiver of seeds waiting under the rich soil, assaulted him. Farms had always struck him as places that were just crouched and poised to strike forward, waiting to explode into a verdant flare of life.

He had yet to see this particular farm in any season beyond autumn—golden and hushed—but fully intended to watch it push out new buds, watch young calves frolic and graceful deer munch and whatever other sort of idyllic shit these sorts of places invested in. He was going to see this place year round because he and Gwen were going to visit here, often. Gwen had reached out that first tentative hand of reconciliation, and Basil wasn't going to let her screw it up again.

He *liked* the Piersons, damnit.

He liked Canada too, at least what he had seen of it, despite the horrid, horrid tea.

He heard Gwen's door slam shut, felt the empty truck rock slightly, and then the crunch of gravel under broken-in military boots heralded Gwen's slow walk around the nose. She had to squeeze between the grille and the door of the barn, leaving a low, long swipe of age-greyed dust along the thighs of her jeans. They were in civvies for this operation, and they'd come in a rental U-Haul with wheat stalks painted on the side; they wanted it to look like the Piersons' daughter had returned home to fetch some furniture, not a three-decade-buried space craft. The Institute and the Piersons might know why they were here, but that didn't mean the neighbours had to. And small communities talked.

"Great," she sighed, and tried to bat the dust away. It just spread out more. She pinched the bridge of her nose and Basil had to choke down a gasp; Kalp used to do that.

"It's fine," he said, wrapping his arms around her shoulders and nuzzling at the spot under her ear. He'd claimed that spot for himself, ages ago. That was Basil's spot.

"Right, right," she said, but didn't sound convinced. "It's not like I put on clean, new jeans for my mother."

"Your mother has seen you in a filthy uniform. I don't think a little barn dust is going to make much of a difference, issit?"

She reached up and squeezed the hand he had hooked around her shoulder fiercely. He squeezed back, strong and stable and there.

Then Gwen let go and Basil dropped his arms and she walked towards the house, head high and hands jammed into her pockets to hide the way they were trembling.

Evvie Pierson was standing on the front porch in her overalls, a shovel in one hand, and a pot of tea, tags fluttering beautifully in the light morning breeze, in the other.

Basil really did almost cry at the sight.

Really.

THE DIGGING took half as long this time around. Partially it was because Basil didn't have to stop to measure the depth of the hole versus the height of the ship to make sure it would be buried deep enough to not leave a lump, and partially because Mark had seen them coming up the drive with the U-Haul and had already puttered his backhoe tractor over to the dead patch of grass above the raspberries.

By the time Basil had finished his first cup of Evvie's glorious tea and Gwen had finally said more than "hello," and "surprise?" to her mother, Mark had the canopy of the long thin ship exposed. With the four of them digging together, they had the sides freed and part of the undercarriage excavated within the hour. It was a one-man ship—one-woman ship, really, and something at the back of his tongue turned sour. It was just long enough for a seated body and the fuel generators in the back, somewhat circular but more of a cigar shape when viewed up close. Aerodynamic.

With the backhoe as muscle and the shovels and some old boards as levers, they slid the ship out of the hole to loll on the grass, one wing pointing up, the weight of the craft resting on the other, and the nose pointed away from the house.

Basil clambered up the side and released the catch that made the clear canopy hiss and slide backwards. He folded himself in half, legs dangling out, and looked inside. Twenty-nine years buried above the garden had not changed the interior at all. He could still see the place where he had ripped out half of the control box for parts, the wrench he had forgotten and left behind, the long thin strip of fabric that had been shredded off the sleeve of his uniform still hanging by a few fibres on the edge of the lateral control stick, the gap in the dash where he'd removed Aitken's Flasher and most of the interior cabling to get them home.

He reached into his pocket and pulled out a dark lump of metal. It was now totally useless as a Flasher trigger, but it had travelled across the decades more than once.

He hadn't even recognized it for what it was, hadn't put together this last strange puzzle, until he'd begun dismantling the Flasher in preparation for the court case. Basil thought that the poor little thing deserved a reward, or at least a frequent flyer time traveller's points card.

If he allowed for the warping that the intense process of Flashing imprinted on the trigger, he could see where it still fit in the console. He put it away, carefully wrapping it back in its evidence bag and tucking it into his coverall pockets, then turned his eyes to the other evidence inside the ship.

The mysterious music deck was still hooked haphazardly into the console system, held together with duct tape and wire clamps and something Basil vaguely recognized as bubblegum. He resisted the urge to tear it out and throw it to the ground and smash it repeatedly with the flat of his shovel.

This—*this*—was why his lover was dead, his son had never been born, his whole life had gotten so *crappy*. This stupid deck in a stupid ship, and stupid Raquel Winkelaar.

Instead he took a hundred photos on his digital camera of the deck rigged into the cockpit sound system from all angles, then lifted it gingerly with gloved fingertips, wrapped a plastic bag around it, and set it securely on the cockpit seat. There would be fingerprints on that deck, and those fingerprints would condemn the people who had almost taken the last precious thing from Basil's life. They would prove that the pilot had been Agent Aitken.

The woman who had almost killed Gwennie. Gwen.

Everything inside sorted and secured, Mark hooked a chain up to the winch in the inside of the truck's box, and the other end to the nose of the ship. Along with the help of the truck's fold-out ramp, they got the ship safely secured in the wooden crate. An ungodly amount of foam peanuts and bungee cords later, Basil was fairly sure that if the ship didn't make it back to the UK in one piece, it was because the plane it had been in would have been bombed.

He shuddered at the careless thought.

A few months ago, someone out there would have given anything for the opportunity to take out both Gwen and Basil so easily, in one fell stroke. There would have been no regard for the other passengers, of course, and that's what scared Basil most.

That other people—like Kalp—would be killed and just regarded as collateral damage.

Other people with lovers and children and…

No.

But it was over; over forever, he hoped.

And this was the last winding string, the loose end. With the ship as evidence, the whole lot of the wankers who had killed so many innocent people would be sent up the river for life. For the first time, Basil almost regretted that the U.N. had rallied the nations of the world together to ban capital punishment across the globe.

The Institute had demanded that its own special ops and clean up teams do the retrieval, once Director Addison had revealed what Gwen and Basil were going to do, but Gwen had insisted on going alone. She had withheld the location until they gave in. Basil was sure they'd been followed via satellite GPS the whole time. Her parents' address had to be on file somewhere, so no doubt the clean team was already en route, but Gwen's desire had been partially fulfilled already: private time with her parents to patch and pack up the last of a hurtful and terrifying past.

There would be all of today: the rest of the afternoon, talk at the dinner table with the French wine Basil had smuggled into his luggage, conversations late into the night and breakfast in the morning to ward off hangovers.

There would be *time*.

The revelation smacked Basil in the forehead and he stood and stared up at the sky, blue and deep and *forever*. Gwen had almost died, and then she had not. Basil still had her. If he had lost everything else, he still had *her*. Basil still had time.

The first bang of a hammer slamming against a nail brought him out of his stupor and he went into the box of the truck to help Mark nail the crate shut. When it was done, they came out and watched as Evvie brushed the back of her hand over her sweating forehead, pushing aside the raucous humidity-induced curls. Gwen echoed the gesture unconsciously, hand in similar curls, and Basil swallowed heavily.

"I was standing right here," Evvie said. "Right here, by the raspberries, when it happened."

Gwen folded her hands over the top of the shovel and rested her chin on them.

Evvie pointed up, sketching hope and memory in the air with the movements of her fingers, outlining the remembered hulls of the first of the ships that broke through the light, early evening cloud cover that not-so-long-ago night.

"'Look, Mark,'" she said. "That's what I told him. Just like you said. *Look*."

THE PIERSONS had a wall-mounted HDTV, so the television stand sitting abandoned and bare under it was a bit ridiculous all alone, collecting dust and age-yellowed television guides, left over pennies and elastic bands, and a dollar-store basket full of curled take-out food receipts.

Basil stopped at the foot of the stairs, sock toes on the edge of a carpet that could have once, reasonably, been called cream. It wasn't that the basement was dirty. It was just that it was thirty-odd years old, padding the memories of a family home.

Basil could imagine little Gwennie there, easy as anything, even though he'd never actually seen her in this particular room. He could imagine the first steps, the first tears, the first fights. He bet Gwennie had learned to walk on this carpet. She'd probably also learned to projectile vomit on this carpet, too. She'd yelled at him in this room. He'd yelled at her. She'd probably had equally loud fights with her parents, standing in the exact same spot, hands on her hips and the curl of weave under her toes. They'd probably had fights over allowance, car keys, clothing choices, school and boys.

And one memorable, haunting twenty-four hours when everything went terribly wrong, and then terribly right. His eyes traced the old, worn black scuff on the wall where a toolbox had once been kicked against it.

The Betamax was staring at him, lying in wait on the top of the television stand; waiting for the moment he walked into the basement.

"Oh, come on," Basil said, throwing up his hands but turning to smile at Gwen's father. Mark Pierson stood at the top of the stairs, hands on his hips, dirt under his nails, and a smile curling one side of his mouth.

There was more of Mark than when Basil had last seen him: decades of nightly beer had rounded out his belly above the jeans, but still left him with knobby skinny-man legs. There was also less: Mark's once-thick mop of careless brown hair had started its steady, silvery retreat backwards, particularly thin in a band where a ball cap had been rubbing against his scalp for the last thirty years, and his forehead was now higher than Basil's.

Basil took a sort of perverse pleasure in that.

The last time he'd seen Mark, Basil had been almost a decade his senior, which had been all kinds of odd. Now their roles were reversed and Mark was the one who was a decade (or more) older, and Basil decided—in light of this thing with the Betamax—that he was going to remind Mark of that age gap mercilessly, and at every opportunity.

"You promised me a new one," Mark said.

"I did not," Basil protested. "Your memory is faulty."

Mark grinned wider. "You said you'd pay me back. I remember that clear enough. With interest."

"Bollocks," Basil cussed under his breath. He felt his cheeks start to splotch. He didn't blush often, but when he did, he knew it wasn't with Gwen's even, attractive flush. It was mottled and painfully bright.

"Okay, fine," he conceded and pulled his wallet out of his back pocket. Now that they had discarded the coveralls, streaked with dirt and sweat from digging up the past, he was in much-loved jeans with a faded wallet-mark on the back pocket, and a wash-faded brown tee-shirt that said *Roses are #FF0000, Violets are #0000FF, All my base are belong to you.*

"How much?" Basil asked, fumbling past his pound notes to the Canadian tender. He pulled out a violently purple bill. "Is this a ten or a one?"

"Ones're coins, just like where you come from," Mark said, shaking his head again. "An' I don't want yer money."

Basil frowned, one corner of his perpetually crooked mouth pulling down. "Well, I guess I can fix the Betamax, but what you would play in it, I've no idea."

"No, I still want you to pay me back."

"So then—?"

"Gitcher boots on." Mark smiled fit to put the devil ill at ease. Basil, being only human, was understandably discomfited.

"Oh, no," Basil said, presenting shovel-blistered palms in supplication. "I've done my heavy lifting for the day. Can't I just pay you? S'okay, innit?"

"No," Mark said, and the *no fun that way* was unspoken but no less present.

"But," Basil tried, grasping for an excuse and knowing that he was cornered all the same. "I really am not the rough trade, here."

"Are now."

Basil swallowed once. "What if I break your tractor?"

"You'll know how to fix it, I reckon."

"What if I kill a cow!"

"You'll learn to butcher it."

"What if—"

"Boots, Specialist Doctor."

Basil sighed and shoved his wallet back into his pocket. He walked up the stairs into the kitchen, when Gwen and Evvie were sharing a pot of tea in awkward, freshly reunited silence.

There was an old yellowed piece of paper on the table between then, with time-faded brown squiggles that might have once been writing, and a hotel receipt with HILTON LONDON written across the top in black sharpie. There was also a plane ticket stub for a round trip, used, obviously. And Evvie's name was on it.

Basil wanted to pause, to read what the papers said, to decipher the puzzle of Gwen's stunned expression. Her eyes were round and wet, and she looked faintly shocky. Basil wanted to stop to ask what the matter was. But Mark shook his head once, mouthed "not now," and tugged him into the mud room. Mark didn't pause, just slipped on a pair of wellies and ambled down the concrete stairs and across the lawn, so whatever it was, Basil thought that Evvie and Gwen probably needed to work it out on their own.

Basil followed him out the back door, feeling nothing so much as like a man going to the gallows.

"SO, YOU want to marry my daughter."

Basil felt all the colour slide off of his face. Mark reached into a cabinet just inside of the barn's wide front doors. "Oh, God," Basil blurted before he could get the brain-mouth disconnect under control. "You...this is the part where you threaten me with the shotgun, isn't it? You're going to—to blast me full of grapeshot for taking your daughter's virtue!"

Mark paused, one hand on the knob of the cabinet, the other arm hidden up to the elbow by the angle of the door.

"*Did* you take her virtue?" Mark asked, the wicked gleam back in his eyes.

"What? No!"

Another lazy smile tugged at the side of Mark's mouth. "Didn't think so—Gwennie had a pretty handsy boyfriend in grade ten."

Basil clapped his hands against his ears. "La la la! I'm not hearing this! If you're going to shoot me, shoot me, but don't torture me first!"

Mark grinned harder and shook his head a little and withdrew his arm. In his hand were two pairs of heavy, worn-in work gloves. Basil dropped his own hands back to his sides, feeling suddenly ridiculous.

"Not going to shoot me then," he said.

Mark raised an expressive eyebrow. "Disappointed?"

"Not as such, no."

Mark dropped one pair of the gloves into Basil's hands, and clapped his shoulder manfully. Basil had never quite understood the masculine urge to beat the crap out of one another for fun or camaraderie, but suffered gamely.

"C'mon, Bay-zil," Mark said, still pronouncing his name with the rural drawl, "I've known you'd end up with my daughter since before she could say 'Papa.'"

"And that *doesn't* make you want to shoot me?" Basil asked uncertainly. He had been picked on by enough people like Mark in grammar school to have left him with a healthy self-preservation instinct and an aversion to jocks and soldiers. Farmers didn't quite fit the type, but they were close enough to make Basil twitchy.

Mark tugged on his gloves. "Don't push it."

"Yessir," Basil replied, using a more formal address partially out of fear, partially out of respect for the man who had raised Gwen, and partially because, well, this was also a man who had known for twenty-nine years exactly what the future held, and it hadn't driven him crazy. Moreover, now Mark and his wife Evvie had no clue what came *after*. After the return, the hasty phone call, the quiet desperation of reaching across an ocean to patch up a family, after a humid day of digging. And *that* wasn't driving Mark nuts, either.

It took a strong person to know the unknown and live with it. It took an even stronger one to suddenly come to a point where nothing replaces everything, and the once-sure future suddenly becomes chaotic chance.

"None of that 'yessir' crap," Mark said, turning towards a heavy door at the far end of the barn and gesturing Basil to follow. "I ain't my father. 'Mark' is just fine for my Gwennie's..." His voice faltered on the honourific, "her Ag-lu-nated."

Basil couldn't help the sharp hot welling at the back of his eyes but he blinked rapidly to push it back. He smiled sadly. "Just 'husband' is fine. We...we're not an Aglunate anymore. Not without..."

Mark acknowledged the rest of the sentence with a grunt, sparing Basil having to vocalize it. When they reached the door on the far end of the cavernous grand barn—Basil's nose was tickling from the hay already—they stood in a shaft of dust-mote speckled sunshine for a brief moment as Mark yanked up the ancient iron handle.

"No ring, though," Mark said, pointing over his shoulder at Basil's hand. Then he pulled back the door and began to walk down the revealed stairs to a lower level. He half vanished into the darkness, and Basil couldn't help the flash of apprehension, the memory of one too many horror movies that featured dark stairs and empty barns and crazed cannibals.

He was so wrapped up in his own illusions that it took Basil a second to realize they were still talking about marriage.

He was going to answer, but the earthy and overpowering scent of cows and their crap buffeted Basil in the face and he held in a cough instead. It would only make him suck in more of the stench. He rubbed the bare skin of his left ring finger. Then he decided in for a penny and all that, and yanked on the slightly loose gloves. Holding his breath, he descended into the dim cattle hold after Mark.

Basil's hands gripped desperately to the natural timber railing of the narrow, gapped stairs, hoping fervently that there were no splinters lying in wait. It was absurd, an absurd fear—the rail had grown smooth from thousands of such journeys, and he was wearing gloves, but Basil was a consummate worrier. He had accepted it years ago.

"No, no rings," Basil confirmed, feeling a strange sense of déjà vu. He'd already had the rings conversation with Evvie two weeks—and twenty-nine years—ago. "We never bothered. K-Kalp couldn't wear one," he admitted and was surprised that his tongue still tripped over his lover's name.

"So it wasn't a real wedding then," Mark said, coming to a stop at the bottom of the stairs and flicking on hanging overhead lights. The cows didn't react to the sudden brighter-than-day-light. Basil bit back a wince and narrowly avoided scrubbing his eyes with the hay-covered, manure perfumed gloves.

"It *was* a real wedding, just not an Earth one, and stop it."

"Stop what?"

"Stop trying to wind me up!" He pointed a finger at the back of Mark's head. "I know what you're trying to do."

Mark turned around, face carefully, suspiciously expressionless. "What am I trying to do, Bay-zil?"

Exasperation pressing at the back of his tongue, Basil flapped his hands in the air, feeling ridiculously ungraceful as the oversized gloves made an embarrasing *flap flap* sound as a result. "You want to get me mad so you have an excuse to get in a fight with me!"

"Fight with you?"

"Yes! You know, throw a punch, knock out my teeth, all that manly crap that you jocks like to do to prove that you're bigger and scarier than me, innit! That's what all this 'gitcher boots on and come to the barn of allergy-ridden cow death' is all about, innit? So you can intimidate me into never hurting precious Gwen, but I tell you, I've been trained to be a combat engineer and I could turn a milking machine into a compressed air explosive before you could manage to find a pitchfork and—"

A flash of something positively stormy passed over Mark's face. Basil broke off his tirade and gulped. Then Mark's expression smoothed out, carefully blank and slightly harmless looking. Back to the innocent man-of-the-land, everybody's-buddy farmer. It was even more terrifying than the devil smile.

"If you ever hurt precious Gwennie," Mark said, voice deceptively light and cheerful, which made Basil's short hairs jump up, "I won't have to find an excuse to throw a punch or knock out your teeth or all that manly crap. I won't need to prove anything and I won't use a pitchfork. They will not find your body."

Then he smiled, wide and sharkish, and Basil considered himself warned. And pretty lucky that it had ended there.

He also felt a sudden ringing pity for the handsy grade-ten boyfriend.

"Right," Basil said, rubbing the back of his neck and then regretting it. He had *just* gotten clean, too, taken a relieving warm shower to wash off the garden mud, and the hair at the nape of his neck was still a bit damp. Prickly barn dust smeared along the moisture there, coating his skin with gritty grime. And now he smelled of cow. God, he hoped Gwen didn't find that a turn on, or he might have to dump her. After everything they'd been through together, that *would* be a shame. "So, ah, about the milk machine thing, I didn't mean—"

"I know what you meant," Mark said. He walked away, back to the other side of the barn and Basil wondered if this was supposed to be an exercise in futile movement rather than the torture of physical labour. So far all they'd done was pace. "You're willin' to fight me back, that's what's important."

"I, well, uh...yeah," Basil said, his usual verboseness stymied in the face of Mark's natural stoic demeanour. For the first time in his life it felt rather foolish to be so wordy. Basil debated whether or not to follow Mark back to the far side of the barn, warily eyeing the rear ends of the cows and their slapping tails, their powerfully heavy hind feet. But none of them seemed to be kicking Mark. Basil shrugged and followed. He watched the cows carefully, though, for any signs that they thought it would be fun to play kick-the-Welshman. It wasn't like the walking would be bad for him—he could do with burning off a few extra calories, especially if Evvie was thinking of serving them that strawberry rhubarb pie Basil had spotted cooling on the counter in the kitchen.

He did like that about Gwen's parents being rural. Fresh pie. Mmm.

Everything Basil's mother had served when Gwen first met her had come from a shop. Not that Basil was embarrassed that his mother couldn't cook—it was really rather better that she just not try at all, especially on a day when Basil wanted to impress his then-girlfriend—just that he felt a bit cheated of a staple childhood memory. Everyone's mother is supposed to be able to cook better than one's wife, and well…Basil would have taken Gwen's cooking over his mother's any day. Basil would have taken fast food over his mother's, honestly, which was probably why he fancied the chippy down on the corner of their street so much. Probably also why his tummy wasn't quite as toned as the other Specialists', who had to do just as many laps around the gym as he every morning. Luckily, Gwen found his beer-pooch cute.

Mark stooped to lift two pitchforks—actual, honest-to-god pitchforks!—and tossed one in Basil's general direction. He managed to catch it out of the air, but just barely. His hands were made for writing equations and finagling electronic systems, not so much for catching things. Fine motor skills, Basil excelled at. He was a wiz at the art of the video game controller. Gross, not so much.

Without a word, Mark turned to the first stall to his left, prodded the cow inside gently on the hip, inciting it to move over, which it did with no more than an ear flick, and went in for the first paddy.

"Oh, no," Basil said miserably. "Seriously?"

"Either this or we send 'em to the field and do the whole stall."

Mark lifted his pitchfork and emptied its congealed burden into a waiting wheelbarrow. The bin of it was already crusted with proof that it had been used for this purpose for many, many years. Basil debated holding his breath against the pungent warmth of the stink, but that would require sucking in a big one to start with—if it was through his nose, he would smell it, and if it was through his mouth, he would taste…

Gagging slightly, Basil pulled the collar of his tee-shirt up over his nose with a delicate pluck, cursing himself for wearing the one with the thready holes along the seam, and turned to nudge his own cow out of the way.

The stubborn thing didn't move.

"Oi!" Basil said, poking it harder. "Shift."

TRIPTYCH

The cow, a great spotted black and white beastie, craned its neck to stare at Basil over its shoulder. Basil thought cow eyes were supposed to be big and wet and docile, but this one looked annoyed. It chewed ominously.

"Say, uh, Mark," Basil started.

Mark looked up over the back of his own cow and frowned.

Basil hastily muttered, "Never mind."

Reaching carefully around the cow's legs with the tines, Basil set to work. The cow pats were heavier than he expected, and before long he started to sweat. Basil didn't relish the idea of rubbing at his forehead with gloved hands or arms that had brushed cows, so he let the salt sting his eyes and frowned. He looked over. Mark wasn't sweating at all.

Bastard.

"So," Basil said, trying to break the monotony of the repetitive action of stooping and scooping, filling the silence the only way he knew how: chatter. The top of his shoulders and the bottom of his spine were already starting to pull and ache. "Uh…so, it…I guess that's it, innit?"

Mark grunted, and Basil fancied he heard a question mark at the end of the sound.

If he didn't, he was going to keep talking anyway. The silence was slightly eerie. "I mean, for thirty years you've known, more or less, what the future held. Gwen was gonna grow up, be Fall Fair Queen, do her Masters, lie and get in a fight with you, and travel back in time. And that's it. Now all of that's over, and the future is just… blank."

Mark grunted again, this time in affirmative.

"It would drive me bonkers," Basil admitted. "I like knowing what's coming."

"Who says I don't know?" Mark asked, turning for a moment to readjust the position of the wheelbarrow closer to the new stall he was moving to.

Basil gawped. "What, have you had more visitors? Did we come back and bug you again?"

Mark grinned mischievously and waggled a glove-clad finger. "Temporal Time Directive."

Basil's mouth fell open, then he scowled. "You're putting me on, aren't you?"

Mark said nothing, only bent again to his task, his shoulders shaking with something that Basil suspected was suppressed laughter.

"No, seriously, it doesn't bother you?"

Mark sighed and paused again. "Bay-zil, I've never known the future. I've known a couple things, but your trip back didn't tell me everything. Gwennie was in a car accident once, you know that? Busted her knee. Thought she was gonna die."

"You weren't sure that the future we'd come from would happen?" Basil asked, following Mark's logic to its endpoint.

Mark shook his head. "After that, we just took it as it came. 'S what I'll do now."

Basil nodded to himself. It made sense, of course. Yes, Basil would be going bananas, but not Mark. Not solid, steady Mark. Mark, who was making him do a shitty job to repay an equally shitty video player.

Basil groaned.

By the fourth stall, the small of Basil's back ached sharply and his palms were sore, and he'd let the tee-shirt drop back onto his chest because it was just making him hotter, breathing into his own clothing. He could see the damp vee forming down the front of his chest and stomach. Mark, on the opposite side of the concrete walkway that ran between the two rows of stalls, had finished nearly ten more stalls than Basil and had already gone outside to empty the wheelbarrow twice. Basil wanted to be the one to take it outside, get the breeze and the fresh air, but then he'd just have to turn right back around and come inside to the close, damp stink, so maybe it was better to stay here, where he was getting accustomed to the smell. Besides, it looked heavy. Even Mark grunted when he lifted the handles.

Basil stood straight and popped his back, the vertebrae snapping satisfactorily all along his spine. He was going to have to beg Gwen for a massage tonight. She'd learned a wonderful technique for getting at the knots that Basil cultivated under his shoulder blades from Kalp and—

Oh.

Basil cupped the top of the pitchfork handle with both hands and rested his chin on top. Kalp would have loved the farm. The low steady thrum of the machinery, the slow pattering of cow hearts, the relaxed lows that sometimes broke the air. The whole barn felt lazy and comfortable. Basil could see Kalp right there, standing at the end of the row, crouched down to stare into the face of a heifer and her calf, stroking his finger pads down a long, velvety nose, smiling fit to split his face open when the calf sucked on the hem of his shirt...

Kalp would have liked cows.

Kalp would have liked Mark, too, Basil thought. And vice versa. Men of few words, both of them, but communicative all the same, sure and steady and expressive in their slow movement. Kalp had always been able to make himself understood, even if he hadn't the words for what he wanted to say. Mark seemed that way, too.

A soft smile tugged at Basil's mouth as he conjured an image of Kalp and Mark holding an entire conversation solely in eyebrow waggles.

Kalp's ears had always reminded Basil of a cat's; that made Basil wonder if there were any fresh litters of kittens in the loft. Kalp would have liked the cats, would have twitched his ears in time and learned to purr in an effort to communicate with the queenly creatures.

Maybe Gwen would like to take a cat back with them—something to put another heartbeat in the house. Wood had kept the chickens, in the end, and it felt too empty in the house.

A cat might be good for them, something small and vulnerable, something that needed...taking care of. Something just theirs.

Mark moved over to the next stall, rubbing an affectionate hand across the rump of the inhabitant as he passed, calm and gentle. Gwen rubbed Basil's shoulders like that, used to rub Kalp's head with the same affectionate motion. For a moment, Basil allowed himself to be miffed that she stroked him like she stroked a cow, but decided to be flattered by it instead.

"Not done yet, Baz," Mark said without looking up.

Basil jumped, startled by the sound of a human voice cutting through the gentle calm of the quiet barn. "Oh, I...uh, just needed a break for a second, eh?"

Now that Basil had spent so many hours lifting and pushing, the muscles in his back and arms, while still sore, seemed to be shifting easier, stretching and pulling with a burn that was starting to feel kind of nice.

Endorphins, Basil decided. Endorphins *rocked*.

By the time Basil made it to the end of the row, Mark had already finished his side and gone along a third aisle by the cows' heads, breaking up bales of hay and balling up all the twine that had bound them. Mark had shoved all of the twine into a hole in the cement wall that was already filled with more of the same from previous feedings. He pulled a handkerchief out of his other pocket and wiped his face and arms with it. Basil glared at the handkerchief covetously.

"So, I've been thinking," Basil started quietly, and Mark blinked and nodded, encouraging him to go on. "Why all this talk about me and Gwen and marriage today?"

Mark's mouth slid upwards at one corner. "Evvie and me, we were talkin' about it last night. About Aglunates and stuff, and wonderin' if it was still official. That's all."

Basil stripped off a glove and rubbed the back of his neck free of gritty sweat, and then put the glove back on, just in case Mark was going to send him off to do another torturous chore. Oh God, what if he wanted Basil to do the milking next?

"It is official," Basil said. "I mean, on paper and all, Gwen and I are husband and wife, even though we're both…uh…widows. It's no different from, um, a husband dying before his…his wife. They're still married, you know…sort of."

Mark shrugged. "We wondered if Kalp dyin'—an' I'm sorry, I know you guys both…well, I know." He didn't seem to be able to say it—*that you loved him*—but Basil forgave him that small thing. What did vocalizing it matter, anyway?

Then Mark shoved his handkerchief back into his pocket and ambled in the direction of the open door that led out into the paddock. Basil followed at a small distance, just in case another pitchfork was about to come flying at him. Instead, he found Mark waiting in the sunshine just on the other side of the rickety fence.

Basil scrambled over a set of narrow wooden steps that had long ago dried into greyness, and stood beside Mark. He scratched his chin with the back of the glove.

"We assumed it was still on," Basil added, because he didn't feel like he had really explained enough in the barn, a habit left over from grad school, where any silence was treated as one last chance to make the evaluator understand his brilliance. "But I guess we should go check to be sure. Go wait in line at the government office, yeah?"

Mark shrugged again. "Yeah," he said, which Basil thought meant "you're welcome." "C'ept, you know, Evvie was wonderin'…"

Basil groaned.

"She'd just like to see her daughter's wedding, is all," Mark said softly. "It was hard, you know—watchin' her on TV, know'n what she was doin' with her life and not…bein' there to help. I'd, uh… wouldn't mind givin' away my girl, neither."

Basil narrowed his eyes. "You want us to have a wedding?"

Mark nodded once, firmly, as if he'd said everything in the world worth saying, and moved towards the house with that swinging, slow and proprietary stride with which he seemed to stalk his land. Over his shoulder, when Basil failed to follow, he added:

"M' sure your family would 'preciate it, too."

Well, yes, Basil conceded, speeding up to walk in step with Mark. His sisters and mother had been a bit put out to learn that Basil had gone and gotten married without a wedding for them to fuss over. Not even so much as a celebratory bridal shower. It was just that Aglunate ceremonies were only attended by the participants and an officiate, and they had wanted Kalp to feel comfortable. They had wanted to keep his customs alive.

But Kalp was gone.

And maybe, yes, maybe Basil wanted to marry Gwen, too. It was true, Basil was *that guy*, the one who wanted the picket fence and the cats and the babies. He wanted to play ball in the yard and curl up with his wife on the sofa and do the dishes after dinner. This was something he wanted, the affectionate curl of warmth in his chest when he realized just how damn much he loved Gwen, the stupid grins, the silly fights. He wanted it. He wanted it *proper*.

They had a house. They could get kittens. They could adopt a child. Maybe Ogilvy's.

They could get married.

It would be nice, a ceremony with a party, a chance to show his family and friends how freaking awesome his wife was (still mostly in the biblical sense, there, too). Something to take their minds off of the hurt, the big gap that had been left between then. Something special and joyous and *for them*. Something to celebrate Gwen and Basil.

Just Gwen and Basil.

They would never forget Kalp, of course, but…he wasn't here.

And they were.

Mark and Basil came around a corner of the house, and were met with a window that looked into the kitchen. Basil suspected that Mark had done this on purpose, but was too stunned by the sight of Gwen—her arms wrapped hard around her mother's shoulders, crying into her neck—to say as much. Evvie Pierson had one hand in Gwen's hair, the other smoothing up and down the hitching length of her daughter's spine. They were still seated at the table, pie and tea and a jumble of papers all around them. Evvie pulled back and the tips of her fingers brushed the edge of the lingering bruise on Gwen's cheek, a keepsake from Aitken's effective blackjack.

"Yeah," Basil said softly, eyes riveted. "Yeah, I guess it's a good idea, innit? I should propose."

"Okay," Mark said. Then he pulled one of his gloves off with his teeth—Basil gagged again—and jammed it into yet another pocket. Out of the same, he pulled a small object. "You could use this," he said. Splaying work-calloused and dirt-lined fingers open, he revealed his treasure. It was a small maroon velveteen box, incongruously luxurious looking in Mark's rough-worn palm. "That would pay me back."

"I…you!" Basil spluttered and tore his gaze from the reconciliation going on in the house. "You!"

"I?"

"You…the payment is the proposal, innit?"

"Sure."

Basil stripped off his gloves and slapped them down on the lawn under his feet. "So I've been sloughing through cow shit for your sheer amusement?!"

"Yup."

"Sonofa—!" Basil started, but then he remembered who he was talking to. The man who was asking Basil to marry his daughter. To heal the hurt of a whole family. And offering a ring to do it with. "Fine then," he huffed, reaching out and snatching at the box, even as he said "Ta." Basil pushed open the stiff hinges, and Mark dropped his free hand back into his pocket.

"Whoa," Basil said, staring at the cluster of small blue and white. "That's flash. Real sapphires?"

"Yup. Was my mother's," Mark said, and now he finally sounded sheepish. "It was supposed to go to Gwennie, but then she ran off to…teach aliens n' stuff, n' I thought…she should have it, you know? And you're already with her, so you know, it should be you, I reckon. Seems sorta fair. Gwen Grey—sounds nice, yeah?"

It was the longest stretch of words Basil had heard Mark utter yet, and from his downcast, anxious eyes, the firm line of his mouth, it was a stretch he'd been practicing.

"Yeah, okay," Basil said. Something warm and wonderful was blossoming in his chest, an affectionate feeling of finally being welcomed to the family.

Inside the house, Evvie leaned back and raised a thumb to clear her daughter's tears off of her cheeks. They smiled at each other, broken and awkward, but genuine. Trusting.

Trying.

"One thing, though…" Basil said, snapping the ring case shut with a sharp click. He grinned, because he was about to be cheeky. "What if I don't want to?"

Mark looked back up, eyes devilish and mouth pulled wide with little-boy mischief once again. "I've still got that shotgun."

About The Author

J.M. Frey holds a BA in Dramatic Literature, where she studied playwriting and traditional Japanese theatre forms, and a Masters of Communications and Culture, where she focused on fanthropology. She is an active in the Toronto geek community, presenting at awards ceremonies, appearing on TV, radio, podcasts, live panels and documentaries to discuss all things fandom through the lens of Academia. She loves to travel (disguising it as research), and has visited nearly every continent. She also has addictions to scarves, *Doctor Who*, and tea, all of which may or may not be related.

Triptych is her first full-length novel. She has previously published poems, academic articles, and short stories.

http://www.jmfrey.net

Thanks to...

Elizabeth, who gave Kalp his body and sexuality, and lent me some of her incredible words; Stephanie, who was the first to mourn for Kalp; Karen, whose passionate knowledge of sci-fi helped to flesh out the plot; for all those who did read-overs and made suggestions, and whose names pepper the text in thanks.

The stunningly clever Gabrielle Harbowy, the lovely editor whose interest in the novel helped make it strong.

And especially to my mother and father, who'd had me by my age; the realization of this fact gave me the impetus for this story.

CPSIA information can be obtained at www.ICGtesting.com
226031LV00001B/55/P